BOX 731

PAUL McKELLIPS

iUniverse LLC
Bloomington

BOX 731

iUniverse books may be ordered through booksellers or by contacting:

iUniverse
1663 Liberty Drive
Bloomington, IN 47403
www.iuniverse.com
1-800-Authors (1-800-288-4677)

Because of the dynamic nature of the Internet, any web addresses or links contained in this book may have changed since publication and may no longer be valid. The views expressed in this work are solely those of the author and do not necessarily reflect the views of the publisher, and the publisher hereby disclaims any responsibility for them.

Any people depicted in stock imagery provided by Thinkstock are models, and such images are being used for illustrative purposes only.

Certain stock imagery © Thinkstock.

ISBN: 978-1-4917-0280-2 (sc)
ISBN: 978-1-4917-0273-4 (hc)
ISBN: 978-1-4917-0272-7 (e)

Library of Congress Control Number: 2013914328

Printed in the United States of America.

iUniverse rev. date: 08/12/2013

Also by Paul McKellips

"This is a stunning biomedical thriller that will keep the reader on edge as scientists race to save the world from the plague. The setting of the book is not static as it moves rather quickly from one end of the United States to another and then expands to the outer reaches of the globe. *Uncaged* is presented as a thriller but also leaves the reader trying to piece together a mystery."

—Amazon Top 50 Reviewer

"*Uncaged* by Paul McKellips is a medical and military thriller that won't only keep you up at night turning pages to find out what happens next but will have you wondering if something like this could really happen. It's a fast-paced book that really does leave one wondering 'what if?'"

—Amazon Top 1000 Reviewer

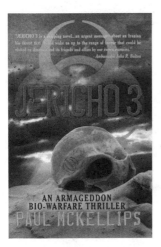

"While the mortal peril of Iran's dangerous regime getting nuclear weapons is now gripping the civilized world, Iran's nuclear threat is not the only danger. Biological and chemical weapons are also on Tehran's to-do list, just as they are for murderous terrorists from Taliban to al Qaeda. *Jericho 3* is a gripping novel about an Iranian bio threat that should wake us up to the range of horror that could be visited on

America and its friends and allies by our sworn enemies. *Jericho 3* has an urgent message. It is both a great read and serious effort to alert us to the false sense of security spun by political leaders who say the terrorist threat to America is essentially over. Scaring people may be the necessary first step to the effective defense of the United States."

—Ambassador John R. Bolton

ACKNOWLEDGMENTS

A work of fiction that deals with biological weapons, medicine, and the American military requires a level of accuracy and plausibility that only biomedical researchers, physicians, and US military veterans can provide. I am indebted to the following for lending their expertise and knowledge on all fronts: COL Ron Banks, US Army (Ret.); LtCOL Mike Motley, USMC; MAJ Curtis Klages, US Army (Ret.); MAJ Michael Stany, MD, US Army; SFC (E-7) Bill Wade, US Army (Ret.); Robert Baker, DVM; Donna Clemons, DVM; Stephanie Morley, DVM; Joy Rostron, PA; Toni Mufford; Angela Stoyanovitch; Stacy LeBlanc; Deborah Donohoe; Rebekah Lovorn; Bonnie Sutherland; Christopher Hummel; and Andrew McKellips.

To
Patricia A. Brown
(1959-2012)

PROLOGUE

Tokyo, Japan
September 1947

Yoshino Matsumoto stood in the center of the one-window office as overhead ceiling fan blades cut through the silence of the room. A Japanese interpreter sat quietly at the table next to three American investigators, Judge Advocate lawyers with the US Navy.

"Does the witness understand that he is not going to be prosecuted for war crimes if he tells us the entire story truthfully?" the American lieutenant commander asked.

The interpreter translated the question and Yoshino nodded.

"What is your full name and rank?"

"My name is Colonel Yoshino Matsumoto. I was the pilot of a Nakajima A6M2 bomber for the Imperial Japanese navy."

"A Rufe pilot?" the commander asked.

Yoshino shrugged. He didn't understand the Allied code name for his plane.

"Tell us about the Unit."

"We needed to keep our biological and chemical weapons work secret, so we built the laboratory in the conquered area of Manchuria, China. We wanted land that was isolated but also had an unlimited supply of test subjects for the research. We chose Ping Fan, a suburb of Harbin, which had more than two hundred forty thousand Chinese and eighty thousand Russians living in the area."

"What kind of research?"

"Human experimentation."

"How did you persuade people to participate in the research experiments?"

"We told the local people that our facility was a log factory. Our center could only hold five hundred people at one time, but there were two thousand to three thousand dead bodies that needed to be burned each month. The smoke stacks were always working . . . like a log factory."

"And you called the people you were experimenting on *maturas*?" the commander asked.

"Yes, it means logs."

"Colonel Matsumoto, what was your job at the Unit?"

"Since I was a high-ranking officer, I was assigned to guide other high-ranking officers through the Unit."

"Prisoners?"

"Yes. Prisoners that became logs."

"And this is how you came to know the Russian colonel?"

"Yes. The secret police picked him up at the train station. I don't know why he came to Manchuria. But I was assigned to guide him through the laboratory."

"And the Russian colonel then became one of your lab animals?"

Yoshino shrugged when the interpreter said "lab animals."

"He does not understand the term lab animals," the interpreter said as Yoshino appeared confused.

"Okay, log. What happened to the Russian log?"

"General Ishii wanted to show proper respect to the Russian log so he was not used in the frostbite or bomb fragment studies. Instead, he was put in a separate room for a defoliation bomb experiment."

"A biological bomb?"

"Yes, it was anthrax."

"What happened to the Russian colonel?"

"He suffered for more than a week. Scientists watched as his body began to show black lesions and he began to scream in pain."

"You could see the lesions?"

"He was naked the entire time."

"Just lesions on his skin?"

"No, he was having trouble breathing. He got very tired and was always vomiting and had diarrhea all the time. He lost weight very quickly."

"And what did you do while he was suffering?"

"I just watched and guarded him. That was my duty. I gave him some water once, but that was not authorized."

"Then he died?"

"Not exactly." The three Americans stopped writing notes and waited for Yoshino to continue. "The Russian log was in bad shape. He was near death, so I was ordered to take him into the dissection chamber. He was strapped to a metal table, and I scrubbed his body with a deck brush, which caused many of the black lesions to open up and bleed. Once he was washed, his wrists were tied to the buckles hanging from the ceiling. His naked body was only a few inches off the ground. One of the researchers held a stethoscope to his heart. One was holding a long knife. At the precise heartbeat, a signal was given and the Russian log's stomach was cut open from side to side and his organs poured out on the floor as he screamed. The researchers quickly examined the liver, pancreas, and kidneys for visible signs of decomposition from the anthrax."

The three horrified American naval officers sat in stunned silence until the interpreter began to vomit in the trashcan next to the wooden table.

"Anesthesia? Did he receive any medicines for pain?"

Yoshino shook his head.

"A precise heartbeat?"

"Yes," Yoshino said. "The timing was very important. If they cut at the wrong time, then blood would have sprayed everywhere and all of us could have been infected. They wanted to see the organs while the log was yet still alive."

The three Americans nodded and whispered quietly among themselves.

"Colonel Matsumoto, did you know that the Germans and Josef Mengele were doing human experimentation on prisoners in the Auschwitz concentration camp at the same time as your Unit?"

"I know that now."

"Have you heard about the Nuremberg trials and the Code?"

Yoshino shook his head.

"Thank you, Colonel Matsumoto. You are free to go."

PART I

CHAPTER 1

Desert Rose Inn
Reno, Nevada

Oleg unzipped the small case, took a short pull on a Budweiser long neck, and kept his eyes fixed on the TV chef who was preparing a "Flaming Beehive."

He glanced at his watch and then back to the TV as he began to assemble the parts.

"You can start with an eight-inch sponge cake, but I prefer Genoese pastry about a half inch thick," the chef said.

He connected the gas piston and the pusher with the spring and then fit the spring to the rear side of the pusher. The front end of the pusher went into the gas tube. He compressed the spring and inserted the rear end of the pusher together with the spring into the passage of the sight bar. He pulled the pusher back and removed it from the gas tube, inserted the gas piston, and then slid the front of the pusher into the piston socket.

"So here's what we'll need for a perfect Flaming Beehive. I suggest a quarter cup of Irish Mist whiskey and a quarter cup of fine sherry. Now let's grab eight egg whites, a half cup of sugar, one quart of vanilla ice cream, two egg yolks, and one-and-a-half cups of whipped cream."

He connected the hand guards, left side first, into the lower band and pressed down until it clipped into the lugs on the supporting ring. He fit the upper band to the end pieces of the

1

hand guards and then turned the axle pin on the gas tube to let the lug enter the recess on the band.

"Now, we place the Genoese pastry cake on a round wooden board."

He connected the firing and trigger mechanism. Engaging the recesses of the firing and trigger mechanism body with the stop-pin, he pressed them into the receiver, inserted the safety lever pin into the hole of the receiver, and turned the safety lever in the clockwise direction.

"I'm going to prick the pastry in several places with a fork. Pour the Irish Mist and sherry over and chill for one hour," the chef said, reaching into the refrigerator. "Since watching a Flaming Beehive chill for an hour is not exactly compelling television, we'll use the one I made just before we went on the air."

His mind began to recite the assembly instructions with the same military cadence he had heard a thousand times before. *Connect the bolt to the bolt support, insert the bolt into the passage of the bolt support, turn the bolt so that its driving lug enters the shaped recess of the bolt support, and move the bolt forward as far as it will go.*

"Let's preheat the oven to four hundred degrees. Beat egg whites until stiff. Gradually beat in sugar."

Connect the bolt support and the bolt. Insert the guiding lugs of the bolt support into recesses of the receiver and move the bolt support forward. Connect the receiver cover together with the retracting mechanism.

"Now we top the pastry with a mold of ice cream. Beat egg yolks and add to the meringue."

Insert the return spring into the passage of the bolt support, insert the lugs on the front end of the cover into recesses on the lower band; press the rear end of the cover to make the cover fit tightly to the receiver, turn the axle pin of the receiver cover forward to set it on the cheek plate limiter.

"It's best to pastry-tube this stuff on, using a plain tube, beginning at the top of the ice cream mold and continuing around and around to the base to simulate a beehive."

Box 731

Connect the butt cheek plate. Put the cheek plate on the butt with its fastener to the right, fit the loop onto the hook of the clip, and turn fastener upward. Connect the optical sight.

"Be sure the ice cream and pastry are fully covered. Scoop out enough meringue from the top so you have the space to hold a half eggshell later."

Match the slots on the sight bracket with the lugs on the left wall of the receiver; shift the sight forward as far as it will go and turn the handle of the clamping screw toward the objective, and let the handle lug enter the recess of the bracket.

"Bake two to three minutes or until meringue is pale gold. Garnish the base with maroons in syrup and colorful glazed fruits."

Connect the magazine. Insert the front hook of the magazine into the opening of the receiver, and turn the magazine toward shooter to let the latch engage the rear hook of the magazine.

He carefully mounted the Pritsel Snaipersky Optichesky PSO-1 optical sniper sight and inserted one round of the 7N1 variant of the 7.62 × 54mmR rimmed rifle cartridge.

"Now let's place that half eggshell in the top space of the beehive."

Oleg stepped over to the second-floor window on the backside of his guest room at the old Desert Rose Inn on West Fourth Street in downtown Reno, Nevada, lifted the lower pane, and checked his watch one more time. Thirty seconds.

"Fill the half eggshell with warmed Irish whiskey."

He rechecked the flash and sound suppressors one final time. Placing his right cheek on the cheek pad, he casually looked through the PSO-1 reticle. The bottom left corner properly ranged the seven hundred meters between him and the target, a 1.7 meter man. The top center chevron was the main aiming mark. The horizontal hash marks for wind and lead corrections wouldn't be necessary given the weather conditions in Reno.

Oleg inserted the small point-of-view camera into the scope and verified the image was recording on his laptop.

"Now we're ready to go. Serve flaming, sauced with sweetened vanilla-flavored whipped cream."

The outside door to the laboratory opened and a five foot, six inch Japanese scientist walked out and down the sidewalk the same way he had done the previous three days. As his hand touched the door handle of the white Toyota Camry, a single 7N1 variant bullet from the 7.62 × 54mmR rimmed rifle cartridge entered and exited his brain just above the right eye, rendering the Japanese scientist immediately deceased with neither bang nor flash.

Oleg turned back to the TV before his target hit the pavement, and he began to disassemble the rifle. His Dragunov SVD sniper rifle had now successfully terminated seven biomedical research scientists around the world.

"With some French couverture chocolate, pipe out some bees on paper and arrange them around the beehive after flaming. Magnificent. Next time you have a party, knock 'em dead with a Flaming Beehive and feature a vivacious twist of Irish whisky."

Oleg took another long pull on the Budweiser and then flipped the channel.

CHAPTER 2

Camp was dead.

He stepped off the road into the full darkness of night, down through a shallow ditch, and up into some tall grass. He could see a faint white glow on the other side of the evergreens. Passing through the trees, his senses exploded with the cleansing smell of pine needles and a unique freshness in the air, aromas he had never before inhaled.

The reunion experience was overwhelming.

Camp was overcome with joy as his oldest and closest friends, now gathered at the edge of the pond, stood waiting for him. A thousand years seemed to pass with each long embrace, deep smile, unhurried laugh, and the touching of hands. Hands were holding hands, and none of the fourteen people were letting go of each other.

"How was it, Camp? Was it everything you dreamed of?" Liza asked, blue eyes piercing his thoughts.

"It was incredible! Liza, Enod, James, Nahla, Margaret . . . I can't even find the words." Camp reached over and caressed each face as he moved down the greeting line. "Micah, Daniel . . . oh my, Rebekah . . . Landon . . . even Thomas. It's so good to see my old friends again."

Camp's eyes lifted above his friends' faces and beyond the pond to the slope that led up the hill. He saw a large building. He felt the music that was beginning to surround his senses.

Liza reached out and took Camp's hand and led him past the pond and over toward the old wooden footbridge that crossed the stony brook.

"Come on, Camp, everyone is excited to see you," Liza said as she tugged on his hand.

Camp stood mesmerized. He couldn't take his eyes off the building. It was so beautiful, so perfect, and so alive with emotion and music.

The others passed by and stepped over the bridge to the other side of the brook. His friends parted down the middle to make way for a woman who walked slowly through them. She stopped at the center crest of the wooden footbridge.

Liza lowered her eyes as she let go of Camp's hand and stepped over the bridge to where the others had gathered on the other side.

Camp pulled his eyes down from the building and over to the woman. He opened and closed his eyes slowly, methodically, just to make sure he wasn't dreaming. A rich, warm oil of eucalyptus filled his nostrils and saturated his body as he looked into the eyes he had known for a million years.

"Jane," he whispered.

"Hello, Camp. You're still beautiful," she said, taking a step closer.

Camp reached out to touch her, but she gently held her hand out to stop him.

"The dinner is almost ready, Camp; most everyone is here. They're all anxious to see you again." She turned to look back at the building where the music was coming from.

"Jane, I've missed you. Not a second has passed that I didn't think your name or see your face," he said as he stepped closer, moving higher up the footbridge.

"Are you sure?"

Camp was perplexed. He looked over at his fourteen friends, but their auras of unconditional love neither betrayed Jane's question nor solved Camp's confusion.

Box 731

"Am I sure of what? Why won't you touch me? It's almost as if you're blocking me."

Jane smiled, reached out, and softly brushed the back of her hand against his cheek.

"No, I'm not blocking you. You can come now, if you want, but you need to be sure."

"Sure of what?"

"Are you finished? Is your work done? Has the whole story been written?"

Camp lowered his eyes with uncertainty. Music filled his mind, and he was drawn back to the image of the building.

"Well?" she whispered patiently.

"Yes, I think my work is done."

The fragrance of the pine needles and the poetic babbling of the brook were shattered by a desperate scream.

"*Camp!* Do you hear me? *Do not let go!*"

Camp's eyes snapped over to Jane, who was already focused on the chaotic scene behind him. She motioned for him to look.

He slowly turned around. A few feet behind him, a stretcher was being wheeled into the Gettysburg Hospital emergency room. Leslie Raines was holding US Navy Captain Seabury "Camp" Campbell's lifeless hand and screaming at him, as paramedics and doctors worked frantically to get his heart beating again.

"What's going on?" Camp asked quietly with his back to Jane. "Why is everyone so upset? Why is Leslie crying?"

"You're dying, Camp. *They* love you. *She* loves you."

"But I'm happy. Don't they know I'm happy? I'm home. I'm finally home with all my friends."

"Yes, you're home. If you want to cross this bridge, then you are home now and forevermore. You're welcome to stay here. But you must be sure."

"What are you saying?"

"You've always been a fighter. What if you have more work to do, more life to live, more lives and dreams to save? Perhaps you need to fight one more time. What if more people and the precious innocence of their children are in danger? Too many of us leave unfinished work and unrealized dreams too early. You'll be home soon enough. Just make sure."

"*Camp!*" Leslie screamed from the emergency room as he saw his body on the stretcher. A curious feeling dashed through his mind as he viewed his body, his life-shell. It was nothing more than mortal clothing that moved him from experience to experience.

Camp shook his head in dismay. The ER doctor quickly inserted an endotracheal tube so Camp could be ventilated.

"Look at that young ER doc. He's lost . . . He's panicking. Jane, look . . . he doesn't know what to do. He's *letting* me die!"

Jane took a few steps over the bridge and stood next to Camp.

"Come on, kid . . . I'm in hypovolemic shock," Camp said to the young ER doctor who could not hear his words. "I've lost too much blood, the heart is trying to pump, but there's not enough blood left in my body."

"Then tell him what to do, Camp. He's searching his mind, recalling his cases, flipping through old textbook pages still printed in his mind. A million voices are going off in his head all at once. Let him hear yours, and every other doctor who guided his hands before," she said as she reached out and took Camp's hand.

"I need four units of emergency release O negative blood STAT!" the young ER doctor yelled.

Leslie looked up at the EKG monitor as Camp's heartbeat crashed. Eileen's arm was wrapped around Leslie's shoulders.

"He's only got one IV in. Come on, buddy, put another eighteen-gauge IV in the other arm . . . There ya go . . . Now get a liter of lactated ringers running . . . That's it . . . Come on, wide open on both sides."

"You want to go back," Jane said with calm assurance.

BOX 731

"I just don't want to see this kid screw up," Camp said as he couldn't pull his eyes away from the scene. "He's the one who's gonna have to live with this, not me."

"Doctor!" Leslie screamed as she pointed to the EKG.

"Wake up kid; I'm in V-fib. Give me one milligram of epinephrine . . . That's right, now five cycles of chest compressions, one hundred times a minute."

"Will that be enough?" Jane asked.

"To save me? Hardly. I have classic tension pneumothorax. My right lung is collapsed, leaking like a balloon, and putting too much pressure on my heart. When I breathe, air escapes the lung, but it's trapped inside the chest cavity. With each breath, the amount of air around the lung increases, and the amount the lung can expand . . . decreases."

The ER doctor listened to Camp's chest with a stethoscope. "I've got nothing!" he yelled.

Jane leaned in and rested her head on Camp's shoulder as they watched.

"You are an amazing man, US Navy Captain Campbell. The best trauma surgeon I ever saw. Tell him what to do, Camp. Help him remember everything he was taught."

The doctor grabbed a sixteen-gauge needle from the tray, felt for Camp's clavicle, and then walked his fingers down just below the second rib. With a quick jab, the doctor thrust the needle into Camp's chest, sending a rush of air out and through the needle as his chest expanded.

"You should go back now," Jane whispered. "A major storm of evil is brewing. You might be the only one stubborn enough to stop it."

Camp turned toward his former fiancée and then looked back over the footbridge at the others. Their faces were full of smiles and encouragement. *A major storm of evil?* He struggled to even comprehend the thought. "If we all come from the same place, the same God, how can there be evil, Jane?"

"Choices—we all make choices."

A surge of understanding and enlightenment filled his thoughts. "So is this where premonitions come from? Curtains pulled back slightly from the hereafter, to warn us, to guide us in the here?"

Jane let go of Camp's hand and walked back to the crest of the old wooden footbridge.

"You are a special one, Camp. God's gift to each of us is one life. You've been granted two. What will you do with that gift? Who will you save to live another day?"

He looked back into the emergency room. Leslie and Eileen held each other crying as the young ER doctor and his staff worked frantically on Camp's lifeless body.

"She loves you," Jane said with penetrating admiration.

Camp paused for what seemed an eternity as he straddled the here and the hereafter. "What about us?"

"We had our season and it was wonderful. But Leslie is your soul mate, Camp. She always was. You have more work to be done, more life to be lived."

He turned and glanced at his friends and reluctantly raised his hand to wave good-bye.

"We'll see you soon!" Liza called out as they all inched closer to the babbling brook.

"We'll be waiting for you when you get back," Enod shouted as he put his hand on Liza's shoulder.

Camp looked into Jane's eyes. "How long have I been gone?"

"In life time? Three minutes."

Camp dropped his head and smiled. "Funny, isn't it? But I feel like I've been here for an eternity."

"You have," Jane said, smiling as Camp turned and started walking slowly toward the evergreen trees and the tall grass. "We all have."

Box 731

Camp turned and took one final look at the building that was all aglow. He closed his eyes and printed the sound of the music and the fullness of the air. He was consumed with peace, joy, and assurance.

He stepped through the trees, walked down the slight hill of long grass, and moved through a shallow ditch, across the street, through the doors, and up into the family waiting room next to the ER at the Gettysburg Hospital. He walked through the double-swinging doors and over by Leslie and Eileen, who stood holding each other. He paused next to them and watched. They looked frightened and sad.

Camp sat on the edge of the stretcher, hesitated, and finally lay down back into his body.

The EKG spiked instantly and corrected to a normal rhythm.

Camp's body twitched uncontrollably. His eyes fluttered open as his hands clawed violently at the endotracheal tube that had been shoved down his throat.

Tears gushed out of Leslie's eyes as she collapsed to the floor in relief. Eileen dropped to the floor on her knees as the women wept together.

Two trauma nurses pulled Camp's hands away from the intubation tube back down to the gurney. His eyes opened and closed rapidly in panic. He raised his index finger, thumb, and middle finger and started writing in the air.

"Get him a tablet," the doctor ordered as a nurse grabbed the small dry erase board and marker from the counter.

Camp closed his eyes and wrote: *36 FRENCH, 6TH RIB, MID-AX.*

The doctor read the scribbles and stepped back. He looked at Camp's side and then back at the small white board.

"How the hell . . . ?" The doctor's faded mumble was quickly replaced with orders. "Okay, prep his side. I need a thirty-six French thoracostomy tube, STAT."

The doctor made a three-centimeter incision over Camp's sixth rib, in the mid-axillary line, on the right side of his body just below his armpit. He pushed a clamp over the rib and pushed down into the thoracic cavity. Sticking his latex-gloved finger into the hole in Camp's body, the doctor pushed it open wide enough to handle the tube, but no larger. The thirty-six French chest tube was inserted and then sutured to the skin, allowing blood to be suctioned out and creating enough negative pressure to persuade the lung to remain open.

"Okay, he's stable. Let's get him to x-ray and see where the bullet is. Get OR number two on standby."

CHAPTER 3

Indian Creek Island
Miami Beach, Florida

Ekaterina opened the plantation blinds, stepped out, and looked down from her second-story bedroom veranda over the expansive lagoon-style pool that held more than one hundred thousand gallons of water. Six bikini-clad South Beach bimbos—"business associates" who "worked" for her husband, Viktor—pranced in and out of the water as Viktor worked his cell phone, chugged Beluga vodka like water, and nodded his approval with each stupid splash and giggle.

She took a quick glance at her Cartier Ballon Bleu wristwatch. Ekaterina—or Rina, as Viktor would call her whenever he needed something he was too fat and lazy to fetch for himself—had waited long enough. She was growing impatient.

Rina walked past the iPhone sitting silently on the white vanity desk with inlaid pearl and reached into her red Tignanello handbag. The Velcro behind the prepaid TracFone ripped away from the hidden compartment in the bag. Rina opened the double doors to her bedroom and walked across the Italian marble floor to the top of the split-curved stairways.

Viktor and Ekaterina had purchased the *Castello Del Luna* three years earlier after a quick business deal and an even faster exit from a secret city for billionaires, deep in the forests outside of Moscow, near Izmaylovsky Park.

Rina missed her old palace of marble and gold and twenty-foot green walls and gates, as well as the weekend shopping trips to Milan and Paris on Viktor's private jet. Their $37 million "cottage" on an island just off South Miami Beach, complete with eight bedrooms, nine baths, and the three-story foyer with fresco ceilings she was standing in felt more like a dull, dank Gulag for a Russian woman of means, one who was accustomed to so much more.

Viktor kept her somewhat happy and partially appeased with a $1 million per month allowance, money she was finally putting to good use.

Her TracFone vibrated just as all six business associates removed their tops for a competitive game of bimbo volleyball, with Viktor serving as line judge and scorekeeper.

"You're late."

"The bus stopped in every town."

"No more buses, Ekaterina."

She fell silent. Boiling heat blew out of her eyes, though her store-bought face, with no lines or wrinkles, remained expressionless.

"Do not ever say my name again. Where are you?"

Now Oleg grew silent.

"I'm petting the blade of a Spetsnaz Smersh tactical knife, as travelers walk past the pay phone outside the Greyhound Bus Terminal, in downtown Albuquerque."

"And?"

"The seventh Bushido sleeps."

"Yes, I know, I saw the video. There's an old post office at 1050 Sunset Road. Box 189 has a dial combination; right seven, left three, and right one. There's a key inside that opens safety deposit box sixty-seven in the vault at Sunrise Bank. You'll find your seventh payment and instructions for the next three jobs. I'll be waiting for your call."

Box 731

National Interagency Biodefense Center
BSL-4 Facility
Fort Detrick, Maryland

Lieutenant Colonel Raines got her coffee from the atrium's barista, scanned the security badge and processed her biometric, and rode the elevator without floor buttons to her cleared location.

Dr. Ernst Groenwald's door was open as he talked with Masahisa "Martin" Ishii, an infectious disease expert and microbiologist from Kyoto, Japan. Martin had managed Fort Detrick's biocontainment level-three laboratory for more than a decade and was one of the most brilliant scientists on staff. Leslie smiled and waved as she passed.

She settled into her office outside the inner sanctum of the BSL-4 and stared at the calendar photos for November and December, images of holiday feasts and a winter wonderland that offered anything but holiday cheer as she sipped coffee.

Leslie was exhausted.

The push to find a workable vaccine for *Francisella tularensis* had been draining enough, but the horror that unfolded at Lightner Farms on October 27 was beyond her ability to cope. In a split-second reaction, she shot the man she had fallen in love with before burying the next bullet into Miriam's neck. Miriam was the Afghan woman hell-bent on killing the Navy SEAL-turned-trauma-doctor who had valiantly extinguished the flames on her suicide vest in Afghanistan, before she could transform a hospital of healing into a corridor of hell.

Every night for two weeks after the shooting, Leslie Raines made the thirty-four mile drive to Gettysburg Hospital after work and slept in a chair next to Camp's bed, until she had to get up and drive back to Detrick and report for work each morning.

Most nights she held Camp's hand as he called out *her* name from the depths of a drug-induced stupor. He called *her* name with tenderness and longing, pleading that *she* wait for him.

Each time she heard the name, tears trickled down Leslie's cheeks. The man she loved was not calling her name. He was calling for Jane.

Eileen had tried to comfort Leslie. Jane's older sister, and a former trauma nurse, explained to Leslie how the human mind sorts through old data like a computer trying to reboot. Random things are sometimes spit out in FIFO—first-in, first-out—fashion.

It had been more than a year since US Army Captain Jane Manning, a MEDEVAC helicopter pilot who crashed in Iraq, had been laid to rest in Arlington National Cemetery. Camp had stayed by the side of his fiancée, on and off for more than a year, as she lay in a persistent vegetative state in room three at Lightner Farms Bed and Breakfast.

Leslie never doubted Camp once loved Jane. Jane was his first love. Leslie and Camp had long tried to resist the feelings that pulled them together, until—at last—their love would not be denied.

But as Camp straddled the fine line between life and death from a bullet Leslie fired accidentally into his chest, he called out for one as the hand of another held him through the long nights and frequent setbacks.

Leslie looked at the days of December in front of her. Nothing was written on the calendar. It was empty, just like her spirit. US Army Lieutenant Colonel Leslie Raines was spent.

Groenwald had been standing in Leslie's doorway for a minute or two, not sure if she was sleeping, praying, or just lost in her thoughts.

He finally cleared his throat.

"Dr. Groenwald, good morning. I didn't hear you come in."

"Mind if I take a seat?"

"Please, by all means," Leslie said as she rubbed her eyes awake and summoned new energy into her soul along with a surge of caffeine through her veins.

Box 731

"I just had a very difficult meeting with Dr. Ishii."

"Martin? Is there a problem?"

"Not of the infectious disease variety, more like the infectious fiscal sequester variety. We've been given budget cutbacks from the Department of Defense."

"Oh my," Leslie said, concerned. "What's going on?"

"I had to reduce senior staff by four people, as well as two veterinary technicians."

"Dr. Ishii? But he's an expert on Dengue fever and several other tropical diseases and viruses."

"Trust me, I know," Groenwald said with more than a hint of sadness. "But I had to choose four."

"That's crazy. We were already in need of six *more* scientists on staff. Now this? How did he take it?"

"It's all about *mentsu*, or face, for the Japanese," Groenwald said. "Martin is only sixty-two and it's too soon for him to retire. He believes his termination is *mentsu wo ushinau*."

"And that is?"

"Losing face. It's an insult and an embarrassment to him and his family."

"But it has nothing to do with him. It's about money, budget dollars, just numbers on some bureaucrat's spreadsheet," Leslie said, beginning to feel Martin's pain. "How long does he have?"

"We'll pay him for ninety days, but he'll have to clear out his office today, and security will escort him to the checkpoint gate where he'll turn over his badges."

"Geez, no wonder he feels like he's losing face; escorted off the property like he got caught with his hand in the petty cash drawer!"

"It's standard operating procedure, Leslie. You know that. But we did give him an airline ticket back to Japan. Thought it was the least we could do."

Groenwald got up to leave as Raines looked back at her empty calendar.

"Dr. Groenwald? I want to put in for leave. I've got twenty-one days on the books, and I need to get away from all this for a while."

"Well, that's the best thing you've said in weeks. You definitely need a break. When were you thinking?"

Raines reached out and tapped the box on her wall calendar just below the photo of children zipping down a snow-covered New Hampshire mountain on a toboggan. "Next Monday, December 9."

"Well, that's sort of a short notice, but I'll see what I can do. Heading home to New Hampshire?"

"Probably. For a few days anyway," Leslie said as she drew a black line through Monday and the next twenty days thereafter. "Then off to someplace where cell phones don't ring."

ISAF Headquarters
Kabul, Afghanistan

US Army General Jim Ferguson and retired FBI Special Agent Billy Finn waited anxiously for the encrypted, and highly secure, video conference call to begin as two coffee-pouring majors made sure the connections were ready.

Secretary of Defense Pennington had scheduled the call and was linking in the commanding officer of Forward Operating Base Roaring Lion, Colonel David Sparling.

If the SECDEF was linking with the CO from FOB Roaring Lion, a covert base of special operators inside Jordan and nestled along the Syrian border, it couldn't be good news for either General Ferguson or Billy Finn.

Ferguson and Finn observed Colonel Sparling on the right side of the split screen waiting as SECDEF Pennington finally found his empty chair.

"Gentlemen, I'll make this brief," Pennington started. "Central Command is worried about chemicals and biologicals

BOX 731

in Syria as Bashar al Assad's regime spirals out of control with civil war. Colonel Sparling's got a hundred or so SPEC OPS boys ready to go in from Roaring Lion if it looks like Assad is going to use, or move, those stockpiles."

"Use or move, sir?" General Ferguson asked.

"Use them on his people, use them on the rebels, or move them to one of their proxies like Hezbollah in Lebanon."

"How does that impact us here in Afghanistan?" Ferguson pressed.

"Like it or not, Jim, you've got more practical experience with biological weapons than just about anyone else out there right now."

"And as the secretary pointed out, I need experienced operators," Colonel Sparling said as coffee was poured for Secretary Pennington on one side of the split screen. "I'm putting a small team together for a quick infiltration into hostile territory. We're based five kilometers from the Syrian border, outside the village of Albaej, near the dam of Sarhan. I've got plenty of tactical fighters. I need chem and bio experts."

"Jim, I need your guy to go to Roaring Lion to advise Colonel Sparling on this incursion," Pennington said as he signed a paper pushed in front of him during the video conference.

"Roger that, sir, I can MILAIR to Amman within thirty-six hours," Billy Finn snapped.

Pennington looked into his split-screen TV monitor and squinted. "Who are you?"

"Billy Finn, retired FBI. I partnered with Captain Campbell on the tularemia threat from Iran earlier this year."

"That's mighty nice of you to offer, Mr. Finn, but I was actually referring to Campbell. Jim, I need you to get Campbell hooked up with Sparling."

Pennington noticed the long pause.

"What is it, Jim?" Pennington asked.

"Captain Campbell was shot in the chest and seriously wounded. He's out of the hospital and back home recuperating now, but he won't be cleared by medical for a while."

"What the hell happened? The Iranians?"

"No, sir, Lieutenant Colonel Leslie Raines, US Army; Camp was—well—collateral damage when she took out a terrorist threat."

"Well, I can't wait. Who else do we have? Who else understands infectious diseases and weaponized biologicals?"

"Sir, Colonel Raines is our expert. She's working on Marburg and a host of other diseases in the BSL-4 at Fort Detrick."

"Fine. Get her out to Colonel Sparling."

Ferguson and Finn exchanged glances.

"Mr. Secretary, I just signed her leave papers. She's on R&R for twenty-one days."

"Then rescind it. Anything else, gentlemen?" Pennington asked as he pushed his chair back slightly.

"Sir, is there any specific threat, or are we just trying to keep the lid on a boiling kettle?" Finn asked.

"They're all specific, Mr. Finn, but take your pick. Anthrax, smallpox, camelpox, crystalline botulinum, and even plague; we believe the Syrians have had an advanced biowarfare program for years. If Assad feels cornered by these rebels, he may preemptively go after the Golan Heights by attacking the Israeli Defense Forces, or even contaminate the water supplies in Lebanon with biologicals. It buys him time and curries favor with his proxies in the region. We can't take any risks," Pennington said as the TV monitors went dark.

General Ferguson quickly tasked one of his majors to find Lieutenant Colonel Raines.

CHAPTER 4

Lightner Farms
Gettysburg, Pennsylvania

The dream was more than he could handle. He woke up startled, drenched in sweat. His heart was pounding too fast, and his chest was heaving in duress.

It was a few minutes shy of two o'clock in the morning.

Propped up on his hands, Camp tried to remember where he was, what had happened, and why he was in a strange room. He sorted through images of Tora Bora, trauma tents in Iraq, a terrorist laboratory in Yemen, and a third-world village of Datta Khel in the Hindu Kush before settling in on Miriam's distorted face and her .38-caliber revolver in the living room one floor beneath his bed.

Eileen had finally weaned him off the Percocet after he was discharged from Gettysburg Hospital. He was drug free, which made this the first night for flashing neon signs in his mind to welcome all new nightmares that might be out traveling on the closed highways of Camp's thoughts and fears.

"Reality bites," Camp muttered as he pushed the blanket down and sat up in bed. But for the first time in almost six weeks, he felt awake. The dull "perky" edge was gone, the pain and stiffness more pronounced, but he was fully awake.

He rubbed his temples as his hands began to shake. *It was more than disturbing,* Camp thought with words that seemed to scream in the silence of the room. *What was I dreaming?*

Camp stood up and staggered in his boxers over to the bathrobe that was hanging on the hook behind his bedroom door. He tightly held the rail and walked down the split foyer steps into the main lodge. Embers in the Civil War-era hearth were still orange with fading heat. He wadded up a few pages of newspaper and threw them on the coals along with some dried sticks of kindling.

The fire breathed to life, and Camp put two birch logs on the hungry flames. He walked into the kitchen and rummaged through the cabinets, searching in the glow of the fire that danced in silhouette against the kitchen walls.

"Looking for something?" a familiar voice sounded from the top of the stairs.

Camp sighed. "I'm just getting some water; go back to bed."

"Oh, I keep my *dry* water up in the cupboards and the *wet* water in the faucet by the sink."

"That's hysterical, Eileen. Now go back to bed."

"Camp . . . the Percocet is gone. I buried them in the backyard. So unless you want a flashlight and a shovel, I suggest you give it up."

Camp slammed the cupboard door, rattling the glasses as he staggered back to the oversized leather chairs by the hearth, and sat down.

Eileen kissed him on the forehead, covered him with a blanket, and went to the kitchen to fill a kettle with water. She turned the stove light on and readied two bags of tea.

"What are you fixing now?"

"Herbal tea. It'll help you sleep."

"I'm losing my mind, Eileen."

"That was a preexisting condition, Camp. Can't blame that on the gunshot."

"No, I'm serious. I've had this . . . this dreamlike thing . . . the exact same—it's not even a dream, it's more like an experience—sort

Box 731

of a thing. I see it. I smell it. I feel it. I'm in it and all around it and then suddenly . . . it's gone. It's incredibly familiar and comforting yet so vague, but the details escape me when I wake up."

Eileen walked over with a wooden tray and two cups of hot tea, in the cups and saucers that once belonged to her grandmother, along with milk and sugar. She placed the tray on the ottoman between their chairs.

"Do you remember anything specific?" she asked, steeping her teabag against the side of the cup.

"Yes . . . a few things."

Eileen paused and waited. "Can you tell me?"

"No . . . not yet."

"Why?"

Camp looked over at her and smiled uncomfortably. "I'm afraid."

"US Navy Captain Camp Campbell is afraid of something for the first time in his life. Well, now I have lived long enough to see everything. Afraid of what, Camp?"

"Afraid of hearing the words come out of my own mouth, words that are true beyond my ability to understand them, and more unsettling than anything I've ever experienced."

Eileen got up and walked behind the chairs to warm her hands by the fire. "Okay, now you're freaking me out just a bit here. Let's talk about something else until you're ready to stop talking in codes and symbols."

Camp cradled the hot cup of tea in both hands and closed his eyes as the warm herbal mist filled his airways. It brought back a familiar smell. "Where's Leslie? She hasn't returned my calls in more than five days. I've sent her e-mails and text messages. Nothing. I haven't seen her in more than two weeks. What's going on?"

Eileen moved behind Camp's chair and started to massage his neck and his shoulders.

"Leslie is struggling right now. She almost killed you. She feels responsible. She shot and killed Miriam, who was dead set on killing both of us until Leslie put a bullet in her neck. Give her a little time and space. She loves you. She'll come around."

"I know this has been tough on her, I really do. But . . . I need her. I want her to be with me."

Eileen picked up the wooden tray, took it back to the kitchen, and turned out the light over the stove. She walked back through the lodge and took a few steps up the stairs and stopped. "Camp?"

"Yes."

"Every night you were in the hospital, Leslie slept in the chair next to you holding your hand. I took the day shift, Leslie took the night shift."

"I know, Eileen, you're both saints."

Eileen moved up the stairs to the upper level and called back down. "Come on, sailor, you need to get back to your room and get some sleep. Your parents arrive tomorrow morning for their five-day vacation to watch you recover. The last time they were here, you and your Percocets slept through their entire visit."

CHAPTER 5

Indian Creek Island
Miami Beach, Florida

Ekaterina sipped on a fifty-two-dollar glass of Pinot grigio while sitting poolside at the Biltmore Hotel's Cascade Grill in Coral Gables, Florida. She was disgusted by the children of low-class scum who splashed in the pool while their overweight parents ate burgers and chugged cheap beer, all the while thinking they were *somebody* for only $359 per night. Rina knew they were all *nobodies.* The spicy mango ginger soup with fresh scallions and avocado was almost worthy of the two tablespoons that Rina tasted, but the Mediterranean salad with baby greens, feta cheese, imported black olives, piquillo peppers, tomato, lemon, and oregano dressing with four small island-spice rock shrimp looked nothing short of pitiful. She snarled her lip and with one push exiled the salad plate to the back side of the glass patio table.

If it weren't for the low-key discretion that the historic Biltmore offered, Rina wouldn't have been caught dead at such a Motel 6 for the rich and famous of South Miami Beach. Besides, the Biltmore was just a short taxi ride from Miami International Airport, perfect for an afternoon roundtrip with no bags to check.

Rina hardly looked up and preferred not to notice Semyon, who passed through the wrought-iron patio gates, and walked poolside over to her table. She winced as he kissed her on the cheek, as any gentleman would. Semyon was a senior-level operator within the Russian "organizatsiya," the Red Mafia, and a no-nonsense, detail-oriented manager, one who always got things done. He had the ear of the sixty-one-year-old Ukrainian-born Russian who ran the bratva, and was himself a major figure in the international mafia world.

Rina had done a deal with the devil himself. Semyon had been instructed to give her everything she wanted—for a price—and for as long as she needed, until the project was finished. In exchange, Rina need only provide one small final payment: her husband, Viktor.

"Well?" she said as she sipped her wine.

Semyon reached over and pulled the abandoned Mediterranean salad over to his place setting and shoveled a huge forkful of piquillo peppers and baby greens into his mouth as crumbles of feta fell to the glass table. Rina feigned nausea as Semyon spoke.

"The first seven have been concluded, just as you asked. We have now found the next three."

Rina perked up. "Where?"

"One is in Spain . . . Barcelona . . . works at a university. One has been recruited to work with us in the Middle East. The other is the problem."

"I don't pay for problems."

Semyon lifted a ripe grape tomato off the plate with his fingers and bit into it with his front teeth. The seeds and juice splattered in all directions, but most notably over the left breast pocket of Ekaterina's pink blouse.

She neither flinched nor acknowledged the flying insult.

"He works at a US military base as a scientist. That will be difficult."

"I know where he works, you idiot. Don't lecture me. I want them all together . . . in the same place. I want them to experience everything together."

"I know what you want, Ekaterina."

BOX 731

She looked up, made contact, and glared into Semyon's eyes for the first time. "Don't *ever* . . . say my name . . . again," she scolded with a slight smile creasing her lips.

Semyon grabbed the island-spiced rock shrimp, one at a time, pinched the tails, and sucked the meat out of the shells until all four were devoured. He pushed his chair back.

"I have a flight to catch, Ekaterina."

"You just landed."

"And now I am full."

Semyon stood up and pushed his chair in. He stood next to Rina and caressed her cheek. "I'll call you soon, Ekaterina."

Miami International Airport

The limousine pulled up to the departures level and parked as Semyon waited for the sixty-one-year-old head of the Russian syndicate to finish his cell call. The driver and Semyon sat motionless until the call was ended.

"How was your lunch at the Biltmore?" the man asked, looking out his window and away from Semyon as he adjusted his Detroit Tigers baseball cap and pulled it down low over his sunglasses.

"Fine. She will not be a problem," Semyon said as he reached for the door handle.

"Her project must come off without a hitch. It will be the diversion we need."

"I understand."

"We meet next week in Damascus . . . at the university."

Semyon nodded and got out as the limo pulled away.

CHAPTER 6

The White Birches of Hillsborough County
Weare, New Hampshire

Karl Raines dropped the needle down gently onto the vinyl album now spinning on the 1940s–era Decca record player. The old phonograph was built inside a decorative faux alligator-skin case with genuinely aged brass hardware and a thick celluloid handle that made music and memories more portable. Christmas music from the 1944 Kraft Music Hall show, featuring Bing Crosby, the John Scott Trotter orchestra, and the Kraft Choral Group from Chicago filled the heated porch as Karl and Lydia Raines watched the snowfall cover the white birch trees out their back window.

"December 21, 1944 . . . I remember the day like it was yesterday," Lydia said as the music came to life.

"So do I, Lydia . . . so do I," Karl recounted as he stared through the snow and the trees, not quite sure if he was in New Hampshire or back in the Ardennes mountain region of Wallonia in Belgium.

"Are you thinking happy thoughts?" Lydia asked.

Karl smiled, reached over, and kissed his bride of seventy-two years on the lips. Their eyeglasses clinked, and they both laughed as John Scott Trotter's orchestra was interrupted by the ringing telephone hanging on the wall in the kitchen.

"I'll get it," Karl said as he got up. "Hello?"

Box 731

Lydia was lost in her thoughts. Her mind worked frantically to recall any good memories, only the happy times that filled December 21, 1944, when her husband enjoyed his last full day of freedom during the Battle of the Bulge.

Karl came back and covered Lydia's lap with a blanket she had knitted after her granddaughter's unexpected front-door arrival back in 1973.

"Who was it, Karl?"

"Hmmm?"

"The phone. Who was calling?"

"Oh, some major from the army. I think he said he was calling from Afghanistan."

"Afghanistan?"

"I think that's what he said. He wanted to speak with Leslie."

"Well, for heaven's sake. I wonder why he called us."

"Well, she said she was going on vacation for several weeks. Maybe she didn't take her phone with her," Karl said as the magic-hour sunset began. The freshly fallen snow and white canoe bark of the trees were a perfect canvas for hues of gold, pink, red, and purple.

"Did Leslie mention where she was going?"

"No, no, I don't think she did. But I sure hope she has fun. I told her to take a camera."

"For heaven's sake . . . Afghanistan? Karl, how much do you figure it costs to make a phone call from Afghanistan?"

Karl raised his shoulders, clicked his tongue, and shook his head from side to side as they both pondered the cost of such a telephone call, just as the Kraft Choral Group began to sing. Karl stood up and reached his hand out for Lydia's.

"You are the most magnificent lady I have ever laid my eyes on, Mrs. Karl Raines. Would you honor me with a dance? I think this is one of our favorites."

Lydia blushed as Karl pulled and she pushed herself out of the chair. "I would be delighted, Mr. Raines."

Lydia and Karl walked into the empty living room they had shared for more than seventy years. Lydia lit several candles as Karl straightened his cardigan sweater and bow-tie in the mirror. Then they danced.

Lightner Farms
Gettysburg, Pennsylvania

Camp sat across from his father at the wooden dining room table as Seabury Campbell Sr. plowed through his breakfast of bacon, eggs, and toast.

"Did you have a good walk, Dad?" Camp asked, though somewhat disgusted by his father's lack of table manners.

"Not much walking really," the elder Campbell said between bites of peppered bacon. "We usually fire up the woodstove and just talk in the machine shop."

"We?" Camp asked with a curious smile, as more bacon was shoveled in.

"He's crazy in the head, Junior. Don't pay him any attention," Ruth called from her chair as Eileen walked back with a tray full of cups, brewed tea, sugar, and milk.

Camp laughed. "Who've you been talking with, Dad?"

His father waved his hand and tried to dismiss the question.

"Seriously, I want to know."

Seabury cleaned his gullet with a heaping gulp of warm coffee. "Some spook."

"A ghost?" Camp asked smiling.

"No, a spook . . . You know . . . spook . . . a spy?"

"Sea Bee, did you take your pills this morning?" Ruth yelled from the leather chair. "If he misses his morning pills he talks like a crazy man," Ruth said quietly to Eileen.

"How do you know he's a spy, Dad?"

Box 731

"He told me. Well, not in so many words but I could tell. The accent is a dead giveaway."

"He's a foreign spy?"

"I 'spect so. When we were talking yesterday, he said something about 'A-rabs' and Egypt. He seems foreign to me," Sea Bee said as he slathered two slabs of butter across one wedge of white toast.

"Yesterday? So you've been talking with this spy for a few days now?" Camp asked playfully as his eyes met Eileen's just before Ruth rolled hers.

"Lord, help me," Ruth mumbled under her breath.

"Does your spook have a name, Dad?"

"Of course he has a name. Everybody's got a name. He's still out in the shop. If you want to know his name so badly, go ask him yourself," Sea Bee griped, fully aware that he was becoming the butt of everyone's joke.

"No, he's your friend. It wouldn't be proper to intrude."

"Makes no difference to me, Junior. Go talk to him. He's got a secret code name, Molly Bloom, or something like that."

Camp sat back as the smart-ass grin on his face was extinguished faster than a candle on a birthday cake. "Molly Bloom?"

"You heard me . . . I thought it was a stupid name too," Sea Bee said as he reached for another strip of bacon.

Camp pushed his chair back, grabbed his coat off the hook, and walked briskly through the kitchen and out the back door.

National Interagency Biodefense Center
BSL-4 Facility
Fort Detrick, Maryland

Oleg pulled into the checkpoint circle, parked his newly acquired DHL delivery van, and reviewed the file Ekaterina had left for him in safety deposit box sixty-seven at Sunrise Bank in Albuquerque,

New Mexico. He wanted to make sure he pronounced the name correctly.

Oleg's next assignment would be considerably more difficult than the others and was probably why, he surmised, Rina saved it for the end. Abducting a government scientist working at a maximum security military base in the United States would not be easy.

"Yes, sir," the guard from behind the visitor's desk said as he greeted Oleg. "How may I help you?"

"I have a personal package, probably a Christmas gift if I were to guess, for one of your scientists. Is this the best way to get it to him?"

"Sure, I can sign for it. Who is it for?"

"Ah, let me see . . . ah, yes, a Dr. Martin Ishii."

The guard frowned and then quickly scrolled through his computer roster. "Sorry, buddy, but Ishii no longer works here."

Oleg was genuinely surprised. "Really? Since when?"

The guard looked back at Oleg with a bit of suspicion.

"I mean, the package appears to be from his wife in Japan. Guess he forget to tell her he was changing jobs."

"He wouldn't be the first," the guard said as he started to dismiss the DHL driver.

"Any forwarding address for Mr. Ishii?"

"Right, I'm just going to tell you all of that. I suggest you return the parcel to sender. Have a good day, sir."

Oleg walked back to his hyper-yellow van, picked up the phone, and quickly dialed Rina.

Lightner Farms
Gettysburg, Pennsylvania

Camp suspected he had probably uttered some nonsense during his modulations between sleep and consciousness as his body healed from two gunshot wounds and narcotics dulled the pain

Box 731

while fogging his mind. Surely he must've said the name "Molly Bloom" out loud as he was recovering.

Perhaps he had, unfortunately, mentioned some names in his stupor that otherwise would never have been spoken. Old Sea Bee must've heard some tall tales from Camp as he took an occasional shift at his son's bedside during recovery.

Camp looked through the window pane door leading into Eileen's shop, the infamous shop that once held two hundred lab rats and led to a pilot vaccine for an avian influenza strain during the president's ban on animal research. His heartbeat accelerated as he saw a man sitting on a stool, warming himself by the old woodstove, just as his father had said he was.

Camp turned the door handle. The door opened and creaked with an obnoxious sound.

The man did not turn around.

"I have a gun," Camp said, hoping to stir the intruder while wishing he did in fact have a gun with him.

"I doubt you would know where to load the bullets," a familiar voice said as the man continued to warm his hands.

"I don't believe it. Molly Bloom?"

Reuven stood up and turned around. His trench coat collar was turned up, and frameless spectacles rode low on his nose.

"Hello, Shepherd's Pie."

Camp walked over as Reuven extended his hand. Camp brushed his hand aside and hugged Reuven with the warmth of a long-lost friend.

Reuven was caught by surprise. "You must be feeling better. Your embrace is what I would expect from my sons after a special gift."

"What are you doing trolling around the hills of Gettysburg and cavorting with my father out in the shop?"

"Top-secret mission," Reuven said as a sly smile darted across his face. "How are you doing, Camp? You gave us all quite a scare."

"I'm feeling better, stronger every day. How did you find out?" Camp asked with legitimate curiosity in his voice.

"We're Mossad . . . and Shepherd's Pie is my brother. Since you're not going to invite me into the lodge, why don't you sit with me by the fire?" Reuven pointed to the chair where Sea Bee had been sitting and visiting with him for two days.

Camp sat and reached his cold hands out toward the warm fire. They sat in silence for a few minutes.

"Are you going to be able to continue in the navy?" Reuven asked as reflections from the flames in the woodstove danced across his spectacles.

"Sure . . . if I want to. After I get medical clearance, they'll probably give me light duty at Walter Reed for three months. I doubt they'll let me operate for a while, so I'll review case files until I die of boredom."

More silence filled the shop as Reuven added another handful of sticks to the fire. "So I must ask you . . . why did you let her go?"

"Miriam the Terp? The Afghan suicide bomber?"

"No. Leslie Raines, the woman I thought you loved."

Camp looked over at Reuven and shook his head. "I would think Mossad might be more interested in the Iranians, Hezbollah, and Hamas. Now you're telling me you've been spying on my love life?"

"We had to add an additional agent just for that job." Reuven laughed.

"Well, it's all good. You can dismiss the agent. Besides, I didn't let her go."

Reuven looked over his spectacles and into Camp's eyes. "Then where is she?" Reuven saw the deep, sick feeling fall over Camp as he was instantly panicked. "Relax . . . She's all right."

"What's going on, Molly? I haven't heard from her in almost three weeks now. She stopped coming over to see me a month

BOX 731

ago, and then she stopped taking my calls. Now her office phone goes to voice mail and so does her iPhone."

Reuven looked down at his watch and then gently stroked the crown of his head with one finger. "Do you love her?"

"You're the spy . . . What do you think?"

"I think you do . . . That's why I'm here."

"I'm listening . . ."

"I know where your Lieutenant Colonel Leslie Raines is. If you were a smart man, you'd go to her now."

"Man, how does your wife tolerate you, Molly? Do you always speak in riddles?"

Reuven smiled. It wasn't the first time Camp complained about the Israeli's penchant for painting pictures that others would be left to decipher. "She's in Israel, Camp."

"What?" Camp asked in utter shock. "Why? What's going on?"

"Nothing. She's on holiday. She took all of her unused leave, unplugged her phones, and bought a gallon of suntan oil. She wanted to get away from it all. To think things through, I suppose."

"Get away from it all? Or get away from me?"

Reuven raised his eyebrows and wouldn't answer.

"Well, even if she's in Israel, there's not much I can do about that. Last I heard, Uncle Sam put me on the DO NOT FLY list. Maybe I can send her a postcard," Camp said with bleeding sarcasm.

The machine shop grew silent.

"The DO NOT FLY is a problem, at least for commercial airliners. Fortunately, we have an open seat on our executive jet, which is parked over at the Gettysburg Airport. I even brought a doctor along in case you need additional care."

Camp looked at Reuven as shock and disbelief raced across his face. "I get critically wounded—two gunshots less than two months ago; I lose a few liters of blood, flatline, and have a near-death experience; Uncle Sam puts me on a medical hold with weekly follow-up visits; and you just expect me to hop on your plane, travel illegally to Israel, and search for Leslie Raines along the Mediterranean? As my good friend Molly Bloom likes to say . . . that is not possible."

Reuven reached out toward the woodstove and warmed his hands. He let silence fill the room as a million thoughts filled Camp's mind.

"Tel Aviv Hilton . . . room 4310," Reuven said as his voice trailed off.

Camp sat still. He walked through a myriad of memories and images. He remembered the covert trip to Morocco where the undercover couple—posing as Canadian veterinarians—stayed at the Royal Hotel Rabat. He flashed through the trip to Yemen on A'zam's jet and then the tour of Aden Sea Pharmaceuticals before A'zam's brother Umer thrust his jambiya deep into Leslie's chest. He remembered her face at Arlington National Cemetery, when Leslie became his strength as he buried Jane. Camp remembered her dedication at Fort Detrick and in Lyon, as she worked twenty-hour shifts to develop a lethal strain of tularemia, and then the vaccines that would protect against the weapon, and ultimately serve as a biomedical shield over the Israeli coast.

And he closed his eyes and remembered her gentle touch and the soft fragrance of her hair as they made love in Old Town, Alexandria, two hours before Miriam unleashed hell and Camp walked into heaven.

He remembered it all. He had been too busy sorting through his own pain to notice that Leslie was drowning in hers. Camp stood up and walked to the door of the shop. Reuven kept staring at the fire.

"Give me ten minutes to pack."

CHAPTER 7

FOB Roaring Lion
Albaej, Jordan

Colonel David Sparling started the briefing. Twenty individual augmentees from different agencies and branches were joined by a man and a woman, both "by name" requests from SECDEF Pennington for the mission. Maps of Syria, Jordan, and Turkey were tacked to the wall in front of the U-shaped configuration of tables.

"All right, let's get after this. Gentlemen, this is Billy Finn, retired FBI and now deputy director for General Ferguson at ISAF headquarters in Kabul. Finn got here late last night after the Jordanians brought him over from MILAIR in Amman. You met Fallon Jessup at our briefing last night. Special Agent Jessup is a CIA asset and an expert on biologicals."

Billy Finn was a bit surprised to see Jessup but hardly disappointed. Her tall slender figure, muscular legs, and long blonde hair promised to make any mission more than palatable, even if he was in his early sixties, three inches shorter than Jessup, and sporting less than a full crop of hair. But just how Fallon Jessup was going to "sneak" into an Arab culture like Syria, given her Nordic look, was an entirely different proposition.

"Our NATO partner—Turkey—has granted us permission to launch from Kilis, a small town just six miles from the Syrian border," Colonel Sparling said. "Aleppo is a quick sixteen-mile drive in from there. For mission plan, I'm going to turn it over to Master Sergeant Rickman."

The twenty-member team quickly opened their briefing books as Billy Finn looked around the room with a smile on his face. "Sir, did you say the mission will start at 'kill us' in Turkey?"

Finn started laughing. No one else found the humor.

Kyoto, Japan

The Kintetsu Railways train pulled into Kyoto Station, and Dr. Martin Ishii walked two blocks in the brisk December air until he found his childhood *machiya*. The traditional wooden townhouses were scattered throughout Japan, but this area of townhouses in the historical capital of Kyoto held special significance to Martin. It was the home that he and his brother had been raised in, the home where his own father had been raised, and the home where his grandfather died in 1959, when Martin was only seven years old. Along with farm dwellings known as *nokas*, the machiya and noka made up the *minka*, or the "folk dwellings" of Japan.

Martin unlocked the door and entered the front room, a small retail shop area where his ninety-year-old mother still operated her sewing business. The wooden home had a narrow street frontage but stretched back deep into the center of the block. Martin's townhouse had a small courtyard garden, or *tsuboniwa*, and the one hundred-year-old earthen walls, though cracked by a century's worth of earthquakes and tremors still supported the baked tile roof on top of the second story.

He walked past his mother's lower-level apartment, slid the door open, and looked in. She wasn't home. He walked through the garden and back to his apartment in the rear of the machiya. A bowl of fresh fruit was on the table along with a note from his mother.

Welcome home, Masahisa.

BOX 731

His *kyoshitsubu*, or living space, looked the same as it did when he was a child. The raised-timber floors were still in perfect condition. Tatami mats were clean and configured around the raw earthen service space in the kitchen. Martin walked through the kitchen and back to the *kura*, the storehouse where his mother had already stocked him with supplies of rice, fruits, and vegetables.

He paused and looked up at the old chimney through the kitchen skylight. He remembered gazing at the *hibukuro* as a child, watching smoke and heat leave his mother's kitchen as the thin glass skylight brought them light.

The family machiya was a comfortable home, but it seemed like a million miles away from the luxury and comfort of Martin's condominium in the Rock Creek Estates subdivision of Frederick, Maryland, and his national security job at Fort Detrick.

Martin walked over to the steps that led to the second story. He stood there for several minutes wondering if he would ever have the courage to go up there, slide the door open, and enter the unlocked kyoshitsubu that once belonged to his grandfather.

When he was seven, Martin's father warned the young child that entering the second-story kyoshitsubu was forbidden. It didn't matter that Martin was now sixty-two or that he had earned a medical degree, a doctorate in biology, and was an internationally recognized scientist just like his grandfather. It didn't matter that anyone who could scold him was already dead.

When his father said "forbidden," it meant forbidden for life.

Andulus University for Medical Sciences
Near the Port of Tartus
Al Qadmus, Syria

Semyon and his six Russian paramilitary crew members snapped to their feet as the sixty-one-year-old "big boss" of the Red Mafia syndicate entered the second-floor laboratory at Andulus

University. He was followed by four bodyguards and Professor Hafiz Haidar.

"Have you run the test?" the boss asked as he adjusted his Detroit Tigers baseball cap.

"We have," Semyon said as he motioned to the boss. They both looked through the glass window into a quarantined and sealed room off the main laboratory. "He was given the vaccine thirty days ago and then full exposure five days ago."

Semyon watched as the boss examined the writhing body of a young Syrian student on the floor in the room. A middle-aged Japanese man sat quietly on a chair next to the student, reading a book.

"The American vaccine for the student?"

"Yes, the same one they give to all their military," Semyon said proudly.

"Looks like he is dying . . . The other is fine?"

Semyon smiled.

"Who is the Asian?"

"He is the military scientist I told you about. He's an expert on biological weapons," Semyon said as Dr. Okito Yamamoto stood up and bowed slightly from inside the contaminated room.

"So this is his new recipe?"

"No one has ever seen anything like this," Semyon said. "Based on test results so far, existing vaccines won't protect against it."

"How much has he made?"

"Fifty kilograms . . . about 110 pounds."

"New vaccine?"

"Dr. Yamamoto was his own lab rat. He gave himself the new vaccine, and the Syrian got the American military's vaccine," Semyon explained. "They were both exposed in the same room at the same time."

The big boss nodded and walked briskly out into the second-floor corridor of the university. Semyon followed at his heels.

BOX 731

"Arrange for a meeting at the safe house in Hadida—tomorrow night—and only with their troika. Tell them the diversion is in place. We are ready to do the deal. Their storm is brewing."

Semyon watched as the big boss marched down the hallway with his bodyguards. The Red Mafia boss of the bratva would never utter a compliment, but Semyon knew he was pleased.

FOB Roaring Lion
Albaej, Jordan

FBI retired Special Agent Billy Finn and the CIA's Fallon Jessup were the last two to board the second Blackhawk for the flight. Israeli airspace had been cleared so that the pair of American helicopters could avoid a much longer mission up and around the Iraqi border and into Turkey. Within minutes they would be over the Mediterranean and then up the northern coasts of Lebanon and Syria before they entered Turkey over Hatay, the ancient port city of Antioch in biblical times.

Finn buckled in next to Master Sergeant Rickman as Jessup took the hurricane seat next to the chopper's window.

"Sir, when do we do a rehearsal on this thing?" Finn yelled to Rickman over the cutting blades as the bird started to lift.

Rickman laughed. "No rehearsal on this one, Finn. Easy in, easy out. It'll be a drive-thru. Oh, and knock off the 'sir' thing. I work for a living."

"Roger that, sir, but nothing's easy, Sarge. We even did a rehearsal in the frozen Hindu Kush," Finn yelled.

"That's because you were marching with the army. We're air force, buddy. We don't need to rehearse."

Rickman's confident branch-bravado was anything but consoling for Billy Finn. Finn looked over at Special Agent Fallon Jessup, who just stared out the Blackhawk window, occasionally stroking the 9mm holstered on her hip.

CHAPTER 8

Atlantic Ocean

The Dassault Falcon 7X long-range business jet was cruising over the Atlantic at 560 miles per hour after leaving the Gettysburg Airport two hours earlier. Camp stirred from his nap on the long leather couch. Reuven sat in one of the large cabin recliners, reading a book, a bottle of red wine and a plate of juicy red grapes and white cheese on the tray next to him.

"You're awake," Reuven said without looking up from the book.

Camp rubbed his eyes, checked his watch, and sat up. "I thought you said you had an empty seat for me."

Reuven put his book down and looked around the mostly empty cabin. Four Mossad agents, Reuven's security detail, occupied the first four seats up front. They were the last ones to board and would be the first ones to get off and secure the runway area at TLV, the Ben Gurion Airport in Tel Aviv.

"This thing has fourteen seats and there are only six of us," Camp counted.

"Just as I said then, Shepherd's Pie, I had an open seat for you."

"You flew this half-empty jet all the way to Gettysburg, paid for by the government of Israel, just to see me?"

Reuven filled a second goblet with red wine and walked it over to Camp. He handed him the glass and sat down on the

Box 731

leather couch next to Camp. "Not exactly. I did it for love. Yours for Leslie, and the love and appreciation we have for what the two of you did for Israel."

Reuven raised his wine glass. "Here's to Gabriel X . . . and to our friend, Omid."

Camp hadn't thought about Omid much since the shooting. But he always thought fondly of the Iranian who gave his life to make sure that the "wind of torment" did not lead to innocent deaths in either Israel or Iran.

"To Omid," Camp said as their wine glasses touched.

"Let's just consider this a gift—perhaps a wedding gift," Reuven said, delighted as he baited his American friend.

"Wedding! Leslie Raines bolted in the middle of the night to the other side of the world just to get away from me. I'm not thinking she's much in the mood for a wedding."

"You said you loved her."

"I did. I mean I do."

Reuven sat back and looked out through the windows of the Falcon as he spoke from his heart. "The orthodox Jewish wedding is a spiritual event. Two souls are merged together, bound together physically and spiritually, as one. The idea of being merged moves from concept to reality. In her wedding dress, she prepares for the transition. She recites psalms and prays for the ability to crown her husband. Not to be a decoration on his arm or in his house but to be the tie between his dreams and his consciousness. Just as the crown rises above the head yet connects with it as well, so too does the bride connect the spiritual with the physical. Because she is queen, she allows him to be king."

A solitary tear streamed down Reuven's cheek as he sipped the wine. "She takes off her earrings, bracelet, and necklace. In another room, her *chatan*, her groom, empties his pockets, undoes his tie, and unties his shoelaces. They do not marry for physical beauty or for external jewels. She does not marry him for the money in his pockets. They come to each other unbound, with no ties, and no connection to anyone or anything but for the connection and the love they share for each other. The chatan goes to his bride and covers her face with a veil, an opaque veil that neither can see through. They know they are marrying what they can see, but they are also marrying that which they cannot see. With complete belief and confidence, they know that each of them is but only a half of a complete and mutual soul. They need each other."

Camp sat back and let Reuven's poetic words echo in his heart as both love and self-doubt poured in. "I'm a pretty flawed man, Molly—rough around the edges, broken and empty in more places than you can imagine," Camp said softly.

"She won't be the answer to your incompleteness, but if you love her, she can be the means for you to get better. The bride and her chatan reunite under the *chuppah*, the marriage canopy, to become husband and wife. The canopy is open on all four sides, just as your home and hearts should be welcoming and open to all who are around you."

Reuven poured some more wine into Camp's goblet.

"So what's with the whole glass thing? You guys love to stomp on glass when you get married."

"You guys?" Reuven laughed. "It's the last thing the new husband must do. Everyone becomes silent as though they sleep, as all must hear the shattering glass. It represents the suffering that always must be remembered, even in the midst of our joy. It is our responsibility to remember that as we rejoice, we need to create a world where all can rejoice. We must live our lives sensitive to those less fortunate, and grateful for all the good we have been blessed with."

"I've got lots of shattered glass, Molly Bloom."

"We all do," Reuven said as he turned to look in Camp's eyes. "But if you love her, never forget the shattering pain of Jane's death, Leslie's divorce, or even the shooting; rejoice by allowing your souls to merge. Yes, there were bad things in your lives. But

BOX 731

look closely, Shepherd's Pie, there was much, much more good. Allow your queen to let you become her king."

Camp's emotions were fully stirred. The pain in his chest was replaced by warmth in his heart. He reached with the open palm of his hand toward Reuven. Reuven looked at Camp's hand and then held it tightly for a passing second and released.

Camp took a big swallow of red wine and reached for the bottle.

"So . . . you know about Jane, my fiancée, and Leslie's divorce?"

Reuven smiled and returned to his recliner. "I'm Mossad. I get paid to know these things. I also know that you died and went on a journey. I'd like to know where you went."

Kilis, Turkey

The Blackhawks carrying retired FBI Special Agent Billy Finn, CIA Special Agent Fallon Jessup, and the rest of the infiltration team landed at a NATO base on the northwestern border with Syria where four hundred American soldiers manned two Patriot Missile batteries. When Syrian rockets and mortars aimed at rebel forces "accidentally" landed on Turkish soil, NATO took all necessary precautions to protect Turkey from what might be interpreted as "intentional" Syrian missiles. Syrian President Assad had already mixed the separate components of some sarin gas stockpiles and had begun to fire Soviet-era Scud missiles within his own country. It wouldn't take much to fill the tips of those Scuds with lethal sarin gas and launch them deep into Turkey. Once a shell exploded, sarin vapor attacked victims within seconds. The toxic nerve agent blocks the body's natural "off switch" as muscles, glands, and nerves overstimulate themselves at lightning speed until the lungs can no longer support the speed of breathing.

Finn and Jessup followed the team into the staging tent for the final briefing.

"Okay, listen up folks . . . This mission just got called, and we are 'no go,' clear?" Master Sergeant Rickman said to the group with obvious irritation and disdain in his voice. "We get back on the birds as soon as they refuel. You can leave your kit and gear here. There's a chow tent on the other side of the vehicles. Jessup and Finn, I need you two to stay behind."

The members of the infiltration unit from Roaring Lion filed out.

Finn walked up to Rickman and grabbed the SAT phone off the table. He punched in the numbers to the unsecured line at ISAF headquarters in Kabul.

"Major . . . recognize the voice?" Finn asked.

"Affirmative, sir," the major said.

"Let my friend know the sightseeing trip has been canceled. I'm on my way back to the ranch."

"Roger that, sir." Finn put the phone down as a familiar-looking man walked into the tent.

"Well, that explains everything. Heads-up, Jessup, your boy-toy from Langley is in the house," Finn said as Fallon Jessup snapped her head around to look.

"Daniels . . . what are you doing here?" Fallon asked with a newly discovered softness in her voice.

"Two Russian amphibious vessels are pulling into the Port of Lattakia as we speak," CIA Special Agent Daniels said as Master Sergeant Rickman started to clear the room. "We had to scrap the mission."

"Russian ships are here all the time," Jessup said as Daniels took a seat.

"They are; in fact, they're doing major construction to handle their warships. But all that activity is down in the Port of Tartus, forty-two nautical miles to the south."

BOX 731

"Not exactly the other side of the world," Finn answered, failing to grasp whatever Daniels thought was significant.

"Lattakia puts them much closer to Aleppo and Al Safir."

"Chemical and biological facilities?" Jessup asked.

"Production and storage. Looks like our Russian friends are going to make a play for Syria's WMDs," said Daniels. "We watched them load up, and clearly they are packed with special operators and all of the necessary testing, transport, and storage equipment they'll need."

"You got an eye on the sites, right?" Finn asked.

"Sure, but not a lot of good that'll do us. A Russian-built SA-2 surface-to-air missile site defends the storage area and the underground facility." Daniels pulled out his laptop and quickly booted up. "Here's a close-up of the SA-2 SAM site with Guideline missiles on the launchers, Fan Song Radar, and control vans. These systems were locked and loaded this morning. You can even see the cables running from the command van to the launchers. They clearly don't want any trouble during their mission."

"Underground?" Finn asked. "I thought we were targeting a facility—a university or government building—where twenty of us could just walk in and take a look around."

"Well, that was the military plan. Langley has a different idea, a different building, and a different city . . . so we've got it from here."

"Got what?" Finn asked.

"Syria has always been a fractious country to get a handle on. Libya was a cakewalk. We knew where their VX and mustard gas was, and the storage canisters were so old and compromised that we knew they couldn't use it, let alone load it in a weapon or delivery system. Syria is different. The Russians have been helping them since day one. They've got CHEM and BIO in at least three different locations: Damascus, Hama, and Safira Village near Aleppo. They've got three main locations and dozens of facilities. Al Safir is the most interesting. There's a large electric substation right next to the warehouse complex and an elaborate tunnel system for underground storage. A normal warehouse complex would never require that much electricity."

"So what's the Russian play?" Jessup asked.

"Hard to say for sure but easy to speculate on, I guess. Assad has lost all control of his country since the Syrian uprising hit full throttle. The demise of the current leadership regime in Damascus is inevitable, but the revolution will be an unpredictable and messy affair."

"Wasn't any different with Qaddafi in Libya. A thousand splinter groups claiming control, while the CIA tried to buy up as many stinger missiles out of the black market until al Qaeda affiliates attacked us in Benghazi. Organized chaos and a total cluster you-know-what," Finn said.

"Except Syria is different. They're one of eight nations that never joined the Chemical Weapons Convention. They have one of the largest and most sophisticated chemical weapons programs in the world. And, we suspect they've got biological weapons. Unlike Libya, these Syrian insurgents are more sectarian and radicalized. Their civil war is being hijacked by jihadists."

"Ergo the Russian interest," Special Agent Fallon Jessup said with punctuation as she got up and paced the dirt floor of the tent.

"Syria has several hundred tons of blistering agents and deadly nerve agents like VX and sarin. The Russians want to make sure the smaller splinter groups don't get their hands on the CHEM, but that's not our major concern," Daniels said as he opened a new window on his laptop.

"BW?" asked Finn.

"Until Syria's Foreign Ministry deputy, Jihad Makdissi, assured the world that they would never use their chemical or biological weapons on their own people in July 2012, we were not totally convinced that Syria even had BW," Daniels said. "But that's what the man said."

Box 731

"And now you believe him?" Finn asked. "So Langley wants to send a CIA team into an underground weapons facility, guarded by SAMs with seventy-five Russian SPEC OPS boys on their way in, just to see what they've got? I, for one, am thrilled this mission was scrubbed."

"Not exactly, Mr. Finn. Syria has invested heavily in their pharmaceutical industry since 1992. The sector has exploded both in size and output."

"That's great. At least the Russians and the jihadist groups can get their prescriptions filled when they get back to their ships in the Port of Lattakia. Listen, I'm going to get some food out of the chow tent before we fly back to Jordan," Finn said as he got up to leave.

"Which is why we need you and Jessup to stop by and visit the Andulus University for Medical Sciences in Al Qadmus . . . down closer to the Port of Tartus . . . the Russian port *without* any Russian ships . . . at least right now," CIA Special Agent Daniels said as Finn stopped dead in his tracks.

"Excuse me?"

"If there's a Syrian government-sanctioned BW program, Andulus is the only research university that could possibly be doing the necessary work. We'd like to send in a TV news crew to find out how this major research university is coping with the civil war; conduct a couple of interviews, film some b-roll, plant a few hidden cameras, and then go home."

"Geez, Daniels!" Jessup started to protest but was quickly outpaced by Finn.

"Right, an American TV news crew walks into Syria to file a science report. That worked really well for the NBC news crew recently."

"Not American, French. Jessup is fluent in French, and we have a Syrian operative who can produce the segment. I need a man of color who will shut up, keep his eyes open, and investigate while he holds a camera. As I recall, you were in the Montreal field office for a few years before Manhattan. I'm guessing you know a little French too. Besides, I would think an old organized crime investigator like you would enjoy being back in the saddle."

Finn and Jessup exchanged glances as an uneasy tension filled the tent.

"Then again, maybe I was wrong," Daniels said as he closed his laptop.

Finn turned around and sat on the folding chair in the back of the tent.

Jessup blew the tension out of her mouth and sat down as well.

CHAPTER 9

Lightner Farms
Gettysburg, Pennsylvania

Eileen heard the landline ringing as she shuffled through the back kitchen door of the lodge with two bags of groceries.

"Hold on, I'm coming, I'm coming," she yelled to the ringing phone as she put the grocery bags on the counter and rushed over to the desk in the dining room by the long wooden table. "Hello, Lightner Farms Bed and Breakfast."

"Ma'am, please hold for General Jim Ferguson," the major at ISAF headquarters in Kabul, Afghanistan, said as he quickly put the call on hold.

"Eileen? How are you doing? This is Jim Ferguson in Afghanistan."

Eileen started to panic. "General Ferguson, how nice to hear from you. Merry Christmas!"

"You're right . . . It's not that far off . . . Merry Christmas to you, as well. Eileen, I was trying to get in touch with Captain Campbell, but he's not answering his cell phone. I wanted to make sure everything was okay."

Eileen ran her fingers through her hair as nervous tension took over. She had warned Camp that this might happen. Eileen refused to bless Camp's spur-of-the-moment excursion, regardless of assurances that he would have access to the best medical care available in Israel. More than his health, Eileen told Camp she would not lie to anyone about his whereabouts. Eileen was a straight arrow, and she wasn't inclined to fudge the truth about anything or for anybody.

"Eileen? Are you still there?"

"Yes, sir, um . . . Camp enrolled in a residential physical therapy treatment center. The program lasts about two weeks and patients are somewhat isolated so they can focus on rest, recovery, and getting their heads cleared out. He should be discharged in about two weeks. Can I have him call you?"

Now Ferguson's line went silent for a moment. "Yes, yes, please, have him call me."

"Yes, sir, I will."

"Eileen?"

"Sir?"

"Is this a military program?"

"The physical therapy program? Well, it's a joint civilian-military program. He's doing great, so I suspect he'll come back feeling better."

"Well, let's hope so. A few weeks ago I signed off on an R&R request for Lieutenant Colonel Raines, who took twenty-one days of leave from Fort Detrick as well. The timing is coincidental, isn't it, Eileen?"

Eileen felt her heart beating in her throat. "Well, sir . . . I need to tell you the truth," she said as she took a deep breath. "Leslie stopped calling a few weeks ago, and neither Camp nor I have seen her since the day he came home from the hospital. I think that's been part of the problem for Camp."

Eileen held her breath and grimaced as she waited for Ferguson's silence to end.

"Well, I wasn't expecting that. Merry Christmas, Eileen. Please have the captain call me when the PT program is complete."

Box 731

Tel Aviv, Israel

US Navy Captain "Camp" Campbell walked out of Talin's at 231 Ben Yehuda Drive, into the high-noon sunshine and right into the backseat of the waiting black Mercedes.

"Did you find what you were looking for, Shepherd's Pie?" Reuven asked with a mischievous smile as the driver pulled away from the curb for the four-minute drive to the Tel Aviv Hilton.

"I think so," Camp said as he exhaled loudly.

"How's your chest? Feeling okay?"

"Chest is good . . . Heart is a bit jumpy. You said room 4310?" Camp asked, hoping to confirm the simple details that were becoming harder to remember.

"You'll be fine," Reuven said as the driver pulled up.

The bellman from the Hilton opened Camp's door as the driver popped the trunk lid.

"You know how to reach me," Reuven said as Camp's single navy seabag was placed on a brass luggage rack and his car door was closed. Camp tapped on the backseat window glass and walked through the automatic stainless steel revolving doors and into the expansive Hilton lobby.

On cue, the hotel manager was waiting for Camp directly inside the lobby. "Mr. Smith, welcome to the Hilton Tel Aviv. My name is Benyamin Asher. Your arrangements have all been handled. Our bell captain will take you to your king corner suite on the top floor. Here's my business card. Please call me directly if you need anything. Mr. Smith, we have you staying for ten days. Is that correct?"

Camp was immediately overwhelmed. He hadn't even thought through reservations or using his real name. He was still on the US government's "do not fly" list into Israel. Fortunately, Reuven had handled everything.

"Yes, thank you."

The bell captain put Camp's solitary bag on the luggage rack inside the hotel suite, opened the sliding door overlooking the pure blue Mediterranean Sea, and left the room before Camp could dig out any tip money. The fresh sea salt cleansed his lungs and brought back vivid memories of the night he met Reuven.

Camp was the odd man out during that high-level security meeting with Daniels and Jessup from Central Intelligence, General Ferguson and Billy Finn from ISAF headquarters, Reuven and Yitzhak from Mossad, and their counterparts from Shin Bet and the Israeli Defense Forces, IDF. Camp and Reuven were the only ones who appeared to understand the gravity of the Iranian tularemia threat. But Reuven and Camp had come to verbal blows during the meeting. Camp walked out hastily and bolted for his room at the same Hilton Tel Aviv. Camp smiled as he recalled his "accidental" encounter with Reuven in the hotel lobby later that night and the "covert" trip over to Molly Bloom's Irish Pub, which was the beginning of their friendship over shepherd's pie and Guinness beer.

Reuven, one of the most senior members of the world's most effective and ruthless intelligence agencies, had become one of the best friends US Navy Captain Camp Campbell, a former SEAL and a decorated trauma surgeon, had ever enjoyed.

It was an unlikely friendship that centered on coming face-to-face with the woman Camp was in love with, the same woman who now wanted to be left alone.

He removed the binoculars from his bag and explored the sea and beaches that rolled for as far as he could see from north to south. His eyes scanned back toward the hotel and to the pool below. Tourists and their children enjoyed the pool and the warm salty air that blew in from the Mediterranean. Camp's binoculars panned the deck until he found a solitary figure, isolated on a lounge chair. The book she was reading covered her face, but the long legs and brunette hair pulled back in a ponytail could not betray the identity of the woman.

Box 731

It was Leslie Raines.

Camp's heart missed a beat as he quickly pulled Asher's business card out of his front pants pocket. He walked over to the room phone and dialed the number.

"Yes, Mr. Asher, this is, um, Mr. Smith. I just checked in . . . Listen: could I get a bottle of Turonia Rias Baixas Albarino and two glasses?"

"Certainly, Mr. Smith. If we don't have that bottle will another fine Italian Pinot gris meet your needs?"

"Actually, no . . . It really needs to be the Turonia."

"Any preference on the year?"

"No. Whatever you can find will do."

"I will send it up immediately, Mr. Smith," the hotel manager said. "Is there anything else?"

"Yes . . . you have waiters at the pool bar?"

"Yes, sir, would you prefer the bottle be delivered poolside?"

"Ah, no, but could you send me one of the hotel's waiter uniforms as well?"

"Yes, of course," Benyamin Asher said after a brief pause. "As I said . . . anything you want."

Camp hung up and reached into the Talin's shopping bag, removed the gift box, and put it on the nightstand.

CHAPTER 10

Hadida, Syria

Six Russian paramilitary soldiers and four Red Mafia bodyguards patrolled the perimeter of the safe house in Hadida as twelve Hezbollah soldiers watched from their three vehicles. All weapons were drawn, though neither side expected trouble from the other.

The "deal" going down inside the safe house was much greater than the tension outside the house.

Semyon and the Bratva's big boss sat on floor pillows on one side of the room and faced the troika from Hezbollah on the other side. The commander of Assad's underground mercenary group sat in the middle. He was the mediator.

As was customary with such meetings, no weapons were allowed in the room. Semyon stroked the pistol grip of the 9mm stowed in his black combat boot and wondered where the three Hezbollah commanders had hidden their weapons.

Hezbollah, the party of God, was a Shia Islamic militant group politically rooted in Lebanon. They received political and financial support from both Iran and Syria. Hezbollah, Syria, and Iran had a common cause—they all hated Israel.

Muslim clerics created Hezbollah, and the Iranian Revolutionary guards trained them, after the Israeli invasion of Lebanon in 1982.

Box 731

What started as a resistance force soon morphed into Hezbollah going on the offensive and calling for the destruction of the Zionist entity.

The "evil storm" would finally give them the overwhelming power they needed.

"I presume you brought the money?" the boss asked as he tipped his Detroit Tigers baseball cap back and looked into the eyes of the troika leaders.

Two large, soft-sided satchels were pushed to the center of the floor.

"That's half of the money," the oldest Hezbollah leader said calmly. "One for brother Assad, and one for the devil."

"Half? Not even the devil takes half his money," the boss said as Semyon stroked his boot.

"Our apologies . . . but I do not see my R-17 Scud missile launcher parked outside the commander's safe house. I do not see my two Scud missiles with their Agent 15 chemical warheads."

"You aren't getting R-17s. The deal is for the Scud-B."

"They are old."

The Red Mafia boss reached out and pushed the two bags of money back toward the Hezbollah leaders.

"A Scud is a Scud. The Scud-B is more than capable of meeting your needs."

The room remained silent as a veiled woman entered with a tray of hot chai tea poured into small Turkish cups that were made of porcelain and decorated in gold.

"What about the Zionists?" the Hezbollah leader asked.

"We have crafted a diversion. They will be focused on biological weapons when we transfer the missile system into your control."

"Protection?"

"We'll deliver the product safely to you, five hundred meters away from the border. Once it is in Lebanon, you're on your own.

But I wouldn't hang on to it very long. The Israelis have many eyes in the skies looking down at you."

"When?"

"President Assad's commander will contact you. It won't be long."

The troika rose to their feet, followed by Semyon and the boss.

"Don't forget to bring the rest of your money when we meet again."

The Hezbollah leaders left the safe house as the commander quickly opened the satchels and began to count the money.

"Ekaterina's project is ready to go. Oleg is in position," Semyon said as the boss watched the red taillights of the Hezbollah vehicles drive down the dirt road and cross over the border between Syria and into Lebanon.

"Good. Get started."

Lightner Farms
Gettysburg, PA

The caller ID on Eileen's landline indicated the same number as before so she let it go to voice mail. She knew it was General Ferguson's office again.

Eileen had never been angry with Camp before. She had watched him lay on the floor by her sister's bed for more than a year. He had taken care of Eileen by making sure everything Jane needed was taken care of and paid for. Camp never asked for anything in return. But now he had gone too far. Camp's spontaneous—and unauthorized—excursion to Israel while he was supposed to be in her care during recovery put Eileen in an awkward situation. She wasn't willing to lie to General Ferguson again.

Box 731

Eileen pulled out her iPhone and scrolled down to her last text message to US Navy Captain Camp Campbell. She read the message and found the words she never wrote. They were Miriam's seeds of evil that almost cost Camp his life: Love you too . . . Just wanted to say good-bye . . . My life is not worth it anymore . . . Tonight I will meet god . . . Peace be with you.

Eileen cringed as she read it. She imagined Camp's horror as he drove frantically to save his deceased fiancée's sister, only to come face-to-face with the disfigured face of the devil herself.

Eileen's initial anger with Camp over Ferguson's call simmered. She typed out a new message: Sailor . . . Ferguson's office has called 2x looking for u . . . Told them u r in a 2-week residential pt program . . . U need to connect with him ASAP.

She pressed send and deleted the new voice mail without listening to it.

CHAPTER 11

Tel Aviv Hilton

Camp was admiring his new waiter's uniform in the bathroom mirror as the iPhone began to vibrate on the granite countertop next to him. He picked it up and quickly read Eileen's message. He knew General Ferguson and his coffee-pouring majors could be a problem if they learned he was traveling. But it would cause an international crisis if they discovered he was in Israel.

Camp opened the e-mail icon on his phone and carefully selected his Gmail account instead of his official US Navy e-mail service. His message was short and succinct: Sir, Eileen said you called. Thanks for checking up on me. This pt program is excellent. Feeling much, much better. Will call you when they release me in two weeks. V/R, Capt Campbell.

Camp placed the corkscrew, two glasses, and the box from Tanil's on the service tray, covered as much as he could with a white cloth napkin, and held the bottle of Pinot gris in his free hand as he left the suite and headed down the corridor to the elevator bank. Camp reasoned that keeping two empty wine goblets secure on a tray while walking created more personal anxiety for the combat trauma surgeon than either combat or surgery ever had. He reminded himself to be more generous with gratuities in the future because of it.

The elevator doors opened in the lobby and Camp emerged in full "pool boy" regalia. He was convinced everyone was looking

Box 731

at him, especially curious as to why the pool bar waiter was leaving the guest tower with a full bottle of wine and two empty glasses.

Mr. Benyamin Asher looked up from behind the concierge desk as Camp walked past. Camp knew the hotel manager would be more than curious as to why Mossad's American guest with a grizzled beard wanted to wear a staff uniform only to deliver a bottle of wine to a poolside guest.

Camp felt Asher's gaze on the back of his neck and assumed the manager would be following him from a safe distance.

Camp didn't care. He was on a mission.

The glare from the early afternoon sun reflecting off the sand and the Mediterranean was instantly blinding. Camp balanced the tray against the wall and quickly pulled the Oakley shades down over his eyes. His heart raced frantically when he realized "the woman" was in the same spot, reading the same book, on the other side of the pool.

He walked past several tourists reclining in the sunshine. An older gentleman raised his hand and called out to Camp.

"Waiter," the man summoned.

Camp was oblivious and had already forgotten that he was in uniform.

He placed the tray down on the glass table next to the woman, reached under the white cloth napkin, and removed the corkscrew. Without saying a word, Camp held the bottle out for her to inspect.

The woman lowered her book, looked at the bottle, and then pulled the book back up.

"Nice selection. Turonia Rias Baixas Albarino is my favorite Italian Pinot gris . . . but I didn't order it," she said dismissively.

"Compliments of the house," Camp said in the most ridiculous attempt at an Israeli accent he could invent on the fly. "I was told the wine is for US Army Lieutenant Colonel Leslie Raines. I presume that's you?"

Raines sat up suddenly and slammed her book closed. "Excuse me, but I did not check in with military affiliation," Raines said indignantly as she scanned the others around the pool.

Camp poured the first glass and then pulled out the second glass.

"Excuse me? Two glasses?"

"For your guest," Camp said as he filled the second glass.

Raines held out her hands. "No, no, no . . . some guy out here sends me a bottle of wine and thinks he's just going to join me because I'll be flattered? Take it back. I refuse it."

Camp pulled a chair over close to Leslie's recliner and sat down. He reached for Leslie's glass of wine on the table.

"Just what in the hell do you think you're doing?" Leslie demanded with highly visible, self-righteous indigantion painted across her face. Her rising voice was drawing idle stares and the concerned attention of Mr. Benyamin Asher.

Camp pulled his sunglasses up and reached out with the wine glass. "Leslie," Camp said softly, all traces of the Israeli accent gone.

Anger and irritation dissolved from Leslie's face and was quickly replaced with shock. "Camp?" Leslie asked as she lowered her sunglasses, trying to convince her eyes that what she saw was, in fact, real. "How did you find—"

"I finally found the woman of my dreams and I almost lost you in Yemen. I grew to admire your strength in France where I fell in love with you. You're my soul mate, Leslie Raines, you—and only you—you are the only reason I came back. And I won't leave this world again unless you're in my arms."

Leslie's lower lip started to quiver and tremble uncontrollably. Tears filled her eyes and began to stream down her cheeks. She struggled to hold back the sobs. "What about—"

"Jane? I saw her. I talked to her. Yes, I'm sure I called her name out while I was in the hospital. I'm sure that fact still hurts you . . . and confuses you. Maybe it was the drugs . . . or maybe

BOX 731

it was a near-death experience. Call it what you want, but I came back for you. I'm in love with you, Leslie."

Leslie covered her mouth and nose with both hands as she could no longer restrain the deep cries that started to escape from a broken heart that was quickly healing.

Camp was tempted to reach out and comfort her but he wasn't ready to touch her yet. He pulled the napkin back from the service tray and grabbed the box from Tanil's. He opened the lid and got down on one knee.

"Be my best friend. Be my compass. Be my soul mate, companion, and lover. Be the mother of my children and the grandmother of our children's children. Grow old with me, Leslie. Laugh with me, dance with me, and drink wine with me until we're old and tired. Leslie . . . please . . . will you marry me?"

Leslie Raines was hysterical. Though she lost all decorum, poise, and military bearing, she was no longer the least bit confused. She threw her arms around Camp's neck as thirty-six poolside sunbathers, tourists, authentic waiters, and Mr. Benyamin Asher all heard US Army Lieutenant Colonel Leslie Raines say yes.

Part II

CHAPTER 12

Universitat de Barcelona
Bellvitge Institute for Biomedical Research
Barcelona, Spain

Professor Jouta Tanaka glanced at the clock on the back wall of the lecture hall. He had fifteen minutes to wrap up his lecture on selectively targeted muscle regeneration. Dr. Tanaka believed his findings could be used to develop new treatments to help regenerate muscular injuries and bridge the muscular challenges associated with dystrophies. The professor's wide array of post-doctoral and graduate students, were trying to focus on alpha-enolase proteins and plasmin.

Tanaka, however, was focused on lunch.

It was, after all, Friday, and Friday was sushi day at his favorite Japanese restaurant Bonzai Sushi in Barcelona.

Dr. Tanaka rose through the faculty ranks at the University of Barcelona for more than twenty-two years. He started at the Barcelona Science Park's Institute for Bioengineering of Catalonia. But once the prestigious Bellvitge Institute for Biomedical Research offered him his own laboratory for muscle growth and regeneration, his life—and his career—took off on a different trajectory.

Jouta Tanaka and his wife had two children. His two sons were members of the latest incarnation of sixty-three thousand University of Barcelona students pursuing seventy-five undergraduate degrees, more than three hundred graduate programs, and ninety-six doctorate studies. Even though it was one of the oldest universities in the world, UB was only the fifth oldest in Spain and was considered the "youngster" among Spanish universities. The first class of students walked through the ornate gates and entered the lecture halls with soaring ceilings in 1450.

Neither history nor tradition was lost on Jouta Tanaka. He had plenty of history and tradition himself. But none of that mattered on Fridays.

Tanaka dismissed the class promptly at noon and nearly sprinted down the center aisle as students casually gathered up papers, folders, cell phones, and computers.

A line of three taxis was waiting outside the institute as they did every day at lunchtime.

"*Calle Sarajevo Cuatro*," Tanaka said to the driver as he sat back for the short ride.

Tanaka was out of his taxi and walking into Bonzai Sushi seconds after his cab driver pulled into the parking lot next to the eight-story red brick building that housed apartments, restaurants, and patio cafes.

Bonzai Sushi Restaurant

Oleg had been following Professor Tanaka from the second taxi that was waiting in the queue at the university.

"*Parque en la parte de atras, por favor*," Oleg said in a thick Russian accent as his driver pulled around to the back of the building near the loading docks. Oleg reached between the seats and offered ten euros with his right hand as he planted the needle of a syringe deep into the driver's neck with his left.

Oleg stepped out of the taxi, opened the trunk, and walked around to the driver's door. Within a few short seconds the

BOX 731

sleeping driver was safely stowed in the trunk, and Oleg pulled "his" taxi around to the front and just a few steps from the glass entry doors of Bonzai Sushi. He opened his newspaper and waited for his only passenger of the day, Dr. Jouta Tanaka, who was already eating his Friday special: the three-and-three tray with six pieces of salmon and six pieces of spicy tuna, nigiri rolls of raw fish. Tanaka's second Kirin beer hit the table as Oleg flipped through the newspaper and waited.

Within twenty minutes Dr. Jouta Tanaka checked his watch and then exited the front door of Bonzai Sushi and stepped out into the sunlight. Oleg noticed that he appeared to be delighted to see a waiting taxi. Tanaka opened the back door and got in.

"*Universitat de Barcelona, Bellvitge Institute*," Tanaka said to the taxi driver through the six-inch payment window between the Plexiglas dividers that provided security for cabbies against thieves who knew they were often loaded with cash.

Oleg nodded.

The taxi headed down the main road toward the university as Professor Tanaka checked voice mail on his cell phone.

Oleg looked through the rear-view mirror and smiled as he noticed the professor was using a Net 10 Motorola GSM phone. Global System Mobile phones simply searched for open cell connections in the local vicinity and dropped the calls just as fast. They weren't nearly as robust as a 4G phone, which uses the mobile wireless broadband network infrastructure.

Oleg took a hard left off the main street, which rocked his untethered passenger into the middle of the back bench seat.

"No, no, no . . . wrong street," Tanaka yelled as he folded up his phone.

Oleg pressed the automatic door locks. Tanaka saw the locks go down.

"This is good here," Tanaka said as he looked for familiar buildings about a mile from the campus.

Oleg kept driving.

Tanaka opened the phone again and punched in the numbers for university security.

Oleg removed the nineteen-dollar portable cell phone signal blocker from his shirt pocket and pushed the button until the green light illuminated.

Tanaka heard the ringing tone just before the call was lost.

Oleg made two more turns and started to drive faster.

Tanaka redialed. Nothing. "Please, stop the car. I want to get out," the passenger said with heightened tension.

Oleg stared straight ahead.

Tanaka looked at the cab driver's GPS device in the window. They were nearing the water, the deep sea Port of Barcelona.

Tanaka pulled up violently on the door handle.

Oleg pulled a hard right and accelerated the speed of the stolen taxi.

Tanaka pounded on the windows and pressed his face against the glass. He screamed for help.

Oleg drove past the cruise ship and charter Terminal D, and over to Port Vell, the old port. The commercial terminal had two marinas for yachts, fishing boats, and a maritime station for ferries traveling to the Balearic Islands and other destinations in the Mediterranean.

Oleg hit the number three speed dial key on his phone. "*Bot*," he said quietly and ended the call.

The taxi stopped at the edge of the dock on the third pier. Tanaka was left to watch in terror as two men got off of the first moored yacht and ran toward the taxi. The lettering on the side of the vessel read *заход солнца*. Oleg whispered "sunset," and Tanaka screamed when the automatic door locks disengaged and both back doors opened simultaneously.

No one said a word as the real cab driver started banging on the trunk lid. And no one was around to hear any of the professor's muffled screams or witness his duress as he was thrown onto the yacht with both engines idling before he was stowed beneath the

BOX 731

main deck. Ropes were loosened from the steel ties on the pier, and within seconds the yacht was in the channel bound for the Balearic Islands.

Oleg called Semyon first to confirm the package and then dialed Ekaterina's number as the coast of Barcelona started to fade behind the yacht that was named *Sunset*, which was now at full open throttle.

Andulus University for Medical Sciences
Near the Port of Tartus, Al Qadmus, Syria

Two armed bodyguards led the three-member freelance "TV news" team of Fallon Jessup, Billy Finn, and their CIA producer and interpreter, Walid "Wally" Jamil, to the doorsteps of Andulus University. The old and well-worn Land Rover Discovery made the 336 kilometer drive through the dark Syrian night in fewer than seven hours. Leaving the Syrian refugee camp near the Oncupinar border crossing, the bodyguard drivers were only stopped twice by various rebel groups.

Billy Finn was more than just a bit concerned that the rebels "recognized" both bodyguards yet gave them all quick and safe passage. He noticed that even Wally, a Syrian schoolteacher turned CIA recruit, was pleasantly relieved.

Rebels and journalists usually got along well together. But Finn was more concerned with Assad's Syrian government forces. The rebels wanted media coverage and publicity. The Syrian army wanted to hide the entire revolution behind the fog of war and out of the eyesight of an international television audience.

Andulus was a private university and, though only established in 2005, enjoyed a nice reputation for their schools of dentistry and pharmacy. With the pharmaceutical sector of the Syrian economy expanding at a rapid pace, the CIA took special interest in Andulus, not because of good drugs and medicines but rather because of their new laboratories with their inherent ability to concoct lethal biological weapons under the guise of good public health.

The two bodyguards with concealed weapons led Wally and the freelance TV news team through the front doors and inside the university.

"We have an appointment with Professor Hafiz Haidar," Wally said in Arabic to the front desk manager, who stood to greet them. "We are with the French media *Agence France Presse*."

The manager picked up his phone and dialed the professor's office. After a short conversation, he led the team up three flights of stairs to Haidar's office and laboratory. Fallon Jessup carried the microphone, a clipboard, and a makeup bag, just as any good reporter would. Billy Finn carried the television camera and a rickety old tripod. The two bodyguards carried a 9mm automatic pistol each with extra clips hidden beneath their untucked shirts.

Dr. Haidar welcomed the crew into his office with gracious hospitality and a large smile. He immediately dispatched his assistant, who returned with six cups of hot chai tea. A too-close-for-comfort mortar explosion jolted Billy Finn's hand as he reached for his tea. Professor Haidar was undaunted and hardly noticed what had recently become an hourly occurrence.

"It is an honor to meet all of you. Andulus is delighted to host such a prominent media group as AFP," Haidar said in Arabic as Wally translated in French for Jessup and Finn. Fallon Jessup was fluent in French. Billy Finn had enjoyed more than his fair share of French fries and French toast, but unless they were all going to sing *"Frère Jacques,"* he knew he was shit-out-of-luck with anything that Wally might translate in French.

"Thank you for agreeing to meet with us, Dr. Haidar," Jessup said in French as Wally translated back in Arabic. "As we promised, we are not here to talk about the rebels or their rebellion."

BOX 731

Haidar nodded and allowed manufactured remorse to fill his expressions. "Yes, these are sad days in Syria. But, God willing, we will prevail."

"Inshallah," Wally added.

"We would like to interview you on camera here in your office," Jessup continued. "We want to know about your students, your university, and how you can improve the lives of the Syrian people. I know that you are training pharmacists who will mix the compounds and produce the medicines for your people. Are you also doing any research here?"

Haidar waited for the complete translation and then quickly shook his head. "Not yet. When we open our School of Medical Engineering, then we will have a full research program."

"After we film our interview with you in here, we would like to film some b-roll of you walking in your labs and in the classrooms where your students study," Jessup finished.

"Yes, but as I said before, we are not allowed to film students or speak with them."

Billy Finn set the camera on the office floor and unfolded the tripod just as he had practiced numerous times before in Kilis. The camera snapped perfectly into the head and powered up just as it was supposed to. Fallon Jessup took the SLR cable out of her makeup bag and connected one end to the microphone and the other directly into the camera. Just as they had rehearsed, Wally pointed to Fallon's face, and she quickly reached for a foil pouch in her makeup bag and tore it open. She set the makeup container on Haidar's desk and quickly applied some more powder as Wally apologized to the professor, who didn't seem the least bit put out by Fallon Jessup's beauty or primping.

The interview lasted fewer than ten minutes. Haidar seemed pleased and proud of his performance. Finn just hoped he had pushed all of the right buttons to record.

Haidar led the news team down the hall, down one flight of stairs, and into the main classroom. Finn held the camera down by his side with one hand and just kept the camera recording as he nonchalantly flashed the lens in and out of rooms in the hallway as they walked by.

Holding the microphone close, Jessup conducted the interview as Professor Haidar stood in front of the empty classroom and explained how a Syrian education at Andulus was far superior to most places in the world. Finn didn't understand a word he was saying but understood "pompous" as a personality trait that translates perfectly in all types of body language.

Haidar toured the team through two laboratories, where students learned how to mix various ingredients into ointments, lotions, pills, or other medicaments. The professor paused in the first lab and gave another speech for the camera. The lab looked pristine, as though no one had actually ever worked in it before or Haidar had it scrubbed to perfection for a TV news crew.

The second lab was messy. Haidar stuck his head inside and waved his hands with an Arabic explanation that suggested ongoing work prohibited an interruption. The office door in the back of the second lab closed abruptly as Haidar tried to hustle the news crew out.

Jessup made eye contact with Wally. "I'd like Professor Haidar to tell us in this lab what university he attended and how he earned his credentials," Jessup asked Wally in French, who started to translate quickly. "We have heard that no one is more qualified to lead this program in Syria than Dr. Haidar."

Wally translated, and Professor Haidar immediately seemed to grasp the importance of such a question. His ego was sufficiently stroked. He moved over in front of the messy lab bench and waited for the microphone. Billy Finn put the camera back on the tripod.

On cue, Wally pointed to Fallon Jessup's face again and then started to apologize profusely to Haidar about female vanity in France as Jessup the reporter removed another foil pouch from her makeup bag.

Box 731

As Wally stroked the professor's imagination, Jessup opened the silver resealable foil pouch and removed a Pro Strips 5 Biothreat Detection Kit, complete with a testing compact, moisture pouch, the swab micro-tube, and liquid buffer. She pulled out a powdering sponge for good measure. Jessup set them all on the lab bench counter.

The Biothreat Detection Kit compact looked something like an early pregnancy test device. Five colors—blue, red, black, purple, and orange—coincided with five biological weapons— Bacillus anthracis, ricin toxin, botulinum Toxin, Y pestis plague, and staphylococcal enterotoxin—and would register positive, negative, and inconclusive results just like an EPT.

Fallon unscrewed the cap from the diluent tube and removed the swab. Finn started humming *"Frère Jacques"* as Wally dove deep into Dr. Haidar's childhood history.

While powdering her nose and forehead, Jessup ran the swab over a sizable area of the lab bench and then back into the diluent tube and tightened the cap. She shook the tube up and down for five seconds as she started to close her makeup bag. Jessup removed the clear protective cap from the top of the swab device and then snapped the tip off the top of the tube, which transformed the bottle into a dropper. She squeezed ten drops into the sample basin, put the plastic protective cap back on, and placed all the items back into the silver resealable foil pouch.

"Pardon me, I'm ready now," Jessup said in humble apology for the twenty-second delay.

Wally moved aside and offered the Arabic translation as Jessup created some quick questions in French.

After brief farewells and another round of mutually expressed gratitude, the bodyguards got them back inside the Land Rover and ready to depart within forty-five minutes from the time of their arrival. The exit out of Syria would be much more dangerous under the light of day.

"Well? Anything?" Finn asked as Jessup removed the Pro Strips 5 Biothreat Detection Kit from the silver pouch.

Jessup held the compact up in the light near her back seat window. The team had trained with the detection kit and already knew that two lines indicated a positive for that particular analyte, or substance. One single line under the C, with no visible line under the T, meant the test had worked correctly but the test sample was negative.

Finn rewound some of the tape in his camera and set the camera on VCR mode. There was something that bothered him in the second lab and he hoped he'd caught it on tape.

Jessup examined the results and then looked out the window.

"Wally, take a look at this and tell me what you see," Finn said as he pulled the LCD screen out from the camera body and pushed play. "Somebody's face can be seen before the back office door closes."

Wally examined the footage carefully as Finn kept rewinding it.

"It's a man," Wally finally said.

"I know that," Finn said, exasperated. "Anything unusual about the man?"

"He's not Middle Eastern . . . maybe Asian?" Wally answered as Finn verified his own hunch.

"Come on, Jessup . . . are we pregnant or not?"

Jessup placed the compact back into the silver resealable pouch that also served as a biohazard bag.

"Four negatives," she finally said.

"And one positive? For what?" Finn begged.

"Anthrax."

As the Land Rover pulled away from the front of Andulus University for Medical Sciences near the Port of Tartus, retired FBI Special Agent Billy Finn, CIA Special Agent Fallon Jessup, and CIA operative Wally Jamil did not notice the two military transport vehicles parked and waiting down an adjacent side street.

Box 731

Andulus University for Medical Sciences

Semyon stormed through the front doors of the university, past the front desk manager, and up two flights of stairs followed by six heavily armed Russian paramilitary soldiers. They entered the second lab where Dr. Haidar was talking with Dr. Okito Yamamoto, recently freed from self-imposed exile in the lab's back office.

"Who was here?" Semyon barked as the Russian soldiers fanned out in the lab as Haidar cowered in fear.

"French TV news . . . they're doing a story on Andulus," the professor tried to explain.

"*Aypak*," Semyon grunted. He pulled his Makarov PB suppressed pistol with a secondary suppression out of his belt and fired at point-blank range into Dr. Haidar's forehead. Yamamato was hustled out of the lab by two overpowering Russians as the other soldiers carried four thirty-pound sealed containers down the stairs and into their waiting vehicles.

"Where are we going?" Yamamoto begged as he was pushed into the back of the second vehicle.

"Port of Tartus, a little boat ride, and then the Balearic Islands," Semyon said as he lit a cigarette. Semyon pulled out his two cell phones and called the commander of Assad's mercenary force on the phone with the latest Russian encryption technology.

"*Da* . . . I have a situation I need you to handle for me."

CHAPTER 13

Molly Bloom's Irish Pub
Tel Aviv, Israel

Camp and Leslie snuggled together on one bench in an oversized wooden booth at Molly Bloom's Irish Pub on Number 2 Mendele Street across from the American embassy and Dan Hotel on Hayarkon Street in Tel Aviv. Camp promised Raines it would be a late lunch to remember.

"Incredibly romantic destination to take your fiancée," Raines said playfully as she surveyed the mostly empty pub. "I'm surprised you were even able to get a reservation."

The waitress stopped by the table, threw down two drink coasters, and never uttered a word as she stared at Camp.

"A Pinot gris and a Guinness, please," Camp said as she departed as silently as she had arrived.

"So, do you even know who Molly Bloom was?" Raines asked.

"I don't know . . . The queen of Ireland?"

"Did you ever read any of James Joyce?"

"Did he play football?" Camp asked.

"Molly Bloom was a fictional character who appeared in Joyce's novel *Ulysses*. In the book she was married to Leopold Bloom, an Irish Jew, who was one of the main heroes in the book. It's still a masterpiece in English literature."

BOX 731

"How do you know so much about it? I tried to read *Ulysses* at the Naval Academy and I couldn't finish it. Not the easiest thing to read, if you know what I mean, Les."

"I read it six times," she said with a hint of pride.

"On purpose?"

"My grandparents Karl and Lydia don't own a TV or a computer. Never did. Our only form of entertainment around the house was the radio, old vinyl albums on the phonograph, books . . . and dancing."

"Dancing? You danced with your grandparents?"

"Mostly just with Karl." Raines laughed. "Pops taught me everything about ballroom dancing and swing. As soon as I got home from school I had to do my chores and then my homework. After dinner, Lydia would escort me to the chair on the porch, cover my legs with one of her handmade blankets, and hand me a book of classic literature. I didn't understand *Ulysses* at first, but after my fifth reading the lights went on."

The waitress dropped a mug of Guinness on one coaster and spilled a few drops of the Pinot gris on the other.

"We'll order food in a few minutes," Camp said to the back of the waitress who had all but left the area.

"Everything in *Ulysses* unfolds in a single day, kind of like Jack Bauer and *24* on steroids. Joyce melds Celtic lyricism and vulgarity into an overpowering experimental work of realism. It's just fascinating. Oh my God!" Leslie squinted as her eyes focused on the front door of the pub. "Look who just walked in."

Reuven entered through the red doors of the green-painted pub, stood front and center on the black and white floor tiles, and scanned the restaurant. His eyes fixed on Camp's smile and Leslie's shocked face. He walked over and sat down.

"You knew we were here?" Leslie asked with respectful awe.

"Congratulations, Colonel Raines. I understand the two of you are to be married," Reuven said with a hardy smile cutting through the crease of his lips.

Leslie's head snapped over to look at Camp, who was soaking up the moment.

"Mr. Molly Bloom, here, was discovered by my father as he was covertly sneaking around Eileen's tool shed back in Gettysburg last week. He said he had some INTEL for me; said he knew where a certain love of my life was holed up on a beach in Israel," Camp said as Leslie's eyes widened with disbelief. "After circumventing the do-not-fly list, Molly Bloom brought me to Israel, dropped me off at Tanil's jewelry store, and left me at the Hilton. The rest I did on my own."

The waitress reappeared, and before she could say nothing again, Reuven ordered two more Guinness beers and another Pinot gris to go along with three shepherd's pies.

"Make sure to add a shot of Blackbush to each pie," Reuven said, not looking at the waitress, who walked away not talking. "Have you set a date?"

Leslie's eyes sparkled and she took center stage as Camp held her newly engaged hand.

"My grandparents were married on February 28," Leslie said as she looked into Camp's eyes. "We want to get married on the same day."

"Next year?" Reuven asked as the waitress dropped his beer on the coaster and put another beer and wine glass in the center of the table. He raised his glass.

"No, February 28 as in ten weeks from now," Camp said as Reuven faked choking on his first swallow. "My dad's in failing health, and Leslie's grandparents aren't getting any younger."

"Can you get a church that quickly?"

"We want to be married outside, in the snow, and among all of the white birches in New Hampshire. We're thinking a very small wedding on my grandparents' farm."

"Well . . . I wish you great happiness and I wish I could be there," Reuven said as he hoisted his mug.

BOX 731

"You will be," Camp said smugly. "Molly Bloom . . . I'd like you to come and be my best man."

"I'm afraid that's not possible," Reuven said with a straight face until a rare and unusual smile dashed across his lips. "Actually, I've reconsidered. May I bring my wife?"

Three steaming hot bowls of spiked shepherd's pie were tossed on the table as they enjoyed the engagement dinner.

"Eat up and enjoy," Reuven said, "for tomorrow I have something very special planned for you both."

"An infectious disease?" Raines laughed.

"No. We're going by helicopter to the Old City . . . I want to show you Jerusalem."

Aleppo, Syria

As the Land Rover Discovery entered the outskirts of the war-torn city of Aleppo over the M45 highway, the driver suddenly veered left and to the northwest.

"What's going on?" Wally Jamil, the Syrian CIA operative, asked no one in particular in the front seats.

"Too dangerous right now with rebel factions," the driver answered in Arabic. "We're going to take Highway 62 up to Afrin, then over to the border with Kilis."

The Land Rover continued another twelve miles until they pulled into a fueling station in Dar Ta Izzah. The driver pulled up to the pump, and then he and the other bodyguard got out and walked up and inside the small fueling station just as fourteen armed rebels ran out with weapons drawn.

Billy Finn rolled his eyes and bowed his head.

"Oh sweet mother of God," Finn whispered as the butt of a rifle shattered the glass window by his head and the back door opened violently.

Indian Creek Island
Miami Beach, Florida

Ekaterina heard the prepaid TracFone vibrating. She ripped the phone off the Velcro and looked down at her Cartier Ballon Bleu wrist watch. It was almost five o'clock in the afternoon. Viktor hadn't returned to the *Castello Del Luna* from his latest business trip, but she expected him at any moment.

"Yes."

"Ekaterina . . . we have one of your friends on a Russian yacht heading for the Balearic Islands," Oleg said.

"I've told you before . . . do not use names," Rina scolded as she looked through her open bedroom windows just as Viktor's car pulled through the gates. "What about the other two? When will you have them?"

"Don't worry your pretty little head off, Ekaterina. Semyon has a plan too. Meet us in four days . . . change of plans . . . we will meet in Ibiza."

"What's wrong with Mallorca?" Rina asked as she heard the front house door open and close.

"Nothing's wrong with Mallorca . . . Semyon feels like some nightlife before we do your dirty little deed and he finally gets his hands around Viktor's neck. That's all."

"Where?"

"Rina!" Viktor called upstairs from the foyer entrance.

"The Hotel Corso, dinner, Thursday night at eight o'clock, in the outdoor restaurant overlooking Marina Botafoch Harbor," Oleg said as Rina closed her phone and threw it into the red Tignanello hand bag. Viktor's heavy steps started to ascend the marble stairway.

Rina stepped quickly out of her room to greet him at the top of the stairs. "How was your trip, Viktor?" she said with a sudden flurry of dispassionate interest and calmness.

Box 731

"Just like every other trip, Любимая моя."

"You haven't called me sweetheart in fifteen years," Rina said with suspicion.

"That's because you haven't acted like one in sixteen," Viktor said as he handed Rina the file. "There you go, just as you wanted. You are now the proud owner of a laundry detergent company in Sault Ste. Marie, Michigan."

"Me?"

"Yes. It was too complicated to use my name. Besides, I will never visit there again, and I don't want to hear about it again. It felt like Siberia up there."

Viktor walked into his bedroom and started to change as Rina stood in his doorway.

"A strange birthday gift, don't you think, Ekaterina? Last year you asked for a condo on the French Riviera. Two years ago, I give you African safari with thirty-five servants and deluxe accommodations. This year, for your fiftieth birthday, you ask for a soap company in Michigan . . . a soap company that was in bankruptcy. A bit strange, no?"

Viktor pulled off his boxers and reached for his Speedos.

"I'm bored, Viktor. I want to do something. I want to try my own business. I want something that belongs to me, that I'm responsible for."

"Hmmm . . . perhaps you're finally growing up, Любимая моя," Viktor said as his protruding belly folded down and over the low-rise band of the Speedos. "It only took fifty years."

Viktor walked past her and down the marble stairway toward the bimbo-infested pool as Rina planned her trip to the Balearic Islands, an archipelago of Spain in the western Mediterranean Sea, near the eastern coast of the Iberian Peninsula.

Kyoto, Japan

The Kintetsu Railways train stopped at the Kyoto Station and Dr. Martin Ishii held his ninety-year-old mother's hand as they slowly walked the two blocks to his childhood *machiya*.

The doctor had assured Martin that his mother was in excellent health and could possibly live another thirty years.

Martin wasn't sure if that was supposed to be the good news or the bad news. The world-renowned infectious disease scientist had been unemployed for fewer than six weeks since Fort Detrick dropped the sequestration ax on him and several other "nonessential" US government employees. Finding a suitable job for a sixty-two-year-old PhD wouldn't be easy, Martin reasoned, but perhaps easier than tending to his mother for another thirty years.

Amaya Ishii walked immediately over to her kitchen, started a fire in the *hibukuro,* and began to heat a pot of water for green tea.

Martin's cell phone rang. The screen read "Unknown Caller," so he decided to let it go to voice mail.

"Masahisa, go get some mint out of the *kura* for our tea," Amaya directed as only a mother could do.

Martin put the phone in his pocket and begrudgingly walked through the house and outside to the storehouse with the same childhood obedience he had demonstrated for six decades. He may have been an accomplished scientist with international degrees and accolades, but Amaya was still the boss.

The phone rang again.

Martin looked up and saw the smoke starting to escape the chimney above the *hibukuro*. He could buy a new house for both him and his mother, but he knew that family tradition would never allow it. He had offered a new house to his mother multiple times over his career. She wouldn't leave.

But he had to. "Hello?"

Box 731

"Hello, my name is Richard Williams, and I'm the executive vice president at Science Search here in Chicago. I'm looking for Dr. Masahisa Ishii," the voice said over Martin's phone.

"How did you get this number, Mr. Williams?"

"Well, your name and telephone number were given to me by a Dr. Ernst Groenwald in Maryland. He said you might be looking for a new opportunity."

"What kind of opportunity?"

"A job, Dr. Ishii. I'm a recruiter—headhunter if you prefer—and I'm looking for a microbiologist to fill an executive position in Michigan. It's a CEO position for a small lab and they're offering a $325,000 base salary plus benefits. Are you interested?"

Martin reached into the *kura* and pulled out a handful of mint leaves. He had never earned that kind of money and had never been chief executive officer of anything before.

"Masahisa! Where's the mint?" Amaya yelled from the kitchen.

"Why does the position pay so much money?" Martin asked as he walked back toward the kitchen.

"Probably because it's located way up in the Upper Peninsula of Michigan, basically the middle of nowhere. That's the downside," Williams explained. "Nobody really wants to go there. What do you think? Care to explore it? The client is willing to fly you out here for interviews."

"What do I think?" Martin asked rhetorically as he stopped in the hallway. The doctor's words echoed in his thoughts. *She could live another thirty years.*

"Dr. Ishii?"

"Yes, I would like the interview."

CHAPTER 14

Tel Aviv, Israel

Three black Mercedes were parked and waiting outside the Hilton as Camp and Leslie emerged through the revolving glass doors. Camp suspected another half-dozen cars were in the area and out of sight. Mossad never took any chances, especially in their own backyard.

"Good morning, Leslie . . . Good morning, Shepherd's Pie," Reuven said with a nod to his driver as they took off for the short ride to the Palmachim Air Force Base. "It's a short flight to Jerusalem from Palmachim. We'll see some sights, take lunch, and have you back in time for your romantic dinner or room service, whatever you choose."

"I'm so excited, Director Shavit. Visiting Jerusalem has long been a dream of mine," Leslie said as she snuggled into Camp's arm.

"Please call me Reuven. We are now good friends," Reuven said, scanning the buildings and cars that passed by as his car headed toward Palmachim.

"You never said I could call you by your name," Camp feigned in protest.

"We are not good friends," Reuven deadpanned. "Have you two decided where you will live after the wedding?"

Reuven watched through the long rear-view mirror panel that hung above the windshield from the driver's door to the

Box 731

passenger's door as Camp and Leslie exchanged glances. Reuven had noticed the indecision, Camp observed quickly.

"Ah . . . still working through the minor details of merging two military careers and your Uncle Sam's assignments, I see."

"Well, Leslie is two years short of retirement, whereas I could drop my papers today. If we're lucky, Leslie can stay at Fort Detrick and I can finish out at Walter Reed."

"So will you stay in Washington after your careers?" Reuven asked.

"Maybe not," Leslie explained. "I was raised in New Hampshire and I'd like to settle there. I want to apply for a teaching position at New Hampshire State University."

"NHSU is only a five-mile drive from the town where Leslie's grandparents live," Camp added.

"And what about you, Shepherd's Pie? Are you going to clean rodent cages at NHSU?" Reuven asked, looking straight into Camp's eyes through the mirror.

Leslie reached out and held Camp's hand as his fingers tapped nervously on his knee.

"Still working through that one too, Molly Bloom. But Hillsborough County would be a great place to raise our children," Camp said.

"Children!" Leslie choked. "Who said anything about having children?"

The conversation grew quiet as the Mercedes passed through the checkpoint at Palmachim.

Dar Ta Izzah
Syria

Billy Finn, Fallon Jessup, and Wally Jamil were pulled from their Land Rover and dragged behind the gas station building. One of the abductors carried the TV camera and the other had Fallon

Jessup's makeup bag. Finn saw the Land Rover being driven into the field behind them. An RPG round was fired into the fuel tank. The fireball stayed in the sky long enough for the three to be searched and cuffed with plastic restraints behind their backs.

"Get your dirty hands off me," CIA Special Agent Fallon Jessup screamed a second before the butt of an AK–47 rifle smashed across her high cheekbone, spouting blood from a new four-inch gash on her face.

A blindfold was tied around Finn's eyes and a rag of some sort was tied as a gag across his mouth. Finn assumed Fallon and Wally received the same treatment when Fallon's excruciating pain was muted to muffled groans.

The three were thrown into the back of a box truck and driven immediately down a bumpy dirt road.

ISAF Headquarters
Kabul, Afghanistan

One of General Ferguson's coffee-pouring majors answered the telephone ringing on Ferguson's desk.

"General Ferguson's office," the major said and then put the call on hold. "Sir, CIA Special Agent Daniels on the line, says it's urgent."

Ferguson shuffled through a stack of papers he hadn't touched in weeks, held up his coffee mug for Major Spann, and answered the call as hot coffee was poured into the general's cup from the decanter on the conference table.

"Ferguson."

"General, we've got a situation."

"We've all got situations, Agent Daniels; what's yours today?"

"Bill Finn and Fallon Jessup . . . they've gone off the grid."

BOX 731

"What the hell? What do you mean they've gone off the grid?" Ferguson demanded as he bit off the tip of an Ashton Belicoso and torched it three times. "In Jordan?"

"No, sir, in Syria. They were making a fifteen-hour incursion into Syria, a university near the Port of Tartus that we suspect is producing biologicals. They were supposed to be back in Turkey three hours ago."

"Turkey?"

"Yes, sir . . . of course we had GPS tracking on their vehicle and had been in COMS with their Syrian operative until they got to Dar Ta Izzah. Then we lost them."

"Lost them?" Ferguson asked with irritated emphasis. He put the call on speakerphone and paced the room behind his desk and in front of the classified maps on the wall. "Spann, get me a map of Syria!"

"Satellites detected an explosion in Dar Ta Izzah at exactly the same time their GPS and COMS went dark."

Ferguson rubbed his balding head rapidly while his fingers massaged a forehead that had just become very tense. "Status?"

"Unknown, sir. But I thought you should know."

"Hell yes, I should know. Billy Finn is my asset," Ferguson barked.

"Actually, sir, he's an asset assigned to both of us."

"That may be, Daniels, but I've also been calling Billy Finn my friend for nearly seventeen years. Keep me posted."

Ferguson pushed the button and terminated the call as Major Spann walked back into the office with a freshly printed and rolled map in his hand.

"Get it up and put a flag-pin on Dar Ta Izzah, or whatever the hell it's called."

Ferguson took a quick swallow of the hot coffee and another pull on his Ashton before he started dialing Lightner Farms in Gettysburg, Pennsylvania. Ferguson looked at the wall clock. It was six thirty in the morning.

"What time is it in Gettysburg?" Ferguson asked as the phone started ringing.

"Nine-and-a-half hours later, sir, it's just past four o'clock in the afternoon."

Port of Tartus
Syria

Dr. Okito Yamamoto was ushered past the steel storage containers down the center aisle of the ship. He watched as the gigantic overhead crane dropped another container into the cargo hull of the massive ship. Yamamoto was led up the stairs and into a large internal cabin on the MV *Chariot*, a rusting red Russian freighter built in 1984, flagged out of St. Vincent in the Grenadines, and ported permanently in St. Petersburg, Russia.

The MV *Chariot* was a well-known Russian vessel and was often called upon to do the dirty work, usually nefarious deeds that always seemed to raise the ire of international observers. After the fall of the Egyptian government in the summer of 2011, the *Chariot* transported tons of consignment to the Democratic Republic of the Congo, including tons of grenades, rockets, mortars, and more than four million rounds of ammunition. The *Chariot* had been a frequent guest in the Syrian Port of Tartus, delivering arms and weapons to the Syrian government that quickly fell into the hands of various rebel factions. In February 2012, the *Chariot* called at the Iranian port of Assaluyeh for thirty-three hours after completing a four-week voyage from the Ukraine.

The Russian paramilitary soldiers started changing out of their uniforms and stowing their weapons as Yamamoto watched. Within minutes the soldiers were transformed back into casual crew clothing and returned to the deck of the ship to finalize the loading process.

BOX 731

Semyon pulled out his two cell phones and checked his watch as the call connected.

"Da," the voice said on the other end of the call.

"The ghost commander has the Americans," Semyon said cautiously, hoping not to provoke another tirade from the big boss.

"Good. Move them down to the safe house and hand them over to the troika."

Semyon paced on the deck of the *Chariot*. He assumed a quick execution and buried bodies in the Syrian Desert would be his next order.

"Okay," Semyon said with obvious uncertainty.

"We can use this situation to our advantage. Don't hand them over to the troika until I give the order. Semyon?"

"Yes."

"Use the nonencrypted phone for all further conversations about the Americans and the troika."

Semyon was shocked. The speed of his pacing doubled as he pulled out a cigarette and lit it quickly.

"But the Americans will be able to listen to our conversations."

"Da . . . and so will Mossad. Where is Oleg?"

"He's in position. Ekaterina is flying in."

"Good."

Old City of Jerusalem

Reuven walked slowly next to Camp and Leslie as a circle of Mossad security agents engulfed them from all sides, though they all remained unnoticed by the thousands of tourists and religious pilgrims visiting the Temple Mount.

They started up the rising pathway to the right of the Western Wall.

"The Temple Mount is one of the most historic and significant places for Jews, Muslims, and Christians," Reuven explained. "I believe it is the holiest place on earth."

"Jerusalem is so hilly," Leslie observed as she looked out over the old city. "But this area is flat, almost perfectly flat."

"After David conquered Jerusalem, he purchased the flat rock at the top of Moriah from a Jebusite who had used it as a thrashing floor," Reuven said as they meandered along the path. "It was here that David's father, Solomon, built the first temple, which was destroyed by Nebuchadnezzar around 586 BC. Herod enlarged the spot and rebuilt it into the most massive religious venue in all of the eastern Roman Empire. The vast Temple Mount you see now, Leslie, was artificially created with flat, stone-paved platforms. Herod expanded the Temple Mount to almost thirty acres in order to handle all of the religious pilgrims in his time."

"Then more destruction?" Leslie asked.

"Yes. The Romans destroyed the temple complex in 70 AD. The Muslims conquered Jerusalem in 638 AD then built the Dome of the Rock and the Al Aqsa Mosque."

"Can we go inside?" Leslie asked, pointing to the mosque and the Dome of the Rock.

"Not right now. It has been open in the past, maybe once again in the future," Reuven said as he looked over at Camp. "You're pretty quiet today, Shepherd's Pie."

"I'm just taking it all in. It all seems so oddly familiar to me," Camp said.

"These images have been on your television screens since you were a child. The Temple Mount is familiar to billions of people," Reuven explained.

"Probably so," Camp said as he opened and closed his eyes and squinted toward the Western Wall.

"Al Aqsa is the third–holiest place of prayer for Muslims after Mecca and Medina. The building was completed in 720 AD and

Box 731

it's where King Abdullah the First of Jordan was assassinated in 1951, in the presence of his then fifteen-year-old grandson, the late King Hussein of Jordan."

"Why was he killed?" Raines asked.

"There were those in Islam who were afraid he preferred peace in this area, peace with Israel. That was deemed unacceptable."

Reuven led the entourage of Camp, Leslie, and Mossad security down a stairway to the subterranean chambers called Solomon's Stables.

"Some believe these were the stables that housed King Solomon's one thousand horses. Others do not."

"What do they believe?"

"Many Muslims believe Israel's Solomon was in fact their Ottoman Sultan Suleiman the Magnificent, who rebuilt the walls that surround the present Old City and who repaired the Dome of the Rock during his reign in the mid-sixteenth century."

Reuven led the group across Temple Mount Plaza and past a fountain surrounded by pink marble seats.

"What are those?" Raines asked softly as Reuven kept walking.

"*El-Kas*, where Muslims perform their ritual ablutions before entering the holy places," Reuven said as he stopped and looked skyward at the shiny gold dome. "Even though they assassinated his grandfather up here, King Hussein of Jordan completely rebuilt the dome and regilded it with 176 pounds of twenty-four-karat gold in 1994. Pretty impressive."

"Can we see the Wailing Wall up close?" Leslie asked.

"Kotel, the last remaining remnant of the second temple . . . Herod's Temple. Let's go."

Reuven led the way down the descending path from the Temple Mount until the entourage stood one hundred feet away from the center of the wall. They stood in silent, reverent awe.

Leslie reached out and squeezed Camp's hand. "Isn't this amazing?" she whispered.

Camp felt distressed. Though nothing was between him and the Western Wall, he struggled to see it. A sharp pain filled the right side of his chest near the spot of the gunshot wound. Camp squinted and tried to focus, but the Western Wall was partially hidden, and his view was blocked by trees that didn't exist. He grimaced, let out a slight groan, and then dropped to one knee. He heard the sounds of a babbling brook beside him.

"Camp!" Leslie yelled as Reuven quickly turned. Reuven made eye contact with the physician who was traveling with the Mossad agents, and she immediately ran over to Camp's side.

"Are you in pain?" the physician asked as Leslie pulled back and the doctor moved in and felt Camp's neck for his pulse. Tears poured out of Camp's eyes.

"Talk to us, Shepherd's Pie. Are you in pain?" Reuven insisted as the doctor examined her partially collapsed patient.

"I've seen this," Camp uttered through a fog of competing emotions.

"This is a very holy site. Pilgrims of all faiths travel here to experience it. You are not the first to be overwhelmed," Reuven said, trying to reassure his American friend.

"No . . . I've seen this temple before . . . I couldn't go in . . . but now I can see it clearly," Camp said as Leslie moved closer and the doctor pulled back.

"Tell me what you've seen," Reuven said as he helped Camp back to his feet.

"It was massive . . . A warm glow emanated from within . . . Music filled the courts all around it; the music filled me . . . The building was tall . . . The floor inside appeared to be elevated and built with cedar, and the floors and walls were overlaid with gold," Camp described as the group of Mossad agents, who were supposed to be inconspicuous, inched in closer to listen. "There was a cherubim, one on each side of the building—angels made of olive wood—with outstretched wings that met below the ceiling in the center of the room . . . I saw a two-leaved door

Box 731

between the room and the holy place and it was covered with gold . . . There was a veil, like a fine linen curtain, it was blue, and crimson and purple; blue for the heavens, crimson for the earth, and purple for the bond between heaven and earth."

"Did this place have a name?" Reuven asked as Camp took a few steps closer to the Western Wall while his eyes gazed up and beyond.

Camp pointed to the east. "There was a gigantic porch on the east side . . . It must've been the entrance."

"The Ulam," Reuven whispered.

"I saw two large pillars inside . . . beneath the porch. They were shiny, almost glowing, like brass . . . but different than brass," Camp said as he visualized that which did not exist.

"Jachin to the south . . . and Boaz to the north," Reuven said knowingly.

"The pillars were only a few inches apart . . . They seemed to be marking time, some kind of a sun clock and their shadows revealed time. But when I saw them, time no longer moved."

Camp turned toward Leslie, held out his arms, and she fell deep into his embrace.

"Are you upset?" Leslie whispered as Camp held her tighter.

Reuven moved in close next to both of them.

"I saw what I saw, Leslie . . . I can't explain it. I didn't ask for it. It just is."

"I know what you saw, Camp."

"Did you just call me by my name, Molly Bloom? Now I know I've died and gone to heaven." Camp laughed.

Even Reuven couldn't hold back a smile. "You have given a perfect description of Solomon's Temple . . . the first temple. This is a gift, Shepherd's Pie . . . It is not a curse."

Camp let go of Leslie and the three stood shoulder to shoulder looking at the Western Wall and the shiny gold top on the Dome of the Rock.

"Molly Bloom . . . the place was full of people . . . all sorts of people . . . people who were men and women, people who were children . . . people of color . . . people who were Christians, Jews, and Muslims . . . all sorts of people."

Reuven's face didn't flinch. He let Camp's words swirl around his mind as he tried to contemplate Camp's vision from the depths of a near-death experience. "I don't know if that's possible," Reuven finally said as his colleague, Yitzhak, ran up and pulled Reuven Shavit, director of Mossad's kotsas in the Middle East, away from his deep thoughts and the solemn company of US Navy Captain Camp Campbell and US Army Lieutenant Colonel Leslie Raines.

"What is it?"

"Syria. Human intelligence in Aleppo reports that two Americans have been abducted."

"Not my problem," Reuven said with obvious irritation for being disturbed.

"They are CIA assets," Yitzhak pushed.

Reuven was still not interested and walked away.

"They've got FBI retired Special Agent Billy Finn," Yitzhak said as Reuven stopped dead in his tracks.

Camp heard Yitzhak speak his friend's name. He walked over to Reuven as the sun started to get lower in the skies of Israel. A golden hue of orange, yellow, and red started to dance on the Western Wall.

"Did he just say Billy Finn?" Camp asked.

CHAPTER 15

Dar Ta Izzah
Syria

Billy Finn guessed they had driven fewer than twenty miles when the truck finally stopped and the engine was turned off.

Daylight filled his blindfold when the back door of the box truck was opened. Finn felt the rough pull from one of the captors as he rolled off the freight deck and into the sand below. He heard the others falling and groaning next to him. The blindfold had shifted, and the sunshine penetrated his retina with blinding heat. He saw one of the captors jerk Fallon Jessup to her feet using her long blonde hair as a handle.

Finn sensed the clay and straw walls he was bumping into until he was pushed forward and fell face first into a larger room. Wally and Fallon landed on top of him before rolling off to the sides. The room was filled with excited and agitated Arabic chatter. A single gunshot rang out, followed by immediate silence that governed the chaos.

Billy Finn's blindfold was removed. His eyes adjusted and he saw blindfolds being removed from Wally and Fallon.

The apparent commander moved to the center of the room. The barrel of his pistol was still smoking.

"*Agence France Presse?*" the man asked in English, reading the ID badges belonging to Wally, Fallon, and Billy Finn. "I don't think so. Who are you?"

The commander motioned toward Fallon Jessup, and two captors quickly untied the gag from around her mouth.

"Who are you?" the commander asked again.

"Nous sommes des journalistes de l' AFP, qui font un reportage sur Andulus Universite," Jessup said in perfect French.

"Nice French. Where did you learn the American accent to go with it?" the commander asked as Fallon's gag was tied back around her head and mouth. "Anyone else want to try this simple question? Who are you?"

Finn dropped his eyes. He didn't think a round of "Frère Jacques" would help the cause given current circumstances.

"How about you? Are you a Syrian brother? Maybe you can tell me who these people are?" the commander asked as Wally's gag was removed.

"I work as the escort. They are journalists from AFP. She is the reporter. He is the cameraman," Wally said in Arabic.

The commander did not seem satisfied. Finn watched his every movement and his interaction with the other rebels.

"Fine. Then you shall die first," the commander said as Wally's gag was restored. Two rebels pulled him to his feet and took him into the next room.

Finn and Jessup flinched as a single gunshot rang out and a large thump hit the dirt floor of the building.

"So let me ask again . . . two more chances . . . who are you?"

Finn and Jessup exchanged nervous glances, but neither spoke. The commander motioned toward Fallon, and she was pulled to her feet by her hair and hustled out and into another room. A gunshot rang out and Finn heard her body hit the dirt floor.

Finn's eyes filled with tears. His heart raced and pounded through the walls of his chest. His breathing was heavy and labored.

"Last chance, my friend . . . who are you?"

One of the captors pulled the gag down from his mouth. Finn looked around the room at all of the rebels and the AK-47s

BOX 731

pointed at him. The commander's face was expressionless. Billy Finn cleared his throat.

"*Frère Jacques, Frère Jacques, dormez-vous? Dormez-vous?*" Finn sang enough to irritate the commander before the butt of another rifle came down across the crown of his head and the lights went out.

Mossad Headquarters
Tel Aviv, Israel

Camp Campbell and Leslie Raines paced back and forth in the conference room. They watched through the dividing glass walls as Reuven Shavit, director of Mossad's kotsas in the Middle East, received the situational report from his staff and field operatives in the region.

Reuven removed his wireless spectacles, stroked his nose with the tips of his fingers, and then got up and walked toward the conference room door.

"What's the status, Reuven?" Camp asked, foregoing all "Molly Bloom" nonsense.

"We have an asset on the ground there in Aleppo. The man says he's hearing that Fallon Jessup and Billy Finn posed as French journalists and conducted a television interview of sorts at Andulus University."

"What on earth?" Leslie gasped.

"They were escorted by a Syrian, a CIA operative by the name of Walid Jamil, and two armed bodyguards."

"Jamil turned on them?" Camp pressed.

"Didn't appear to. More than likely their hired guns took a higher fee," Reuven said as a map of Syria emerged on the flat panel monitor in the conference room. "This is Aleppo . . . It was one of the first cities to fall during the uprising. This village off to the west, Dar Ta Izzah, is probably where they were abducted."

"What the heck were they doing in Syria?" Camp muttered as Reuven pulled up another photo.

"Guess you'd have to ask Agent Daniels . . . or even your good friend General Ferguson."

"Why this university?" Leslie asked.

"Andulus has been on our radar screen for a long time, too. We know the Syrians have an advanced chemical weapons program. We suspected they had biologicals as well; BW they acquired from Russia as well as BW they were developing on their own. Andulus would be a great location for some pioneering research work," Reuven said as several photos of the university filled the flat panel TV screen.

"So what can you do about it?" Camp asked.

"Me?" Reuven asked without waiting for a response. "As you Yankees like to say, 'I have no dog in that fight.' At least for now, the abduction poses no national security risk for the state of Israel. I suggest you ask that question of Daniels and Ferguson."

Reuven turned the monitor off and gathered his papers.

"Well, let's get you two back to the Hilton for your romantic dinner."

"Sorry, Les, but I'm feeling less than romantic right now," Camp groaned as they followed Reuven out into the hallway, down the elevator and into the waiting Mercedes outside the building with no signs.

O'Hare International Airport
Chicago, Illinois

Dr. Martin Ishii handed his passport to the US Customs agent and declared no duty-free goods.

"Welcome back, Dr. Ishii. How long will you be staying this time?" the customs agent inquired.

Box 731

"Just a short trip for a meeting, actually a job interview, in downtown Chicago. I'm flying back to Tokyo tomorrow morning."

The agent stamped his passport and smiled. "Well then, good luck."

Martin passed under the security signs and rode the escalator down to the baggage claim area. As promised, a Town Car driver was standing amidst the throng of other drivers wearing black suits. He spotted the sign that read DR. MARTIN ISHII, nodded, and the driver carried his small suitcase out to the Lincoln Town Car parked in the second lane outside O'Hare.

The Town Car weaved in and out of traffic on the Kennedy Expressway, took the Wacker Street exit, and arrived at the Willis Tower, formerly the Sears Tower, in forty-five minutes.

Martin checked in with the guard desk, received his badge, passed his small suitcase through the security scanner, and then rode the elevator up to the sixty-third floor.

The name on the glass doors read Science Search Consultants, LLC.

Martin was checked in at the front desk and hadn't even sat down before an attractive young intern escorted him back to the video conference room.

"Can I get you anything to drink before Mr. Williams joins you?" she asked as Martin put his suitcase in the corner of the room.

"A bottle of water would be great, if you don't mind."

Richard Williams entered the video conference room carrying the bottle of water as Martin stood to greet him with a slight bow and a handshake.

"Dr. Ishii, it's so good to meet you. I appreciate your making the trip on such short notice," Williams said as he handed the water to Martin. "Were your travel arrangements satisfactory?"

"You can't go wrong with first class. I don't think I've ever traveled first class before. Thank you."

"Well, the owners of the company are holding back no expenses to fill this key position."

"Who are the owners, Mr. Williams?"

"Please, call me Richard. The company is held by a private equity group. Several on the ownership committee will be watching our interview over the Internet via a video conference call today. If they have specific questions they'd like me to ask of you as we're going along, they'll send them to me via text message. Are you ready, Dr. Ishii?"

"Please call me Masahisa, or Martin, if you prefer a more Anglicanized version."

Williams clicked on the video link, and within seconds Martin noticed the red recording light on the monitor in front of him. The images of three men and one woman in professional business suits popped up on the screen. Pristine blue water, perhaps a sea with palm trees blowing slowly in the breeze, danced in the background behind them. The four offered a subtle wave as Martin nodded with a friendly smile.

The interview lasted sixty minutes and covered a broad range of topics including management philosophy, financial reporting, and the mission of the company.

"I think that concludes all the questions that the ownership committee has for you, Martin. Do you have any questions for them?" Williams asked.

"Yes, I do, just a clarification really. You indicated that this laboratory is supposed to operate like a Department of Defense contractor doing research work on biological weapons and infectious diseases. But it operates inside a soap company that makes detergent? I'm still not clear on that," Martin said as one of the suited businessmen started typing on the virtual keyboard in his iPhone.

"Your existing security clearances make you a perfect fit for this position," Williams read as the first message came through. "Due to the nature of this work, we need a commercial front that

Box 731

is more amenable to the public, especially in this small town in Michigan."

Martin nodded. He certainly understood the rationale.

"Why Sault Ste. Marie, Michigan?" Martin asked as the woman typed her response and sent it to Williams.

"Anywhere but the Washington, DC beltway . . . if you know what I mean," Williams read. "And she offers a 'smiley face' as well," Williams added.

Martin laughed. He knew exactly why the private equity group wanted to be as far away from Washington as possible. He did too.

"Martin, the ownership committee has one more question," Williams said as he looked at his text message.

Indian Creek Island
South Miami Beach, Florida

Ekaterina typed away frantically on her phone, looking up occasionally as Martin waited for the final question.

What is your experience with anthrax?

Rina listened as Williams repeated the question, and Dr. Martin Ishii gave some long-winded, technical answer that was lost on Rina but verified that he knew what he was talking about.

"Yes, I am very familiar with anthrax," Martin said as Rina watched on her computer screen as she started typing another text message. "But I never worked directly with that bio agent. I do, of course, have the latest anthrax vaccine from the US military."

Midway through Martin's answer, Rina sent the other text.

Hire him. $325k base. All relo paid. I'm wiring your fee in 10 minutes.

Rina closed the teleconference video window on her computer and then pulled out the TracFone and called Oleg in the Balearic Islands in the Mediterranean Sea.

"Yes," Oleg answered quietly.

"Pay your four actors and send them home. See you tomorrow."

Rina looked out over the pool where Viktor was carrying a topless "business associate" on his shoulders in another game of pool chicken. She smiled thinking about Oleg's "ownership committee" actors who probably had to borrow business suits for an hour of video acting and received three hundred euros each. Rina logged in to her bank account and wired 33 percent of Martin's starting salary as a retainer fee to Science Search and Richard Williams. It was the easiest search fee they would ever earn. Rina thought about Martin's Town Car ride back to the airport and his first-class flight back to Tokyo. She imagined he would go home, celebrate his career break with his ancient mother, and then pack for a very short life in Michigan.

CHAPTER 16

ISAF Headquarters
Kabul, Afghanistan

General Jim Ferguson dismissed his coffee-pouring majors and
sent them off to the dining facility to eat and pick up a boxed
lunch for him while he tried to figure out what to do about Billy
Finn. He reasoned that since Finn was a "schedule A" civilian
in theatre, Central Intelligence had just as much right to use his
talents and skills as did Defense.

But as with most security and covert operations that are
initiated in Washington, fiefdoms spring up as interagency players
all jockey to avoid falling on the sword. In Washington, no one
is ever accountable. Ferguson imagined himself being called to
testify at a Senate intelligence committee hearing only to be asked
if he had prior knowledge of the CIA mission and incursion into
Syria. He of course knew something about the initial military
plan from FOB Roaring Lion in Jordan, but he knew nothing
about the ultimate CIA plan out of Turkey.

Everything would've been fine had Billy Finn not gone off
the reservation.

"Ferguson," the general snorted as he answered his own desk
phone.

"Sir, Captain Campbell . . . how ya doing, you old buzzard?"
came the familiar voice from the other end of the line.

Ferguson allowed himself a rare smile and a brief moment of levity. "Well if it isn't Lazarus himself. Nice of you to finally check in with your commanding officer."

"Sir, my commanding officer right now is a drop-dead gorgeous physical therapist by the name of Brandi."

"Is that right? I assume Colonel Raines hasn't met this Brandi, or Brandi would no longer be associated with your morale, welfare, and recreation."

"Negative, sir, Raines has not. But methinks the general is meddling in my love life again," Camp said playfully.

"Far be it from me to meddle in romance given my track record. How are you feeling, Camp?

"Much better, sir. Greatly improved. And I have some good news for you."

"Good news? I need some today, Campbell. Please tell me that you're retiring so I can shred your file."

"Well, it's not *that* good, sir. I'm engaged. We're getting married."

"To Brandi?" Ferguson asked, hardly able to contain his laughter.

"No! To Raines," Camp said.

Tel Aviv Hilton

Raines covered her laughter behind the pillow she held over her mouth as she listened to Camp and General Ferguson over Camp's speakerphone.

"Raines has time to accept your proposal but she can't return my phone calls? I thought she was on vacation, twenty-one days of leave and not even her grandparents know how to reach her."

Raines pulled the pillow away from her face with "what the hell" hands raised toward Camp.

BOX 731

"She did go to Costa Rica sometime back and then came to see me in Gettysburg," Camp said as he carefully parsed the truth. "Were you trying to reach her, sir?"

"I wasn't calling her grandfather in New Hampshire just to talk about fishing. Is she there with you now?"

"Where, sir?"

"There!"

Raines jumped off the bed, ran, opened the door to the hotel suite, and then stepped outside in the hallway, leaving the door open to listen.

"Actually, she just stepped out, sir. I can have her call you if you want."

"No need. The situation passed. So have you set a date?"

Camp motioned and Raines walked back into the room and sat back down on the king-sized bed next to Camp.

"Affirmative, sir. We're looking at Friday afternoon, February 28 at 1630 hours. Leslie wants to be married outside in the middle of her family's white birch trees."

"In the snow? What year?"

"This year, sir." Camp smiled as Leslie laughed out loud.

"Captain, that's in—what—a few weeks? Who the hell can attend your wedding on such short notice?"

"Well, actually in fewer than two months, sir. Hopefully you, Billy Finn, my parents, and a few friends can join us. Just a small wedding and some fun parties. Sir, put Billy Finn on so I can tell him the good news myself."

Mossad Headquarters
Tel Aviv, Israel

The technician heard the preplanned cue and motioned to Reuven and Yitzhak. The audio feed from Camp's mobile phone call was pumped into their command center. They heard General Ferguson sigh.

"Bad news, Camp. Billy's unavailable."

"Sir? Unavailable?" Camp asked, hoping to get some information.

"Can't discuss it on this line, Camp. Suffice it to say, we're trying to locate Finn as we speak."

"Any word on his condition, sir?"

"Negative. No word on anything . . . not a damn thing. Your old buddy Daniels has grown silent and doesn't know how to return phone calls either. I suspect his ass is in the proverbial meat-grinder right now."

"Sir, please keep me informed. Let me know if there's anything I can do to help," Camp said with complete sincerity.

"Your job is to recover, Captain. According to my calculations, your medical leave expires soon. As soon as you are cleared, we can talk."

The audio feed went dead and Reuven paced the room for a few minutes. "Get Langley on the line, Yitzhak, I want to speak with Special Agent Daniels."

Yitzhak started to dial the number when Reuven lifted his hand. He hung up. "Give me the file with all of our assets on the ground in Syria, especially those around Aleppo and Dar Ta Izzah. Then we'll call Daniels."

Dar Ta Izzah
Syria

Billy Finn sat against the dirt wall gagged and blindfolded. He couldn't be sure but he thought he heard the sounds of others breathing in the room around him. Footsteps approached. He heard several people stand and the sound of weapons clanging on buckles and clothing.

BOX 731

The gag around Finn's mouth was suddenly removed, followed by the blindfold. His eyes spent several seconds adjusting to the dim light in the room. He saw the commander standing in front of him. Finn looked around. Fallon Jessup was a few feet away and very much alive. Wally Jamil was next to her. Finn watched as rebels removed their gags and blindfolds as well.

The commander motioned, and three cups of dirty water were hoisted to each mouth as heads were forcibly tilted back.

"Don't want you to die before we kill you," the commander said.

Finn tasted the foul water but decided it was better to swallow and live another day than spit it out and die of dehydration.

"You two are Americans," the commander said pointing at Finn and Jessup. "You are a traitor, and a Sunni," he said pointing to Jamil. "And for that, you will be hung tomorrow morning and your body will be plucked by the birds for seven days until all Syrians know what treason looks like."

"So you're not rebels, are you?" Wally asked defiantly as he intensified his stare into the commander's eyes. "You're not even good enough for the Free Syrian army. You wouldn't have the courage to fight with the Ahrar Al-Sham brigades. You are nothing more than criminals, hired mercenaries, pathetic ghosts who rape, torture, steal, and murder our children. You are *shabiha*."

"And you're not journalists, so I guess that makes us even. Tonight my brothers will enjoy some fun with the woman and tomorrow we'll take a small drive. Sleep well."

The commander left the room as six armed captors kept their eyes focused on Fallon Jessup.

"What do we do?" Finn whispered as the abductors congregated, and as Finn suspected, made their plans and registered their claims for first rights with Fallon.

"Stall," Fallon said as her eyes never moved from the horror that was unfolding in front of her.

Finn heard the sound of a ringing cell phone in the other room as the commander's voice echoed above the growing chorus of abductors as their plotting grew more animated. Finn struggled to listen.

"Did you hear that?" Finn asked.

"I'm hearing lots of things and none of them sound very good," Wally said as he checked the tension of the plastic restraints that bound his hands behind his back.

"He said hello."

Jessup and Jamil looked over at Finn with not-so-subtle contempt.

"привет . . . that's hello—in Russian."

MV Chariot
Mediterranean Sea

"Dah," Semyon answered as he shoveled another spoonful of meat stew into his mouth. "Tell me the status." The galley kitchen on the *Chariot* was filled with the six Russian paramilitary crewmembers and Dr. Yamamoto, who ate silently by himself.

"We have them . . . just as you ordered," the commander said as Semyon listened and ate.

"Who are they?" Semyon asked before he took two long swallows from a German beer.

"Americans. One is Syrian . . . a Sunni."

"What was on the camera tape?"

"Nothing really. Looks like an interview. But the woman had a kit."

"What kind of kit?"

"Like testing. It had lines and letters with different colors."

Semyon took another large spoonful and spoke through the stew. "Take a picture and send it to me. Send it to this phone number."

BOX 731

Semyon waved to the cook and held up his empty beer bottle. A replacement beer was delivered to his table just as the shabiha commander's text message and photo pinged his cell phone. Semyon looked at the photo. It made no sense to him.

"Yamamoto san!" Semyon yelled to Dr. Yamamoto as he held up his phone.

Yamamoto walked over not knowing for sure if the call was for him or if his Russian employer was finally going to kill him.

"What is this?" Yamamoto examined the photo thoroughly for several seconds and then nodded.

"Well?"

"It's an inexpensive biodetection kit. It gives measurements for positive, negative, and inconclusive for several biological agents. This one shows a positive reading for *Bacillus anthracis*," Yamamoto said as he handed the phone back to Semyon.

"What's that?"

"That's anthrax."

Semyon pressed the redial on the phone.

"Yes."

"They're CIA. Take them down to the safe house in Hadida and have your Hezbollah brothers take them to Lebanon and kill them. Make sure their blood cannot be traced back to you or the Assad government. Let them blame it on terrorists. But don't hand them over to the troika until I give you the command. Do you understand?"

"Yes. What about the woman?" the commander asked.

"I don't care . . . but she doesn't die on Syrian soil."

Semyon ended the call and then picked up his encrypted phone and called the big boss.

Mossad Headquarters
Tel Aviv, Israel

Reuven and Yitzhak removed their headsets as Semyon terminated the call. With a simple nod, Reuven dismissed the technicians from the Middle East-Russian desk who had intercepted the call.

"Call the sailor and interrupt his romantic dinner. Tell him to meet me at Molly Bloom's . . . alone," Reuven said as he left the surveillance room.

Molly Bloom's Irish Pub
Tel Aviv, Israel

Camp was deep into his third round of Guinness when Reuven finally arrived. "This better be good. I'm not even married yet, and she's already pissed that I left her for work."

Reuven smiled. He knew *those* conversations all too well. "Get used to it, Shepherd's Pie. It never stops until we die."

Reuven pointed to Camp's beer as the waitress walked away without a word. "We intercepted a call. The Syrian abductors are working with Russians. They have your Billy Finn."

Camp pushed back in his seat and vigorously rubbed his sculpted, short beard. "Whoa, wait a minute. Syrian rebels and Russian military?"

"I didn't say that. I doubt the Syrians are rebels. This is not the typical style of the Free Syrian army. They're probably progovernment militia. I'd guess shabiha."

"And the Russians? What's their role? Why are they in Syria?"

"No idea . . . yet. Satellite positioned the call in the sea, just off the coast of Syria. We think it came from a Russian cargo ship, the MV *Chariot*."

"Who is shabiha?" Camp asked.

Box 731

"Shabiha means 'ghost' in Arabic. They began as invisible criminals out of Syria's coastal region in the 1970s. Their young men earned livings by smuggling electronics, drugs, and weapons between Syria and Lebanon."

"They're mafia . . . organized crime?"

"Yes, and they're Alawites. Alawites are a Muslim minority group, about 12 percent of Syria's population. They line up with the Shiites in Iran, but they're much more liberal. They have no problem with alcohol or celebrating Christmas. Most of the rest of the Syrians, and even the rebels themselves, are Sunnis."

"So what does that have to do with Billy Finn?"

"The family of Syrian President Bashar al Assad is Alawite. If the Assad regime falls, the shabiha falls as well. So they do the dirty bidding of the government because Assad is one of them. They repress the opposition to the Arab Spring, just as progovernment thugs did in Egypt, Yemen and Iran. In each case, the government outsources repression during public uprisings with a keen eye out for ethnic cleansing."

"What about Billy Finn?" Camp asked without trying to hide his growing concern.

"Mr. Finn and his friends apparently discovered some biological weapons while posing as TV journalists."

"Biologicals? I thought the Syrians favored chemicals, Agent 15 and all that other crap they were trying to fit on the warheads of their Scuds."

"Me too. We knew the Syrians were quite fond of their chemicals, and obviously we changed their nuclear ambitions at al-Kibar in 2007. We have long suspected they were pursuing biologicals but didn't really know that for sure, until your Mr. Finn got a positive test. And now *we're* interested."

"Positive test? Billy Finn? I doubt Finn passed any of his high school tests. What did he find?"

"Anthrax."

Camp sat back and soaked it all in. He knew enough about the anthrax attacks in Washington after 9/11 to know it was lethal. Given Syria's close proximity to the Golan Heights of Israel, he also knew why Reuven was suddenly interested in Billy Finn.

"So Billy's alive?"

"At least for a day or two. They're taking him down to a safe house in the south and handing them over to Hezbollah. The Russian told them to execute the hostages in Lebanon. I called Daniels at Langley. His folks had obviously intercepted the same call. We're trying to put together an operation."

"To rescue Finn?"

"No, to find out more about this anthrax."

CHAPTER 17

Kyoto, Japan

Dr. Martin Ishii received the official job offer even before he got off the Kintetsu Railways train in Kyoto Station. He didn't know all that much about the company, but the opportunity to be the president and chief executive officer of any company was beyond his wildest dreams.

His ninety-year-old mother was out running an errand, so Martin quickly logged in to his computer. He was still bitter that the Department of Defense had cut the funding for his position at Fort Detrick. Martin wasn't angry with Dr. Ernst Groenwald, but he would take great satisfaction informing Groenwald, and his close colleague Lieutenant Colonel Leslie Raines, that he'd been recruited to run his own company for $325,000 per year. The new job offer validated his self-image.

Neither of them made half that much.

He sent the e-mail and pulled two suitcases out of the closet. If he hurried, Martin could be packed and gone before his mother got home and shamed him into staying and caring for her.

**Miami International Airport
Miami, Florida**

Rina settled into her first-class seat for the flight to Madrid. After a short connecting flight to the Balearic Islands, she'd be enjoying dinner with a man she thoroughly despised but was determined to put up with.

Rina reached into her red Tignanello handbag and pulled out the thirteen—by twelve-inch aluminum and steel box that was three inches deep and put it on her lap as the flight attendant topped off her glass of wine.

Uncontrollable rage seeped into the dark recesses of her mind as she gazed down at the setting sun over the waves of the Atlantic.

Rina tilted the case up and looked at the scrambled numbers on the first combination lock through her reading glasses. She knew all too well that her rage lived inside that box, just as it did for her father until he died a broken man with his head on the curb and his body in a Moscow gutter as snow fell across his face in 2003. Dmitry was wealthy by most Russian standards but he too was consumed by the box. The police pried the frozen box out of his dead fingers that night as his ice-cold eyes stared upward at the rage that had finally consumed his life.

Rina's only brother, Ivan, was supposed to be the family's standard-bearer. He was supposed to have been entrusted with the box. But that was before the 1994 Chechen rebellion when a sniper's bullet put an end to Ivan's rage and his Russian military career near the city of Grozny.

Rina remembered Dmitry's hesitation when she first begged to be given the box.

"You're still young, Ekaterina. You have a new husband. Maybe I will have grandchildren one day. The box will only kill you like it kills me every day."

She started to spin the numbers on the combination dial. One. Zero. Two. Five. The Bolshevik Revolution began with the October uprising. The old-style Julian calendar marked the armed insurrection in Petrograd as beginning on October 25, 1917. But it was November 7 on the Gregorian calendar for the rest of the world, and the beginning of what would soon be Soviet Russia.

BOX 731

Rina's grandfather Pavel was a young officer in the Red Guards and had joined forces with Vladimir Lenin and Leon Trotsky to win the bloodless revolution that gave the Bolsheviks power and gave birth to the Soviet Union in 1922.

Rina started to spin the numbers on the second combination dial. Zero. Seven. Three. One.

That's when her rage boiled up to the surface. Every time she entered those numbers—seven, three, and one—the only thing she could think about was revenge. She was consumed with revenge.

As she did each time she opened the box, Rina reached for Pavel's old black and white photo, slightly bent and well-worn, but safely tucked away beneath the inside flap on top of the box. Tears rolled down her cheeks. Her fingers trembled.

The family photo was taken in 1943, just before Pavel received his military orders to visit Harbin, the largest city in Manchukuo in northeast China, as part of a diplomatic mission. The Imperial Japanese army had invaded Manchuria in 1931, and the Soviets wanted assurances that the Japanese weren't going to keep marching over the border and into the Soviet Union.

Pavel was forty-eight years old in the photo. Rina's grandmother and namesake, Ekaterina Tatyana, had a round, full face with a welcoming smile. Her father, Dmitry, was just an eleven-year-old boy in the photo. He stood proudly next to his father, with his hand on top of his father's, as they both cradled Pavel's military sword.

Pavel was a *polkovnik*, a highly decorated colonel in the Soviet army. He was known more for his diplomatic style than his tactical substance.

The Manchurian mission should have lasted but a few weeks, most of that occupied by long train rides across the frozen Siberian tundra of Russia and down into northeast China.

The official word the Soviets gave Dmitry and his mother was that Pavel was being held against his will by the Empire of Japan.

The Soviet Union and the Empire of Japan had signed a Neutrality Pact in 1941, two years after the brief Soviet-Japanese Border War and the battles of Khalkin Gol. Colonel Pavel Shmushkevich was not technically categorized as a prisoner of war, but his whereabouts were completely unknown.

When the Soviets finally declared war on Japan and invaded Manchkukuo and Mengjiang in August 1945, the family eagerly expected Pavel's liberation and a joyous homecoming.

What they got instead was an envelope. An envelope Rina kept inside the box of rage. An envelope simply labeled "731."

Palmachim Air Base
Israel

Leslie and Camp stood on the tarmac next to the steps leading up to the Dassault Falcon 7X long-range business jet as Reuven waited in the Mercedes.

Raines was upset. "I don't like this, Camp," she said as a Mossad agent took her suitcase into the plane. "I should be staying with you. Hell, you should be coming home with me. Just what in God's name do you think you can do to help Billy Finn?"

"I'll be fine, Les. I'm going to stay another two, maybe three days and see what happens. Ferguson won't tell me anything, and none of the Americans know nearly as much as these guys do. Besides, you've got a wedding to plan."

"Speaking of General Ferguson . . ."

"If he calls, just tell him I'm out and I'll call back. But make sure he gets a wedding invitation. Les, when you get back to Detrick, you need to bone up on anthrax. I have an uneasy feeling about this."

Camp pulled her close. With both hands he grabbed her face and kissed her. She wrapped her arms around him and squeezed as though she might not ever let go.

Box 731

"I called Eileen this morning," Leslie said with a sudden surge of disjointed excitement. "I asked her to be my maid of honor."

"And?"

"She screamed! She was so excited. I'm going to stay at Lightner for the next week and commute to Detrick. We can work on the guest list, invitations, decorations, and all of the other details. Oh my God!"

"What's wrong?"

"I haven't told my grandparents yet."

"Ah . . . aren't we having the wedding at their house? In the white birch trees, with snow? Don't ya think they might need to know?"

Leslie let loose with her trademark little smirk and picked up her handbag from the tarmac. "Oh, and I suppose 'Mr. D. Tails' has already told Ruth and Sea Bee?"

Camp rubbed his beard and smiled. "I will, I will . . . as soon as I get home. I promise. Enjoy the flight, Les. I swear private spy jets are the only way to travel these days."

With one more kiss and a quick wave to Reuven, Leslie climbed the stairs and the door to the Falcon closed.

Camp got into the backseat of the Mercedes next to Reuven as the Falcon reached speed and pushed up into the sky.

"Now what?" Camp asked as the driver put the car in gear.

"Now we go to work."

CHAPTER 18

Hadida, Syria

Billy Finn, Fallon Jessup and Wally Jamil had been bouncing around in the back of a dark truck for several hours. They were still bound, gagged, and blindfolded. Above the din of the truck speeding over dirt roads, vehicles passing by, and an occasional all-too-close explosion from an ongoing civil war, Finn heard whimpers and random sobs from Fallon.

He could only imagine the hell she'd been through the night before.

The truck bounced up and the drive got suddenly smooth. Finn felt the acceleration and assumed his death might be coming that much quicker as well.

The vehicle dropped off the pavement again and back onto dirt roads before several turns and an aggressive skid and stop in the sand. The engine was turned off.

The back door opened, and Finn felt sunlight seeping through the blindfold. He heard the sounds of Fallon and Wally being pulled out of the truck just before he felt two sets of hands pulling on his camera vest and shirt.

Finn was carelessly banged against the walls in the building and then shoved violently to the ground where he thought he must've fallen on Fallon—at least it sounded like her groan. He sat up and waited.

BOX 731

The footsteps that ran out of the main room were replaced by slow and methodical steps that entered. The person next to him was dragged to the other side of the room. Finn heard the sound of a tactical knife blade opening and then heard a cut followed by another. He was pushed forward and the plastic strap around his wrist was cut as well.

"You can uncover your eyes and your mouth," sounded the familiar voice of the commander.

Finn reached up and pulled the blindfold up and over his head. He squinted tightly to gradually allow light in. He reached back and untied the gag. Light started to filter in as Finn looked around the room. He was sitting next to Wally. Fallon was on the other side of the room. She was leaning against the wall, and a woman was cleaning the cuts and bruises on her face. The room was filled with floor pillows.

Finn grimaced at the sight of Fallon's facial injuries. Her right eye was completely swollen shut. Her lip was swollen, and the open cut was still bleeding. Her khaki pants were covered in blood from her groin down to her knees. Fallon's breathing was labored.

Two men entered the room with a pot of rice and a kettle of water. They put it down between Finn and Wally.

"Eat and drink. I don't want you to die before you're executed," the commander said as the room emptied.

The woman tending to Fallon put some salve on her eye and lips and then lifted a glass of water to her mouth. Fallon tried to swallow but most of the water dripped down over her blouse.

"Any idea where we are?" Finn whispered to Wally.

"I have a guess. Once we got off the dirt road and hit smooth pavement, I think we were on the M5 highway," Wally said as he grabbed a handful of warm but soggy rice and put it in his mouth. "Then our speed got faster. That means we didn't go through Homs, we went around it."

"Around it which way?" Finn asked.

"Had to be to the west based on the speed and the pavement."

"I smelled oil at one point," Finn observed.

"Me too; that must've been the Homs petroleum refinery. It's where the Ring Road and the M1 highway intersect. I think we headed west toward the sea from there."

"Are we still in Syria?" Finn asked as he put some rice into his cupped hand and into his mouth.

"Maybe . . . but just barely if we are."

"What do you mean?"

"I started counting once I smelled the refinery. Each time I reached seventy-five, I counted it as one kilometer. We turned left toward the south after sixteen kilometers. I think we got off the M1 and onto Highway 9. Then we stopped about five kilometers later."

"Thanks for the travelogue. So where the hell are we?"

"I'm guessing Hadida . . . about one thousand meters from Lebanon."

"Meters? You mean I could hit it with a three iron," Finn said as he got up and walked over to Fallon. Her head was resting against the wall with her legs straight out.

"Fallon," Finn whispered as he put his fingers inside her open palm. She closed her hand around his fingers. "You need to drink. Can you take another drink?" Fallon squeezed his fingers slightly. Finn raised the cup the woman had left up to Fallon's mouth and put his other hand gently behind her head. He felt the crusted blood on the back of her head and the missing patches of hair. He tilted her head back and poured some water into her mouth. She swallowed and opened her lips for another drink.

"They gave us some rice. Can you eat?"

Fallon shook her head slightly and then let go of Finn's hand. Finn scooted back over next to Wally as the commander's cell phone rang in the other room.

"That's Russian again," Finn whispered.

"What's he saying?" Wally asked.

BOX 731

"I think he said three days is too long. He wants them to come get us sooner. Fallon won't last three more nights with these pigs. Who do you think will come to get us?" Finn asked.

"Probably Hezbollah. Highway 9 cuts right through a little section of Lebanon in the north and then right back into Syria heading to the sea."

"How far is the Mediterranean from here?" Finn asked.

"More than fifty kilometers to the sea—first on Highway 9 and then Highway 3—but there's not much around there. One small village if I remember. You have to go another twelve kilometers or so north on Highway 2 until you reach the Port of Tartus."

"Tartus? So we've gone in a big circle. Isn't that just where we were at Andulus University?"

"Not really. We were in the Tartus Governorate, but Qadmus is another hour northeast of the port. Why are you so curious?" Wally asked as Finn poured some water in his cup.

"I want to know how far away we are from a rescue."

Wally shook his head. "No one is coming to rescue us, Mr. Finn. Better get used to it."

Finn listened as the commander was speaking on the phone.

"How is it you can only sing one stupid song in French but know Russian?"

"There wasn't a lot of French mafia in New York, if you know what I mean. And I don't know Russian, but I understand some of it," Finn said as he moved closer to Fallon in order to hear the phone call.

"What's he saying?" Wally whispered.

"Nothing about us, other than laughing about their evening with Fallon. He asked when he would get his money and told someone to enjoy dinner."

Mossad Headquarters
Tel Aviv, Israel

Reuven told Camp that Mossad routinely tracks and intercepts all Russian calls in and out of Syria. The Syrian desk scans through as many Arabic calls as possible, but the revolution had created a massive amount of frantic chatter that all pointed toward more internal strife and less international terrorism. Mossad was interested in anything that might foretell an attack in the Golan Heights, or anything related to the Russians who had become increasingly fond of docking both military and Russian-flagged cargo ships in the ports of Lattakia and Tartus.

Camp watched through the glass walls as Reuven took his headset off and read the short-hand report from the technician who intercepted the call then started to walk toward Camp and into the briefing room.

"Well?" Camp asked.

"Same two guys talking."

"Satellites?"

"One of the men has moved down to the southern border with Lebanon, probably the village of Hadida, between Homs and the sea. The other was in the Balearic Islands, off the coast of Spain, maybe in a hotel. It was a very short call. Not enough time to pinpoint everything exactly."

"So he's off the ship . . . That's a good thing."

"Maybe. The MV *Chariot* is heading back toward Turkey and Syria. But maybe not. Who else got off the ship? More importantly, what did they take off the ship?"

"Anything else? Anything about Billy Finn?"

"Nothing about Finn, but I suspect plenty about Special Agent Jessup. The one guy was bragging about how much fun they had with her the night before. Said she was roughed up and barely conscious, but he was looking forward to another night."

BOX 731

Camp dropped his head and closed his eyes. After his near-death experience he hadn't spent much time contemplating the realities of evil. He had journeyed to the other side where peace and kindness was the ultimate reality; where fragrance and texture filled every thought. He had a new lease on life and a rebirth of purpose. His heart was filled with love for Leslie Raines and his thoughts were occupied by an outdoor wedding in the snow, surrounded by white birch trees somewhere in New Hampshire.

Camp had all but forgotten that humans were brutal and the world was filled with pain between fleeting moments of happiness. But Camp also knew Reuven would never forget. That's what Mossad dealt with every day, shielding Israel from several hundred plans of terror and evil each moment of their fragile existence.

"So what do we do?" Camp finally asked as he raised his head.

"I'm calling Daniels at Langley. We need to do a joint operation, maybe IDF and some of your special forces."

Camp got up and paced the room. He cackled out loud. "A joint operation to rescue Finn and Jessup . . . with Russians in the mix? No way. We didn't even do that sort of thing in Libya. Look what happened to the ambassador in Benghazi! We even stood down there, for God's sake. They'll just laugh at you and send you over to the State Department and *they'll* just protest the detention, which means Finn and Jessup will be executed."

Reuven sat and slowly rubbed his fingers together. He wasn't one for showing emotion. "Then what do you suggest, Shepherd's Pie?"

"Plausible deniability. Keep this thing off the grid and out of the SECDEF's office. Get an ambitious undersecretary to buttonhole someone on the Joint Chiefs. Come up with some overarching reason why US national security is at risk, and then . . . then . . . maybe you've got a 5 percent chance that we'll do anything."

One of the Mossad technicians from the Spain desk tapped lightly on the door. Reuven nodded and the young woman entered. She spoke quietly in Hebrew and handed Reuven some photos as she left and closed the door.

"Maybe you do have an overarching national security interest," Reuven said as he pushed the first satellite photo over the mahogany table to where Camp was standing.

"Three ships docked close together. What are these? That one looks like a cruise ship," Camp said.

"The cruise ship is the Costa Serena. Next to it . . . that's the MV *Chariot*, the Russian cargo ship. And on the other side . . . that's a Canadian cargo ship."

Reuven pushed the second photo down.

"This is a high resolution close-up from our Ofek 9. Four small canisters are being loaded onto the Canadian ship next to the *Chariot*."

"Okay. Not seeing your point here, Molly Bloom. Are you suggesting these canisters are full of anthrax?"

"Andrea, the woman who runs our Spain desk, pulled archived imagery from the Ofek to determine when those canisters were loaded onto the *Chariot*."

"And?"

"Three days ago . . . in the Port of Tartus . . . Syria."

"Okay. And that's significant because . . . ?"

"Because they've now been taken off the Russian *Chariot* and put on a Canadian ship."

"So intercept all three dang ships."

Reuven got up and walked to the door. "If it's anthrax . . . we can't assume they off-loaded all of it. After all, the MV *Chariot* is already heading back this way. I'm going to call Daniels and your General Ferguson. Would you like to be in on the call?"

"To listen, yes . . . but I'm on medical leave and getting physical therapy in Gettysburg from an attractive and fictitious therapist named Brandi, remember?"

BOX 731

Hotel Corso
Ibiza, Balearic Islands

Ekaterina was the first to arrive at the outdoor restaurant overlooking Marina Botafoch Harbor at the Ibiza Corso Hotel and Spa. The host seated her at the open-air table against the partial glass wall. The round table was covered with an expensive white linen tablecloth, and the matching napkins were pressed and neatly folded in each wine glass setting.

Rina occasionally heard the pulsating beat and pounding music from the two clubs in the hotel. She had walked past the neon signs that indicated IBIZA STATION CLUB and LOVE POWER CHAPEL.

At least now she knew why Semyon wanted to meet at the Corso.

Oleg and Semyon were escorted over to Rina's table. Both were dressed in sleazy-looking Italian suits, hair gelled back, and open shirts unbuttoned down to their bellies. As pathetic as they looked, Rina thought it was a dramatic improvement since the last time she had seen either of them.

"You look nice this evening, Ekaterina," Semyon said with sufficient sincerity to pass as believable. "I trust your flights were good?"

The waiter arrived before Rina was forced to answer any small talk. She ordered a bottle of wine for the table. Oleg and Semyon ordered "keep them coming" double shots of the Corso's most expensive vodka.

"So what's the status of our project, gentlemen?"

Oleg lowered his head. He wasn't about to speak a word with someone like Semyon next to him. Oleg did Semyon's dirty work. He pulled the trigger when necessary and cleaned up messes. But he did not handle client relations.

"All three are in place, Ekaterina. We leave tomorrow."

"And the product?"

"Yes, well, Dr. Yamamoto and the shabiha have been very productive. We have more product than our contract called for. If for any reason we have a squabble over money, then I will take the extra product and sell it in the marketplace. I'm sure you can understand that even someone like me needs to hedge risk."

Rina reached down and removed a white business envelope from her red Tignanello handbag and gave it to Semyon.

"There's your second payment. If you try to sell any product in the marketplace that puts my project at risk, I will personally remove your eyeballs with a corkscrew."

Oleg couldn't resist a smile as he pounded his shot and signaled the waiter for more.

"Tell me about the three," Rina said as she opened her dinner menu.

"All three have been enlisted in the project, just as you specified. Two are coming by choice. Professor Tanaka wasn't quite as easy, but he's onboard."

"Literally," Oleg whispered before catching an angry glance from Semyon.

"Dr. Ishii has accepted his new job and is flying to Michigan. Dr. Yamamoto thinks he works for me, so he does whatever I tell him to do. It's all unfolding just as you wanted, Ekaterina. There is nothing to worry about."

"How will you get the product to the lab?"

"It's on a Canadian cargo ship with my team and will be arriving at the Port of Barcelona right about now. It's being transferred into eight suitcases that my guys will take on the Madrid to Toronto flight."

"What about the test?"

"Two of my men will fly with Dr. Yamamoto to Atlanta from Madrid. They will run a small 'proof of concept' test there. Yamamoto calls it a lethality test."

"And the professor?"

BOX 731

"We have a new passport for him and many lovely drugs. He will enjoy a long sleep all the way to Canada."

"And after the test?"

"Yamamoto and my two men will drive north to our factory and join the seven of us for the project."

"You seven are flying commercial into Canada, with the product in suitcases?"

"No, Russian Aeroflot Cargo. The plane gets into Toronto at three in the morning. Our friend in customs will allow our crew members and their bags to move quickly into our Suburbans. Then an eight-hour drive on the Trans-Canada Highway."

"I thought you were going in by boat?"

"Change of plans. Too slow. The winter weather is bad right now."

"Lots of ice," Oleg chimed in as Semyon shot him down with a glance. Oleg took another double shot of vodka.

"The US Coast Guard would grow very suspicious of a boat out there in those conditions."

"How will you cross the Sault Ste. Marie International Bridge and get the product through customs?"

"In our Suburbans. We have a Cessna, a boat, and four snow machines staged and ready to go on Saint Joseph Island. There's only four hundred feet of water, ice, or snow between Canada and Michigan. The weather will determine which one we choose. Since six Russian guys and a Japanese professor from Spain might raise suspicions, we'll cross with clean papers and pick up the product in Michigan, just south of the city."

Rina ordered sea bass with peach salsa. Semyon and Oleg ordered more shots.

"And how will the three fly to Atlanta?"

"Delta Airlines. They have clean passports and first-class seats," Semyon answered.

"You will both personally run the project, correct? That's what I'm paying for."

"Yes, Ekaterina. You're a sick lady. You seem to enjoy watching people suffer. Me? A quick cap to the forehead is all I need to see."

"My preferences are none of your concern. Have the cameras been set up and tested?"

"I believe you saw what we did for Dr. Ishii's job interview right here at this restaurant. We've got it handled."

"I must see everything."

Oleg and Semyon kept drinking the vodka, but were more anxious to get to the Love Power Chapel than spending anymore time with their client. Semyon tapped Oleg's shoulder and held out his open hand. Oleg reached into his Italian suit and removed an envelope. He gave it to Semyon, who handed it over to Rina.

"Here are the first seven, by name, location, photos, obituaries, and as many local newspaper stories describing their families' pain as possible."

Rina took the envelope and placed it on the table next to her as she ate her meal.

"Listen, ah, you might want to stow that in your dirty little box. Most police agencies call that sort of thing evidence."

Rina abruptly pushed her chair back, stood up, and put the envelope in her red bag.

"Call me when the soap factory is open for business," she said and briskly walked away.

Oleg and Semyon sat in stunned silence as they watched her leave.

"Guess you're buying," Oleg said as he reached over and grabbed Rina's plate of food.

CHAPTER 19

Lightner Farms
Gettysburg, Pennsylvania

US Army Lieutenant Colonel Leslie Raines and Eileen had papers, folders, photos, and two laptops sprawled out across the large wooden table in the dining room. Leslie kept scanning through her e-mail contacts and reading off names to Eileen, who was creating the first draft of the invitation list.

"Okay, so much for the small private wedding in your grandparents' backyard," Eileen said as she got up and pulled the boiling tea kettle off the burner. "We've got 406 people on the list so far, Leslie. Have you thought about just having this thing in Madison Square Garden instead? Maybe halftime during a Knicks game?"

"I know, I know . . . We'll pare it down, but I just wanted to create a master list first. I didn't realize I knew this many people."

The bells hanging around the back kitchen door handle started jingling as the door pushed open.

"Hello? Eileen?"

Leslie and Eileen recognized "that voice" and both sprang to their feet. Eileen went to the door as Leslie did a massive sweep, lift, and dump of all the papers on the dining room table.

"Ruth!" Eileen said as she gave Camp's mother a hug. "Is Sea Bee with you?"

"No, the girls are over at the house watching him. The boys are out fixing the fence. Too darn cold to fix a fence in January, but can't let the cows get out either."

"What brings you out this way?"

"Just wanted to check up on my son. Is he back from his spy trip?"

Leslie walked around the corner and into the kitchen.

Ruth's eyes lit up like a Christmas tree. "Sweet Jesus," Ruth said as she moved toward Leslie and held her hands out. "Come give this old woman a hug, Leslie."

"You look wonderful," Leslie said as Ruth held the embrace for an awkward second too long before she pulled back and held Leslie's hands.

"Look at you . . . I was scared to death that I might not ever see you again . . . Let me look at you." Tears started to trickle down Ruth's cheeks as her old arthritic fingers started to rub Leslie's hands and then suddenly stopped. Ruth let go of one hand and placed both hands on Leslie's left hand and then her ring finger.

Leslie felt a rush of heat flush through her face.

Ruth pulled Leslie's hand out, turned it over, and looked at the engagement ring. Ruth looked horrified.

"What happened? Where did you disappear to?"

"I'm engaged, Ruth."

"I can see that. To whom?"

Leslie and Eileen exchanged glances. Leslie realized Ruth hadn't made the connection.

"To Camp, I mean Seabury . . . He found me in Israel . . . He gave me the ring, even got down on one knee, and he asked me to marry him."

The fear Leslie saw in Ruth's face started to subside as clouds of doubt were replaced with shock and joy. Ruth looked quickly over to Eileen for confirmation. Eileen's hands were clasped under her chin as she affirmed the engagement with a big smile and electric eyes.

BOX 731

"Finally!" Ruth yelled. She reached out to both Leslie and Eileen as the three hugged and bounced in the kitchen. "Eileen, can we put some music on? I've got my eye on that bottle of brandy up in your cupboard. I think it's time for a bit of a celebration."

Leslie and Eileen broke into laughter.

"Ruth, it's not even noon yet," Eileen said as she opened the cupboard, moved the molasses, and pulled down the dusty bottle of brandy.

"I don't care. This old bag could be dead before supper. This is one of the greatest days of my life. Where is that kid of mine? Tell him to come down here and have a drink with his old Mom."

Leslie turned some music on as Eileen poured three very small servings of brandy into the orange juice glasses.

"He'll join us later," Leslie said as her country music playlist kicked in over the speakers. She hoisted her glass. "It's girl time right now."

Ruth raised her glass too. "To the greatest marriage there will ever be," she said as all three juice glasses clinked.

"That's a pretty tall order. Greatest marriage ever?" Leslie asked playfully.

"It will be, trust me," Ruth said. "The man already knows you'll shoot him if he gives you too much crap."

The three roared in laughter.

Mossad Headquarters
Tel Aviv, Israel

US Army General Jim Ferguson and US Marine Corps General Lexington Smith could be seen in the secured video conferencing room from Afghanistan. Special Agent Daniels, CIA Director Kensington, and Undersecretary Blair Hurst from the Department of Defense had each joined the call. Reuven and Yitzhak were on the call from Mossad in Tel Aviv.

Camp watched the call from the side of the room and out of view from the video cameras.

"There's no situation, under any circumstances, where American assets will be on Syrian soil or in Syrian air space. It's not going to happen, folks," Undersecretary Hurst warned with an added exclamation point that wasn't lost on anyone.

"With all due respect, Secretary Hurst," Yitzhak countered, "you already have two American assets on Syrian soil, and they're about to be executed."

"We intend to deny that assertion," Hurst responded.

"I'm sure Special Agent Fallon Jessup and retired FBI Agent Billy Finn will find your denial quite comforting when Hezbollah puts their images up on Al Jazeera TV," Yitzhak summarized.

"So we're left with no options? Just wait it out and see what happens?" Ferguson asked.

"Not completely," Hurst responded. "If the shabiha hands them off to Hezbollah in Lebanon, we may have more options."

Reuven nodded in agreement. "The secretary is correct. Once they are in the hands of Hezbollah, there'll be many more optional places where we can gather their bodies."

The video conference call went silent.

"Director Shavit, given the reality of the American government's nonintervention policy in Syria and given the poor planning and execution of this mission, what approach would you take, sir?" Central Intelligence Director Kensington asked as Special Agent Daniels fidgeted in his chair.

Camp could spot a public ass chewing and shakedown a mile away. He had to admit that he was pleased to see a pound of flesh being removed from Daniels's hide for public viewing, even if it was a private and secured call.

Reuven stared straight ahead at the camera. His face was expressionless, and his voice lacked any hint of inflection. He was methodical, by the book, and matter of fact.

BOX 731

"I regret to say that agents Jessup, Finn, and Jamil are expendable. And while the mission design was elementary— school level at best—the team did get a positive ID for anthrax."

"Have we really seen any proof of that, Director Shavit?" Hurst asked with accentuated skepticism.

"That was not my conclusion, Secretary Hurst; those were the words of the shabiha commander and the Russian on the intercepted call. If we let Jessup and Finn die, we lose all access to the biological weapon. I think we must assume that Jessup and Finn have more information that might be of use. We must assume the Russian and the shabiha commander know the entire story."

CIA Director Kensington responded, "Sir, your classified brief identifies a cargo transfer between the MV *Chariot* and a Canadian cargo ship."

"Yes, two of my agents joined the Comisaria, Guardia Urbana, and the Port Authority in Barcelona early this morning and only two hours after the Canadian ship reached the Port of Barcelona," Reuven said. "The captain allowed us to do a complete sweep of his ship, even without a warrant. We also intercepted the MV *Chariot* after it started its return loop back toward Syria and Israel. I'm sure the Russian captain thought we were looking for illegal weapons and munitions bound for either Syria or Iran. He let us board too, with not so much as an argument. There was nothing. No weapons, no traces of anthrax."

"Then, sir, I am simply not willing to risk an international incident and worldwide condemnation for Americans violating Syrian sovereignty," Hurst summarized as he closed the binder on the table in front of him for all to see.

"Then we will go in and rescue your people, Mr. Secretary," Reuven said as video screens in Afghanistan and Washington fell silent again.

"May I ask why?" General Jim Ferguson finally asked.

"Because your government continues to be naive, and you prefer to play defense. Like it or not, wish it were not so if you prefer, but evil exists and intends to annihilate you at the first opportunity. We don't play defense in Israel, not within Mossad at least. And I'm not convinced that the anthrax is not ultimately intended for Israel."

Marine Corps General Lexington Smith was overcome with energy. He leaned forward in his chair. "Director Shavit, you're speaking my language now, brother," Smith said in his thick South Carolinian drawl. "I can't put my leathernecks in Syria, but I can sure as God put 'em in Jordan at FOB Roaring Lion or amphibious units off the Syrian coast. Tell me what you need, and I'll make sure you've got some support."

"Gentlemen, I think we should move this off video and get face-to-face," Ferguson said as he started to close the call.

"General Smith, you're welcome to visit us in Tel Aviv tomorrow if you wish. But we will launch a mission within thirty-six hours regardless."

"I'm sending Agent Daniels as well," CIA Director Kensington said as he stood up. "He'll be bringing a broom and a dustpan."

Camp stepped out of the shadows behind the cameras in Mossad's video conferencing studio as Reuven ended the call.

"I want high resolution photos from the Ofek of every house, building, shack, car, clump of dirt, or pile of goat dung that can be found in the village of Hadida." Yitzhak was taking the satellite order over to the Ofek desk before Reuven could finish speaking.

"What do you think?" Camp asked as he moved toward Reuven, who sat fixed and focused on the TV screens that had gone dark.

"Americans are so worried about how others will perceive them on the small things. Then you broadcast a shock and awe invasion of a second world dictatorship on 'live' TV while Geraldo draws operational battle plans in the sand. Your foreign policy is very curious to me."

"You hadn't mentioned that you were contemplating a rescue attempt," Camp said as he sat down across from Reuven.

Box 731

"This is cold to say, Shepherd's Pie, but I only care about the anthrax. If we happen to rescue some Americans . . . that would be nice."

"What's your plan?" Camp asked.

"I'm your best man, Shepherd's Pie—not your partner. Some things are still secret."

CHAPTER 20

Sault Ste. Marie, Michigan

Dr. Martin Ishii got into the Hertz rental car from Chippewa County International Airport in Kinross, Michigan, and out of the subzero, frigid, early January wind for the twenty-mile drive to Sault Ste. Marie, Michigan, his new home. The tear ducts in Martin's eyes were frozen by the time he made the short walk from the parking lot to the front door of the property management office on Armory Place in Sault Ste. Marie. Everything was covered in snow no matter which direction he looked. Most of a nearby church steeple was covered in snow and ice.

He opened the solid wood door to Chippewa Real Estate and Property Management and walked in. Baseboard heaters surrounded the open room with two Steelcase desks.

A very large man with a huge smile got up. "Oh, geez, where's your coat, eh?" the man asked as he reached out his hand to greet Martin. "That little strip of leather won't do you any good up here in these parts. You must be Dr. Ishii. I'm Darrell; I run the place, in case you hadn't figured that one yet."

"It's a pleasure to meet you, Darrell. Please call me Martin."

"Hey, your English ain't that bad, ya know. When I found out you were from Japan I thought, hey, jeepers, this could be a problem."

Box 731

"Well thank you. I've been living and working in the United States for the better part of thirty years. It's my Japanese that isn't so good anymore."

"Well, how 'bout that. Well, come on over here and sit down. This'll only take a few minutes, and then you can head over to your new house. But I'd stop at ShopKo first and get a parka or something, ya know?"

Martin sat down as Darrell handed him a folder.

"What's that buzzing sound?" Martin asked as he looked up and around the room.

"Buzzing? Oh, geez, I'll betcha you're hearing the I-500. It's the forty-sixth annual International Snowmobile 500 race. People come from all over the world to see it each year."

"A snowmobile race?"

"You betcha. It takes about three weeks to build the track. They pump in almost two million gallons of water and build a one mile oval ice track. Just like the Indy 500 but on ice. First one around five hundred times is the winner. You could probably get over and catch the last part of the race, but you'd need a snowmobile—or a rugged four-wheel drive—to even get in there."

Martin smiled. "Perhaps next year."

"Well, you'll be sharing the executive house on Riverside Drive. It's waterfront property, don't you know."

"Sharing?"

"Don't worry. That house is sixty-two hundred square feet, and the executive manager is only here about one week out of four. They own several businesses around the world."

"Should be fine, I suppose. Can't beat the price, I guess."

"You got that right. Free is a great price to live in a mansion on the water." Darrell handed him the keys. "Here are the keys to your house and keys to the office. And hey, this is nice . . . here's your signing bonus. It's a check for $10,000. Are you believing that?"

Martin was genuinely surprised. "I guess I can afford that parka now. Does the house have Internet?"

"You betcha. DSL and WiFi everywhere you go, even outside by the hot tub."

Martin stood up and shook Darrell's hand one more time.

"So how many people live here in Sault Ste. Marie?"

"The T is silent. Folks around here just call it The Soo. I 'spect there's fifteen thousand folks or so. A lot more today, given the I-500."

Martin got back into the Hertz rental car, which was already frozen after a brief, ten-minute stop. He entered the address into the GPS and took off for the six-minute drive to his new mansion next to the frozen water.

Franklin Landing Strip

Semyon, Oleg, four Russian paramilitary crew members, and Professor Tanaka—who was starting to wake up near the end of their five hundred-mile drive from Toronto and over the Trans-Canada Highway to the International Bridge—were parked in two black Suburbans next to the Franklin Landing Strip, as headlights from four Arctic Cat snowmobiles grew in the horizon against the cloudy afternoon sky.

Four canisters were loaded in the back of the SUVs and next to the luggage. The Suburbans headed off the island at East Neebish Ferry Road and up South Scenic Drive, as the snowmobiles disappeared in the opposite direction.

"Drop me off at the Riverside Drive house," Semyon said. "We meet in the office tomorrow morning at eight, and then we'll bring our new president over to the soap factory."

Box 731

Palmachim Air Base
Israel

US Marine Corps General Lexington Smith walked out the back of the American C130 and into the backseat of the waiting black Mercedes.

"Welcome to Israel, General Smith. I trust your trip was smooth," Reuven said as the driver left the tarmac and passed through the checkpoint.

"As good as it gets, at least when Uncle Sam is footing the bill. Pleasure to meet you, Director Shavit. So what's the plan and how may we assist you?"

Reuven handed a classified folder to Lexington Smith, who already had his reading glasses on and was ready to get to work.

"It appears that your Amphibious Ready Group is already forward deployed in the area."

"Roger that, the LHA 1 Peleliu Amphibious Ready Group has the amphibious assault ship, the USS *Peleliu* with four thousand Marines on her. We've also got the amphibious transport dock USS *Green Bay*, and the dock landing ship USS *Rushmore*. This ARG has the Helicopter Sea Combat Squadron 23, Assault Craft Units One and Five, and Beach Master Unit One. We've got plenty of Harriers, Sea Stallions, and Super Cobras as well. What did you have in mind?"

"I need your Amphibious Ready Group out in the intercoastal waters. No direct action or involvement."

"Just presence for the Syrians?"

"Actually for the Russians and the Iranians. Your battle groups routinely patrol the Mediterranean and down through the Straits of Hormuz. You always pass through these waters."

"And if your mission heads south toward hell in a handbag?"

"That's for you and your Department of Defense to decide," Reuven said. "But I do need one specific piece of assistance."

"Name it."

"I believe the LHA 1 Peleliu Amphibious Ready Group also contains the Marine Corps's Fifteenth Expeditionary Unit and elements of Fleet Surgical Team One. I need them. There will be casualties."

General Smith removed his reading glasses and closed his classified file folder. "That might be a problem, Director Shavit."

"What's the problem?"

"We have a couple of docs on board, but we're down two surgeons for another three days. One had to be airlifted out for a family emergency back home. The other ruptured a disc in his back and is on restrictions to quarters."

"Can I send one of my surgeons?"

"Well, I'm not sure. I can check with the captain of the ARG and see what he says."

"My surgeon is actually an American. A US Navy captain who was a highly decorated trauma surgeon in Iraq, a Navy SEAL before that. He happens to be in Tel Aviv on holiday."

A large smile broke over General Smith's face. "Then that won't be a problem. I assume we're talking about Captain Campbell? I work very closely with Jim Ferguson and know how Camp helped you guys out last year."

Reuven remained silent.

"Ah, roger that, and understood," General Smith said without Reuven uttering a word. "We'll just keep that little detail out of my After Action Report."

"Do you need a hotel first, or are you ready for the mission brief?"

"I came here to work, Director Shavit. But I do need to get our assets in position. We're off the coast of Cyprus right now. Can probably be repositioned within twelve hours."

Sault Ste. Marie, Michigan

Semyon put his key in the deadbolt and opened the front door as the Suburbans drove off. Martin heard the noise and walked over to the front entrance foyer.

"Dr. Ishii, you made it," Semyon said with manufactured excitement. "I'm Simon Dresgal, one of the members of the executive committee."

Martin grabbed one of his suitcases and walked up and shook hands with Semyon. "Yes, Darrell at the property management company said I would have a roommate. It's nice to meet you."

"I trust the accommodations are to your liking? I hope the refrigerator and the bar were both stocked as I requested."

"Yes, everything is fabulous. Amazing, actually. I can't wait to learn more about the business."

"Absolutely. Perhaps you'd indulge me for a long, hot shower first, and then let's throw some steaks on the grill and open a bottle of something."

"Of course, I'm sure you had a long trip," Martin conceded. "Take your time. I'm rather handy with the grill. I'll get it started."

CHAPTER 21

Mossad Headquarters
Tel Aviv, Israel

General Smith was ushered into the inner sanctuary of Mossad's headquarters in Tel Aviv. Eight analysts, technicians, and planners were gathered in the room as Yitzhak began the brief.

CIA Special Agent Daniels was already seated but stood as the general sat.

"This is a very simple operation. The chaos that already exists on the ground caused by the civil war plays to our advantage. Explosions, gunfire, helicopters, speeding vehicles; unfortunately for them, the Syrians see and hear this sort of thing all the time. But it gives us tactical cover and advantage for this mission."

Reuven pointed to the TV monitors and the screens came to life.

"We have culled through hundreds of Okek 9 satellite photos," Yitzhak narrated. "Two days ago we intercepted a cell phone call from the village of Hadida. There's only one house in Hadida that has the footprint and the vehicle traffic we're looking for. If you look at this photo, you'll notice that there are several armed men standing outside, apparently smoking."

"Rebels?" General Smith asked.

"Negative, sir. Shabiha, government mercenaries. That's why they're anxious to get your folks off Syrian soil and into the hands of Hezbollah."

BOX 731

"How many people are we looking at?"

"Fifteen, maybe twenty. Mostly small arms, probably some RPGs but nothing terribly fancy."

"But that's not the real problem, is it, Yitzhak?" Daniels asked from the back of the room.

Reuven closed his eyes in anguish the moment he heard Daniels's shrill voice. It was his schoolboy mission that caused this mess in the first place. Then again, Reuven reasoned, it may have uncovered a biological weapons plot.

"No, Agent Daniels, it isn't. The border with Lebanon is exactly a half-kilometer from this house. The boys from Hezbollah could sweep down on us in fewer than two minutes."

"So what's the plan?" General Smith asked as he checked his watch. "Once these folks are transferred over to Hezbollah, we can kiss their mama's ass good-bye."

Reuven wasn't sure what the general's South Carolina metaphor meant other than that time was of the essence.

"There are three components to the mission. Director Shavit?" Yitzhak handed the brief over to Reuven.

"We'll be using Shayetet 13 navy commandos coming in from the sea and Sayeret Matkal, a Special Forces unit within IDF, from the air. The footprint will be very small. Sayeret Matkal is much better suited for counterterrorism and hostage rescue missions. They have the lead. Shayetet 13 commandos will handle infiltration and exfiltration."

"Air?" Special Agent Daniels asked.

"One, an Israeli reconnaissance plane will fly up the coast at thirty-three thousand feet then make a hard bank to the east over Syrian airspace for seventeen minutes. At 0100 hours tonight, they'll descend to twenty-eight thousand feet, and eight paratroopers from Sayeret Matkal will do a military freefall, high-altitude, low-opening dive directly over the house in the village of Hadida. They'll be in HALO freefall for about three minutes, or 95 percent of the dive. They'll pull cords at one thousand feet for near silent insertion into the drop zone. They'll avoid radar detection and have minimum exposure until the very last minute."

"Pretty cold up there, Director Shavit," Lexington Smith said. "I assume some small arms and flash-bangs are about all they can carry?"

"That's correct. But if the mission goes as planned they won't have to fire a shot. A little Kravis Maga goes a long way when you're dealing with sleepy mercenaries in the middle of the night."

"Two?" Special Agent Daniels asked from the back of the room.

Reuven closed his eyes in disgust.

"Two . . . at 0035 hours . . . fourteen hours from now, Shayetet 13 commandos will beach at al-Hamadiyah on the Syrian coast, ten kilometers north of the coastal border with Lebanon. Mossad assets on the ground have already staged three, up-armored, civilian vehicles at the entry point. They're painted with tracking beacons so your Amphibious Ready Group can keep an eye on us. The commandos will need to drive 55.7 kilometers in forty minutes. The HALO paratroopers will secure the area and eliminate the threat in fifteen minutes, or by 0118 hours on the mission clock. The commandos will arrive, load and go by 0125 hours."

"Seven minutes? You're building a seven-minute window, a seven-minute margin of error?" Daniels asked as he stood up. "Your plan is way too aggressive. If something goes wrong, our people are dead in a second."

Reuven put his papers down and slowly turned around to face Daniels. He held his remote control clicker up and offered it to Daniels. "By all means, Special Agent Daniels, please share with us the CIA plan. I'm sure your assets are in position, and both Langley and the Pentagon have offered blinking neon green lights of approval for your mission."

Daniels sat down.

BOX 731

"Better yet, why don't you just dress up as a TV reporter and knock on the door in Hadida. Tell them you want an exclusive interview."

Mossad's technicians and analysts fought back the laughter as Reuven returned to the screens in front of him.

"Three, exfiltration is forty-five minutes back to al-Hamadiyah. They'll be carrying eight paratroopers and three hostages. We assume the woman has been injured. There may be other injuries. Three steps, a seventy-minute mission, out at 0210 hours."

"At 175 miles per hour, we can have two AH-1W Super Cobra's spitting hellfire fifteen minutes after you give the word," General Smith said with great pride. "What else do you need?"

"MEDEVAC to your Fleet Surgical Team. Two of the hostages are Americans and the third is a CIA asset from Syria. I'd like to debrief the hostages on your ship."

"Roger that. We'll have a couple of Sea Knights staged and ready for a quick beach grab at 0210."

Reuven dismissed the group. A technician was assigned to General Smith and would have him back to Palmachim by eight p.m. Israeli helicopters would take Reuven and General Smith out to the Amphibious Ready Group for the mission.

Daniels walked up to Reuven as Yitzhak stepped in to buffer. "What about CIA? We'd like to debrief the hostages as well."

Reuven's patience had expired. "Special Agent Daniels . . . you and Fallon Jessup have had an unprofessional relationship for more than eighteen months. You are emotionally vested in this operation. I'm sure you are concerned, but you are of no practical or professional use to me or this mission. I'll send you a report. But you're welcome to stay here with Yitzhak and watch."

Sault Ste. Marie, Michigan

Semyon and Martin finished their steak dinners in relative silence.

"So, Simon, tell me about the business, the manufacturing facility, and the lab. I think you know much more about me than I even know about our business model."

"That's easy. Let's leave the dishes for the maid in the morning. Do you like scotch?"

Semyon poured two tall snifters of Johnnie Walker Black Label and walked into the expansive yet comfortable living room. With a flip of a switch the gas fireplace roared to life as heavy snowflakes began to fall outside the large glass picture window overlooking a channel on the St. Mary's River.

"We function like a CRO—a contract research organization."

"I'm very familiar with CROs," Martin chimed in. "So we're testing drugs, compounds, and biologicals for safety, efficacy, and targeting."

"Precisely," Semyon answered.

"Who are our clients?"

"Up until last month, most of our clients were pharmaceutical and biotechnology companies in Europe. Most of our other facilities are in eastern Europe."

"What changed?"

"Well, we secured a very large government contract."

"American?"

"Actually, from several NATO countries. Due to the nature of the contract research, we needed a facility that was on US soil, out of the spotlight of Washington but located fairly close to where most of the other defense contractors operate."

"That's why my security clearances were important to you."

"Yes, but also your expertise with biological weapons at Fort Detrick."

The picture was starting to emerge in Martin's mind and he was beginning to get excited. A multinational NATO research contract was huge, and he was the man selected to run the entire organization.

Box 731

"I assume typical CRO work for defense, like antibiotics, vaccines, pathogenicity, and all the other usual suspects?" Martin asked as his enthusiasm grew.

Semyon leaned forward with a very serious look in his eyes. "Not exactly. This work is also for offense, and I need to know that you're okay with that before I reveal the rest of the research contract."

Martin sat back in his Queen Ann chair. He had never worked on the development of an offensive biological weapon in his entire career.

"Citizen population centers within most NATO countries have grown tired of multiple deployments to various hot spot regions throughout the Middle East," Semyon explained. "The citizens of the United Kingdom and the US are tired of seeing their soldiers blown up from cowardly IEDs and suicide bombers. They send their sons and daughters off to places like Algeria, to work an honest job in a natural gas plant, only to have thirty-five terrorists descend out of the shadows of the Sahara and leave nothing but blood and carnage behind. There needs to be a weapon. A weapon that takes out the threat, leaves the environment in good shape, but prevents the bloodshed of NATO troops."

"I'm not sure what I think about that," Martin said as he stared into the flickering flames of the gas fireplace.

"I felt the same way, Dr. Ishii, the exact same way," Semyon said as Martin perked up. "The scientist who creates the cancer drug hopes that no one will ever need it. The assembly-line worker at an army tank plant hopes there will never be a war. The final inspector of a bulletproof vest hopes that no bullets will ever be fired. And the war planners at the Pentagon or 10 Downing Street, who have asked for an offensive biological weapon, hope they will never have to use such a weapon. But like all of the other examples, they must be ready."

"Aren't there already enough biological and chemical weapons out there? Do we really need more?" Martin asked with hints of exasperation in his voice.

"Our contract does not call for the creation of a new biological weapon."

Martin was visibly relieved.

"Our job is to create a new mechanism for targeted delivery, so that innocent populations can be spared the impact of an indiscriminate weapon. Our job is to cook up a new recipe for an old biological weapon, one that existing vaccines cannot protect against."

"Okay, I get it. I think I can handle that. But changing delivery mechanisms also has potential consequences to the lethality of the pathogen."

Semyon tried to follow along, but Martin could see that he was not a scientist. "Let me put it this way," Martin said as he regrouped. "A CRO such as this will need to test the potency and impact of a biological weapon if we change the delivery method. We'd need to know if it still worked. Does it still kill?"

"I understand," Semyon said, nodding.

"We'll need lab animals for testing."

Semyon poured some more Johnnie Walker Black into his glass. He raised the bottle toward Martin, who declined.

"We have a lab in place, Dr. Ishii, and you'll see it in the morning. The lab complex is still in development, but our NATO contract requires that we get moving quickly. We also have rodents coming so we are ready to begin."

"Rodents are fine for some of the basic testing, but we'll need nonhuman primates for advanced targeting work."

"This week you will meet two other scientists we have recruited for the project. Between the three of you, we'll implement all of your recommendations to make sure our work is both safe and effective."

Martin felt somewhat reassured and satisfied that Semyon understood his concerns. Likewise, he understood that governments don't mess around with their contracts. Once a contract has been received, it's better to get to work before the funding is pulled.

Fort Detrick was a prime example of that.

Box 731

"Well, we should probably get to bed. Tomorrow will be a long day," Semyon said as he downed the last of his scotch.

"One more thing," Martin said as Semyon flipped the switch and turned the fireplace off. "What's the delivery mechanism?"

"The what?"

"You said our mission is to create a targeted delivery mechanism for an existing bioweapon. Has it been specified?"

Semyon walked through the foyer and locked the deadbolt on the front door at the bottom of the steps.

"Soap. Nonchlorinated laundry detergent."

Indian Creek Island
Miami Beach, Florida

Ekaterina shut down the video feed and turned her computer off as soon as Semyon locked the front door and turned the lights off.

She thought Semyon had done an admirable job and was really quite believable, in spite of his slovenliness.

And Rina already hated Dr. Masahisa Ishii. She planned to enjoy feeling her rage bubble to the surface.

Hilton Tel Aviv
Tel Aviv, Israel

Camp was lounging on the king-sized bed in his rather empty and somewhat cavernous suite when the call came in.

"Shepherd's Pie?"

"Hello, Molly Bloom. Are we going to grab some dinner or what?" Camp asked.

"Did you pack a uniform?" Reuven asked.

"Is the Pope Catholic? Of course I packed a uniform. Why?"

"Shave your beard and get packed. We'll be there in twenty minutes to pick you up. We'll both be at Palmachim waiting for you."

"Both, ah, Raines is gone. Remember?"

"Myself and Marine Corps General Lexington Smith. From Palmachim, we board Israeli helicopters out to the LHA 1 Peleliu Amphibious Ready Group."

"Excuse me?"

"The Marine Corps's Fifteenth Expeditionary Unit is down two trauma surgeons on their Fleet Surgical Team One. You have been volunteered for duty."

"By whom?"

"Me."

"I'm on medical leave. I could get court-martialed for this."

"Get over it. Shave and get dressed. You've only got eighteen minutes now."

Lightner Farms
Gettysburg, Pennsylvania

Eileen and Leslie went over the final invitation list one last time.

"That's 220 names. Let's say 20 percent actually attend. That's about forty to fifty people," Eileen said.

"Perfect. Just a small wedding. That's exactly what I want."

"So let's send the informal invitation via e-mail attachment so people can save the date. Folks are already making their plans for February."

"That's fine. As long as we can send the printed invitations this week, I'm okay with that."

Leslie pressed send and 220 e-mails with invitations attached crisscrossed the world.

BOX 731

Sault Ste. Marie, Michigan

Martin had just turned his bedroom light off when he heard his iPhone vibrate. It was a message from US Army Lieutenant Colonel Leslie Raines.

"Getting married?" Martin read quietly. He sent the attachment to the printer in his room and printed out the invitation. He was pleased Leslie hadn't forgotten about him, and he looked forward to telling her all about his new job.

Palmachim Air Base
Israel

Camp looked through the window as his Mercedes and driver from Mossad pulled onto the tarmac. Reuven, Yitzhak, and General Smith were deep in conversation and standing next to two helicopters.

Camp had already decided his fate and hoped Reuven would cooperate.

A broad smile dashed across Lexington Smith's face as Camp exited the back of his car. Camp snapped a swift salute that was quickly returned by General Smith.

"Camp, you look great."

"Sir, I feel great."

Reuven appeared impatient with the reunion as the mission clock ticked in his head. "Gentlemen, we need to board."

"Director Shavit," Camp said as Reuven stopped in his tracks. Camp realized he had never used the honorific with Reuven. "With all due respect, sir, I'm not going."

Reuven turned and glared at Camp and then over to Lexington Smith, who was genuinely surprised.

"Camp, I've got this covered," Smith said with assurance. "If anything comes up, I'll take full responsibility."

"Captain Campbell . . . we need a surgeon," Reuven added.

"I was a Navy SEAL before I was a trauma surgeon, sir. Either I go in with your Shayetet 13 naval commandos, or I don't go at all."

"That is not possible, captain," Reuven exclaimed as he turned back toward the helicopters.

"Depending on the injuries, they may not survive long enough to get back to the *Peleliu*. I want to be there—with them—on the ground. That's what a Navy SEAL does, sir."

"And what if our only surgeon takes another bullet in the Syrian Desert? Then what do we do, Captain Campbell?" Reuven asked as the helicopter blades began to spin. "They'll leave you behind if you can't keep up."

"No they won't."

"You're out of shape. You're recovering from serious gunshot wounds."

"This is my fate, Molly Bloom. This is why heaven's doors opened and let me come back. Let me go in . . . please."

Reuven looked at Camp and then back at General Lexington Smith. Smith shrugged.

"Yitzhak, get the captain a proper Shayetet uniform and put him on a bird. They're staging now," Reuven said as he stepped over to the helicopter.

"Director Shavit!" Camp yelled over the whirling rotor blades of the helicopter.

Reuven turned. Camp smiled and saluted his friend.

Reuven just shook his head and got on the helicopter.

CHAPTER 22

LHA 1 Peleliu Amphibious Ready Group
Mediterranean Sea off the Coast of Syria

Two Israeli helicopters landed on the deck of the USS *Peleliu*, a Tarawa-class amphibious assault ship belonging to the US Navy and named for the Battle of Peleliu during the Second World War. The helicopters left as fast as they had arrived.

General Lexington Smith was greeted by the captain of the *Peleliu* as he and Reuven Shavit, director of Mossad's kotsas in the Middle East, were escorted to the ship's command center.

"I thought you were bringing a navy surgeon," the captain said as they entered the command center.

"He joined the assault mission, sir. In case they require immediate medical attention on the ground," General Smith said as they took their seats. Smith was already having second thoughts about letting Camp join the Israeli commandos. The captain's question didn't help matters.

Hadida, Syria

Billy Finn had lost track of time in the darkness of the center room as he, Wally, and Jessup sat in the dark world that had become a never-ending cycle of impromptu faked executions, blindfolds, gags, and plastic restraints.

The lights in the room were throttled to full and several Arabic-speaking men entered the room with a sudden burst of energy. Finn's blindfold and gag were removed. As his eyes adjusted to the introduction of light he saw blindfolds and gags removed from Wally and Fallon. The same woman Finn saw before sat down next to Jessup, who was lying motionless on the floor.

"I have enjoyed our brief relationship," the commander said as he entered the room, "but the time has come to hand you over to our friends from the south. They will be here in an hour or so."

Finn and Wally made instant eye contact. Fallon's eyes were swollen shut.

"The woman needs to see a doctor," Finn said as the commander started to leave the room.

"Amazing. The black man from America speaks," he said with as much sarcasm as he could muster.

"I'm grateful for the nurse you have provided, but she needs to see a doctor. Your men acted like barbarians."

The commander edged forward and bent down near Finn's face. "My men take what is theirs when an infidel woman comes to their land."

Finn filled his mouth with saliva and hoisted a wad of spit directly into the commander's face before a shabiha boot struck the side of his cheek, snapping his head against the back wall. Warm blood trickled down his face.

"You are very tough and an incredibly brave commander. You won't be so tough when our drones blow you out of your vehicle," Finn stammered.

"Our? You said 'our.' Who are you?"

"My name is Billy Finn, FBI special agent. That woman? She's Fallon Jessup with the CIA."

Wally tried to motion to Finn to get him to shut up, but Finn ignored him. Finn knew this was the end game, and the only chance he had was to stall for any chance that might still exist.

BOX 731

The commander looked at the other abductors around the room and smiled.

"I knew they were CIA. That's what I told you," the commander said with great pride. "Then it is an honor to kill some American spies. This is, indeed, a great day."

"I heard you speaking to your friend in Russian," Finn said as the commander's face grew solemn. "I speak and understand perfect Russian. French? Not so much. I heard about your plans. I know all about the anthrax."

Billy Finn was making it up as fast as he could. He knew time was running out. The commander edged in closer.

"You don't know anything, Mr. Finn."

"I know this much . . . twice I have planted devices in your vehicles, tracking beacons that I kept hidden in my mouth. As soon as you start one of those vehicles outside, a hellfire missile from one of our drones will light you up like the Fourth of July."

The commander's nod sent four mercenaries out to search and scour their vehicles for tracking devices that didn't exist.

"The others? I swallowed. Wherever I go . . . the tracking device goes."

"Then you will be the victim of your own drone."

"Makes no difference to me; I'm not living either way. You've already put us through three mock executions, firing your damn guns in other rooms trying to scare us to death. Well, we're already dead. Your Hezbollah brothers are really going to love you when your ignorance rains hell down on their heads in a few hours."

The commander got up and paced the room. He motioned for one of the other captors to come forward. "Cut him open . . . Find the tracking device."

Finn wasn't planning on such an abrupt interruption to his stall tactics, nor did he relish the thought of his bowels being examined for a nonexistent device while he was yet awake.

"Wait," Finn said. "Maybe we can make a deal."

CHAPTER 23

LHA 1 Peleliu Amphibious Ready Group
Mediterranean Sea off the Coast of Syria

General Lexington Smith, the captain of the *Peleliu*, and Mossad
Director Reuven Shavit were positioned in the operations center
aboard the USS *Peleliu*. Reuven had opened a channel to Israeli
special ops communications so that the Americans weren't forced
to eavesdrop as they would typically do. Reuven was also linked
in to Mossad's command operations center in Tel Aviv.

"Air status," Reuven commanded softly as the Americans
watched several linked-in TV monitors from Mossad's mission
control center.

"RECON plane at thirty-three thousand feet, thirty-five
kilometers from drop zone, twelve minutes to freefall."

"Sea?"

"Two Morena-class rigid-hull inflatables beached, eight Bats,
and one coalition-force SEAL loaded in three up-armored civilian
vehicles, five kilometers down highway, currently thirty-four
minutes to extraction."

"Ofek 9?"

"Four vehicles at target. No movement since 2200 hours."

"Thermals?"

"Four hostiles on the outside perimeter, eight hostiles inside.
Three friendlies in center room, no movement from the friendlies
since 2330 hours when one friendly was moved briefly and then

Box 731

returned to center room. All eight hostiles and three friendlies now in center room."

Reuven was only partially relieved that Camp had made it safely into the vehicles with his Shayetet 13 commandos. But the real fight hadn't even started.

Hadida, Syria

Billy Finn's arms and legs were extended and secured by a shabiha mercenary on all four corners. His shirt was off. The commander stood off to the side and gave the order to the mercenary standing over Finn, who was holding the tactical knife.

"Find out if he has a tracking device, but try not to kill him."

Sweat poured through Finn's anxiety as he felt the cold steel of the blade against his abdomen.

"I heard you talking to that Russian. I heard you say his name. We all know his name," Finn quickly divulged, hoping to buy seconds or even change the commander's mind.

"I don't think so," the commander said nodding as Finn felt his gut being ripped apart.

"*Semyon!*" Finn screamed through the pain as the commander held up his hand to stop the dissection. "Russian mafia, organized crime. Just like you."

"Then take his name to your grave."

"I know who the Asian is as well. I have already told Washington," Finn said as blood poured out of the cut in his abdomen.

"That's impossible," the commander said as he motioned again to the knife-wielding mercenary to stop.

"It's true," Wally pleaded in Arabic to the room full of abductors. "The black man has communications technology inside his body. He called in a raid from the Americans. You must leave quickly."

The commander considered Wally's words. Finn could see that the rest of the shabiha mercenaries were clearly agitated as well.

"That's not possible," the commander said. "Our brothers will be here in a few minutes. Let them handle the Americans."

Finn felt his strength draining as his head grew lighter. He bought some time at the expense of his gut, though he didn't know what good it would do. He heard the commander on the phone in the other room.

"Semyon?" the commander asked as Finn started to lose consciousness.

LHA 1 Peleliu Amphibious Ready Group
Mediterranean Sea off the Coast of Syria

Reuven and the Americans watched the reconnaissance plane drop to twenty-eight thousand feet.

"Sir, go or no go?"

Reuven didn't hesitate. "Go," he said over the microphone to the jumpmaster in the plane.

The top left TV monitor lit up with a green glow from the unit commander's night vision camera goggles as he and eight other Sayeret Matkal paratroopers plunged through the Syrian night in silent freefall.

The top right TV monitor tracked the movement of the Shayetet 13 "Bat" commandos in their three vehicle convoy exiting the M1 highway, cutting through the Syrian Desert to Highway 9, and over toward the target house in Hadida. The onscreen digital mission clock indicated that they were seven minutes out from the target.

BOX 731

"Mr. Director!" a voice yelled urgently from Mossad's operations center in Tel Aviv. "We've got four vehicles crossing over the border from Lebanon, moving directly toward the target house, closing in less than a minute."

"Thermals?" Reuven asked softly.

"Not enough time."

"Assume four hostiles per vehicle and send."

The Mossad operations center opened all COMS channels to the paratroopers in freefall and the commandos closing in from the desert.

"Four new vehicles. Hostiles: sixteen new arriving, four on the perimeter, eight inside target."

"Pull," sounded the voice of the paratrooper commander as seven chutes opened below and around him with one thousand feet remaining before silent insertion. The target house and the four vehicles parked outside began to fill the screen rapidly on the top left TV monitor as the headlights of four new vehicles flashed the ground with blinding light through the night-vision camera.

Eight smaller TV monitors mounted on the lower rack in the observation room went "active" as General Lexington Smith, the captain of the USS *Peleliu*, Reuven, and the others watched the assault and extraction through the eyes of each paratrooper.

Paratrooper THREE landed directly on the dirt road in front of the Hezbollah lead vehicle and two hundred feet from the target house. The headlights of the vehicle blinded his night vision camera. Each of the four vehicles stopped as starburst patterns of gunfire were sprayed from the vehicles toward THREE.

Reuven took the audio feed from the commander's COMS.

Hadida, Syria

Billy Finn stirred with the sound of gunfire. He braced for the next plunge of the tactical knife as chaos erupted outside the house. The shabiha mercenaries froze in silence and then quickly got up and pulled their AK-47s that were leaning against the wall near Fallon Jessup's lifeless body.

"I told you," Wally screamed defiantly as the shabiha commander pulled the pistol out of his waistband and ran out the door.

LHA 1 Peleliu Amphibious Ready Group
Mediterranean Sea off the Coast of Syria

"THREE is down," the voice of the Sayeret Matkal Israeli paratrooper commander called over the audio feed. "Repeat, THREE is down."

The seventh and eighth paratroopers belly-crawled to the rear vehicle as four Hezbollah gunmen emerged from each door. Four suppressed pops could be heard as video cameras from SEVEN and EIGHT watched while four Hezbollah soldiers dropped in their spots, next to open car doors, before firing a shot.

"Bats?" Reuven asked calmly into his headset as his eyes briefly met those of General Lexington Smith.

"Two minutes," came the voice of the Shayetet 13 commander in the lead vehicle. "We've got picture and audio."

The remaining twelve Hezbollah gunmen fanned out around their vehicles, staring blindly into the black cloak of the Syrian Desert.

Monitors from helmet cameras on ONE and TWO showed the commander and his tandem TWO paratrooper moving quickly toward the front door of the target house.

"One man down, four hostiles down, and you're leaving five men to handle twelve hostiles," Lexington Smith narrated with no hint of a question in his voice as he watched the assault unfold. "I love it."

Reuven allowed his eyes to smile for a split second at the general's pleasure.

The front door of the target house flew open, and light flashed through the night vision cameras on monitors ONE and TWO.

"Muay Thai," Reuven whispered in his headset, thinking out loud as paratrooper commander ONE unleashed a barrage of fists, elbows, knees, shins, and feet on two mercenaries, followed by two lethal head snaps. AK-47 fire sprayed out of the house as the six remaining mercenaries emerged. Tandem TWO stood next to the door and thrust a tactical knife in and through the first man's throat with decapitating force.

The night-vision monitor from the first Shayetet 13 commando vehicle showed the four perimeter hostiles sprinting toward the original four parked vehicles outside the target house. Two Shayetet 13 snipers in each of the trailing vehicles took out two of the hostiles with single suppressed, long-range moving shots over the choppy Syrian Desert at night.

Tandem FOUR hovered over his fallen THREE partner and administered aid as he held a perimeter of protection around him.

"Status, THREE?" Reuven asked calmly.

"AK round upper left chest, no exit wounds, MEDEVAC," FOUR said calmly as he turned.

Reuven pulled his headset off and looked over at General Smith. No official request was either made or acknowledged as Smith looked over at the captain of the USS *Peleliu,* who was waiting for an order.

"Hold the Sea Knights for now," General Smith said as Reuven's face grew agitated. "Send two AH-1W Super Cobra's instead . . . They can get there faster."

Reuven offered a subtle nod of gratitude and then put his headset back on.

"Two friendly AH-1Ws en route," Reuven said.

Shayetet 13
Vehicle 3

Camp heard the description of the wounds to THREE and the announcement of inbound Cobras from the USS *Peleliu* over his headset as he rode in the back of the third Shayetet vehicle.

"Hostile vehicle egress." Reuven's voice erupted with calm as the third Shayetet 13 up-armored civilian vehicle started to break formation while the other two Bat commando units slid to a stop outside the target house.

Camp opened his door, jumped, and rolled into the sand of the Syrian Desert from the moving vehicle as the commandos cut a path diagonally through the desert on an intercept angle with the Hezbollah terrorists.

Camp rolled onto his feet as he ran through sporadic gunfire carrying his medical bag around the side of the complex to where THREE was down.

Paratrooper FOUR was talking on his COMS and keeping pressure on THREE's upper left chest wound as Camp closed to within thirty yards. As Camp approached from the back of one of the parked Hezbollah vehicles, the front door opened and a terrorist carrying his AK-47 started sprinting toward THREE and FOUR.

Camp ran faster and pulled the tactical knife out of his waistband. The terrorist slowed and lifted his weapon. Camp pushed the button on his tactical and went airborne six feet from the attacker as the AK-47 discharged.

LHA 1 Peleliu Amphibious Ready Group
Mediterranean Sea off the Coast of Syria

A flash filled FOUR's video frame. The terrorist fell next to THREE as Reuven and Lexington Smith watched Camp Campbell

Box 731

pull his knife out of the abdomen of the attacker, throw the AK-47 out into the sand, step over the injured Hezbollah terrorist, and begin to render aid to the fallen Israeli paratrooper.

Reuven couldn't help but notice the look of shock on General Smith's face.

The monitors tracked as FIVE and SIX jumped the two closest terrorists and wrestled their hands and arms around fingers on triggers and used their attackers' weapons to mow down three more terrorists. The FIVE and SIX Sayeret Matkal commandos grappled their way to the ground and inflicted terminal knife wounds on each of their attackers in another split-second.

The seven remaining Hezbollah terrorists ran back and crammed themselves into one of the running vehicles, spun around wildly in the desert sand, and sped back down the road for the short drive over the border and back into Lebanon on Highway 9.

"Four hundred meters to the border crossing," Reuven said as the black sky of Syria and Lebanon was lit up with a fireball from the RPG fired out of the trailing Shayetet "Bat" commando vehicle. Fire-engulfed debris of seven Hezbollah soldiers and their one vehicle floated down to the desert sands on both sides of the border.

The shabiha commander and four of his mercenaries ran back into the house as the bodies of his first two comrades and the head of the third piled up in the front doorway. They ran through the center room, past Fallon Jessup's body, and Wally, who was applying pressure on Billy Finn's abdominal wound.

Wally looked up at the fleeing shabiha mercenaries. "Should've listened to me."

The commander fired one round from his pistol into Wally's forehead.

ONE and TWO followed the five hostiles through the center room and took a few steps down the hallway then dove to the sides.

"Grenade!" screeched a voice over the audio feed as a flash of light filled monitors ONE and TWO.

FIVE and SIX gave chase on foot through the dark desert as the remaining shabiha perimeter guard ran through the dunes and small brush.

"Zero-one-twenty-three," Reuven said calmly as the mission clock showed two minutes remaining before exfiltration.

A quick flash was seen over monitor SIX as the fleeing shabiha mercenary fell to the ground and was still struggling until FIVE bent over and finished the kill.

The lights from the shabiha commander's truck flashed by the side of the house through FOUR's camera as FOUR remained vigilant and stood guard while Camp worked frantically to keep THREE alive. A Shayetet 13 commando vehicle gave chase as AK-47 fire erupted out of the open bed of the fleeing vehicle.

"Get out of the sand and get up on Highway 9," Reuven said as the Syrian commander's vehicle began to pull away from the commandos. The Bats' commando vehicle pulled to an abrupt stop as the taillights of the shabiha vehicle faded in the horizon as they got away.

"Damn it," Reuven shouted with his first real hint of emotion as he pounded the desk in front of him.

The skies above the shabiha vehicle quickly lit up with a solitary floodlight before a burst of fire from the hellfire missile that was launched from the AH-1W SuperCobra decimated the fleeing truck down below, sending a thunderous explosion into the black Syrian night sky.

Reuven snapped his head over at General Lexington Smith, who was beaming from ear to ear.

"All clear," came the audio feed from paratrooper ONE inside the house and verified by FIVE and SIX outside on the perimeter.

"Status?" Reuven barked.

BOX 731

"One friendly dead, one unconscious but alive, and one with a major abdominal wound. THREE is down. Status unknown."

Reuven looked over at Lexington Smith. Neither knew which friendly was dead but both knew Camp was alive as they watched him help load one of the victims into an AH-1W Super Cobra.

"Immediate egress," Reuven said into the COMS. Camp ignored the order and ran back out of the helicopter and into the Syrian Desert. Reuven became instantly agitated. "Repeat! Immediate egress!"

"Negative, sir," Camp said as the command center watched the video from his helmet camera.

"THREE has combat clot applied to the wound. Bleeding stopped and IV started," Camp yelled as he rounded the house and sprinted toward the area where THREE had fallen.

Reuven and General Smith watched through Camp's helmet camera as he neared the wounded Hezbollah terrorist who was trying to belly-crawl away from the scene. Camp turned the terrorist over on his back and pulled out his pistol.

"Get in the chopper now!" Lexington Smith ordered over the COMS.

Camp pulled out a stick of morphine and injected the dose in the center of the attacker's abdomen, where he had stuck his tactical blade. Camp pulled out a new bag of powdered combat clot, a powder that when applied to a wound instantly stopped the bleeding and would hold for two to three hours. He ripped the package open and poured it onto the wound.

The command center watched the horrified eyes of the Hezbollah agent as Camp held the pistol over the terrorist's face for security while he stopped the bleeding for his adversary.

Camp turned and sprinted back to the helicopter.

Talkalakh, Syria

The man adjusted his Detroit Tigers baseball cap and held his encrypted phone silently in his lap. The windows in the car were down and they listened. Two AH-1W Super Cobras flew over them as three civilian up-armored vehicles, carrying Shayetet 13 commandos and Sayeret Matkal paratroopers, raced by on the highway in front of them.

The Syrian Desert grew quiet once again. The big boss opened his phone and dialed the Russian GRU, the Glavnoye Razvedyvatel'noye Upravleniye. The GRU was Russia's largest foreign intelligence agency. The GRU never "formally" worked with the Red Mafia, but the big boss was one oligarch that the Kremlin wanted to keep happy, especially on this project.

"Ground radar?" the boss asked quietly.

"Clear."

"Satellite?"

"Their Ofek 9 is now out of range. No eyes in the skies."

He closed his phone and gave the signal over the radio.

"Go."

Car doors in twelve vehicles opened simultaneously as thirty-six Russian paramilitary soldiers ran over to the metal building next to the Red Mafia boss's car. The lean-to tin walls of the building were pulled down quickly as pieces of metal were removed from a makeshift roof.

The 38.9 liter D12A-525 diesel engine sputtered to life as the 1965 era MAZ-543 Scud launcher rumbled down Highway 9 for the four-thousand-foot drive to the border with Lebanon. One truck hauling two Scud missiles, each mounted with an Agent 15 chemical warhead, followed behind for the short drive to the Aarida border crossing between Syria and Lebanon.

Headlights from the Scud launcher truck flashed across the Hezbollah vehicles that were staged and waiting for them in Lebanon.

Box 731

The boss got out of the vehicle as weapons were drawn on both sides of the border.

"You have the rest of my money?" the boss asked.

The leader of the Hezbollah troika looked at the launch vehicle and the truck carrying chemical Scuds. He pointed to his truck and two Russians ran to the back and removed a trunk and put it in the boss's car.

"Your plan worked," the troika leader said.

"They'll be chasing anthrax in America for a while. Don't wait too long."

The boss pulled the cap down over his eyes and got back into his vehicle.

PART III

CHAPTER 24

Hartsfield–Jackson Atlanta International Airport
Atlanta, Georgia

Dr. Yamamoto and his two Russian paramilitary colleagues cleared international customs in the Maynard Jackson International Terminal without even so much as a question or suspicious glance. According to their new passports, the three business executives at the front of the customs line, dressed in expensive Brooks Brothers' custom-tailored suits, were making their third trip to the United States in fewer than three months. All three made sure their first-class boarding passes were visible inside the passport jackets.

They rode the airport tram to baggage claim and watched the carousel spin around and finally drop their three bags.

Yamamoto and his two colleagues rode the escalator up one level to ticketing and found the domestic departures monitor. None of them bothered to view the destinations or the airline name. They were looking for one word: CANCELED.

"That one. Delta canceled their next flight to Washington Reagan," Yamamoto said as the three business executives left the international terminal and stepped into the shuttle bus for the twelve-minute ride back to the domestic terminal.

Yamamoto and the two Russians stood in the long ticketing line for United Airlines and made sure everyone observed them repeatedly checking their watches. All three stepped up to the desk of the first available ticket agent.

"We just got off our flight from Madrid and saw that Delta has canceled their flight to Washington Reagan. Do you have any seats on your next direct flight?" Yamamoto asked as the agent pulled up flights.

"We don't have any directs to Washington with available seats, but I can connect you at Baltimore at seven thirty tonight if that would work."

The three well-dressed business executives feigned serious contemplation and finally agreed to take the flights.

"One way or roundtrip?"

"One way," Yamamoto said as all three placed their passports on the counter. He handed the agent the prepaid Visa card Oleg had given him for the trip.

"Checking bags?"

"No. We'll just carry on."

After a long wait through the TSA lines and a quick tram ride to the concourse, the two Russians took seats in the boarding area as Dr. Yamamoto went to the men's restroom. He searched through feet on the floor until he found an open stall, went in, and locked the door.

Yamamoto took his suit coat off and hung it on the hook of the stall door. He reached into the side pocket of his coat and removed two latex gloves and put them on. He pulled the paperclip out of his passport, straightened one length, and then pried open and lifted the hidden lid from inside his top suit coat button. He reached inside the button and pulled out two postage stamps that were taped together as well as the small piece of double-sided tape that held the stamps against the back of the button. Yamamoto reached into the toilet seat cover dispenser box anchored to the wall above the toilet paper rolls, and counted back through five paper covers. He gently cut two of the taped sides of the stamp sandwich with the paperclip and then placed the dot of double-sided tape back onto the stamps. Careful to make sure

Box 731

the open side of the stamps faced up, he taped them to the fifth toilet seat cover.

Yamamoto flushed the toilet as he removed the latex gloves and then flushed again as he dropped the gloves into the toilet bowl and put his suit coat back on.

Soo Marie Soap Labs
Sault Ste. Marie, Michigan

Dr. Martin Ishii was escorted into the front lobby of Soo Marie Soap Labs. It was an old brick-and-mortar building in the original warehouse district of downtown Sault Ste. Marie. The three-story building shared a parking lot with the main post office. Finnegan's Tavern and Walleye Grill sat kitty-corner across the street from Martin's new company.

There's was nothing about the building that seemed to come close to justifying Martin's new salary, but the $10,000 signing bonus went a long way toward dispelling any cosmetic concerns he had.

The front lobby was small and led into a narrow hallway that housed three executive offices. The third office was the largest. Raised bronze letters on the door read Dr. Martin Ishii, President & CEO.

"Why don't you drop off your briefcase and papers and we'll take a quick tour?" Semyon said as Martin put his briefcase on the steel desk, as well as his folder of papers. He paused to glance at the wedding invitation from Leslie Raines that he had received the night before, printed from his iPhone, but hadn't had the chance to read or respond to. He wondered who the lucky guy was.

Semyon conducted the brief tour and started in the manufacturing facility at the end of the hallway past Martin's new office, where eight employees were working on the floor. Semyon waved and a man walked off the floor and over to Semyon and Dr. Martin Ishii.

"Chip Bremmer, let me introduce you to Dr. Ishii. He's the new president and CEO of Soo Marie Soap Labs."

"Dr. Ishii, it's an honor to finally meet you. I took a peek at your resume, and, well, all I can say is wow," Chip said.

"Tell Dr. Ishii about our business," Semyon injected as Chip led them out and onto the manufacturing floor.

"We've got about twelve thousand square feet dedicated to the manufacturing process. Up until last month, this was a small family-owned business since 1937. That was until Simon's investment group bought us."

"And we make laundry detergent?" Martin asked.

"Not just laundry detergent, Dr. Ishii, but family-value detergent. We are on the verge of exploiting a real niche in the market."

"Explain."

"Well, we're targeting trade-down American consumers. In good economic times, they have brand loyalty. For example, if it doesn't say Tide, people won't buy it. But these are new economic times, uncertain times. People are willing to trade-down from high-priced and even mid-tier laundry detergents, to what's considered value. That's what we sell. Value."

"What's our market share?" Martin asked.

"Right now? Nil, next to nothing. We were teetering on the edge of bankruptcy until Simon's investment group made the acquisition."

"So what's the marketing plan? How are we going to create customers and market share?" Martin prodded.

"Free samples by mail with a four-dollar-off coupon. We have negotiated premium shelf space with several 'big box' retailers in our market test areas. We are giving a 75 percent commission on every unit sold during the first ninety days."

"So essentially we're buying our way into the market."

Box 731

"Precisely," Semyon echoed as Chip continued the tour down the assembly line.

"So customers will be driven to Soo Marie Soaps simply because it's cheaper?"

Chip smiled at Semyon before he delivered the epiphany. "Actually Dr. Ishii, we have created a new formula that far and away exceeds anything on the market. We've branded the product as '731 Power,' a brand name that has done extremely well in focus group testing. Seven specially formulated cleaning agents guaranteed to knock out grease, grime, and that hard to reach dirt; three color-revitalizing ingredients that restore the true colors of the original fabric; and one powerful fragrance that keeps your clothes smelling fresh long after a hard day of work is complete."

"Sounds like a TV commercial already," Martin said, laughing.

"That's the beauty of the free sample of 731. Once people smell it, they'll be hooked," Semyon said as he handed Martin a sample from the manufacturing floor.

"Hmmm . . . that *is* good."

"Thank you, Chip," Semyon said as he led Martin out of the main floor.

"How many employees do we currently have?" Martin asked.

"Eight on the floor, four technicians in the lab, a chief technical officer, a chief research scientist, and yourself," Semyon said as he climbed the carpeted steps to the second floor.

"What's this?"

"That's our executive bunk room. As you know, research can be a twenty-four-hour proposition some days. The executive committee wanted a facility where you could stay on the premises, if you so desired. Let's head to the Ice House."

"Ice House?"

"Well, that's what this space was used for in the 1940s. Basically a cement-sealed, inner sanctum where they kept their blocks of ice for the manufacturing process," Semyon said as his crewmembers hung oxygen lines and put up HEPA filtration units.

"What are the workers doing in here now?"

"This is where we're building the BSL facility, the biosafety lab. Dr. Yamamoto is supervising construction and will walk the permits through the approval process."

"Dr. Yamamoto?"

"Yes, you will meet Dr. Yamamoto and Dr. Tanaka soon."

Indian Creek Island
Miami Beach, Florida

Ekaterina watched the video feed from Martin's office on one screen as Chip Bremmer and seven other temporary workers from Manpower Staffing were paid and dismissed on the other screen.

LHA 1 Peleliu Amphibious Ready Group
Mediterranean Sea off the Coast of Syria

US Navy Captain "Camp" Campbell, former SEAL and decorated trauma surgeon, ripped off his latex gloves and scrubs and then exited the operating room on the USS *Peleliu* after conducting three surgeries in fewer than four hours.

General Lexington Smith and Reuven Shavit were waiting for him in the outer chamber.

"Sir, your paratrooper is going to be just fine. The bullet entered above his Kevlar vest, bounced off his collarbone—which created some fragments—and then lodged in his shoulder. He lost a little bit of blood so we filled up his tank with some A-negative, per his chart, started him on some antibiotics, and sewed him up. He can travel in three days."

Box 731

"Thank you, Shepherd's Pie. We are most grateful," Reuven said as Lexington Smith was a bit confused by the honorific.

"General Smith, Special Agent Fallon Jessup has been through hell but she's alive. She has four broken ribs, trauma to the eye socket with an orbital fracture, and internal bleeding; she was torn apart and beaten repeatedly."

"Prognosis, captain?"

"Her physical wounds will heal in six weeks. Her psychological trauma may last decades. She's going to require a lot of work when she gets back to DC. But there may be a silver lining."

"What's that?"

"Sir, I think she was unconscious most of the time. Her body was assaulted, but hopefully her mind was asleep. She is extremely dehydrated. She needs to see an internist and a gynecologist to evaluate any internal organ injuries."

"When can we transport her?" the general asked.

"I'd give her ten days to two weeks. Have the ship docs make the final call," Camp said.

"And what about Billy Finn?"

"I'm heading over to recovery right now . . . I'll let you know, but he should be ugly, annoying, irritable, and just fine."

"Captain Campbell, I need you to join me in the video conferencing room," Lexington Smith said before Camp could walk away. "We need to debrief General Ferguson with our After Action Report."

"Sir, I thought this was going to remain under the radar," Camp said as he looked to Reuven for support.

"Captain, I said we'd keep it under the radar going in to the mission. Asking for forgiveness, now with success under our belt, puts us in a much better position than asking for permission up front."

"Aye, aye, sir," Camp said as he excused himself and entered the recovery bay where all three of his patients were recovering and resting comfortably.

He leaned over Billy Finn's bed and spoke quietly into his ear. "Special Agent Finn?"

Finn's eyes fluttered open until he finally fixed on Camp's face staring back at him. "Jesus, help me. I done died and went to hell," Finn whispered with dry mouth and parched lips.

Camp started laughing. "Hello, Billy."

"Where am I?"

"The USS *Peleliu* out in the Mediterranean, about thirty nautical miles from the Syrian coast."

"Am I going to make it?"

"Unfortunately . . . yes. They tried to give you a C-section, but the good guys got there in time."

Billy Finn's eyes fluttered and closed.

"Rest up, brother, I'll see you back at Walter Reed. I need you rested and recovered. Looks like we've got an anthrax mission to solve," Camp said as he stood and left the bay.

An ensign from the command center on the USS *Peleliu* rounded the corner with news that the Israeli helicopters were twenty minutes out. Camp grabbed his bag and followed Reuven and General Lexington Smith to the video conferencing room.

"This should be interesting," Camp muttered as he trailed behind Lexington Smith and Reuven.

"Our commandos recovered a camera and tape at the target house. I'd like to see it first, and then I'll share it with both of you," Reuven said as they took their seats.

ISAF Headquarters
Kabul, Afghanistan

General Jim Ferguson struggled to hear the details of the After Action Report as General Lexington Smith and Director Shavit explained them. He couldn't take his eyes off Captain "Camp" Campbell, who sat beside them and remained uncharacteristically

BOX 731

quiet. Ferguson's blood was boiling, and he couldn't wait to get Camp alone.

"So all in all, Jim, it was a very successful mission," Lexington Smith summarized.

"But we had American boots on Syrian soil, Lex," Ferguson responded. "The undersecretary will not be pleased."

"I'll handle the Department of Defense, Jim. I authorized Campbell to go in. Besides, he saved an Israeli paratrooper, stabilized Billy Finn and Agent Jessup, and probably saved the life of the Hezbollah terrorist as well."

"I'm sure that'll bless the socks off the secretary. Well, bring Campbell back with you. I'm anxious to chat with him," Ferguson said as Camp shifted uncomfortably in his chair.

"Negative, Jim. Camp has to head back to Washington and over to Walter Reed. I also need him to debrief Langley."

"Let me guess . . . Camp needs to clear medical so he can be authorized to return to duty?"

General Smith smiled and terminated the conference call.

LHA 1 Peleliu Amphibious Ready Group
Mediterranean Sea off the Coast of Syria

Lexington Smith, Reuven, and Camp stood as the screen went dark.

"Could've been worse, I suppose," Camp said as Reuven smiled.

"Captain, once you clear medical I need you to debrief Agent Daniels at CIA. Stand by as I may need your help on the anthrax situation, especially if we have any INTEL that it's headed for American shores," Lexington Smith said.

"Sir, you may need to clear that with General Ferguson. He's got his claws in pretty deep, not to mention we're friends," Camp said as he hoisted his assault pack over his shoulder.

"I've got one thing that Jim Ferguson doesn't have, so I wouldn't worry about it, sailor."

"What's that, sir?"

"An extra star on my shoulder," Lexington Smith said. The general wasn't as nearly concerned about Camp as he was with worse-case scenarios of an evil storm that was brewing.

CHAPTER 25

Baltimore / Washington International Thurgood Marshall Airport
Baltimore, Maryland

Three well-dressed international businessmen exited the secured area of BWI and rode the escalator down to ground transportation and boarded the Avis Rental Car bus.

The three checked in at the customer service office on the lot. The bus driver had assured them that cars were still available for rental. After five minutes of paperwork, two one-way cars with a drop fee were rented and the three men loaded their luggage into the trunks of both cars parked in stalls sixty-one and sixty-three.

"Here are the orders from Semyon," Yamamoto said as he handed an envelope to one of the Russians. "It's a dairy farm about three miles off Interstate 70. It's close enough to Fort Detrick to get their attention."

"Where do we meet?" the Russian asked.

"We'll need a few hours in the Green Ridge State Forest. We'll meet at the US Airways ticket counter in Pittsburgh, tomorrow morning at seven."

Yamamoto got into the passenger seat as the other Russian started their car. He pressed the button and lowered his window.

"Remember, no credit cards. Cash only."

Centers for Disease Control
Atlanta, Georgia

Margaret Tapper read the hand-delivered note from her administrative assistant as the conference room full of international health experts continued to discuss influenza Type A H3N2, and the variant virus H3N2v that were infecting far too many people worldwide. She left her file folders on the table and quietly excused herself to take the call in her office.

"This is Dr. Tapper."

"Ma'am this is Agent Marco Hidalgo. I work out of the FBI field office here in Hattiesburg, Mississippi."

"How may I help you, agent?"

"Ma'am, we have a patient who checked himself into the local ER complaining of flu symptoms. Pretty sick fella."

Tapper exhaled the frustration and quickly checked her watch. "Agent Hidalgo, influenza Type A is a nasty flu strain this season. Unfortunately, some of those who got flu shots are still getting this influenza. But please, sir, the FBI can't call here every time you discover unusual flu symptoms. It hits everyone differently. I'm sure his doctors will take care of him. Now if you don't mind, I'm in the middle of a—"

"Actually ma'am, we thought it was flu at first too. But the black ulcerated lesions on his fanny didn't match up with your normal, run-of-the-mill influenza. So the ER doc sent him over to an infectious disease expert who ordered a chest x-ray, sputum culture, blood culture, and a CT scan."

"And?" Dr. Tapper asked, trying to get to the bottom line as she stood and prepared to end the call.

"Well, ma'am, nothing terribly unusual until he did a spinal puncture. The spinal tap was conclusive. It's anthrax, ma'am."

Tapper grew silent. She sat down.

"The doctor calls it cutaneous and inhalation anthrax. He says this could be a national security issue."

BOX 731

"Not necessarily, Agent Hidalgo. Does this patient work with animals? Does he have a farm or ranch there in Mississippi? Or perhaps he recently traveled to South America."

"Actually ma'am, the patient is an accountant and lives in a condo. But he did just return from a trip."

"Where?"

"That's kind of a funny story too, ma'am. Four days ago he took an early morning flight to your town. You see, he's also in the army reserves and his unit is based there in Atlanta. He flew back to Hattiesburg late that night, after his monthly meeting. But he started feeling sick a day later."

Tapper raced through the morning briefs she had received over the last week. There was no mention of anthrax that she could recall. "Agent, no one from airport security, TSA, or our local FBI office has made any mention of anthrax in the last week. I highly doubt the infection took place here. But I will certainly call your office if I hear of any new reports."

"Ma'am, there's one more thing."

"Go ahead, Agent."

"This fella was deployed to Afghanistan for a temporary duty assignment last year. He received the anthrax vaccination. He's not responding to the current antibiotics regimen."

Tapper was quickly lost in her thoughts as she ended the call and returned to a conference room full of coughing and sneezing world health officials.

Soo Marie Soap Labs
Sault Ste. Marie, Michigan

Semyon strolled into Dr. Martin Ishii's office and handed him the memo. Martin read it twice as Semyon looked through the magazines, reports, and books that were now scattered all over the president and CEO's desk.

"I don't understand what they're asking for," Martin said as he lowered his reading glasses. "And who wrote this cable?"

"Well, it's been thoroughly scrubbed since our Brussels office received it yesterday, but I presume the CIA, or maybe even MI-6. We do contract work for both."

"But what are they asking?"

"Apparently, someone sent an anthrax-laced product through the local mail system in some Eastern European country. The bioagent was packaged with regular powdered laundry detergent. The perpetrators added aroma granules as well as high levels of bee pollen. The product was vacuum-sealed in a foil pouch, and the postal system did not detect the anthrax."

"I understand all of that, Simon, but are they asking how such a package could bypass the Bio Detection Systems at post offices? Well, number one, I'd guess they don't have systems that are as sophisticated as we have here in the US. And two, it's the pollen. Natural environmental ingredients can render those BDS devices useless."

"So there's nothing we can do about it?" Semyon asked.

"Biological weapons are released in small quantities every day around the world, and I would guess anthrax is the most common among them. But since it can't be spread from person to person, it doesn't really rise to the level of news."

"What if some group gets their hands on a lot of anthrax?"

"Then that would give the BDS systems greater odds of detecting something. Sooner or later, a vacuum-sealed foil pouch is going to get broken or torn apart on a sorting machine during mail processing. The authorities would know and the population could be warned."

"But many of them would get through, would they not?" Semyon asked.

"Yes . . . probably . . . but someone would need a significant supply of anthrax to cause any real mass hysteria."

Box 731

"How much anthrax would be needed in each pouch . . . to kill someone?"

Martin got up from his desk and walked over to the whiteboard on his office wall. "You know what a kilogram is, right? It's basically equivalent to 2.205 pounds," Martin explained as he drew the numbers on the board. "There are one thousand grams—that's the kilo part—in each kilogram. A gram is basically one-twenty-eighth of an ounce; think about the weight of one postage stamp. The task is to see how concentrated we can get the anthrax spores within one gram of powder."

"So it doesn't take much, does it?" Semyon asked as he sat down.

"No, but a terrorist in a cave is not going to be able to make the high-grade powder required for inhalation lethality. You'd need a laboratory and a military scientist who knows what he's doing. A gram of anthrax needs only ten thousand microscopic spores to be lethal. If a military scientist makes it . . . there may be as many as five hundred *billion* spores in just one gram. I think some scientists can even get one trillion spores in a gram now."

"A military scientist like you?"

Martin was taken aback by Semyon's question.

"Like me, yes, or Dr. Yamamoto, or even Dr. Tanaka, though I haven't been able to discuss our project with him yet so I really don't know much about his background. I understand that Dr. Yamamoto will arrive soon. I'm anxious to meet him."

"I apologize for that, Dr. Ishii; we've been keeping both of them quite busy."

"But the only times I was working with anthrax was to develop vaccines and antibiotics to treat it. I have never worked on it to produce a weapon."

Semyon got up and brushed past Martin's desk. He noticed a wedding invitation sticking out of Martin's inbox. Semyon pulled it out and looked at it.

"Excellent," Semyon said, "who's getting married?"

"One of my former colleagues at Fort Detrick; she's marrying a US Navy captain."

"In New Hampshire?" Semyon read the invitation and then put it back down in the box. "Are you going?"

"I'd like to, but it'll depend on my workload here."

"You should go, Dr. Ishii. Weddings are wonderful events to celebrate. What does she do?"

"Who?"

"Your former colleague at Fort Detrick."

"Oh, Lieutenant Colonel Raines? She's a military scientist. Works on bioweapons and infectious diseases."

CHAPTER 26

National Interagency Biodefense Center
Ft. Detrick, Maryland

Lieutenant Colonel Leslie Raines walked into the atrium lobby and stepped up to the coffee bar for her usual tall skinny latte. She entered the elevator without buttons, performed the biometric scan, and rode the car up to her approved floor.

Raines entered the office with both a sliver of regret and a quiver full of optimism. She had worn the uniform for her entire professional career and loved every day of it. Nothing was more satisfying to Leslie Raines than solving infectious disease and bioweapon puzzles through research with animals, Petri dishes, and computer programs.

There were no exciting projects on her horizon, nothing that could compete, at least, with the wedding excitement that filled her every thought.

"Lieutenant Colonel Raines," she said as she answered her desk phone.

"Good morning, gorgeous."

"Camp? Why are you calling on this line?"

"Your cell keeps going straight to voice mail. Perhaps the colonel has other things on her mind these days other than turning her phone on," Camp teased.

"Where are you?"

"Molly Bloom's pilot dropped me off at 0300. I'm at Langley."

"CIA? What's going on?"

"Long story, happy ending. I'll tell you tonight at dinner."

"Are you asking me out on a date, sailor?" Raines asked.

"Les, I just got out of a briefing with Agent Daniels. I'm not going to call it an attack, but there's been an anthrax incident in Atlanta."

"I'm listening," Leslie said as Dr. Groenwald stepped into her office and sat down.

"A passenger flew back from Atlanta's airport, developed flu-like symptoms, got a full workup, and was diagnosed with both cutaneous and inhalation anthrax."

"Just one report so far?" Leslie asked.

"Affirmative, but that's not the juicy part. The passenger is an army reservist. He deployed to Afghanistan last year. He received the military's anthrax vaccine, Les."

Leslie closed her eyes and rubbed her forehead. She looked over at Groenwald, who was already nodding.

"Les, I need to know if someone could cook an anthrax recipe that renders our current vaccines useless. Daniels will be calling your supervisor. We need to make this a top priority."

Leslie stood up to end the call. "Roger that, I think he did already," she said as she hung up. "Anthrax?" Leslie asked and Groenwald nodded.

"Colonel, have you ever heard of the NCTR in Arkansas?" Groenwald asked.

"Yes, sir. The National Center for Toxicological Research."

"During the Cold War, we had several ten thousand-gallon vats . . . gigantic tanks that were used to grow bacteria for potential offensive biological weapons. Nixon shut the whole project down in 1969."

"Aside from the history lesson, Dr. Groenwald, how does this relate to the anthrax event out of Atlanta?"

BOX 731

"The NCTR is now under control of the Food and Drug Administration, but those Cold War tanks are available. The Department of Defense would like you to head out to Redfield, Arkansas, tomorrow. If we have a previously vaccinated soldier who has now contracted inhalation and cutaneous anthrax, we may have a huge problem on our hands—even if it turns out to be from an agricultural source. We need to get samples of the toxin found in Atlanta and ramp this thing up immediately."

"Sir?"

"New antibiotics . . . a new vaccine. We have no idea what we're dealing with here, Colonel Raines. If this is a new strain of anthrax, we can't risk bringing it here to Detrick. We could end up with contaminated equipment and an internal disaster on our hands."

"Yes, sir, I'll get with the travel desk and make my arrangements."

"Colonel Raines, you need to get over to medical for a full physical before you go. We need a recent baseline on your health and blood work. Just in case."

"Sir?"

"You may be exposed to some nasty organisms. They'll call you in a few weeks with the results."

Soo Marie Soap Labs
Sault Ste. Marie, Michigan

Semyon was talking on his cell phone in Dr. Tanaka's empty office when Oleg walked in with the spreadsheets.

"What?" Semyon said as he ended his call.

"These came in on the FedEx from Ekaterina in Miami," Oleg said as he put them down on the desk.

"What is it?"

"Presorted and targeted populations, cities, neighborhoods, zip codes, and individual addresses," Oleg said as he paged through the first few of more than five hundred spreadsheet pages.

"How many does she want us to hit?"

"Looks like more than five thousand or so in the Chicago area, and another one thousand in Dublin, Ohio. There are fifty names and addresses per page. What's that? Like twenty-five hundred or so?" Oleg asked as he calculated the simple math.

"Try twenty-five thousand."

Semyon waved and dismissed Oleg, who quickly left the office without saying a word. Semyon rubbed both temples as he held his head in his hands over Tanaka's unused desk. He opened the unsigned letter from Rina that was packaged along with the spreadsheets.

Prove the concept. Send unmarked, nontraceable, no return address in a vapor-sealed foil pouch to spreadhseet address #3,012 in Beaverton, Oregon. Have Oleg drive sample to Oregon and drop in local post office there.

"I hate this woman," Semyon grumbled quietly. He picked up his cell phone and dialed Oleg, who had just climbed the stairs to the third floor. "Get Yamamoto. We need to produce a sample. And gas up the Suburban . . . you're driving to Oregon."

"When?"

"Soon."

Indian Creek Island
Miami Beach, Florida

Ekaterina saw her cold, calculated smile in the flat-panel monitor's reflection as she closed the video link on her computer.

"Trust me, I hate you too, Semyon," she said loudly as she heard Viktor laughing and playing in the pool with his colleagues

Box 731

from work. "Just a few more weeks and you'll have the rest of your money, and my beloved husband, and I will have my revenge."

Rina paged through her copy of the spreadsheet until she came to address number 3,012: *Howard and Bonnie Suzuki, 11809 SW Frankston Pond Court, Beaverton, Oregon, 97008.*

The address selection was random, but Rina hoped the outcome would be predictable.

Carolinas Medical Center–Mercy
Charlotte, North Carolina

Frank Makowski rolled over on his side as yet another specialist entered the infection isolation room at Carolinas–Mercy to examine the lesion on his rear end.

"You said you do not work with animals?" the doctor asked for the third time.

"No." Frank grunted in frustration. "What kind of doctor are you?"

"Dermatologist," the physician answered as he pulled the magnifying visor down over his eyes and turned a bright examination light on.

"So you think this is a rash?"

"I didn't say that."

The dermatologist turned off the overhead exam light and walked to the back of Frank's room and stood next to the primary-care physician. They spoke quietly with each other as Frank watched.

"You said you recently got back from a trip?" the dermatologist asked.

"I told you that too. I took the family to Orlando for a week at Disney World."

"Then you came straight home?"

"For God's sake, people! Now you're really starting to irritate me. We flew to Orlando, spent six days, seven nights, and blew about $3,000. Do you want me to engrave it in stone?"

The two doctors talked quietly again.

"Direct?" the primary-care physician asked.

"Direct what?"

"Was it a nonstop flight?"

"Geez," Frank protested as he violently pulled the bed sheets up by his face. "No, we made connections in Atlanta. But we never even left the terminal."

Turner Dairy Farm
Middletown, Maryland

The Avis sedan was parked quietly on the side of the country highway as he finished the last draw on his cigarette. The door to the farmhouse opened. He pulled the keys out of the ignition as he watched an elderly man walk across the gravel driveway and into the milking barn as the lights in the barn illuminated.

He stepped out of the car and stepped into the coveralls he had removed from his luggage and zipped them up over his suit pants, dress shirt, and tie. He ripped the bubble-wrap packaging away from the hunting knife he had just purchased from a Walmart up the highway.

Darkness shielded him from view as his dress shoes crunched the gravel below until he could duck between two strands of electrified barbed wire and into the farmer's dirt and grass pasture.

He looked through the pane glass window next to the barn door. The farmer was on a stool in the back of the barn where he was hooking up the milking machine to one of his cows.

The old wooden door creaked as he entered and quickly crouched in the shadows next to a milking stall. Most of the forty

Box 731

black-and-white Holsteins bellowed as the door closed. Through the board slats in the stall he saw the farmer glance up at the door before he stood up and moved to another stall.

He extended the blade to his hunting knife, moved quietly down one row, across the center connector aisle, and then walked down the second row until he stood quietly behind the farmer and beneath a solitary hanging lightbulb. His shadow danced on the back of the wooden stall, which caused the farmer to lift his head up just as the hunting knife was thrust deep into the back of the farmer's neck.

He put on latex gloves, reached in to his victim's back pocket, and removed an old leather wallet. Two dollars were quickly deposited in his coveralls before the wallet was thrown on the floor by the bellowing Holstein.

He pulled Yamamoto's envelope out of his coveralls, hoping the vaccine was as just as good as the Japanese scientist had promised.

CHAPTER 27

Shelly's Backroom
Washington, DC

The waitress opened Camp's humidor, box eighty-eight. He removed two fifty-gauge cigars and returned to the table as dinner plates were cleared. Two neat, seventeen-year-old Macallan's single malt scotches were waiting at each setting.

Leslie's face was covered with horror.

"What?" Camp asked as he sat down and cut both cigars. "I promised I would dance with you until one of us died. I'll even listen to your country music and go out on hikes to watch birds with you. But there are a few things you need to do with me as well."

Camp lit Leslie's cigar and handed it to her. She stared at it for several seconds and then put it between her fingers.

"I should advise you that these are illegal Cuban cigars. You can tell because the smoke has a blue tint to it."

"Fascinating." Leslie feigned interest as she took her first puff of the cigar. "And what's with the gasoline?"

"It's single malt. No ice. Always neat. Sip. Smoke. Sip. Smoke . . . and talk," Camp said, smiling.

"How's Billy doing?"

"I stopped by his room at Walter Reed just a few hours ago. He should be discharged in the morning. Well, at least he'd better be because we're on a noon flight to Atlanta with Daniels from CIA."

Box 731

"Geez, Camp . . . let the guy rest up," Leslie said as she took a sip of the Macallan's. Her eyes bulged as the scotch trickled down her throat.

"Good, isn't it?" Camp beamed. Leslie shook her head in disgust. "I spoke with the microbiologist at the hospital in Hattiesburg today. They don't have much but they have a few spores they're going to put on a military transport over to Little Rock tonight. It should get to the NCTR before you do."

"Camp, what if this is just random? What if it's, in fact, just natural agricultural anthrax?"

"That's our best-case scenario, Les. But we've got to plan for the worst."

Glendive, Montana

Oleg had been driving for eighteen hours and thirty-nine minutes when his cell phone rang.

"Where are you?" Semyon asked.

"Some dive in Montana . . . Glendive . . . I've never been to Montana before. I think I will retire here and find a nice American wife," Oleg said as the windshield wipers on the black Suburban brushed away the steady snow that was falling on Interstate 94.

"How many miles to go?"

"I'm halfway. Just about one thousand, one hundred miles until I reach the post office in Beaverton. But I'm getting tired. Can I get a hotel room . . . just for a few hours?"

"Keep driving. You can sleep when you're dead."

Oleg hung up, cursed at Semyon, and threw his phone down on the seat next to the package of "Power 731" laundry detergent addressed to Howard and Bonnie Suzuki.

Centers for Disease Control
Atlanta, Georgia

Camp, Billy Finn, and CIA Special Agent Daniels were seated in an empty conference room as Dr. Margaret Tapper finished a meeting in an adjacent conference room.

Daniels turned his laptop on as Camp and Billy watched.

"Director Shavit sent me a video file early this morning," Daniels said.

"What is it?" asked Finn.

"The Israeli Shayetet 13 commandos recovered your camera and the tape you shot. But there's nothing significant from what I can see."

Finn watched the video file. It was all unedited raw footage. He narrated the footage as he, Camp, and Daniels watched it together. "I started recording when we parked outside of Andulus University. Those are the two bodyguards that Wally hired."

"Wally?" asked Camp.

"CIA Syrian operative. His name was something like Walid."

"Must've been the KIA."

"Oh geez, are you serious? How's Jessup doing?"

"She's alive. What's going on here?" Daniels asked.

"Ah . . . we're in the lobby asking for our contact, Professor Haidar. Here we're going up the steps to his office and laboratory. He didn't speak a lick of English, so Wally translated as Jessup did the interview."

"Why were you even there?" Camp asked as the video followed them down one flight of stairs.

"We suspected the university might be hosting a clandestine bioweapons lab," Daniels said.

"Anything?" Camp asked.

"Keep watching. On the second floor he takes us into a perfectly clean lab where pharmacy students work preparing

BOX 731

medicines. Fallon interviews the professor in here for a couple of seconds, but no evidence of any students."

"What's this?" Daniels asked.

"The professor sticks his head into the second lab and then suddenly backs out, saying they are working in there. The lab is messy, I mean really messy, with scattered compounds everywhere, so we bust in. There! Stop the video and back up."

Daniels paused the video and pulled the PLAY bar back a few seconds and let it play again.

"There's an office in the back of the lab. You can see the guy's face for a brief second or two and then he closes the door."

"And that's significant?"

"He wasn't Middle Eastern. He looked Asian to me. After the whole nuclear thing with North Koreans in Syria a few years back I thought that was a bit unusual."

"Molly Bloom intercepted a call between a Syrian and a Russian. They mentioned anthrax on the call," Camp said.

"Molly who?" Daniels asked as Finn and Camp ignored the question.

"Fallon had a little Bio Detection Kit with her. You can see here where she swabbed a sample of the residue on the lab bench. When we got back into the car she tested it and got a positive reading for anthrax."

Daniels closed his laptop and stood up. Finn had a perplexed look on his face.

"You okay, Billy?" Camp asked.

"You mentioned Russian. When I was in the FBI field office in Manhattan we dealt with Russian mob stuff in the city and over the river in Jersey. After fifteen years, I got pretty good with my street Russian."

"And?"

"The leader of the shabiha group that abducted us spoke Russian as well. I was blindfolded and gagged but could hear him in the other room talking on his phone in Russian."

"Did you hear anything useful?" Daniels prodded.

"Not really. But he did say the guy's name at the beginning of the call. Samone, Semyon . . . something like that."

Daniels and Camp made eye contact.

"That might be the same call we intercepted. Mossad did too," Daniels said. "But I'm less than convinced they're heading this way. Doesn't make any sense. If there's going to be an anthrax attack involving Russians and Syrians, more than likely Israel would be the target."

Dr. Tapper entered the room and apologized for her tardiness. "Gentlemen, while I appreciate your interest in this situation, I must tell you there's nothing new to report. This is clearly an environmental incident," Tapper said as Daniels sat down.

"With all due respect, ma'am, we received a report of a cutaneous anthrax infection from Charlotte, North Carolina. The patient—male—was in the Atlanta airport at the same time as the first patient from Mississippi."

"That's true, Agent Daniels. Clearly there was anthrax exposure in that terminal, but it was hardly an attack. As I indicated over the telephone, your office will be notified the minute we have reason to believe this is anything other than a random environmental event."

Tapper dismissed the trio and ushered them to the elevator.

"Camp, we need Molly Bloom to do an image enhancement on that Asian and see if the name Semyon—or this guy's face—ring any bioterror bells," Finn whispered as Daniels stepped into the elevator first.

Beaverton, Oregon

Bonnie Suzuki ran up the driveway and stopped, finally ending her seven-mile run in the chilly forty-three degree mist. She flipped up the cover to the electric garage door opener, entered

BOX 731

her four-digit code, and went inside. The mail basket just inside the garage was full of the day's mail so she scooped it up, pressed the button on the side of her kitchen door to close the garage, and went inside to warm up.

A variety of bills and junk mail were thrown on the kitchen counter and could wait until she'd had a hot shower. But a uniquely packaged sample product caught her eye. She read every word of it: Free load on us . . . $4 coupon inside for your first purchase. Introducing 731 power . . . 7 cleaning agents . . . 3 color guards . . . and 1 amazing fragrance . . . You've got to smell it to believe it.

Bonnie took the sample down to the laundry room. She opened the lid to the Kenmore Elite washing machine, set the water level to large load, temperature to warm, turned the dial to ten minutes, and pulled the knob. As the machine started to fill with water she kicked her Asics off and threw the running socks in followed by her shorts, fleece, sports bra, and four large towels on the floor next to the machine. She grabbed her robe off the hook on the laundry room door, reached for the bottle of liquid detergent, and then stopped when she saw the free sample.

She opened the pressure-sealed foil pouch and stuck her nose in. It was, as advertised, an amazing fragrance. Bonnie reached into the pouch, pulled out the four-dollar coupon, and poured the free sample into the rising water before heading upstairs to call her mother and take a hot shower.

Lightner Farms
Gettysburg, Pennsylvania

Billy Finn walked gingerly behind his wife through the side kitchen door and into the lodge at Lightner Farms. "So this is the famous Lightner Farms," he said as Eileen escorted him to the oversized-leather chairs in front of the hearth.

"In fact, I was sitting in that exact chair when Leslie shot me," Camp teased as Eileen covered her face in mock horror.

"Still too soon, Seabury Campbell Jr. . . . too soon," Eileen said as she retreated to the kitchen.

"Captain Campbell, I wanted to personally thank you for saving my Billy's life," his wife, Madge, said as Eileen handed her a cup of hot tea on her grandmother's saucer. "Although I must say I wasn't thrilled that he had to join you for the meeting in Atlanta yesterday."

"Don't call him Captain, Madge, or it'll just go to his head," Billy said, changing the subject as he eyed the basket of steaming blueberry muffins that Eileen grabbed from the kitchen counter.

"Ma'am, it was my privilege. Hopefully Billy has told you that my participation must remain secret. But it's not what you think it was," Camp said with his trademark grin. "Billy had gotten so doggone fat that the bad guys thought he might be pregnant. They were just trying to give him a C-section to save the baby, that's all."

"You're going to make me pop my stitches," Finn said laughing with a mouthful of muffin.

"Well, I'm excited to have company for a few days," Eileen said as she pulled some keys off the hooks above her desk. "Sailor, Mr. and Mrs. Finn will be in the double in room six. You can have seven."

Camp made two trips upstairs to get the luggage situated but kept a close ear on the conversation below.

"Jim Ferguson called me last night," Finn yelled upstairs.

"What did he say about me?"

"Something about dog meat and Leavenworth," Finn mimicked as Camp came down the stairs smiling.

Camp's cell phone started ringing. The incoming call was an unpublished number and could only be one person.

"Molly Bloom?" Camp answered.

Box 731

"Hello, Shepherd's Pie. How's our friend?" Reuven asked.

"Stubborn, obnoxious, and annoying. Basically, he seems to be back to normal," Camp said as Finn shook his head. "Anything on the image enhancement?"

"No. It's a new face to us. But I do have something on the name."

"Tell me," Camp said eagerly.

"Not on this connection. But I had my team go back to the Ofek 9 archived photos, the short cruise of the Canadian ship to the Port of Barcelona, and then the four vehicles that took ten people from the port to the airport."

"In Barcelona?"

"Actually no. The vehicles pulled up to the departures level and all ten got out, switched vehicles, and left the airport by ground."

"Guess they didn't want to be followed. Where did they go?"

"The Ofek lost them at the airport. But the name has several aliases. Three hours after the vehicle switch in Barcelona, one of those aliases passed through customs at the Madrid airport."

"More international flights out of Madrid, I'd guess," Camp said. "Where did he go?"

"That alias was not used on any commercial passenger flights leaving Madrid. But about an hour after his passport was stamped and swiped at Spanish customs, an Aeroflot cargo plane took off."

"Russian cargo . . . he had to be on there. Where did it go?"

"Toronto, Canada."

"Did you check with Canadian customs? Did the same alias process through Toronto?"

"No, but six new French names did . . . about thirty minutes after the Aeroflot flight landed. Of course the French have no records for these six people. But the interesting thing . . ."

"I'm listening."

"The six French passports were joined by an Asian . . . a Japanese name."

"Do you think it was the guy Finn saw in the lab in Syria?"

"No. Facial recognition software indicates no match with the photo scanned at customs."

"Six French and an Asian . . . that's seven. What happened to the other three?"

"No idea. We're poring through passenger lists and passports now. Could take a few days to reconstruct the pieces."

"So you think seven of them are in Toronto?" Camp asked.

"I doubt it. Ten people travel together by ground to Madrid from Barcelona after making a diversionary vehicle change at the Barcelona airport. Then six previously unregistered French passports and an Asian with an unregistered passport move through customs in Toronto."

Camp paced back and forth in front of the newly repaired French doors on the other side of the long wooden dining room table.

"Should we be concerned?" Camp asked though immediately regretted the naive words that had just left his mouth.

"We'll talk soon," Reuven said as the call ended.

Camp put his phone in his pocket and turned back toward everyone assembled in front of the fire. His eyes met head-on with Billy Finn who had been tracking every move of the conversation he heard while suspecting details from the conversation he couldn't hear, just as any good retired FBI special agent would do.

Madge folded the *Gettysburg Times* daily newspaper and put it in her lap as she shook her head. "Honestly, you expect murder in the big cities. But rural Maryland? On a dairy farm?"

"What happened?" Eileen asked intently.

"A dairy farmer down in Middletown, Maryland, was killed in his milking barn and robbed of two dollars. For heaven's sake."

"Gunshot?" Billy asked.

BOX 731

"No. They stuck a knife through the back of his neck. What is this world coming to?" Madge asked as Camp contemplated the attack.

"Through the back of the neck? Sounds more like a military execution than a robbery," Camp said as his eyes caught Billy Finn's.

CHAPTER 28

Atlantic Ocean
Miami Beach, Florida

The warm Florida wind cut gently through Ekaterina's hair inside the breezeway of the cabin as the captain of Viktor's yacht took her to calm waters three miles offshore as ordered. The seventy-foot Galeon Raptor 700 was one of life's simpler pleasures for Rina but an intoxicating hobby for Viktor. The smoke-black glass gave Viktor the privacy he needed and the two 1550-horsepower diesel engines gave him all the speed and power he could ever use. The luxury yacht was well-appointed with white Italian leather seating, dark-walnut wood trim, and ambient LED lighting for dispersed, though not distracting, illumination.

To Rina it was just a boat.

The captain pulled the engines back and finally cut them as the Galeon floated in absolute isolation and silence off the coast of Miami Beach. Rina looked up through the expansive skylight at the pilot console and nodded. She grabbed her box and walked to the aft of the ship. The captain released the automatic garage and stem platform section as a new section of the yacht pushed out and extended over the water. The captain turned around, pulled out a bottle of Pyrat XO Reserve rum, opened a magazine, and put his iPod ear buds in as Rina stepped onto the teakwood platform.

She put the box inside the rubber raft and then tied it to one of the hooks on the back of the Galeon before gently pushing

BOX 731

the raft out into the warm ocean water. Rina's towel and bikini were stowed inside the raft as it soon trailed the Galeon fifty feet by tether.

She stepped out of her sandals. Her shorts fell to the deck as she unbuttoned the only two buttons that separated her store-bought breasts from a white blouse and freedom.

Rina's body cut through the water with neither noise nor splash before she emerged next to the raft. She bobbed up and reached in for first the top and then the bottom of her suit. She pulled herself into the raft, put her sunglasses back on, and pulled out the thirteen—by twelve-inch aluminum and steel case that was three inches deep.

She started to spin the numbers on the combination dial for the Bolsheviks.

Rina entered the numbers on the second combination dial. Her rage was once again unleashed. Her mind was consumed with cathartic thoughts of revenge.

Rina reached for Pavel's old black and white photo, slightly bent and well-worn but safely tucked away inside the flap on the top of the box. Her fingers began to tremble. She pulled out the almost seventy-year-old envelope, labeled simply with the numbers 731, and pried the clasp open.

Dmitry had told his daughter that she was allowed to look inside the folder only twice in her lifetime.

"The first time . . . so you will know," Rina recalled her father's words. "So you will know what they did to your grandfather."

Rina's breathing became erratic. The ocean was deafeningly silent all around, but her mind was filling with groans and screams from a horror long-since ended.

"The second time . . . it must be the last time," he had said. "The second time must only be to avenge Pavel's suffering."

The envelope contained three photographs, a lab report with two short paragraphs, and a letter from Dmitry. Rina read the lab report first. The first paragraph was written in Japanese kanji, which she could not read.

The paragraph in Russian translated Pavel's horror in exactly forty-five words: *Japanese secret police found six Russian maturas at train depot while on patrol and took them in to work as logs. Five were used in shrapnel tests. Their polkovnik was defiant so he volunteered for seven days of Bacillus anthracis testing followed by live vivisection.*

Ekaterina pulled the three photographs out one by one. In the first, Pavel was stripped to his undershorts and sat alone in an isolated room, as a defoliation bacilli bomb was detonated. His face was frozen in horror not knowing what germs had been released. Rina read the sub-caption on the photo: *bubonic plague, anthrax, typhoid, and dysentery from one porcelain shell.*

Photograph number two showed Japanese scientists dressed in protective suits and goggles as they examined Pavel's arms and legs, now colored in various hues of black with open skin lesions. The sub-caption indicated the photo was taken "DBD+2"— defoliation bomb detonation, plus two days.

The third was the picture that was seared into Ekaterina's mind by her father years before. Pavel's naked body was suspended two inches from the ground. His arms and hands were tied to buckles up in the corners of the room. His eyes were open, and he appeared to be screaming. His body was ravaged with lesions and his body weight on DBD+6 was remarkably reduced since the second photograph. A Japanese scientist held a stethoscope to Pavel's neck. Another was cutting halfway through his stomach as organs began to fall out of his body as the photo was taken.

Still trembling, Rina took out her father's letter and read it one final time.

My father, Polkovnik Pavel Shmushkevich, was tortured and murdered in Unit 731, a top-secret and covert biological and chemical warfare and development facility operated by the Japanese Imperial army in occupied Manchuria, China, during the second Sino-Japanese War between 1937 and 1945 and during World War Two.

BOX 731

General Shiro Ishii, chief medical officer of the Imperial army, and his band of doctors, scientists, and microbiologists, conducted human experimentation, killing as many as twelve thousand Chinese, Koreans, Allied prisoners of war, and Russians in the camp. No one knows for sure how many innocent peasants and farmers in nearby villages were killed by these experiments.

My father was subjected to a defoliation Bacillus bomb detonation in close quarters and was exposed to numerous germ agents. He immediately suffered from cutaneous anthrax exposure through direct contact with anthrax spores. Had he not inhaled the anthrax, his suffering would have been limited to skin lesions and pain. But once inhaled, the spores traveled to my father's lungs, where immune cells carried the spores to his lymph nodes. Once in the lymph system, anthrax spores multiplied and released toxins that created high fever, difficulty breathing, fatigue, muscle pain, nausea, vomiting, diarrhea, and black ulcers. Death was inevitable within seven days.

The Japanese scientists were curious as to the condition of my father's organs as anthrax ravaged his body. Pavel, infected and near death, was led naked into the vivisection chamber. His body was scrubbed with an abrasive deck brush and a water hose. His hands were put into restraints and his body was suspended inches off the ground. Without the benefit of anesthesia, the Japanese wanted to see what the anthrax was doing to my father's internal organs . . . before decomposition could begin. The Japanese had mastered the art of timing. Holding a stethoscope to his neck and listening to Pavel's heartbeat, the doctor gave the signal at the precise moment when my father's stomach could be sliced open without infected blood splashing onto the other scientists.

Ekaterina folded the letter and stuffed it back in the envelope with the three photographs and the lab report. Her body heaved back and forth with internal sobs and anguish, though no more tears could roll down her cheeks. She was empty.

Ekaterina reached over the edge of the rubber raft and grabbed the ski rope that towed her fifty feet behind the drifting Galeon.

She pulled on the rope once. Her mind raged with the war crimes trial that was, and the war crimes trial that never happened. When the Soviets declared war on Japan they invaded Manchuria, as Japanese scientists moved quickly to destroy the evidence. The Russians recovered several files and photographs and arrested twelve members of the Japanese Kwantung army. The Khabarovsk War Crimes Trial was held from December 25 through 31 in 1949, in the industrial city of Khabarovsk, in the far eastern region of Russia. During the trial the twelve accused criminals confessed to dropping plague-contaminated fleas on cities, unleashing biological germs in water systems, and playing with anthrax just to see what it would do.

Ekaterina pulled on the rope. All twelve were found guilty and sentenced to hard labor in Russian gulags. Rina understood why her father, Dmitry, hated the Americans. Most of the scientists who worked in Unit 731 surrendered to the Americans but went on to live prominent lives as politicians, professors, and respected scientists.

Ekaterina pulled on the rope again and floated closer to the Galeon. Dmitry hated America, and one American, in particular. The atrocities of Unit 731 were swept under the American rug because the experiences and data recorded from human experimentation and vivisection, pertaining to biological warfare, were deemed to be of great value to the United States in their biological weapons development program, a program that was developed for potential use against the Russians during the Cold War.

Rina had read the American military letters a hundred times. On May 6, 1947, General Douglas MacArthur, Supreme Commander of the Allied Forces, wrote *"additional data, possibly some statements from Ishii, probably can be obtained by informing Japanese involved that information will be retained in intelligence channels, and will not be employed as 'war crimes' evidence."*

Ekaterina filled with anger as she pulled violently on the rope.

BOX 731

General Shiro Ishii should have been turned over to the Soviets, Rina reasoned, but instead he negotiated immunity for his entire staff and avoided war-crimes prosecution before the Tokyo tribunal. All Ishii had to do was give the Americans all of the germ warfare data he gathered from human experimentation and he could go free, completely unpunished.

Rina's hands gripped the rope with clenched anguish and pulled.

Dr. Edwin Hill, the former chief at Fort Detrick, Maryland, affirmed and supported General MacArthur's position and said Shiro Ishii's information was "absolutely invaluable" and could "never have been obtained in the USA because of scruples attached to experiments on humans." Hill even said the information was "obtained fairly cheaply."

My grandfather Pavel was not a cheap life, Rina's thoughts screamed as she pulled.

Some say General Shiro Ishii traveled to Fort Detrick, Maryland, and served as a bioweapons consultant to the American military after World War II. Some say he stayed in Japan, converted to Christianity, and opened a free clinic for children.

But all say General Shiro Ishii, the mastermind behind Unit 731, and the father of the Asian Auschwitz, was never tried or convicted of anything and died in peace at the age of sixty-seven.

Ekaterina pulled the raft next to the teak platform and stepped onto the Galeon. Her body was silent. Her breathing became normal. She held her hands up to the sunlight and noticed that the trembling fingers had finally stopped.

Ice-cold vengeance pumped through her veins. She was the one chosen to host the war-crimes trial. She was the one who would administer punishment as judge, jury, and executioner.

And she was the one who would exact revenge and avenge the murders of her grandfather and twelve thousand other men, women, and children who were considered nothing more than logs. They were pieces of wood, not humans. They could be cut up and burned in a fireplace. Logs that could be tied to wooden stakes at various lengths and intervals, as bombs exploded in their midst, while scientists measured which logs got hit and which logs escaped the wrath of shrapnel and the fury of a bomb.

For the first time in her adult life, Ekaterina finally felt nothing.

CHAPTER 29

National Center for Toxicological Research
Redfield, Arkansas

Lieutenant Colonel Leslie Raines felt right at home in the Ford 150 rental truck. The rental car company "upgraded" her since she was in full military uniform. Once on Interstate 530 south toward Pine Bluff, Leslie punched the radio on and was delighted to have Trace Adkins fill the Ford's cabin at full volume for the twenty-four mile drive to Chandler Road.

The two-lane road connected to Stagecoach and over to Arkansas Highway 365 north. Leslie slowed down as she approached the NCTR checkpoint. She wondered if she was at the right place as the gate was up and the guard shack was empty.

Tall pine trees lined both sides of Jefferson River Road and NCTR Road as she meandered around curves and bends until she emerged into a clearing where three white water towers and old red brick buildings greeted her. The massive parking lot with grass and weeds breaking through decades-old cement was littered with a spattering of cars and twice as many pickup trucks.

Leslie felt like she was entering 1959.

The guard shack at the complex was void of computers or video surveillance. Leslie presented her credentials, and the elderly woman gave her an ID badge and directed her to room 7G in the main building.

The director of the FDA facility was clueless as to why the Department of Defense wanted to reactivate the bio lab and the tanks. And as far as Leslie could determine, he wasn't very interested or curious either.

"This map will get you out to the back of the property. I sent maintenance out there this morning to make sure the light bulbs were working and the electric was on. Our IT guy is making sure you have a computer or two," the director said as he returned to his computer screen to read more about a bass fishing tournament.

"So I just walk back there?" Leslie asked hesitantly.

"I wouldn't." The man didn't look up from his computer and didn't offer any other salient tips.

"So what would you do, sir?"

"I'd take the service road next to the water towers and drive back there, especially if you're going to be out there working for a spell."

Leslie nodded and started to leave the office.

"Oh, by the way . . . Air National Guard delivered a package for you 'bout an hour ago . . . came from somewhere in Mississippi, I reckon. I had them take it out there to your lab."

Lightner Farms
Gettysburg, Pennsylvania

Billy Finn hung up the phone and paced back and forth inside the Lightner Farms lodge as his wife read a magazine by the fireplace. Eileen had gone outside for a walk in the trees.

"Sit down, Billy, you're driving me nuts," Madge said, never lifting her eyes from the magazine. "You need to learn how to relax."

"I can't relax. I just called the FBI field office in New York . . . I talked to my old friends. Three cases of anthrax have been found."

BOX 731

"An attack?"

"No one's sure. An accountant and reservist in Mississippi got the worst of it. A guy in Charlotte and now another man in Tampa all got cutaneous anthrax lesions too."

"Where?"

"Atlanta . . . at the airport. The FBI sent a special team of biological weapons investigators down to Atlanta. Even the CDC is getting involved."

"No, Billy—where were the skin lesions on the men?"

"Oh . . . I don't know, I think they said on their butts."

As soon as the words left Billy Finn's lips the old investigatory instincts took over, but he wasn't nearly as fast or as sharp as Madge.

"Then they all got it from the same toilet seat," Madge said matter-of-factly as she turned a page in her magazine. "Find the restroom and you'll probably find your anthrax. Sit down, Billy, and let your friends get their work done."

Finn pulled out his cell phone and called Camp.

National Center for Toxicological Research
Redfield, Arkansas

Leslie opened the package from Mississippi. Two slides were the only samples sent. She turned on the overhead lights and put the slides under the microscope. The spore pattern was definitely anthrax, but there wasn't much she could do with such a small sample.

"Dr. Groenwald," Leslie said as her cell call was answered. "Sir, I received two slides from the anthrax patient in Mississippi, but I'm pretty limited in what I can do with these. It's definitely anthrax, but I'm going to need a tissue sample, or at least a culture."

"I'll make some calls, Colonel Raines," Groenwald answered. "In the meantime, make sure you have whatever supplies or animal models you need if this thing escalates."

Leslie pored through some of the classic research on anthrax and made a quick call to a lab animal breeder and supplier. Within minutes, an order for fifty guinea pigs, housing, bedding, and food was placed.

FBI Command Center
Atlanta, Georgia

Disaster communications and rapid response teams were assembled in the three tents adjacent to Hartsfield-Jackson Atlanta International Airport. TV news crews were pushed back a quarter-mile and behind yellow security tape. TV satellite trucks were parked everywhere and beaming coverage worldwide.

Dalton Fischer, the former INTEL chief from the New York office, was given command of the Atlanta situation. Fischer's team emerged from one of the command tents after reaching agreement and consensus for their three main talking points.

Fischer was followed by five agents, Susan Francis, and Dr. Margaret Tapper from the CDC as they walked boldly toward the yellow tape and the bevy of microphones a quarter-mile away as local, national, and international media waited for the press conference.

Lightner Farms
Gettysburg, Pennsylvania

Billy Finn had dozed off in his chair as Madge and Eileen were washing dishes in the kitchen and watching *Dr. Phil* on a small, countertop TV next to the refrigerator. Programming was interrupted for the FBI press conference in Atlanta.

"Billy? Billy!" Madge yelled from the kitchen. "You'd better come see this. Your friends are on TV in Atlanta."

BOX 731

Finn woke up and shuffled over to the edge of the kitchen as the press conference started.

"Good afternoon. My name is Susan Francis, and I'll be handling communications on this situation," the spokesperson said as Billy's eyes widened in disbelief.

"Geez, Madge . . . that's Susan. Remember, she called you several months ago looking for my phone number in Afghanistan?" Billy said excitedly.

"You're right. I remember that call."

"Special Agent Dalton Fischer will make a brief statement, and then I will answer any questions you may have," Susan Francis said as she yielded her position to Dalton Fischer.

"Oh my gosh . . . Dalton must've gotten bored with his DC desk job so he put himself back into field ops," Billy said to no one in particular.

"There are three key points that all of us must keep in perspective," Dalton Fischer started to explain. "First, we do not—repeat—do not believe this is a terrorist attack. Second, there have been no fatalities and thus far only three people are receiving medical treatment. And third, we do not believe the public here in Atlanta, or anywhere else in the United States, is at any heightened risk. With that, I'd like to turn it over to Dr. Margaret Tapper from the Centers for Disease Control."

Billy Finn pulled out his cell phone and started paging through the contact telephone numbers until he found the record for Susan Francis. He pressed her number and watched as she reached down and silenced the call as she stood next to Dalton Fischer and behind Dr. Margaret Tapper on the TV screen.

Billy quickly typed a text message in all caps: Call me ASAP—anthrax—Billy Finn.

"It's important to realize that anthrax outbreaks occur normally in nature," Tapper began to explain. "Anthrax infection is one of civilization's oldest and deadliest diseases. As you know, portions of South America suffered through relentless flooding last fall. Flooding brings fresh shoots of grass, and cattle, sheep, and other livestock go into a feeding frenzy. Alkaline soils are favorable to anthrax spore growth, and when people come in contact with or ingest animal protein that has been infected with anthrax, events like what we are seeing today in Atlanta are not uncommon."

FBI Command Center
Atlanta, Georgia

A reporter yelled out a question and interrupted Margaret Tapper before she could finish.

"Are you saying the three American victims just returned from South America?"

Susan Francis tried to step in and maintain control of the press conference, but Dr. Tapper seemed to be enjoying center stage.

"No, I'm saying it could have just as easily been a farm worker from—I don't know where, let's say Peru—who got infected by one of his sheep the day before he boarded a flight to Atlanta to visit family."

Susan Francis felt Dalton Fischer's elbow pressing against her arm. She stepped up next to Dr. Tapper. "So this Peruvian farmer uses the men's restroom before he leaves the airport and— boom—he leaves an anthrax infection on the toilet seat. That's how easily this type of thing can happen."

Susan Francis raised her hand to interrupt but Tapper continued. "Just today, in fact, we have learned that an entire herd of dairy cows died because of a natural outbreak of agricultural anthrax in Middletown, Maryland. And not far from there, in the Green Ridge State Forest in northern Maryland, fish and wildlife officers have reported as many as one thousand Eastern cottontail rabbits have died apparently from anthrax as well. This

BOX 731

sort of thing happens all the time, but it just doesn't make national news."

Susan Francis physically nudged Dr. Tapper away from the spray of microphones and took over. "Dr. Tapper's hypothetical example is one of hundreds of possibilities we'll be exploring," Susan said as she checked her watch. "With that we plan to give you another update in exactly two hours."

The gaggle of reporters yelled out questions as the FBI and CDC entourage started walking back to their command tents.

"Does the FBI know where the Peruvian farmer is right now?"

"Is he still in the United States?"

"What about the rabbits and the cows?"

"Is America's milk supply at risk?"

Susan Francis felt her cell phone vibrating and chose to answer the call while Dalton Fischer launched a verbal assault on the CDC's Margaret Tapper for straying away from agreed-upon talking points.

"Susan Francis."

"Susan! Billy Finn. Thanks for taking my call," came the old familiar voice.

"Billy, I'd love to talk but I'm up to my eyeballs right now. Can I call you back in a week or so?" Susan said as the others entered the FBI command tent ahead of her.

"Susan, I was on a covert mission in the Middle East. We've been tracking flights and people. Your anthrax is not from a Peruvian farmer."

Susan Francis stood silent as she looked back over the throng of gathered media and listened to an interagency argument that was brewing inside the tent behind her.

"Billy, I appreciate your concern, but Dalton has not received any briefs like that. We haven't heard any chatter from the NSA or even the CIA that remotely points to terrorism."

Susan let her words echo while Billy Finn's silence screamed on the other end of the line. Dalton Fischer opened the tent flap and motioned for her to join them.

"You will, Susan. Call me when you do," Finn said as Susan Francis hung up and entered the tent with renewed intent to regain control of interagency messaging.

Dalton Fischer handed her a folded piece of paper, which she quickly read: *The army reservist/accountant in Hattiesburg just died.*

CHAPTER 30

Office of the Chief Medical Examiner
Frederick, Maryland

The morgue technician opened the vault door and pulled the body of the dairy farmer out so Camp could take a look.

"Kind of unusual to have the Department of Defense involved in a local murder," the technician said as Camp examined the gash wound on the back of the man's neck. "Or was this guy former military back in the day? Is that why you're here?"

Camp ignored the questions and looked up on the x-ray screen. "Are these the x-rays for this guy?" Camp asked.

"Yes, sir. Clean wound, other than the fact that the killer separated cervical three from cervical four. He never even twisted the knife. *Bam*, and the dude was dead."

"Thanks, I really appreciate your time," Camp said as he pulled off his smock, goggles, and threw his latex gloves in the trashcan.

"No problem. That widow got quite the one-two punch this week, didn't she?"

"How's that?" Camp asked with little interest as he opened the door to leave.

"First her husband and then all forty of her dairy cows died."

"What?"

"Some scientist from fish and wildlife says they were exposed to agricultural anthrax or something; same thing for a shitload of rabbits out in Green Ridge. Hell, now my wife is petrified to even buy milk for the kids."

Camp walked through the building and past the office of the chief medical examiner and out into his Defender 90. He noticed a missed call from Billy Finn and pressed redial.

"Billy . . . I just took a look at the farmer's neck wound . . . It wasn't a robbery. It was an execution."

Timberline Lodge
Mt. Hood, Oregon

Howard and Bonnie Suzuki parked their Subaru in the snow-packed parking lot and started the trek through parked cars to get to the ski center and lift-ticket office. Howard tried to persuade his wife of six years to cancel their day trip up to Mt. Hood but she would have nothing of it. Bonnie had never been sick a day in their marriage. She was an avid long-distance runner and meticulous about what she ate. There were no processed, boxed, or frozen foods in the Suzuki household. Bonnie ate six small meals a day including fresh berries, Greek yogurt, raw vegetables, and two ounces of lean protein grilled with fresh lemon as well as four servings of fish every week.

Bonnie's fever had been higher than one hundred degrees for four straight days. She had chills and night sweats that even kept Howard up. Her cough was unusual in that it was nonproductive. Nothing ever came up from her lungs when she coughed. Her chest ached, she was short of breath, she felt incredibly tired, and every muscle in her body ached.

Howard thought it was possible that Bonnie's flu-like symptoms had finally gotten the better of her record streak of continuous health. The sore throat, nausea, vomiting, and diarrhea all indicated that she should be home in bed.

BOX 731

"Gorgeous day on the mountain," Bonnie said bravely, laboring to get the words out as they got into the ticket line.

"Honey, you can hardly speak. How are you going to ski?" Howard asked with concern.

"It's your birthday, Howard, and my gift to you. I'm fine. We're doing this!"

Bonnie removed her gloves and a few layers of clothing so her body could handle the cold once they were back outside and on the mountain. Howard looked down at the top of her right hand. The raised bump she had on her hand since she started feeling sick had become an enlarged ulcer, and the center of it was black.

"Bonnie!" Howard said, focusing in on her hand.

She looked down at the hand and then quickly put her glove back on.

"Two-day passes under Suzuki for will call," Bonnie said as the ticket agent sorted through several envelopes before handing her their prepaid lift tickets.

Howard and Bonnie fastened the lift tickets to zippers on their down jackets and headed outside, snapped on their skis, and shuffled through the lift line until their empty chair circled around and arrived. Bonnie looked over her shoulder at the rooftops down on Government Camp as the historic Timberline Lodge passed slowly by beneath their skis.

"Happy birthday, baby," Bonnie said as she snuggled up against Howard and coughed. The air started to thin. She coughed more. Every hundred feet on the lift she coughed harder and more uncontrollably.

"Bonnie, this is ridiculous. We're turning around and going home," Howard said frantically as he realized they were still less than halfway up the mountain. "In fact, I'm going to have the ski patrol take you back down. You need to see a doctor."

Bonnie's eyes flew wide open and sheer terror covered her face as she could not get any air to breathe. She gasped frantically until her body fell back silently, still snuggled against Howard, as her eyes stared coldly at the beautiful peaks of Mt. Hood rising before her.

National Center for Toxicological Research
Redfield, Arkansas

Four uniformed airmen from the Little Rock Air Force Base entered the main quarry-tiled building and walked down a series of long narrow hallways and outside to the isolated laboratory building in the back of the NCTR property.

Leslie, and fifty guinea pigs caged on the back wall of the lab, were all startled as the four barged in unannounced.

"Good morning," Leslie said as her nerves settled.

"Good morning, Colonel. Ma'am, we have orders to deliver this to you personally with signature receipt," the technical sergeant said as he handed her a clipboard and placed an environmentally sealed container with a biohazard logo on her desk.

Leslie peaked over at the biohazard warning on the container as she signed the receipt. "Hattiesburg, Mississippi?" Leslie asked as her cell phone started to ring. "Colonel Raines," she answered as the four airmen left as quickly as they had arrived.

"Colonel, you should soon be receiving culture vials with lung tissue samples from the patient in Mississippi," Dr. Groenwald said as Leslie stood up and walked over to the container.

"Affirmative, sir, they just arrived. Did you say lung tissue?"

"The patient is now deceased, Colonel Raines."

"Oh my."

"But that's not all . . . The pathologist who took the lung tissue sample during the autopsy has been infected as well."

"Sir?"

"Listen carefully, Colonel Raines. This is not—I repeat—*not* a random agricultural event. We are keeping this off the grid for now, but DOD suspects a national terrorist attack using military-

Box 731

grade anthrax with composition and structure like we've never seen."

Leslie walked over to the guinea pig cages as her thoughts were pulled in a million directions.

"We need you to stay put and isolate the samples in the biosafety lab there. The place is old, but it'll do the trick. We want to keep this low key and off the radar screen for now."

Soo Marie Soap Labs
Sault Ste. Marie, Michigan

Semyon led Martin back to the stairwell and up another flight of carpeted steps. The entire third floor was carved out into a single large room with white boards on all four walls. Six inexpensive folding tables formed a long rectangle in the center of the room. Dr. Yamamoto sat on one side where two of Semyon's Russian paramilitary soldiers stood casually in civilian attire.

Dr. Tanaka sat on the other side with his hands placed firmly in his lap beneath the table. Four of Semyon's men stood behind Tanaka as one copied a formula on the white board.

"Gentlemen, allow me to introduce Dr. Martin Ishii. He is our new president and CEO."

Yamamoto got up and greeted Martin and bowed slightly. Martin did the same. Yamamoto removed a business card from his shirt pocket, placed it in both hands, and presented it to Martin, who studied it in the palms of his hands.

"Forgive me, Yamamoto-san, as I cannot yet complete the *meishi* until I receive my cards."

Yamamoto smiled and returned to his seat. Semyon moved the meeting along before Martin could interact with Dr. Tanaka.

"Each of you received your signing bonuses. I've asked Finnegan's to send over a catered lunch today. If we have time, I'd like each of you to open a bank account at Huntington Bank on Ashmun Street. That's where we bank and it will be the easiest for direct deposit. Dr. Ishii, please sit down at the head of the table. I'd like to get started with our first brief now that you're all here."

Martin sat at the head of six folding tables from ShopKo. A surge of pride filled his recently unemployed veins.

Indian Creek Island
Miami Beach, Florida

Ekaterina watched the video feed from the third-floor conference room on her computer screen as Semyon started the discussion.

"The first phase of our NATO contract is purely theoretical. While we are waiting for the BSL facility build-out, we need to solve some theoretical implications first."

"What's the issue?" Martin asked as Rina watched.

"A terror group in Eastern Europe has found a way to put anthrax into laundry soap. Apparently they intend to launch an indiscriminate bioweapon attack using detergent."

"That would not be difficult to do," Dr. Yamamoto chimed in. "Actually, it is very easy."

"We assumed that, Dr. Yamamoto, but in Western nations, postal services routinely use BDS—Bio Detection Systems—that screen for toxins. For example, look what happened when ricin-tainted letters were sent through the mail to the president and a senator after the Boston Marathon terrorist bombings."

"But these systems are not specific," Martin added. "For example, most BDS systems can't distinguish between a normal biological background and the toxin or agent it's searching for. Heavy dust and pollen might be environmental interferents that could prevent 'positive' anthrax detection. Even water vapor or fog could have a neutralizing effect on a Bio Detection System."

Box 731

"Dr. Ishii is correct," Yamamoto said. "A single system that exhibits high specificity for anthrax detection in the environment does not yet exist and is not commercially available. Sure, if you can get a sample, you can test it. But widespread detection? We're not there yet."

"So if it's so easy to do, why have rogue terrorist groups in Eastern Europe not done this before?" Semyon asked.

Martin smiled and folded his hands at the head of the tables. "That right there, Simon, is what kept us awake nights at Fort Detrick. Unleashing biological weapons is easier than anyone thinks. Detecting biological weapons is more difficult than anyone can imagine. And the effect and impact of biologicals is more evil and heinous than we can comprehend. Worse than that, it's a dumb weapon. It's random. Unlike a bomb that might fall on top of one hundred people, or a bullet that strikes one person, some will be infected with a biological weapon and some will not."

Semyon paused and gave serious consideration to Martin's words.

"So you're saying a biological attack is easy?"

"Yes, if you have the biological agents and a reasonable distribution system. I don't know about Eastern Europe, but here in the states if you send a letter to the president or a senator it takes more than thirty days to get delivered. The post office pulls first-class mail addressed to dignitaries and targets them for selective screening, just as you mentioned. In most cases the letters are opened. The BDS protocols work perfectly there. But look at your own mailbox. Billions of pieces of mail pass through the postal system each year. There's no way the rest of the mail, letters, parcels and magazines can receive selective screening. Large BDS units are set up in the hopes they accidentally detect something of value. In fact, most of the time, they register a false positive for pollen or dust, so yes, it's very easy."

"Then maybe our contract with NATO is easier than I thought," Semyon said with jubilant resignation.

"As you say, Simon, it's all theoretical. Adversaries would first have to acquire quite a stockpile of biological agents, in this case anthrax. That could take years and chances are that some government agency, somewhere, would detect the biological agent long before it could be disseminated. Distribution is relatively easy. But production or acquisition . . . that's an entirely different matter." Martin punctuated his assessment with the confident demeanor of a newly appointed chief executive officer.

Ekaterina closed the window to the video feed. A confident smile covered her face.

CHAPTER 31

Centers for Disease Control
Atlanta, Georgia

The e-mail attachment with the preliminary autopsy and toxicology reports from Oregon Health Sciences University hit Margaret Tapper's inbox as she ended the phone call with the chief medical examiner's office in Portland.

Her fingers trembled as she held Susan Francis's business card and punched in the numbers on her desk phone.

"Susan Francis."

"Susan, this is Dr. Margaret Tapper at the CDC in Atlanta. Are you back in New York?"

"Hello, Dr. Tapper. Yes, after we closed the rapid response command center in Atlanta, I returned to New York and Agent Fischer went back to Washington. May I help you with something?"

There was a long pause as Tapper tried to find the right words. She had already been taken to the woodshed for Peruvian conjecture and didn't want another tongue lashing from the FBI. But she also knew *this* was different.

"Susan . . . we obviously now know that the patient in Mississippi died."

"Yes, ma'am, but we're keeping that information private for the time being," the FBI agent said.

"Did you know that the pathologist who performed the autopsy in Mississippi is now infected as well?"

There was a long pause. "No. That's new information."

"I just got off the phone with the chief medical examiner's office in Portland, Oregon. They have a fatality, Caucasian woman, in her early thirties. First diagnosis was aggressive influenza in the autopsy report. But toxicology shows something different. They suspect it was anthrax . . . inhalation anthrax."

Susan Francis let the words settle for a second before starting to probe deeper.

"Dr. Tapper, did the deceased travel through Atlanta recently?"

"I don't know that answer, Susan. That's why I'm calling you."

Soo Marie Soap Labs
Sault Ste. Marie, Michigan

Oleg got back to Michigan just in time to sign for a truckload delivery to Soo Marie Soap Labs. The driver and his partner spent forty-five minutes hauling twenty-five thousand preprinted foil pouches, packed five hundred to a box, as fifty cartons were stacked in the manufacturing room. Another 625 five-pound boxes of laundry detergent powder were stacked on the other side of the room. Finally, the drivers pushed a 136 pound Torrey EV16 commercial vacuum packing machine into the manufacturing room as well as several other smaller machines and labeling systems.

Oleg handed the driver the clipboard with an alias signature on the bill of lading as the driver's partner handed him one final package.

"That's the last of it, sir," the man said. "I'm allergic to this stuff myself, which must explain why my skin breaks out when my wife changes detergent. Had no idea you needed pollen for laundry soap. But here's almost five pounds of Pure Premium Bee Pollen."

BOX 731

Oleg read the label on the outside of the large plastic canister: *This is a premium, 100 percent Canadian pollen from Alberta with better color, taste, and nutrient levels than our regular North American bee pollen.*

Oleg watched as the delivery crew left and then dialed Rina.

Indian Creek Island
Miami Beach, Florida

Rina reached into her red Tignanello handbag and ripped the TracFone from the Velcro in the hidden compartment. "Yes," she said quietly.

"We received confirmation on the test in Oregon," Oleg replied.

"Was he Japanese?"

Oleg paused and looked at the report his colleague sent him from the coroner's office in Beaverton.

"It was a she . . . She is Caucasian and married to a Japanese American."

"Cause of death?" Rina asked without emotion.

"The report lists the cause as influenza."

"Fine. Execute the plan. Mail twenty-five thousand out but make sure I get my twelve thousand kills."

Rina could hear Oleg flipping through pages of paper. He did not speak.

"You heard me," Rina said as she terminated the call.

Soo Marie Soap Labs
Sault Ste. Marie, Michigan

Semyon walked into the third-floor conference room. His six Russian paramilitary crewmembers relaxed by the door as Dr. Tanaka and Dr. Yamamoto ate carry-out lunches from Finnegan's.

"Yamamoto, talk to me about the product. Tell me what you did to it and how you made it," Semyon said as he pulled a bottle of vodka out of the mini refrigerator and poured a tall glass.

"Well, after you provided the initial stockpile from Russia, I worked with the pharmacy department at the university in Syria to cultivate virulent anthrax spores. It's the same process the pharmacy students would undergo for the purpose of testing the efficacy of anthrax vaccines," Yamamoto explained.

"Except?"

"Except that as a military scientist I'm trying to induce endospore formation," Yamamoto said as Dr. Tanaka glared back at him. "The objective is to dry the spores and then combine them with chemical stabilizers. That helps them stay airborne longer."

"So what we provided you wasn't lethal?" Semyon asked.

"Not exactly. You gave me freeze-dried spores of extremely virulent anthrax strains, Ames and Vollum, if I recall. In order to mass produce for this project, the freeze-dried spores had to be activated and then cultured."

"Which brings me back to my original question: What did you do?"

"Freeze-dried spores are dissolved into one milliliter of saline solution and then spread over a nutrient agar Petri dish and incubated at thirty-seven degrees Celsius for twenty-four hours. From there, the colonies that form are transferred to their own nutrient agar Petri dishes and incubated further."

"Kind of a slow process."

"It took fewer than six months," Yamamoto said with an odd sense of professional pride. "But it is not easy. That's why it is called black art."

"And that's it?"

"Not even close. Once enough colonies formed, I needed to create the same environmental stresses that cause anthrax cells to grow protective endospores in nature. Because anthrax is an

BOX 731

aerobic organism—it's a living bacteria—the spore process begins by reducing the amount of oxygen in the environment."

"Which is why we need to use vacuum-sealed pouches, to keep the oxygen out so the bacteria fights to live and becomes stronger or more—what did you say—virulent?" Semyon asked.

"Partially. But this is only the formation process. They still have to be purified and dried."

"Go on."

"The Petri dishes with new colony formations go in a sealed chamber and carbon dioxide is pumped in until the gas equals 50 percent of the total air pressure. Then the temperature inside the chamber is lowered to twenty degrees Celsius."

"You are a traitor!" Tanaka screamed as a Russian jumped to his feet and delivered a punch to the side of Tanaka's jaw that rendered the Spanish professor both semiconscious and bleeding.

Semyon nodded to Dr. Yamamoto and took another drink of vodka.

"Somewhere between twenty-four and forty-eight hours, the colonies from the Petri dishes are transferred to saline solutions with pH levels that are common to that of an animal host. The solutions are then placed in the centrifuge and spun to separate the spores from other less-dense contaminants. As each layer of contaminants is removed, more deionized water is added to the spores for other rounds of centrifugal separation."

"And then you dry it?"

"The anthrax spores are now pure. I added a special chemical to the spore-water mixture before the next process," Dr. Yamamoto explained as he grew cautious.

"Shut up!" Tanaka yelled as another fist crashed across the bridge of his nose.

"This must be the secret part. Please go on, Dr. Yamamoto, now it's getting good," Semyon said with excitement and another pour from the vodka bottle.

"I add silica," Yamamoto said quietly. "The enriched mixture is then turned into powder using a spray dryer."

"What does that do?"

"The liquid is separated into thousands of microscopic droplets as they pass through a high-precision atomizer. The droplets are sprayed directly into a heated chamber where the combination of heat, low humidity and a large surface area-to-volume ratio of the droplets cause the water to evaporate instantly. The silica and other chemicals form a partial shell around the individual spores."

"And that's good?"

"The shell prevents spores from clumping together. They are static-free. Less clumping equals smaller particle sizes, which means weaponized anthrax spores stay in the air longer and even bypass certain filter detection systems."

Semyon stood up, turned around, and walked over to the camera mounted in the top corner of the adjoining walls.

"Did you get all of that?" Semyon said to the camera, knowing an answer would not be coming his way. "And you duplicated this black art process continually for six months?"

"Yes."

"So what do you estimate the necessary lethal dose needs to be?" Semyon asked.

"The lethal dose is ten thousand spores. Our anthrax has at least five hundred billion spores in each gram. Two grams would be preferable, but one gram is sufficient."

"And you say that with the weight of one postage stamp, in the form of microscopic powder, it will float in the air, and once inhaled, will kill a person within seven days?"

Dr. Yamamoto did not respond. He sat still waiting for the next shoe to drop as Tanaka relaxed his bleeding face and rested his head on the back of his office chair in apparent surrender.

"I assume the anthrax should go in last so the powder can get airborne right away?" Semyon pressed.

Box 731

"It probably doesn't matter. The pouch will be shaken many times before it is opened," Yamamoto said reluctantly. "It's not an exact delivery system. Anything can happen. But we only need ten thousand out of five hundred billion spores in the pouch to be inhaled . . . to be lethal."

"How much product was in the sealed canisters we took out of Syria from your lab?"

"Fifty kilograms, about 110 pounds."

Semyon walked over to the whiteboard on the wall and removed the cap from a dry erase marker. "So if we want to send out twenty-five thousand samples with two grams per sample, we would need fifty thousand grams. Fifty thousand divided by one thousand gives us exactly fifty kilograms. Looks like your calculations were perfect, Dr. Yamamoto."

Oleg entered the room and nodded to his paramilitary comrades as Semyon admired his mathematical calculations on the board.

"What?" Semyon asked without looking back at Oleg.

"The supplies have arrived," Oleg said as he abruptly left the room.

"Good. Then tonight we manufacture," Semyon said as he sniffed the end of the dry erase marker and put the cap back on.

CHAPTER 32

Mossad Headquarters
Tel Aviv, Israel

Reuven Shavit was about to turn the office light off and head home for an uncharacteristically early dinner with his wife and sons. The worldwide chatter was at a suspicious all-time low and no one seemed to be plotting for the annihilation of Israel in the next few hours.

A young analyst from the North American desk rounded the corner only to find Director Shavit locking his office door with briefcase in hand.

The analyst did a quick U-turn without saying a word.

"What?" Reuven asked quietly as he heard the bolt and electronic sensors click in the door lock.

"It's probably nothing, sir; it can wait until the morning," the analyst said as Reuven turned around and looked at her. His eyebrows rose slightly, and she knew not to delay any longer.

"Do you remember the six French aliases and the Japanese passport that were swiped in Toronto?" she asked as Reuven refused to dignify her youthful question with an answer. "Well, they still haven't left Canada."

"And that is somehow news?" Reuven asked as he started walking down the long hallway.

"But the same Japanese passport was swiped with six German passports later that same day."

Reuven stopped.

BOX 731

"Six?"

"Yes, sir."

"I assume the six were leaving Canada."

"Yes, sir."

"And I assume there is no record of them ever arriving in Canada in the first place."

"Correct."

"Where?"

"They were passing from Sault Ste. Marie, Canada, over the international bridge, and into Sault Ste. Marie, Michigan."

"The United States."

"Yes, sir."

Reuven nodded and the analyst returned to her station as Reuven did his U-turn and returned to the office, first to call his wife and then Shepherd's Pie.

ISAF Headquarters
Kabul, Afghanistan

General Jim Ferguson and General Lexington Smith listened to Camp debrief his telephone conversation with Mossad's director Reuven Shavit regarding movement into Michigan as two coffee-pouring majors stood silently behind them.

Ferguson was not the least bit pleased with Captain Campbell, or even Lex Smith for that matter. But given the shroud of secrecy in the states, his back was pressed into the corner.

"CIA has enough to do with the investigation in Mississippi and Atlanta," Lexington Smith said. "I don't think we can count on them for any resources given that this is nothing more than a Mossad hunch at best, and a wild goose chase at worst."

"With all due respect, sir," Camp asserted, "are we content to ignore the INTEL, or do we want some boots on the ground in Michigan?"

"What do you recommend, Captain?" Ferguson finally asked as his tone softened slightly.

"Sir, Billy Finn and I could be in Sault Ste. Marie tonight."

Lexington Smith shook his head. "Negative, Captain. We don't need your names showing up on passenger lists or we'll create another damn interagency war over turf and jurisdiction."

"I understand, sir, so we'll drive. No credit cards, just cash."

Ferguson was not the least bit comfortable with Camp's plan, but he didn't have any better ideas. "Have you cleared medical, Captain?"

"Roger that, sir."

"Okay. Take Billy with you. But no John Wayne shit. That's a direct order, Captain Campbell."

"Aye, aye, sir."

National Center for Toxicological Research
Redfield, Arkansas

Leslie watched as the last of three inflatable biocontainment suites were positioned behind her laboratory.

She walked back into the lab and put on her Level A HAZMAT suit. The HAZMAT suit was top of the line and made of waterproof and vapor-tight synthetic material. The material covered her entire body as well as provided an oxygen tank and breathing apparatus inside the suit.

She carried the biohazard container to the inflatable biocontainment suite first and returned for five guinea pigs. After the lung tissue sample was isolated, Leslie injected each of the guinea pigs with homogenates, cell fragments, and constituents of anthrax that she pulled out of the tissue sample.

Two hours later, Leslie looked through the clear-vinyl windows on the inflatable and got her first look at the infected

Box 731

guinea pigs. They were severely distressed and visibly infected. Within three more hours, all five were dead.

Leslie took five more guinea pigs into the second inflatable suite and injected them with the existing military anthrax vaccine. She waited twenty-four hours and then injected them with the anthrax homogenates.

Six hours later, the second group of guinea pigs was dead as well.

FBI Command Center
Beaverton, Oregon

Howard and Bonnie Suzuki's home at 11809 SW Frankston Pond Court in Beaverton, Oregon, was taped off as HAZMAT site investigators went in and out of the home wearing full protective suits. Howard was forced to watch the activity from the FBI's command vehicles and trailers parked in front of his neighbors' homes. He wouldn't be able to bury his wife for weeks.

Susan Francis felt bad for Howard as she saw him sitting in the backseat of one of the FBI sedans. She assumed she was thinking the same things Howard was. Who could do such a thing to Bonnie? This was clearly no accident, and not even the CDC could reasonably speculate that a fictitious Peruvian goat herder had anything to do with Bonnie's death.

Seventeen representatives from local, state, and federal agencies gathered in the tent in front of Howard's home for Dalton Fischer's briefing.

"Okay, let's get after this. In September and October of 2001, we believe a military scientist at Fort Detrick sent anthrax-laced letters that killed five people and sickened seventeen others. The attack cost billions of dollars in government and private spending designed to defend against biological weapons. And though we've seen hundreds of 'baby powder' hoaxes since then, the

Fort Detrick biologist allegedly proved that it could be done, and done rather easily."

"Agent Fischer, are you suggesting this is a similar attack?" asked one of the FBI field office agents from Portland.

"Too soon to know, but the number of spores in the deceased's body would indicate military-grade, bioweapon anthrax. Same with the deceased guy in Mississippi, and now the guy's pathologist is fighting for his life. This was not an accident."

"What about the media, Dalton?" Susan Francis asked. "Rumors are running wild and media outlets are speculating that Oregon has been targeted. Local emergency rooms are filling up with the worried-well who have flu symptoms just like Mrs. Suzuki."

"We're not making any statements right now, Susan. We don't need national hysteria. Not until this house, her office, the grocery store she shops in, and the salon where she gets her hair done are all completely searched, investigated, and analyzed."

Soo Marie Soap Labs
Sault Ste. Marie, Michigan

Dr. Martin Ishii ruffled through his papers, magazines, folders, and books one more time. He retraced his steps hoping to recall what he did with it. He walked into the main lobby of Soo Marie Soap Labs and looked once again on the reception counter.

Nothing.

He walked over to the small break room next to the lobby and searched the counter by the coffee service, the table by the water cooler, inside the trash can, and he even took a quick look inside the refrigerator.

Nothing.

Martin walked down the hallway past his office and the offices of Dr. Yamamoto and Dr. Tanaka. He didn't bother checking in

BOX 731

either of them because he had never been inside those offices, and to the best of his recollection neither had Yamamoto or Tanaka. Martin thought it odd that they preferred to stay up on the third floor discussing project details with Simon and just write their formulas on the boards.

He stepped into the first-floor restroom, scoured the magazine holder and the stack of magazines on the toilet tank lid.

Nothing.

He walked all the way down to the end of the hall to the door that led out into the manufacturing room. Martin stopped and looked through the glass window built into the well-worn wooden door. Semyon's crewmembers were changing the configuration of the equipment on the manufacturing floor. Martin examined the boxes stacked on one wall and smaller boxes on the other. One of Semyon's men was unloading the contents of a particular box that really piqued Martin's attention. One by one, HAZMAT suits were pulled out of the boxes and hung up on the wooden pegs.

Martin had worked in BSL facilities on and off for most of his professional career. He was very familiar with the personal protective equipment required to work with infectious toxins and bioagents. But these were HAZMAT suits, something he reasoned were more likely to be worn by firefighters than scientists.

Martin stepped back from the window and changed his angle to be more discreet.

He looked closely as the final two suits were hung up. They were definitely Level C HAZMAT suits. They had splash-resistant coveralls and gas masks with filters. The Level C was sufficient to protect against anything touching the skin or being inhaled.

"Anything like anthrax," Martin whispered to himself as he saw Semyon enter the manufacturing room and start barking out orders. The men tripled their speed as Semyon kept slapping his open hand with a piece of rolled-up paper.

Martin stepped back in the shadows behind the glass window of the wooden door in the hallway. Semyon stopped right in front of him as he supervised the activity. Martin saw a partial photo image on the rolled up piece of paper in Semyon's hand and knew instantly that he was holding what Martin had been looking for.

Dr. Martin Ishii ducked under the window and hurried back down the hall to his office. He closed his office door, sat down, and frantically sorted through a million emotions that were competing for his attention simultaneously. *Maybe this job was a bad idea. Maybe Simon accidentally picked up the paper. Maybe the contract is real and there's a good reason for the HAZMAT suits. Maybe Yamamoto and Tanaka just don't like to work in offices. Maybe there's a flight out of O'Hare back to Tokyo that leaves tonight.*

Martin heard the door open from the manufacturing room. Heavy footsteps grew louder in the hall, stopped for a second outside of his closed office door, and then kept going to the front of the building. Martin got up and pressed his ear against the door. His heart missed several beats when he heard the deadbolt being twisted on the front glass door. It was still the middle of the afternoon on Valentine's Day. It was a work day. There should be no reason to lock up that early. His blood pressure spiked as the rattling steel-cage security door was pulled across and secured behind the glass door. Martin heard the snap of the padlock on the cage door, locked from the inside.

His legs froze in panic. He heard two light switches flip. Then more steps. The steps grew louder.

Martin found his legs and sprinted to his desk. He opened a folder, put on his reading glasses, and pulled the long narrow center desk drawer open.

There was a knock at his door.

"Yes," Martin said calmly as he reached inside the drawer and removed a letter opener.

The door handle turned. Martin slipped the letter opener into the open folder, behind some back pages, that were clipped into his binder.

Box 731

Black steel-toed boots stepped in followed by Oleg's face. Oleg opened the door completely and entered Martin's office. "Semyon wants to talk with you three on the second floor in the Ice House. Something about design plans," Oleg said as he walked over next to the white board in Martin's office.

"Semyon?" Martin asked as he kept looking at the papers he wasn't reading while sneaking glances toward Oleg.

"Semyon, Simon . . . same guy . . . you know who I'm talking about," Oleg said dispassionately.

Martin looked up and saw a pistol tucked beneath Oleg's belt on his backside. Martin glanced quickly at the open office door. He knew he couldn't get through the steel-cage security door. He was too new to even know the padlock combination.

"Okay, tell him I'll be up there in a few minutes. I need to finish this report and make one more telephone call."

Oleg turned around and walked slowly toward Martin's desk. "I think he wants to see you now."

Martin's eyes rose up from the papers and into the cold stare of Oleg. "Fine. I guess this can wait for a little bit."

Martin stood up, grabbed his binder, and walked toward the door. "I do want to stop in the restroom for a second. I'll meet you up there," Martin said as he reached into the file folder and got his fingers around the handle of the letter opener.

"No problem. I'll wait for you," Oleg said, nodding as Martin walked down the hallway and into the unisex restroom. He closed the door and turned the lock button knowing it would provide no security if Oleg decided to enter. Martin flushed the toilet and ran the water in the sink. He pulled two sheets of paper towel off the roller and placed the folder on the back of the toilet. He wadded up the two sheets of paper towel and put them in one front pocket and the letter opener down inside the other. He moved the lock latch and opened the door.

Oleg was leaning against the wall waiting for him.

"Let me run back and get my cell phone. I'm expecting a rather important call," Martin said as he started to walk past Oleg. Oleg's powerful arm snapped out and blocked the hallway in a split-second.

Martin reached into his front pocket, pulled on the handle of the letter opener, and swung wildly at Oleg.

Martin had never attacked anyone in his life. Oleg had stopped hundreds of threats and started twice as many more.

Oleg's hand crushed through Martin's sixty-two-year-old forearm as the letter opener went flying through the air, hit the ceiling, and landed quietly on the carpeted floor. Oleg spun Martin around, grabbed him by the nape of the neck, and pushed him to the stairwell and up the stairs to the cinderblock Ice House.

CHAPTER 33

Lambertville, Michigan

Neither Finn nor Camp had uttered so much as a word in the two hours since they passed Cleveland. The Defender 90 was keeping the guys warm, but the hypnotic movement of the windshield wipers brushing off powdered snow was putting them both to sleep.

"Betcha Madge was thrilled that you decided to spend Valentine's night with me," Camp finally said, shattering the silence.

"Brother, I can't do much more of this tonight. My gut is killing me," Finn said as he pointed to four hotel logos on the Lambertville exit sign.

"She'll really be angry if she finds out we got a hotel room together," Camp said as he pulled off Highway 23 North and picked the closest hotel in sight.

"How far did we get?" Finn asked.

"Just about 416 miles from Gettysburg."

"How far to go?"

"I'd guess 375."

"I thought we just passed into Michigan," Finn said as Camp pulled up to the registration circle under the carport.

"Michigan's a big state, and the Soo is all the way up north. That's why they call it the Upper Peninsula, my friend . . . its way up there."

Soo Marie Soap Labs
Sault Ste. Marie, Michigan

Semyon walked into the third-floor conference room as Oleg and two Russian paramilitary crewmembers started to remove Professor Tanaka, to the horror or Dr. Yamamoto.

"Wait. Leave them there. Oleg, I need to speak with you," Semyon said as he left the conference room and walked down the carpeted stairs to the Ice House on the second floor.

Oleg followed and stood next to him as they both watched Martin through the glass above the cinderblock wall, who stood captive in the locked Ice House.

"Change of plans," Semyon said quietly. "Yamamoto is too important to us. He could bring us millions. Maybe more. Besides, he's been vaccinated. I need you and a few boys to go shopping."

"Shopping?"

"Head out into the city. Go through restaurants, stores, wherever," Semyon said as he handed Oleg a wad of cash. "I need an Asian to take Yamamoto's place. Offer him $10,000 for a job."

"What job?"

"Make one up," Semyon said as he dismissed Oleg for his shopping trip.

FBI Command Center
Beaverton, Oregon

Susan Francis checked her watch. It was almost two in the morning on the West Coast, which meant Billy Finn would still be sleeping on the East Coast. Besides, the old bird was retired and she reasoned he was no longer on the payroll, let alone responsible for middle-of-the-night phone calls anymore.

Box 731

She started the rental car and put the wipers on intermittent as she typed the text message to Billy. Call me. Curious about your covert mission in the Middle East.

National Center for Toxicological Research
Redfield, Arkansas

Leslie's hands were locked behind her head as she stared at the ceiling from the army cot in her laboratory. It was close to four in the morning, and though exhausted, Leslie hadn't slept a wink. She couldn't get the sight of ten dead guinea pigs out of her mind.

Though insulated from the outside world, she had made little progress. Leslie couldn't help it when her thoughts wandered and stumbled across her wedding, an event that was only two weeks away. While she rested on an army cot in Arkansas, she was filled with tension just knowing that Eileen was left alone to plan the most special day of her life.

She glanced at her watch and surmised that her grandfather Karl was already up and out in the barn tending to the animals and milking his only cow.

"Milk," Leslie whispered out loud as she jumped off the cot and over to her computer. She entered "Louis Pasteur" into the search engine bar and began to read.

Pasteur was a French chemist and microbiologist, best known for inventing a process to treat milk and wine, a method that came to be known as pasteurization. During an outbreak of chicken cholera, he was studying a small culture of the responsible bacteria, but the sample spoiled and went bad. He exposed healthy chickens to the spoiled bacteria but wasn't able to infect them with the cholera. Thinking he had made a mistake, Pasteur exposed the same chickens with fresh, new cholera bacteria. Though the chickens developed some mild symptoms, they had become immune from the cholera thanks to the weakened and somewhat spoiled first exposure.

Through scientific luck, Pasteur's weakened form of the bacteria essentially became a vaccine rendering the chickens largely immune from the cholera.

In the late 1870s, France suffered an outbreak of anthrax that hit cattle and sheep in particular. Pasteur used the same theory, but this time he artificially generated a weaker form of the anthrax organism by exposing the bacteria to oxygen.

Leslie thought she might be able to do the same thing with this new strain of anthrax, an anthrax yielding more than five hundred billion microscopic spores in each gram.

Leslie put on her HAZMAT suit, grabbed the ultraviolet light wand from her bench, and moved quickly out to the third inflatable biocontainment suite in the dark, cold Arkansas night.

She removed another isolated sample of the lung tissue and passed the UV wand over the live bacteria several times, hoping to weaken the spores and prevent the anthrax from reproducing once she injected them into the next five guinea pigs.

Saginaw, Michigan

Camp's cell phone rang just as Billy Finn handed him another apple fritter from breakfast they bought at the Dunkin' Donuts drive-thru window. He recognized the number.

"Happy Saturday morning, darling," Camp said through a mouthful of apple, dough, and glazed sugar.

"Where are you?" Leslie asked.

"Just passed Saginaw. Less than 240 miles to go. Should be there by noon."

"And then what? Go door to door looking for Russians with anthrax? Camp, turn around and go home," Leslie pleaded tenderly.

Box 731

"How's it going on your end?" Camp asked, completely ignoring the request.

"I think I may have a breakthrough. I used UV light to weaken the bacteria and injected another five guinea pigs this morning around six."

"And?"

"So far, so good. They don't look great, but they're not nearly as sick as the others were after two hours."

"What's next?" Camp asked as he took another bite of the fritter.

"If it works? I'll set up a pipe sequence from these huge ten thousand gallon vats with a series of UV lights and create weakened anthrax bacteria. I'll turn that into a bacterin that can be distributed to the public health service for inoculating the public."

Camp smiled from ear to ear as Billy Finn looked on. "Les, you make me look smarter just by walking in your shadow. You're amazing. I love you."

"Hold on, sailor. It hasn't worked yet. But . . ."

Camp waited as long as he could. "But what?"

"I love you too. I've gotta go. I need to order pipes and UV lights . . . just in case."

Camp put the phone down and took another swig of coffee as Finn pulled out his cell phone.

"Ha! Got a text from Susan Francis," Finn said as he shoved some more pastry into his mouth.

"Who's Susan Francis?"

"You remember. She called me in the middle of the night in Lyon. She said she got a call from Pablo—our Omid—who was trying to get in touch with us."

"Got it. What's she up to?"

"She ran communications down in Atlanta when they got the anthrax event last week."

"Right, the whole farmer-from-Peru thing."

"Well, now she's out in Oregon with the inhalation anthrax case."

"I thought you offered to help your old New York buddies?"

"I did. They said Susan was out in Oregon on a new case and they'd give her the message. Never heard a word from her until now."

"So call her."

Finn looked out the window as the snow-covered farm fields passed by. "Screw her. She can wait until I'm not so busy."

Soo Marie Soap Labs
Sault Ste. Marie, Michigan

Dr. Martin Ishii got up and looked through the half-glass walls of the Ice House and down to the manufacturing floor. He watched Semyon's men load several large canvass carts with thousands of samples of "731 Power" and push them across the parking lot over to the Sault Ste. Marie post office in a convoy of rolling mail containers.

Semyon placed the five hundred-page spreadsheet with fifty presorted, Japanese American names and addresses per page in the empty fifty-five gallon drum in the middle of the manufacturing room. Oleg poured a cup of gasoline into the can, followed by a match.

The fireball lit up the window in the Ice House for a few fleeting seconds as Professor Tanaka jumped. The flames consumed the paper and gasoline quickly before dying down to an orange glow of embers.

CHAPTER 34

Finnegan's Tavern and Walleye Grill
Sault Ste. Marie, Michigan

Camp and Finn sat down for dinner at Finnegan's Tavern and Walleye Grill in downtown Sault Ste. Marie. The Saturday-night regulars had bellied up to the bar and the downtown streets were filling with rusted cars and pick-up trucks.

"Do you folks leave your Christmas lights up all year long?" Billy Finn asked the buxom waitress as she dropped off two menus.

"Naw, soon as the weather changes we take 'em down. Too dang cold to do it now. I'm Beverly. Can I start you boys off with a beer?"

"Any local microbrews you care to recommend, Beverly?" Camp asked.

"I'd go with the Whitetail Ale, it's brewed up here in the UP, Escanaba I think."

Camp held up two fingers. "Any dinner specials?"

"Same as every night. Our twelve-ounce grilled walleye fillets are to die for. We grill them for about fifteen minutes in a marinade of butter, fresh chopped chives, a teaspoon of orange juice, and a quarter-cup of chopped and toasted pecans."

Camp held up two more fingers.

"Camp, check out the bar. It's an Asian guy."

Camp rolled his eyes and smiled at Finn. "Great. I'll stay here while you go up and ask him if he's working with Russians on an anthrax attack in the United States."

"Well, this was a waste," Finn said as he looked around the tavern. "Local police have had no issues and the FBI field office in Grand Rapids couldn't care less."

"At least we got to enjoy a little road trip together before I get hitched. Let's just call it my bachelor party."

Beverly dropped off two Whitetail Ales as Camp and Finn clinked glasses.

"To Leslie Raines," Finn toasted.

"To Leslie Raines," Camp echoed.

Camp took a swig of his Whitetail Ale and then picked up his cell phone.

"Calling to check in with Momma already? Dang, didn't take her long to put a leash and a collar on you," Finn said as Camp dialed.

"Actually, I'm calling the scheduling department at Walter Reed. I'm going to see if someone can cover my Monday and Tuesday shifts until the nineteenth if I trade them for next Saturday and Sunday. That would give us a few more days to troll around Michigan."

"Yippee. Maybe we can go ice fishing," Finn said as he dialed his own cell phone. He held the ringing phone away from his ear as he downed the last half of his first Whitetail Ale. The call went to voice mail. "Hello, Susan . . . guess we're playing voice mail and text tag. I hear you're in Oregon . . . Good luck with that. I'm with a buddy here in Sault Ste. Marie, Michigan, tracking down leads to the Middle Eastern connection I told you about, and, as I recall, you were not interested in. Sounds like your Peruvian farmer struck again. Call me sometime."

Billy Finn hung up and tossed his phone down on the wooden table. "That's why I retired, Camp. I hate the game."

Box 731

"And all this time I was thinking you retired because you got old," Camp mused as two large men entered Finnegan's and walked straight over to the bar. They took bar stools on opposite sides of the Asian.

"Billy," Camp whispered as he nodded toward the bar.

Camp and Finn watched as one of the men pulled out a wad of cash and showed it to the Asian before putting the money back in his pocket.

"That's not good," Finn whispered as he turned nonchalantly back toward Camp.

"He just put money down on the counter. Now they're all leaving," Camp narrated as he took another drink of his Whitetail Ale.

"What do you want to do?" Finn asked.

"Stay here. I'm going to ask them for directions," Camp said as he bolted for the front door after they left the tavern.

"Camp!"

The three were walking down the sidewalk as Camp called out.

"Excuse me . . . *excuse me!*"

They all turned around.

"Do you boys know where I can find a good hotel in town? I'm just passing through for the night."

Two of the men shook their heads and turned to leave.

"If you go straight down Main, you'll find a Quality Inn . . . maybe two, two-and-a-half miles," the Asian said and then turned to join the others as they crossed the street.

"Hey!" Camp pressed. "Don't I know you?"

One of the men turned and walked directly up into Camp's face.

"I don't think so. Now head off and find your hotel, *okey?*"

"*Okey?* Damn if your accent doesn't sound Russian," Camp said loudly as though he were drunk and trying to buy some time.

Camp felt the strong hands of the Russian grab his winter parka, and before he could react, he was pulled behind Finnegan's Tavern and thrown against the trash dumpster.

"Hey, buddy, I'm not looking for any trouble. I like Russia."

The Russian turned to walk away. Camp reached out and grabbed the man's arm. "Hey, you've got some great beer and vodka, don't ya?"

Camp never saw the three fists that connected on his cheek, nose, and lip as his body went airborne and landed inside Finnegan's dumpster surrounded by several half-eaten orders of walleye and coleslaw.

By the time he pulled his bleeding face up to the top edge of the dumpster, the three men were gone. Camp limped back into the restaurant, blood pouring from his nose and lip.

Finn and Beverly reacted at the same time.

"Geez, Camp," Finn said as he helped Camp into his chair.

"I'll get a towel and some ice," Beverly said as she put the walleye specials on the table and ran back to the kitchen.

"I think we found them," Camp said as he struggled through the pain while spitting through the blood.

Soo Marie Soap Labs
Sault Ste. Marie, Michigan

Semyon watched as Dr. Yamamoto took his clothes off and the Russian paramilitary soldiers forcibly dressed the Asian they had just recruited from Finnegan's Tavern. Semyon unlocked the padlock to the Ice House. Martin Ishii stood up and edged cautiously to the back of the room and away from his captors.

Two Russians grabbed Professor Tanaka and tied his hands behind his back with plastic restraints. The Asian wearing Yamamoto's clothes struggled as he was pushed into the Ice

BOX 731

House. His eyes were covered with a blindfold and his mouth was gagged. The Asian was manhandled into the second chair as plastic straps were looped around his hands as well as the frame of the chair.

"Let's get this over with," Semyon said as Oleg grabbed Martin, secured the plastic restraints around his wrists, and pushed him down into the third chair. "We've got a long drive to Miami and a date with Viktor."

Semyon locked the door as soon as Oleg and the four others emerged. Semyon shook his head as Oleg's cell phone rang for a third time, and then Semyon turned the computer camera on.

Indian Creek Island
Miami Beach, Florida

The three Japanese scientists were gathered together and sitting on folding chairs in the old Ice House just as she had specified. But their backs were facing the video camera that was mounted in the top corner of the Ice House. Rina had called Oleg three times but he never answered. It wasn't exactly how she had planned it out, but it would have to do.

Rina saw Professor Tanaka, Dr. Yamamoto, and Dr. Martin Ishii sitting silently with hands bound as they looked straight ahead toward the back wall and away from the camera. Painted cement cinderblocks filled the bottom portion of the wall. Glass covered the rest of the wall up to the ceiling. None of the three scientists could see the red flashing light on the camera.

A large, flat-panel computer monitor had been placed inside the Ice House and against the back wall so the men could see it. Two computer speakers in the Ice House delivered the sound.

Ekaterina put her microphone headset on. Covering her eyes with oversized Louis Vuitton *Soupcon* sunglasses, she initiated the video conference call between her Miami Beach bedroom suite in the Castello Del Luna and the old Ice House at Soo Marie Soap Labs in Michigan.

The computer monitor came to life as Tanaka, Yamamoto, and Ishii heard Ekaterina's voice.

"Gentlemen . . . this is a war crimes trial for the atrocities committed at Unit 731 . . . I am the only judge and jury that history could find. I will finally deliver justice. In the manufacturing room below we already assembled special packages and have mailed twenty-five thousand samples of laundry detergent to Japanese Americans across the United States . . . Each sample was packaged with the same evil your grandfathers tortured my grandfather with."

Rina watched as Dr. Masahisa Ishii and Professor Tanaka immediately dropped their heads in shame. They knew.

Yamamoto looked straight ahead. Unlike the others, his mouth was gagged and he was strapped to his folding chair. Rena presumed he was the fighter.

"Watch carefully as I show you the photos of the first seven . . . They were not grandsons like you, but they were related—great nephews, second cousins, distant relatives—it does not matter to me. The blood of the father is on the hands of the son and the son's son," she said as seven photos scrolled while she narrated.

"Professor Adachi . . . gunshot . . . Tokyo; Dr. Eguchi . . . gunshot . . . outside of his hospital; Mr. Fujiwara . . . gunshot . . . after visiting his accountant in Beverly Hills; Dr. Hamaguchi . . . gunshot . . . after a board of directors meeting in Brussels; Chancellor Kajiyama . . . gunshot . . . after a meeting with his board of regents in Southern California; Professor Miwa . . . gunshot . . . through the classroom window during a biology lecture in the Philippines; and Dr. Suzambo . . . gunshot . . . getting into his car in Reno, Nevada."

Box 731

She watched as Tanaka and Ishii struggled to remove their plastic restraints. She could see them yelling on the monitor, but her audio feed was intentionally muted.

Yamamoto could hardly move.

"They are the symbolic seven . . . the ones who received a painless bullet to the head even though their families caused indescribable anguish and horror for eight years on the lives of countless numbers of Chinese, Koreans, Allied prisoners, and Russians."

She sent the next file of photos, and they played on the monitor in front of Tanaka, Yamamoto, and Ishii.

"But your grandfathers were in charge. They were the ones responsible. They are the ones who took my grandfather's life, and the lives of his children and grandchildren. They were never charged with crimes. They were never put on trial. They never suffered for anything. Today, a guilty verdict has been levied against you in their absence."

The computer monitor showed grisly images of amputations.

"Professor Tanaka . . . it was your grandfather who asked for more 'maturas'—logs—that he could simply cut off one leg and see what happened if he reattached it to the other side. It was your grandfather who froze attached arms and legs and then thawed them on innocent people just to study the effects of gangrene. And you have the audacity to teach muscle regeneration in Spain. Today you are sentenced to death."

Semyon and Oleg edged in closer to the Ice House door as Rina finished her Internet trial on the computer screen.

"Dr. Yamamoto, your grandfather was responsible for shrapnel experiments. Innocent men, women, and children were tied to wooden posts and bombs were set off so he could calculate the best locations for Imperial soldiers to be during an explosion. He tested flame throwers and other weapons on the innocents just to see what carnage they would do to the human body. You have been sentenced to death."

Oleg put his HAZMAT suit on in the hallway as she delivered her final verdict. Semyon handed Oleg three sealed pouches and a tactical knife.

"And Dr. Masahisa Ishii . . . your grandfather was the mastermind behind all of this. He was the father of Unit 731. He was nothing more than evil in the flesh. Take a look at this video, Dr. Ishii. This is your ninety-year-old mother. She looks quite precious as she's being led upstairs to your grandfather's lab in your house . . . the one that is forbidden . . . the one that contains all of his barbaric tools and the results of his experiments."

Rina saw the side of his face and the tears that flowed from Martin's eyes as she presumed he begged for mercy and the life of his mother.

"Your grandfather deliberately infected the logs with syphilis, gonorrhea, and even dropped random flea bombs carrying the plague on innocent villages and towns. Do you see the boils and ulcers on your mother's face, Dr. Ishii? She too has the plague now and will soon join you in death."

Oleg opened the door to the Ice House as Semyon closed it behind him and walked down the steps into the manufacturing room with the others.

"You, Dr. Ishii, will suffer the longest, for it is your grandfather who caused the most harm. Go ahead."

Oleg took his knife and cut Martin's plastic restraints and freed his hands before throwing three pouches of "Power 731" anthrax into the air. Ekaterina saw Martin's wrist bleeding from Oleg's careless cutting. Oleg left the Ice House and was followed by the eyes of Ishii and the tortured screams of Yamamoto and Tanaka as he padlocked the door.

"Seven by gunshot . . . three by their grandfathers' own medicine . . . and one for the Americans and their unwillingness to hold anyone accountable, for their inability to do what was right and hold a war-crimes trial."

BOX 731

Ekaterina terminated the call. Tears flowed down her cheeks as she looked forward to watching the three die slowly over the next few days.

Soo Marie Soap Labs
Sault Ste. Marie, Michigan

Dr. Martin Ishii got up and looked through the half-glass walls of the Ice House and down to the manufacturing floor below.

"Are we infected?" Martin asked as he watched Semyon and Oleg pack up and follow their men out of the room, down the hallway, and out of the building.

Neither Tanaka nor Yamamoto answered him.

Martin walked to the back of the Ice House and looked down at Yamamoto, who was still gagged and blindfolded. He untied the gag and the blindfold and then stepped back.

"Who are you?" Martin asked.

CHAPTER 35

National Center for Toxicological Research
Redfield, Arkansas

Leslie checked and rechecked the vats and the guinea pigs one final time. They had survived more than thirty-six hours and had actually recovered from their symptoms. It was still early Monday morning on the East Coast, but she hoped Dr. Groenwald was already in his office and ready for some "good news."

Groenwald answered on the first ring.

"Sir, this is promising. I'm only a couple of days into this, but the bacterin is safe and efficacious so far. We won't really know for another ten to fourteen days. If it holds, I think we can hand this over to the CDC and FDA, and they can arrange for vaccine and antibiotic production."

"That's fantastic, Colonel Raines. My fingers are crossed. Well done," Groenwald said as Leslie glanced at her wall calendar.

"Sir, my leave technically started about seven hours ago. Permission to hand this off and head for New Hampshire, sir?"

"Ahhh . . . that's right. You're getting married."

"Roger that, sir . . . eleven nights from now and counting."

"Colonel, I'll send some scientists up from Galveston to relieve you. You should be able to leave by noon tomorrow. Does that work?"

"Affirmative, sir. It'll take me three minutes to pack."

"Colonel?"

BOX 731

"Yes, sir."

"I'm proud of you and I hope to see you next Friday night. Thanks for the invitation."

Indian Creek Island
Miami Beach, Florida

For the first time in her life, Ekaterina felt as though seven hundred pounds and seventy years of painful family history had finally been lifted from her shoulders. She reasoned that both Dmitry and Pavel were smiling down on her for finally righting a long-standing wrong. Rina lifted a glass of wine to the heavens in honor of her father and grandfather as she lay in a lounger next to Viktor's quiet pool.

The TracFone in her bag rang. "Yes."

"The second phase is done. All twenty-five thousand samples were mailed Saturday, and your war-crimes trial is over."

"Good. I have already wired the money into the accounts you specified," Rina said as she sipped her wine.

"The final one is a trade."

"I know that."

"A simultaneous trade. You give me Viktor as you watch the final contract for your rage."

"Where are you now?"

"We're in the vehicles as planned and heading your way," Semyon said.

"Call me when you arrive."

"I will, Ekaterina, I will. But don't forget, Viktor is nonnegotiable. That was the deal."

"He's all yours."

Syracuse, New York

The two black Suburbans pulled off of I-690 East at Exit 39 toward the Syracuse Fairgrounds and into the Blue Tusk restaurant on Walton Street as Semyon ended the call.

The hostess pulled two tables together and positioned nine menus for Semyon and his eight guests. Semyon ordered a round of 2X IPA from Southern Tier for the table after a grueling 698-mile drive from upper Michigan.

"Oleg, you keep three men with you. The rest will come with me to Florida. Then we meet back in the Balearic Islands as planned."

"How much farther for you?" Oleg asked as he searched the menu for something exotic.

"Maybe fifteen hundred miles, but we can take our time now."

"We will stay here in Syracuse for the week and then get into position," Oleg responded.

The waitress walked up to the table and introduced herself.

"Remember, she requires a live video feed," Semyon said as Oleg ignored him and ordered.

Soo Marie Soap Labs
Sault Ste. Marie, Michigan

Martin Ishii was seriously ill. He knew he was near death as he struggled to breathe. He had suffered without food and water for more than forty-eight hours as billions of anthrax spores attacked the delicate linings of his lungs. Professor Tanaka was already dead, and the mysterious man next to him was fading in and out of consciousness.

Martin felt bad. At least he had the ability to move around. The other two were still confined by plastic restraints.

Box 731

Martin crouched in the corner of the two walls and then slid slowly down to the floor. He thought about his childhood growing up in Kyoto and recounted his years of faithful service as a military scientist at Fort Detrick. He remembered the phone call from the recruiter and wished that he had rejected the call and just fetched the mint for the tea as his mother had asked. He thought about the exciting first-class flight to Chicago for the interview and the first night in the executive house on the water with Semyon by the fireplace.

He should've known it was all too good to be true. He should have seen it all coming. Semyon was too smooth yet too rough around the edges.

Martin sat in the Ice House dying as Semyon drove to Miami to get someone named Viktor.

"Miami," Martin whispered. He hadn't heard his own voice in more than a day. "Miami," he said again. He thought about the final words Semyon spoke: *We've got a long drive to Miami and a date with Viktor.*

Martin turned his injured wrist over and examined the scab from Oleg's careless knife work as he cut the restraints from his hands. The woman on the computer was right. Martin was able to move around as his body tried to fight the infection. He would indeed suffer longer.

Martin examined the scab on his wrist and then picked at it with a fingernail on his other hand. The blood began to flow freely again.

Martin dabbed at the blood with his index finger and started to write on the cinderblock wall next to him.

CHAPTER 36

FBI Command Center
Beaverton, Oregon

Dalton Fischer and Susan Francis were about to take a break from the command center in front of Harold Suzuki's house and get some dinner at Elmer's Pancake House when the forensics technician walked into the tent.

"I think we've got it," the technician said with some pride. "The inside lid of her washing machine shows a positive reading for *Bacillus anthracis*. The laundry room trashcan was empty, and the rest of her detergent checked out as normal."

"But?" Dalton Fischer prodded.

"Their garbage can is empty too. But the can registers another positive for anthrax."

"So you're saying laundry detergent? Are we looking at a contaminated manufacturing product or an intentional attack?" Fischer asked, knowing full well that no one could answer that question. At least not yet.

Dublin Methodist Hospital
Dublin, Ohio

Kathy Fujima's car skidded to a stop in the handicap-only section outside the emergency department at Dublin Methodist Hospital.

Box 731

She ran around the back of the car and opened the front passenger door and pushed the red release button on Kevin's seat belt.

Kathy draped her husband's arm around her shoulders as she started screaming for help and pulling him closer to the automatic doors. A security guard ran out of the building and quickly radioed for help as Kevin's knees buckled before he fell hard to the cement.

"Please, help him!" Kathy screamed as two nurses ran out and a security guard grabbed a wheelchair.

"What's wrong with him?" the nurse asked as all four tried to lift Kevin into the wheelchair.

"He had the flu. A low fever, chills, sweats. He had trouble breathing and just felt bad so he stayed in bed. Then about an hour ago his fever spiked to 104. He can hardly breathe," Kathy said as they pushed Kevin into the emergency department lobby.

Kathy looked around with confusion then amazement as 186 other panicked patients filled the lobby around her. Every wheelchair was full. People were lying on stretchers and on the floor.

"What the hell is going on?" Kathy screamed as she looked at all the frightened faces staring back at her.

The nurse put two fingers against Kevin's neck. "I've got a real weak pulse but fast at 120," she said as she tilted Kevin's face up and pulled an eyelid back as her pen flashlight illuminated a nonresponsive pupil. "He's going into shock!" the nurse yelled as they pushed Kevin past a lobby full of dying people and through the automatic doors into the examination bays.

"Doctor!" the other nurse yelled as Kathy followed behind. Kevin's upper body folded over and he vomited on the floor in front of the third exam room.

"I've got no more empty beds," the doctor said as he ran over to check Kevin's vitals. He put the stethoscope on Kevin's neck and then pulled his shirt open and listened in three different spots.

Kevin's body went limp. His breathing stopped completely. Kathy saw the doctor shake his head seconds before she crumbled to the floor in tears. The doctor walked over to her and bent down. He reached into his lab coat and pulled out a one-quart ziplocked bag and put it in front of Kathy's face.

"Did you get one of these things in the mail?" the doctor shouted as Kathy focused through the tears at the package inside the sealed bag. "Did you get this '731 Power' sample in the mail?"

Kathy nodded and became hysterical.

The doctor put the bag back in his pocket.

"Tell the FBI and the chief we just got another one," the doctor said to the nurses as he ran back into exam room number three.

Finnegan's Tavern and Walleye Grill
Sault Ste. Marie, Michigan

Beverly spotted Camp and Finn as soon as the jingle bells on the front door rang.

"Hey, I know you boys. You were here Saturday night. How are you feeling? Looks like you got quite a shiner on that eye."

Camp smiled but was in no mood to respond. He was still licking his wounds.

"Hello, Beverly . . . we couldn't resist your walleye and tail any longer," Finn said as Beverly doubled over in laughter.

"My foot-in-mouth friend means your Whitetail Ale," Camp said as they took a seat at the window table.

"I liked it better his way," Beverly teased. "Two of the usuals?" she asked before Camp could raise his two fingers. "How long are you guys in town for?"

"Just until tomorrow. I got a two-day reprieve but I've got to get back to work Wednesday morning," Camp said as Finn's cell phone started to ring.

BOX 731

Beverly took off to grab two beers and drop the dinner orders.

"Bill Finn."

Camp watched as Billy Finn's face grew solemn. Finn stood up and walked over toward the foosball table as he spoke on the phone.

Camp picked up his phone and quickly dialed Leslie as Beverly dropped off two frosty mugs of Whitetail Ale.

Finn came rushing back to the table as Leslie's voice mail greeting began to play.

"What's up?"

"That was Susan Francis in Oregon."

"And?"

"She's sending two field agents from the Grand Rapids office up here tonight. Six post offices reported positive detections for anthrax earlier today. Now emergency rooms are filling up with inhalation anthrax infections in Chicago, Ohio, California, and God-only-knows where else."

"Geez, Billy!"

"All of the packages found so far have the same return address. Soo Marie Soap something . . . right here in Sault Ste. Marie, Michigan. Susan and Dalton Fischer are heading our way too."

"Let's head back over to the police department and see if they know anything about this place," Camp said as Beverly put down two paper placemats and two sets of flatware rolled in paper towel.

"Beverly, have you ever heard of Soo Marie Soaps?" Finn asked as he took a big drink of his Whitetail Ale.

"Sure have. If you look out that window behind you you'll be staring at it. They just changed the name and now some European guys, or something, are running it. We do lots of carry-out lunches for them," Beverly said as she turned and went back to the kitchen.

Camp and Finn wiped the perspiration off the frozen window behind them and saw the faded painted letters on the side of the red brick building: Soo Marie Soaps, A Family Tradition Since 1937.

"Billy, do you see what's next door, on the other side of the parking lot?"

"Sure do."

CHAPTER 37

Soo Marie Soap Labs
Sault Ste. Marie, Michigan

Red and blue emergency lights from the Sault Ste. Marie fire department, police department, and HAZMAT unit flashed and splashed off the walls of every downtown building within two blocks, including Finnegan's Tavern across the street, where Beverly and the cook sat watching the excitement through a frozen window.

Camp and Billy Finn were stuck standing outside with all of the other first responders. Local authorities were told not to go in until FBI agents arrived from Grand Rapids since they had reason to believe that a federal crime had taken place.

Camp cornered the local chief of police. "I understand all that," Camp said, "but what if we have people inside? If they've been exposed to anthrax, we have a very short window, especially if these things were mailed Saturday."

"I have no reason to believe there's anyone inside," the chief answered. "The security cage door is pulled and there are no lights on. We have HAZMAT suits, and we'll enter as soon as we're advised by the FBI."

"I want to speak with your postmaster and I want to speak with him now!" Finn exclaimed as his old investigatory tone bubbled to the surface.

"With all due respect, Mr. Finn, you have no current credentials, and we're all just going to wait this out until the agents get here from Grand Rapids."

"Give me your business card, Chief. If I have to call the president, I will."

Camp and Finn walked back to the Defender 90, started the engine, and put the heat on full blast. Gawkers, and the tavern faithful, watched first responders talk and wait in subzero temperatures.

"What? Now you have the president's cell phone number? I've spent an entire career hurrying up so I could wait. Our hands are tied, Billy, so just hurry up and wait."

"Maybe not," Finn said as he pulled out his phone.

"Don't you be calling General Ferguson. We don't need *that* right now."

"Someone better than that; someone with a dog in this fight and a very dull ax to grind."

"Who?" Camp asked cautiously.

"Special Agent Daniels . . . CIA . . . and I do have *his* number."

Billy Finn stepped out of the Defender and made the call. Camp watched as Finn paced back and forth in the parking lot as emergency lights flashed across his face in numerous patterns. Finn reached into his pocket, pulled the police chief's business card out, and read the numbers over the phone. Finn stopped talking, turned his head, and watched Sault Ste. Marie's chief of police reach for his cell phone. Finn got back in the Defender.

Camp lowered his window. "What's going on, Chief?" Camp asked as the police chief walked over to the Defender.

"I don't know who you two are, but I just got a call from the CIA. Apparently this thing isn't just national . . . it's international. CIA is claiming co-jurisdiction and has authorized the two of you to go in right now."

BOX 731

"We'll need some HAZMAT suits," Camp said as they both got out.

"We'll get you dressed up. Mr. Finn, need I remind you that this is an active crime scene? Make sure you don't disturb any evidence."

"Thanks, Chief, but this ain't my first rodeo. And Chief?"

"Yes, sir."

"Get the damn postmaster out of bed and over here right now."

Camp and Billy Finn got into Level C HAZMAT suits and followed a firefighter and a locksmith to the front door. The locksmith picked the lock on the glass door in fewer than five seconds. The fireman pulled out bolt cutters and cut the padlock on the steel-cage security door and pulled it back.

Camp and Finn entered the darkened building with high-powered flashlights and two-way radios to communicate with each other and the first responders outside. They flipped the light switches but nothing happened. The building wasn't much warmer inside than the air was outside. Their flashlight beams scanned the front lobby, the reception desk, and the employee break room. Finn walked down the long hallway and examined the first office as Camp passed him and entered the second office.

"Not much stuff inside here. There might have been people working in these offices, but the bookshelves are empty, and I've got just a few papers and magazines on the first desk," Finn said over the radio.

"Second office is completely barren. No one's been in here," Camp reported.

Camp followed Finn farther down the hallway.

"Third office empty," Finn said.

"Restroom is clear," Camp called out. "Okay, I've got my flashlight beam through a glass window in a wood door. It looks like we're going into a larger workroom."

He opened the door and stepped into the manufacturing facility as Finn followed behind.

"FBI agents from Grand Rapids are thirty minutes out," the chief's voice erupted over the radios. "They aren't happy."

"Stacks and stacks of empty boxes on both sides of the room," Finn reported.

"What was in them? Any labels?" the chief asked.

"Affirmative . . . these indicate laundry detergent," Finn said from the west wall.

"I've got Pure Premium Bee Pollen over here," Camp added.

"Hang on! I've got something," Finn said as he stood over an old fifty-five gallon steel drum. "Looks like they burned something in the bottom of this barrel, I've got a pile of white ash and nothing else."

"Workroom is clear. We're heading to the stairwell right now," Camp said as they both started to climb the steps.

"Let's get this done before our friendly agents arrive, Camp. I'll take the third floor, you take the second," Finn said as Camp broke off and Finn kept climbing.

Camp walked past a cinderblock and glass room that looked out over the workroom and then walked down the long hallway toward the front of the building. He waved his flashlight beam out of the second-story window and down at the parking lot and the gaggle of emergency response vehicles.

"I'm in the second-floor window and sweeping from front-to-back on the second floor. Looks like dry storage, empty shelves where inventory might've been stored, empty closets. I've got an empty bunk room," Camp said as his flashlight illuminated each room.

"Third floor is one large conference room. Folding tables set up in the middle with chairs scattered around. I've got some writing on the white boards. Looks like calculations. Somebody needs to write this down," Finn urged.

BOX 731

"We're ready," the police chief's voice answered.

"I've got the numbers twenty-five thousand, two, fifty thousand, one thousand, and fifty," Finn read.

Camp walked back toward the stairwell. The nameplate on the heavy steel door said Ice House.

"I've got a large steel door leading into a cinderblock room. The door is labeled Ice House, and it's padlocked. Walking around to the small hallway overlooking the workroom down below," Camp said as he rounded the corner of the Ice House. Camp's flashlight beam panned the walls through the glass window of the empty Ice House and then down below into the work area with the stacks of empty boxes.

"Clear on the second floor," Camp said.

"Clear on the third," Finn said. "Coming down now."

Camp turned to leave as a hand reached up and slapped the glass in front of him.

"Holy shit!" Camp screamed.

"What's going on?" the police chief yelled.

Camp pointed the flashlight beam into the darkened Ice House. "Oh, God . . . I've got three . . . I repeat, *three* men on the ground in the Ice House. One is still alive the others are not moving or responding to the light."

Finn walked up, saw the men on the ground, and returned to examine the steel door.

"We're going to need bolt cutters to get this door open and get them out," Finn yelled over the radios.

"Hold on, hold on," Camp said as his light illuminated the arm and face of the man on the ground closest to him. "These guys are infected . . . repeat . . . I've got *three* males with obvious cutaneous anthrax lesions on their skin. I've got white powder all over the ground. I can't get in to examine, but I'm sure we're dealing with inhalation anthrax as well."

Finn moved over and illuminated the scene with Camp. "They were locked inside."

"Looks like they really pissed somebody off."

"Why not just shoot them?" Finn asked.

"Chief, I need three doses of levofloxacin, stat . . . We're going to need a suitable hospital with an ICU on standby and ready to go," Camp shouted.

"The HAZMAT truck has the levofloxacin but negative on the ICU. Closest one is the VA facility in Iron Mountain. We've got an infection isolation room here at War Memorial Hospital, but we'll need to set up a quarantine first," the chief responded.

"Negative, sir . . . Anthrax infection is not transmittable from human to human. Worst we're looking at is touching it. I need this door opened *now*!"

Finn illuminated the white cinderblock wall in the corner. Someone had written on the wall in blood.

"Camp, check this out," Finn said as Camp read the words.

"Yamamoto Miami Viktor."

CHAPTER 38

Indian Creek Island
Miami Beach, Florida

Ekaterina poured her first cup of coffee of the morning, opened the massive front door of the Castello Del Luna, and walked down the intricately laid brick pavers on her gated driveway to the mailbox. For one of the first times in her life she noticed the purple and pink Madagascar periwinkles that greeted the morning sun and the splashes of dew still on their delicate petals.

Rina grabbed the rolled up *New York Times* out of the newspaper box and a handful of the previous day's mail and strolled back to the house.

She scrolled through her iPod playlists and found the classical music soundtrack for "Tverboul" by Alexander Paperny. Paperny was her favorite modern composer. The combination of driving strings and deep brass accentuated her upbeat mood.

Rina topped off her coffee, pulled a cup of Greek yogurt out of the refrigerator, sat down in a high bar stool at the breakfast nook, and opened the *New York Times* dated Tuesday, February 18.

The front page headline screamed at her: Anthrax Detected in 13 US Cities.

Ekaterina folded the newspaper, stood up, and began to dance around the kitchen, raising her arms to conduct the symphony as Paperny filled her soul.

War Memorial Hospital
Sault Ste. Marie, Michigan

Camp, Finn, and Agent Daniels huddled outside the infection isolation room at War Memorial Hospital. Two FBI agents from the Grand Rapids field office were wading through reports of anthrax detection and infection that were pouring in from around the country as the doctor emerged from the room.

"What have we got, Doc?" Camp asked as Finn and Daniels moved closer.

"One of the males is nonresponsive—alive but nonresponsive. One is in and out of consciousness. I'm not sure we got to either of them in time."

"Anything on John Doe number one?" Finn asked.

"Other than deceased, Asian male, possibly Japanese? Nothing. No identification on him or any of the other three. I'll keep you posted if their conditions change," the doctor said as he tried to excuse himself.

"Doc, I want to see John Doe one," Finn said. "I may be able to recognize him."

"The cutaneous lesions on his face are pretty severe, but I'll let the morgue know."

Camp, Finn, and Daniels walked down the corridor and out of earshot of the two FBI agents.

"So what are we looking at? Terrorists who were trying to kill themselves in some kind of a suicide pact?" Daniels questioned hypothetically.

"Impossible. The Ice House door was locked from the *outside*," Finn answered.

"So these guys were somehow in on the attack but not important enough to keep?" Daniels asked.

"Whoever locked them in assumed they would die long before being discovered. Seems more like an attempt at tortuous murder to me," Finn said.

BOX 731

"What about those numbers, Billy, the numbers you read off from the third-floor conference room?" Camp asked.

"Random. No pattern that I could see. I wrote them down as soon as we got outside. Why?"

"Let me give them to Leslie and see if she can make any sense out of it."

Finn handed Camp the piece of scratch paper as the two FBI agents walked up.

"How bad is it?" Finn asked them.

"Thirteen cities we know of. Gardena, Rancho Palos Verdes, Campbell, and Burlingame in California; Dublin, Ohio; Bellevue and Tacoma, Washington; Beaverton, Oregon; Greeley, Colorado; and Elk Grove Heights, Naperville, Schaumburg and Wilmette, Illinois. This thing has tentacles everywhere with early reports of ER visits in each area. Hospitals are prepped and ready to go, but our existing antibiotics aren't cutting it. There are fatalities."

"I assume those are just the cities where packages broke apart and the Bio Detection Systems flagged the anthrax," Camp surmised. "What about the post offices that processed and delivered the samples without a positive detection?"

"The Sault Ste. Marie postmaster is pulling the records now, but it's quite voluminous. Their small post office isn't quite as computerized as you might expect in larger cities. With budget cuts and all, they are about fifteen years behind the technology curve. We could be looking at tens of thousands of records, based on his description," the FBI agent said.

"Description?" Finn pressed.

"During Saturday hours he had two clerks on duty. They said six or seven men pushed carts through the parking lot full of samples from their factory. They were all mailed first class."

"What about the men?" Daniels asked as Susan Francis and Dalton Fischer rounded the corner and headed down the hallway at a brisk pace toward them.

"He said the clerks didn't notice much, nothing strange, other than their accents."

Camp and Finn made instant eye contact. Daniels knew as well. Camp picked up his phone and quickly dialed Leslie, who answered on the first ring.

"Hey, sailor, what's up? I'm just about to head over to the Little Rock airport. I'm getting married in ten days."

"Have you read the newspapers?" Camp asked.

"No way. I'm trying to have a normal life today. See no evil, hear no evil."

"Les . . . anthrax attacks detected in thirteen American cities. We've got fatalities."

Silence filled the phone line. "Oh, God. Camp, the antibiotics and vaccines . . . we're too late."

"Les, I want to give you some numbers. See if they mean anything to you."

"Okay, I've got a pen."

"Twenty-five thousand, two, fifty thousand, one thousand, and fifty."

"That's it? Any context?"

"No clue, Leslie, but something related to anthrax would be a good starting point."

Camp walked back over to Finn and Daniels as Susan Francis and Dalton Fischer walked down the corridor and stopped to speak with the director of communications for War Memorial Hospital.

"I need some direction here, guys. The phone is ringing off the hook with news agencies calling from around the world."

"A simple 'no comment' ought to do it. This is an active and ongoing investigation," Dalton Fischer said as Camp, Daniels and Finn walked up.

"Wait a minute, Dalton . . . somebody wanted these three guys dead," Finn said without greeting his former colleagues. "If we leak that all three are dead, the terrorists do one thing.

Box 731

But if we leak that all three are alive and talking, they might do something completely different."

"So which is better?" Daniels asked.

"I'm not sure yet. Let me take a look at John Doe number one first and I'll let you know."

"Billy? Why would you know John Doe?" Susan Francis yelled as Finn ignored her and started walking down the hallway toward the morgue.

"Finn!" Dalton Fischer said loud enough for all to know he was assuming control. Finn stopped and turned around. "I appreciate your help, retired Special Agent Finn. But you and your friend should probably be heading back home now."

"You're right, Dalton," Finn said. "It was so nice of you and Susan to finally get plugged into the whole terrorist aspect of this case. You have such a refined knack for showing up *after* each attack. Got any plans to prevent one in the future?"

Billy Finn dropped his head slightly and saluted sarcastically like a good soldier. Camp caught up to him and the two walked down the long hallway, rounded the corner toward the hospital exit, walked down a flight of stairs, and then doubled back to the morgue out of view of Susan Francis and Dalton Fischer.

CHAPTER 39

Chambersburg, Pennsylvania

Camp and Finn were trying to stay awake as the Defender 90 cut through Pennsylvania's Highway 30 toward Gettysburg. Camp planned to drop Finn back at Lightner Farms to hopefully appease Madge, catch a few hours' sleep, and report for his 0700 shift at Walter Reed.

The ringing of the cell phone startled them both. Camp recognized the "no number" data on his iPhone screen. "Molly Bloom?"

"Hello, Shepherd's Pie. I received the photo your friend took of John Doe and we ran it through our database. Nothing. But we think we found a match through Interpol. A professor went missing in Barcelona several weeks ago. Left behind a wife and two college-aged children. Completely stable background and clean record. Photo recognition software gives it a 90 percent match."

"No terrorist connections?"

"None. Clean record, no questionable associations. His name is Professor Jouta Tanaka. He's Japanese."

"Thanks, Molly Bloom. I really appreciate the information."

"Are you hanging up on me already?" Reuven asked.

Camp laughed. "I've never known you to spend idle time chitchatting, Molly. Want to talk about sports?"

BOX 731

"Not really. I called your other friend, the spook who stayed back at the hospital. He went inside the isolation room and took photos of the other two patients and sent them to me."

"Okay . . . I'm listening."

"One seems to have a classified file and a security clearance with your government. He's a military scientist. Worked at Fort Detrick. But his job was terminated about two months ago."

"The other?"

"No idea. But we did finally sort through the more than fifty-six thousand passports that were scanned in Madrid on the day of the flights."

"And?"

"And we have a 70 percent facial recognition match on one business traveler who also matches the image from Mr. Finn's camera footage at the university. He flew first class to Atlanta. His name is Okito Yamamoto."

Camp was silent as Finn reacted to Reuven's words. "Molly . . . we saw some writing on the wall in the factory. It was in blood. Are you sure this Yamamoto guy is not one of the infected guys from the hospital photos you received?"

"Positive. Why?"

"The handwriting read 'Yamamoto Miami Viktor.'"

There was a long pause from Reuven.

"So I presume you're on your way to Miami?" Reuven finally asked.

"We are now."

"Try an airplane this time, Shepherd's Pie. I'll check out the name 'Viktor' in Miami and see what comes up. I'll send a photo of Yamamoto to your e-mail account."

"What about the Russians?" Finn whispered.

"Nothing," Reuven said before Camp could ask the question. "If they're still in your country they are using clean credit cards and IDs. No passports have been used to your north either."

Camp hung up as he and Finn explored the entirely new dimension in silence, a proposition they had not yet considered.

"This thing may not be done, Billy," Camp said as they passed the city limit signs for Gettysburg. "Maybe the attack is just beginning."

"Reuven said one of the guys in the Ice House was a former military scientist from Detrick. Maybe this is just another 'Bruce Ivins' thing—a disgruntled American scientist with a vendetta," Finn said.

Washington Reagan National Airport

Camp and Billy Finn were seated on American's flight 525 to Miami. The PA announcement asked that all electronic devices be turned off just as Leslie's call came in.

"Good morning, darling . . . I've got about ten seconds before I get thrown into flight attendant jail."

"Camp, if those numbers are a production formula, we're in big trouble."

"Talk to me."

"Let's assume they had a quantity of fifty kilograms of anthrax."

"That's a giant leap for a starting assumption, Les."

"Every kilogram of anthrax means one thousand grams. There are fifty thousand grams in fifty kilograms of anthrax. Camp, the lethal dose of inhalation anthrax would require ten thousand spores. You could probably get that much out of one gram easily, but two grams would eliminate any margin of error. That means you could have twenty-five *thousand* lethal doses of anthrax in the US postal system."

Camp fell silent. "I'll call you when we land," he whispered as the terror of an evil storm was now blowing with hurricane force.

Box 731

Indian Creek Island
Miami Beach, Florida

Ekaterina didn't even bother walking down to get the morning newspaper. She jumped from website to website and followed local news stories from around the country. According to *USA Today* there had already been more than four thousand confirmed cases of inhalation anthrax infection nationally and as many as twenty-seven confirmed deaths.

The most interesting news in the lead story that caught Rina's attention was found in the third paragraph. She smiled as she read that the FBI had confirmed three fatalities in Michigan at the Soo Marie Soaps factory where the anthrax attacks were launched.

The TracFone in her red Tignanello handbag vibrated. "Yes."

"Ekaterina, are you enjoying the news?"

"Where are you?"

"On the ocean . . . up the coast and a few hundred miles from you . . . enjoying some rest and relaxation and spending some of your money. I thought I would have received some final instructions from you by now . . . instructions for Viktor. Have you forgotten?"

"You said simultaneous. But you can have Viktor first. I want to watch the last one by myself."

"Nine days. You need to let me know where. But I'll let you know the exact time. Until then, we're going to lay low and enjoy the beach."

Rina hung up. She hated Semyon but despised Viktor more. She would be glad when both of them were out of her life.

War Memorial Hospital
Sault Ste. Marie, Michigan

Agent Daniels pored through the data in the e-mails he was receiving as he sipped coffee in the hospital cafeteria. Neither of the patients was making any recovery progress. Even if they lived, interviewing them didn't seem to be an option for quite a while.

An internal CIA e-mail with the subject line URGENT popped up on his Outlook. The message was as succinct as it was disturbing: John Doe #3 fingerprint match. Dr. Masahisa Ishii, military scientist, Fort Detrick, Maryland; recently terminated.

Daniels immediately called the director's office. The CIA office had already been in touch with security at Fort Detrick. Anthrax samples at Fort Detrick were being examined, and all relevant scientists and potential suspects were being detained. Daniels was being summoned back to Washington, and his flights had already been booked.

Daniels called the chief of police and hospital security and asked them to meet him outside the infection isolation room in twenty minutes. He rode the elevator up to the second floor and waved to the two FBI agents from the Grand Rapids field office as they spoke quietly with Susan Francis and Dalton Fischer.

"Game changer, folks," Daniels said ten feet away and closing fast as the agents stood. "John Doe three is a former US military scientist, an expert with anthrax . . . and he was laid off from his government job fewer than eight weeks ago. He should be considered our prime suspect, and we're going to need twenty-four-hour armed security and video surveillance from this point on."

Dalton Fischer cleared his throat and moved in closer to Daniels. "No need for that. Your John Doe number three just died."

CHAPTER 40

Miami Beach, Florida

Camp and Finn sat impatiently in the FBI's North Miami Beach Field Office on Northwest Second Avenue. The agent-in-charge was on the phone with Dalton Fischer, who was back behind his DC desk.

"Sorry, guys, but I'm afraid the Bureau won't be able to offer you any resources. The primary suspect, though deceased, has been identified," Agent Perez said with little emotion.

Finn was agitated. "Agent Perez, have you taken a look at my friend's busted lip and black eye?" he said as the agent glanced at Camp's face. "A sixty-two-year-old Japanese military scientist did not go all kung fu on my SEAL. I'm telling you, these guys were Russians and we've been tracking them all the way from Syria."

"I'm sorry, Mr. Finn. I don't doubt that this Dr. Masahisa Ishii had help, but our investigation is focused on Fort Detrick right now. Besides, we've got almost six million people in the greater Miami area, not to mention more than six thousand square miles. There are thousands of both law-abiding and criminal Russians living here. If the Bureau's investigation turns south, literally, we'll jump in."

Finn reached into his backpack and pulled a sheet of paper out of the stack. "This is a photo of Okito Yamamoto and my cell phone number. Call me if your paths cross."

The agent smiled and stood as Camp and Finn walked out of the office and onto Second Avenue.

"Now what?" Finn asked.

"Guess we call Ferguson and Lex Smith," Camp said as they waved down a taxi for the quick ride back to the Grand Beach Hotel.

Central Intelligence Agency
Langley, Virginia

Special Agent Daniels arrived at CIA headquarters and was immediately escorted to one of the observation booths above Detention Room Three. Four high-level scientists from Fort Detrick were being detained and questioned independently in four separate rooms. Each would be housed indefinitely in the CIA annex until the investigation was over.

The interrogator in Room Three was starting to get agitated. "Dr. Groenwald, your e-mail log indicates that you received an e-mail from Dr. Masahisa Ishii just two weeks ago."

"Martin was simply telling me he had a new job," Groenwald explained. "He left on good terms. We're friends."

"Martin? So you were close friends? You fired him, Dr. Groenwald, did you not?"

"There were budget cuts. It was all part of sequestration, and the fiscal cliff budget cuts to Defense. It was not a punitive action."

"Masahisa Ishii was a military scientist?"

"Yes."

"He worked with biological weapons?"

"Yes."

"Was he upset that you let him go?"

"Well, he wasn't thrilled. Who would be?"

"Did the two of you ever discuss biological attacks?"

"In the routine aspects of our jobs . . . yes . . . all the time. We all do. We game-play attack scenarios and try to solve them."

Box 731

"Game-play attack scenarios . . . so you try to think like a terrorist?"

"Essentially . . . something like that."

"So you have developed attack scenarios for biological weapons here in the United States? Against American citizens?"

"That sounds worse than it actually is. That's our job."

"Where are you originally from, sir?"

Groenwald shook his head in disgust. "I've been in this country for almost two decades."

"That wasn't my question."

"Germany. I was educated in the Netherlands as well."

"Dr. Groenwald, do you have any reason to hate the United States or wish to cause this country harm?"

Groenwald's chest began to rise and fall as he broke down sobbing.

ISAF Headquarters
Kabul, Afghanistan

Generals Jim Ferguson and Lexington Smith were gathered around Ferguson's conference room table. They had been briefed by the CIA, FBI, as well as Director Reuven Shavit with Mossad in Tel Aviv.

Ferguson's landline began to ring as one of the coffee-pouring majors answered the call. Lex Smith looked up at the wall clock.

"They were supposed to call fifteen minutes ago," Smith mumbled.

"In Campbell's world, he's right on time," Ferguson said as the major put the call on hold. Ferguson shuffled through the reports from the FBI and CIA for several seconds and then finally pushed the speaker phone button. "Ferguson."

"Sir, Captain Campbell and Billy Finn."

"Captain, we're shutting this down. You and Billy head back to Washington," Ferguson said matter-of-factly as silence filled the phone connection.

"Sir?" Camp finally asked.

"Camp, Lex Smith here . . . we've been briefed by both the FBI and CIA. We even had a lengthy conversation with Director Shavit in Tel Aviv. This thing appears to be domestic in nature."

"With all due respect, Jim, I happened to be in Syria when they sliced open my belly," Finn said with no shortage of bitterness in his voice. "I don't recall a Japanese scientist from Fort Detrick holding the knife."

"Billy, I don't doubt this Fort Detrick scientist got some help; maybe from Syria, hell, maybe even from Russians. But he had access, expertise, and motive. Not the least of which, you found him at the crime scene."

"General Ferguson, the three men in the Ice House were locked *inside*. There was a padlock on the *outside* of the door. I'm sure this Martin Ishii was a talented guy. I grant you that he had access, expertise, and motive. But are FBI, CIA, DOD, and Mossad suggesting that he is also Houdini and managed to lock himself in the room from the outside?"

Ferguson and Smith exchanged glances. Ferguson knew Camp was right, but the investigation was now out of their hands.

"I understand, Camp, but the FBI has it now. Langley will follow any other leads with international ties of national security interest. I want you to report back to Walter Reed, Captain. And that's a direct order."

"Sir, you keep reminding me of direct orders." Camp laughed.

Ferguson allowed himself a rare smile. "That's because you have a penchant for selective hearing. Billy, let's talk at Camp's wedding. I need to know if you plan to come back here."

"Sir, you're coming to my wedding?"

BOX 731

"That's my intent, Captain. We'll see if MILAIR flights and the weather out of Afghanistan are both willing to cooperate."

Grand Beach Hotel
North Miami Beach, Florida

Finn pressed the speaker phone button and ended the call. Camp sat still staring out the large, bay-front windows while the sun began to set over Biscayne Bay and Indian Creek.

Finn paced the room.

"Guess we need to check flights," Camp finally said.

Finn's blood was beginning to boil. He paced faster and faster.

"At least it's not as cold as Michigan," Camp added.

Finn pulled out one of the sheets of paper with Yamamoto's photo, his name and cell phone number on it. He looked at the photo and paced.

"Wanna get something to eat?" Camp asked.

Finn stopped walking. "I'm staying here," he finally said. "You got the direct order—not me."

"Billy, in case you've forgotten, this place is running us $249 a night. It's on my government-issued credit card, and we're already busting through the allotted per diem."

"I'm taking vacation, Camp. I'll use my credit card. Hell, I'll cash in my 401K," Finn said as he grabbed a handful of flyers and headed to the door.

"Now where are you going?" Camp asked as Finn opened the door.

"I'm gonna find Yamamoto. That's what investigators do."

"Wait! Shut the door."

Finn allowed the door to close and leaned against the wall.

"Fine. I'll stay. I can check in with Walter Reed every day. Ferguson won't know the difference. If Les is okay with it, I'll stay one week. Seven days, Billy, that's all. Next Thursday morning we're on a flight to New Hampshire. Agreed? I'm not letting Yamamoto, Russians, or anthrax stop my wedding."

Finn closed his eyes and wondered if he was acting like an old retired fool. Either way, he was relieved that Camp was staying by his side.

White Birches of Hillsborough County
Weare, New Hampshire

Leslie and Eileen sat across from Lydia and Karl in the heated porch as Karl's Decca phonograph played a Bing Crosby record from the adjacent empty living room. A gentle snow was falling as a new blanket of white covered the ground and filled the barren limbs of the white birches that covered the forty acres behind Karl and Lydia's old home.

"We're so excited," Lydia said as Karl held her hand and stroked her fingers. "Karl hired a harpist and a student photographer from New Hampshire State University. I hope it warms up a bit for Friday's ceremony."

"Did you find a minister, Pops?" Leslie asked.

"Oh yes, the pastor from the Presbyterian church will be here. He was delighted."

"I booked a block of rooms over at the Red Roof Inn," Eileen added. "I'm not sure how many to expect but I got ten rooms based on RSVPs."

"Will the diner be large enough for all of your guests, Leslie?" Lydia asked.

"There won't be that many, Grams. But a general is flying in from Afghanistan and Camp's best man and his wife are flying in from Tel Aviv, Israel. My maid of honor is already here, and, I'm sorry to say, she has been doing all the work that I should have been doing."

BOX 731

"You were busy saving the world, Leslie," Eileen said. "It was my privilege and I'm honored."

"Save the world . . . guess I wasn't quick enough," Leslie said as Karl stayed focused on the guests.

"Afghanistan and Israel . . . my, my, my," Karl said as he clicked his tongue and smiled at Lydia.

"When will Camp get here, honey? We're anxious to meet him," Lydia said.

"He and his friend are still in Florida. They're going door to door handing out flyers and looking for information. Camp promised me he would be here by Thursday. He's getting married twice on Friday no matter what!" Leslie said laughing.

"Twice?"

"Pops, we're going to have a traditional Jewish ceremony first. Camp's friend from Israel is doing that one. Then we'll go outside and have our wedding in the white birches."

"My, my, my," Karl said as Bing Crosby kept singing.

CHAPTER 41

Pizza Bianco
Sunny Isles Beach, Florida

Camp and Finn put the final touches on the last two slices of a Mediterranean pizza as the waitress brought two more frosty mugs of beer.

"Here," Finn said as he handed her a flyer. "This is my last one. Call me if you ever see this guy."

The waitress walked away smiling as both Camp and Finn watched her drop Yamamoto's photo in the trash can as she stepped up to the serving line to deliver another pizza.

"And that about sums it up," Finn said in surrender as his last flyer was placed in the "circular file."

"We did the best we could, Billy. We hit every restaurant, bar, hotel, and store we could find. We could head out tomorrow morning, you know. A day early. Madge would be happy. I know Leslie would be thrilled."

Finn smiled and took a big swig of his beer. Camp figured Billy was probably just as tired and disappointed as he was.

"Wednesday isn't Thursday, my friend. You promised me seven days," Finn said as a large smile broke across his face. "Besides, I need some pool time to work on my tan."

BOX 731

Indian Creek Island
Miami Beach, Florida

Ekaterina removed the TracFone from her handbag and stood next to the open bedroom window overlooking the pool as Viktor smoked a cigar and sipped on scotch in the darkness punctuated by Malibu lighting around the pool.

"Tomorrow, just before sunset. Exactly three miles out in the ocean due east from Indian Creek Island. We're taking the Galeon out to celebrate our *joyous* anniversary. Pull up next to us and he's all yours."

"We'll follow you from a distance, Ekaterina . . . in case you get any silly notions."

Grand Beach Hotel
North Miami Beach, Florida

Camp was relaxing in a poolside lounger as Finn sat nearby in a straight-back chair beneath an umbrella. A cold drink and a cell phone were on the patio table in front of Finn.

Camp's thoughts beckoned back to the pool at the Tel Aviv Hilton where an imposter waiter served the love of his life with a bottle of Turonia Rias Baixas Albarino and a marriage proposal. He walked through an assortment of memories on the Temple Mount as he contemplated the Dome of the Rock mosque, the Wailing Wall, and the vision of Solomon's Temple.

The fingers on Camp's left hand reached up and touched the new scar on his upper right chest as he recalled the hate in Miriam's eyes and the flash from the French doors behind her as pain filled his body and life began to empty out of him onto the floor beneath.

His mind flipped through the fading photographs of Liza, Enod, James, Nahla, Margaret, Micah, Daniel, Rebekah, Landon, and even Thomas. He felt Jane's hand on his shoulder again as he watched his lifeless body on a gurney in the Gettysburg Hospital.

But it was Jane's words that he couldn't forget most of all. *Are you finished? Is your work done? Has your story been completely written?*

Camp had done all he could, but he couldn't stop the anthrax attack. Thousands were infected and hundreds were either dead or dying. But somehow Jane was able to help him let go long enough for him to find and hold on to Leslie.

We had our season and it was wonderful. But Leslie is your soul mate, Camp. You have more work to be done, more life to be lived.

Camp was lost in his thoughts and didn't realize his phone had already rung three times. He never looked at the caller ID on the screen of his iPhone. "Captain Campbell."

"Shepherd's Pie."

"Molly Bloom. How are you, my friend?" Camp asked, smiling.

"My wife and I are getting ready to fly to America. We're attending a wedding. Will you be there?"

"Wouldn't miss it, Molly. We're flying out in the morning. Any luck finding a Russian named Viktor?" Camp asked.

"I'm afraid not. The name Viktor is a transliteration, probably from the name *Виктор*. I think it's probably a nickname, maybe even an alias. I'm sorry."

"Nothing to be sorry for, Molly Bloom. We tried. We all tried. Safe flight, my friend. I'll see you tomorrow."

Camp hung up and looked over at Finn, who was eagerly waiting to hear good news until he saw Camp shake his head. "Come on, Billy, let's get showered and packed. I'm in the mood for seafood tonight."

BOX 731

Indian Creek Island
Miami Beach, Florida

The captain of the Galeon loaded the catered dinner service and three bottles of wine into the galley of the luxury yacht as Viktor spoke on his phone. The twin 1550-horsepower engines were idling and rumbling as they waited for Ekaterina to arrive at the marina.

The captain stocked the yacht with several large white candles and two plastic lawn chairs and a small patio table, just as Viktor had ordered for their anniversary cruise and dinner at sea.

Grand Beach Hotel
North Miami Beach, Florida

Billy Finn turned the hot water up as high as his body could tolerate while steam filled the bathroom and fogged the mirror. He wasn't surprised that the smoke detector was going off, but he was in no mood to either stop the shower or get out and open the door.

Camp could deal with it, he reasoned. Retired Special Agent Billy Finn was officially off-duty.

The bathroom door opened and Camp burst in. "Geez, Billy!" Camp yelled.

"I know, I know . . . sorry about the smoke detector. Just push the button or see if it has a battery and just yank it out," Billy yelled through the water that massaged his shoulders.

"It's your *phone*, Billy! Where is it?" Camp yelled as he squinted through the fog, pushing things around on the counter.

"In my front pants pocket, on the floor by the toilet," Billy said as he turned the shower off and pulled the curtain back.

"Oh, geez, Billy," Camp said with disgust as he handed the phone to a naked and wet retired FBI agent.

"Bill Finn . . . Are you sure? . . . How long ago? . . . Okay, don't leave. We'll be there in fifteen minutes." Finn hung up and reached for a rolled towel on the shelf above the toilet.

"Who was that?"

"The manager of Solstice Boat Rentals at the Turnberry Isle Marina in Aventura."

"And?"

"When he was out to lunch, one of his staff members rented a yacht to an Asian. They have a photo ID and a credit card on file."

"Yamamoto?"

"No . . . says it's a different name," Finn said as he tucked in his shirt and zipped up his pants. "But the photo is the same guy."

"How long ago?" Camp asked.

"Thirty minutes."

Camp sprinted for the door.

"I'll get a taxi."

"I'm thirty seconds behind you, brother!"

Turnberry Isle Marina and Yacht Club
Aventura, Florida

Fewer than seventeen minutes after receiving the call, Camp and Finn were standing at Luke Mickens's rental counter and had quickly verified that the photo and passport belonging to Tadaaki Tai was, in fact, Okito Yamamoto.

"Luke, did he indicate where he was cruising to or where he was going?" Camp asked.

"We give our renters maps and guidelines, but no, they don't file a cruise plan or anything. He had all of the certifications we require and he paid with cash."

"What about the credit card?" Finn asked.

Box 731

"We keep it on file . . . just in case of damages. But they didn't seem like rich spring break kids that were looking for adventure or trouble."

"They?" Camp asked.

"The Asian was the only one who came inside the store. But there were three, maybe four who got onboard with him."

"How far away would they be by now?" Finn pressed.

"The wake speed in the intercoastal waterway is regulated. Slow going until you're out of the bay and into the channel."

"Luke, we're going to need a boat. Do you have something smaller? A speed boat maybe?" Finn asked.

"Nothing I rent. I've got my personal boat out on the pier, but all we rent is yachts."

Finn reached into his back pocket and pulled his wallet out and opened it. He reached over and flashed an old souvenir badge that his coworkers had given to him at his retirement party. The shield said FBI and the agent number was his retirement date. The fine print around the badge read: Final Big Investigation—Retirement.

Billy quickly flashed the badge as Camp closed his eyes in disbelief.

"FBI?" Luke asked.

"That's what it says. Where's your boat, Luke?"

Luke reached into his pocket, grabbed the keys, and walked around the counter toward the door. "Hey, do you want to take a GPS with you?" Luke asked as he stopped in the doorway.

"We've got maps on our phones. We should be good," Finn said as he stepped outside and into the sun.

"No, I mean our tracker system. I have GPS on every yacht we rent. If they break down, get caught in a storm, or just get lost, the tracker brings me right to them."

Luke grabbed the tracker and led them down the pier to his boat.

"You drive, Camp . . . you're the sailor. I'll navigate," Finn said as Luke turned the tracker on and pinpointed Yamamoto's yacht from three others that were out on rental.

"Just like I thought," Luke said as he gauged where Yamamoto's yacht was. "They're about three miles out and heading toward deeper water."

Camp pushed the throttle down and blasted through the "no wake" and "slow" speed zones as dismayed boaters shook their fists.

"I'd slow it down, sailor. We don't need harbor patrol on our ass," Finn yelled over the engine and the wind.

"You got a gun with you, Billy?" Camp yelled back.

"Shit! Maybe we do need Harbor Patrol."

"Call your friend Perez. Ask him for backup," Camp yelled as Billy found the business card for Agent Perez at the North Miami Beach FBI Field Office.

Finn pressed the numbers frantically and plugged one ear as he waited for the connection. He knew Camp was right. They needed backup.

CHAPTER 42

Atlantic Ocean

Semyon raised the binoculars to his eyes and focused in on the Galeon that was anchored about a half-mile away. He could see Viktor and Ekaterina sitting at a small, white table in the aft of the yacht near the teak platform. The back of the ship was filling with the glow of candlelight as the sun began to drop in the western sky over a bottle of wine that stood perched between them on the linen covered table.

Semyon adjusted his view and looked up into Viktor's pilot house where the captain was enjoying his own bottle of wine, feet propped up and earbuds in for music.

"That's Viktor," Semyon said, lowering the binoculars. "We'll wait thirty minutes, let it get a bit darker, and then we move in. Make sure we're alone out here."

Semyon's three Russian paramilitary crewmembers scanned the ocean horizon on all sides and checked their watches and weapons.

Dr. Yamamoto sat quietly in the cabin below.

The Galeon

Viktor and the captain of his Galeon luxury yacht stood up simultaneously as another yacht approached from four hundred yards out and then slowed to their starboard side.

"What the hell?" Viktor yelled up to his captain.

The captain shrugged his shoulders but quickly reached beneath the control panel and removed the 9mm pistol, one of many guns Viktor kept on the boat at all times. He flashed the gun toward Viktor and Ekaterina and then slid it inside his waistband and beneath his untucked shirt.

Viktor nodded.

"What do you want me to do?" Rina asked nervously.

"Stand inside the galley and stay out of the way," Viktor said as he stepped up on the deck and circled the side of the boat toward the starboard side.

"Should we call the police?" Rina asked as she scurried into the galley.

Viktor snapped his fingers to get the captain's attention.

"Throw me my bag," he said quietly as the other boat cut its engines and floated toward the side of the Galeon. "Get the rifle out of the galley."

Viktor unzipped his leather bag, pulled out his 9mm pistol, and slid it deep into the front pocket of his shorts while keeping a careful eye on the unknown yacht.

The captain climbed down from the pilot house and walked to the aft of the yacht and down into the galley next to Rina as Viktor watched from the smoky glass above. The captain pulled the cushion off the bench seat, removed the rifle, and put it on the galley's countertop. He took a small bottle out of the galley cupboard, unscrewed the metal cap, and filled a dishrag full of the liquid.

"What a horrid smell," Rina complained loud enough for Viktor to hear.

The captain reached out and grabbed Rina violently, spun her around, and covered her mouth and nose with the rag that was saturated with chloroform before she could let out a second scream.

BOX 731

Viktor watched as his wife struggled and then finally collapsed like a rag doll into the captain's arms.

Viktor nodded to the captain of the second yacht and then put his Detroit Tigers baseball cap on his head as the two boats were tied together. Semyon emerged from the stateroom of his yacht and stepped warily over the rails of the two ships and onto Viktor's boat.

"Well, you finally have me, Semyon . . . just like you wanted," Viktor said, laughing as he shook hands with Semyon and waved at the three Russian paramilitary crew members who were still standing on the decks of Semyon's rented yacht.

"What about her?" Semyon asked as they both turned. Ekaterina was already propped up in her plastic lawn chair behind the patio table. The captain had duct taped her body to the arms, legs, and back of the chair. Her mouth was tightly taped around her head and hair. And in the middle of her chest, the thirteen—by twelve-inch aluminum and steel box that was three inches deep was taped inside her hands and against her chest with several rounds of silver tape.

Viktor led Semyon to the back of the yacht and onto the teak platform. He passed smelling salts beneath Ekaterina's nose, and her eyes fluttered open.

"Semyon tried to give you what you wanted, Ekaterina," Viktor said as horror started to fill his wife's groggy eyes. "Seven. Three. And one. I hear that you like to watch everything, Ekaterina. In an odd way, I respect that. But you're going to have to be patient and allow technology to deliver the final verdict for your insanity."

Semyon pulled the TracFone phone out of her Tignanello bag and connected his tablet to the phone. "When the phone rings, it will activate the computer tablet, Rina. You'll be able to watch the whole thing." Semyon nodded to the captain of Viktor's Galeon, bagged the phone and tablet, and taped it into Rina's lap so she could see everything, just as she had demanded.

"It was a good trade, Ekaterina," Viktor said as he caressed the only part of his wife's cheek that wasn't covered with duct tape. "Your little venture was very affordable and quite effective. The entire world is watching and focused on American news right now. That's good."

With a subtle nod from Viktor, the captain lifted his foot and kicked Rina's chair backwards over the edge of the Galeon and into the Atlantic Ocean. Her screams were muffled through the ocean and the duct tape as Rina and her chair slowly started to sink while her eyes—and her rage—pleaded in terrified silence. Viktor watched as she drifted down and out of sight.

Atlantic Ocean

Camp lowered the binoculars just as the splash from Rina's chair settled on the surface of the water.

"We've gotta go, Billy. Is anyone coming or not?"

"I don't know. I called Perez. I gave him the coordinates."

Camp lifted the binoculars and watched as the two men shook hands. One stepped over the rails and walked back to the second yacht. The engines of both yachts were started as bubbling water percolated to the surface around each pair of inboard motors.

"They're leaving," Camp yelled as he handed Finn the binoculars. "I'd get down on the floor if I were you."

"Why?"

Camp turned the key in the boat's ignition. He put it into gear and pushed the throttle all the way open.

"Camp!" Finn shouted as he got down on the floor of Luke's 225-horsepower speedboat.

Camp crouched low in his seat and made a beeline directly toward the starboard side of the second yacht as it was being untethered from the first. Camp watched as three men ran to the side of the yacht as Luke's speedboat began to emerge out

BOX 731

of the darkened horizon and close within five hundred yards. The running lights were off. Camp hoped he could buy a few more seconds before the men could get a clear visual on the powerboat.

Billy lifted his eyes from the floor of the boat for a quick second.

"The first yacht is leaving, Camp. Looks like he's heading out to sea," Finn yelled.

Flash patterns of light illuminated the side of the second yacht. Camp couldn't hear any gunshots over the roar of the powerboat motor, but the explosion through the windshield glass and into the hull of Luke's boat left little doubt they were taking fire.

"Camp!" Finn yelled, pointing to the sky as Camp took a quick glance before setting his eyes back to the yacht in front of him.

An FBI helicopter buzzed over their heads as more gunfire erupted out of the open chopper doors and into the starboard rails of the rented yacht.

Billy and Camp climbed back into their seats as the FBI team engaged the shooters on the yacht.

Camp looked down as ocean water started to gush over his shoes.

"Look!" Billy yelled as the garage on the back of the rented yacht unfolded and extended. A small inflatable boat was pushed out and two men got in. They started the outboard motor and soon disappeared behind the yacht on the portside.

Camp swerved away from the gun battle and steered the powerboat to the bow of the rented yacht.

"Billy, take the wheel. Get me up next to them," Camp yelled as he stepped up on his seat cushion and over the shattered windshield glass to the bow of the speedboat. Billy jumped into the driver's seat and squinted through the darkness until he spotted the small inflatable boat that was heading out into the Atlantic.

"We've got a foot of water in here," Billy yelled as an enormous fireball lit up the sky behind them.

Camp saw the terrified reflections of an Asian and another man as they glanced back to see their yacht in flames.

"One hundred feet," Camp yelled as two shots flared toward him from the inflatable boat. Camp got down low on the bow as Finn crouched down in the driver's seat.

"Twenty in the magazine clip," Finn yelled. "That's two."

Finn steered the boat away from a direct path of intersection and stayed parallel for several hundred feet. Two more shots were fired.

"That's four," Finn yelled.

"Move in, Billy!"

Finn turned and pulled back on the throttle. Six more shots were fired in rapid succession. The portside of Luke's power boat was sprayed with new holes.

"That's ten, Camp. We're filling up quickly."

Finn took a quick glance behind and saw the FBI helicopter hovering above the burning yacht and debris that was fading against the Miami Beach skyline in the distance behind them.

Four more shots rang out.

"Come on, Billy, get me up next to them," Camp yelled as Finn pushed the throttle back to open. The power boat sloshed through the sea like a cullender. Five more gunshots ripped through the Atlantic air as both boats heaved and jerked over four-foot swells.

Camp stood up on the bow of the boat as Yamamoto's eyes came into focus. Semyon held the steering bar on the inflatable's outboard motor as he raised the gun one more time.

"He's still got one bullet, Camp!" Finn yelled just as Camp jumped through the air off the front of the boat. Semyon's gun flashed but was quickly covered by Camp's body as he landed on the shooter.

BOX 731

Finn pulled the throttle way back as ocean water began to surge over the sides of Luke's powerboat.

Camp threw wild punches and finally wrestled the shooter to the floor of the inflatable. Camp and Semyon tossed around on the floor, in and out of seawater, as Yamamoto stepped up and over their fighting bodies and grabbed the steering bar on the outboard motor.

Semyon got his forearm around Camp's neck. Camp struggled and pushed against Semyon's forearm to keep it from closing too tightly. He saw the approaching lights of the FBI helicopter in the distance behind Yamamoto's frightened eyes.

Camp struggled to release Semyon's forearm but his grip was fading. Camp's oxygen started to fade as his strength began to drain. He felt weak and lightheaded as his grip on Semyon's arm started to slip.

Camp's eyes stared back into Yamamoto's eyes. The Asian looked at the approaching helicopter, back to Camp's desperate eyes and then down to a small anchor by his feet.

The nine-pound, fluke-style galvanized anchor was sitting on the boat's floor, in the middle of fifty feet of neatly coiled rope.

Camp couldn't hold out any longer.

He let go of his grip as Semyon's forearm tightened around his neck with excruciating strength. Camp reached out wildly, grabbed the stem of the anchor, and threw it back violently over his head. The flukes on the anchor penetrated the back of Semyon's neck and his grip released as Camp fell to the bottom of the boat, gasping for air.

Camp pulled himself up and rested his head on the side of the rubber boat as the running lights of Viktor's Galeon faded over the horizon and out into international waters.

CHAPTER 43

Lydia's Diner
Weare, New Hampshire

The wedding party and most of the family guests arrived by noon on Thursday, the twenty-seventh day of February. Reuven and Dalia Shavit and Mossad's personal security detail landed at a private airstrip Thursday night after making a detour to North Miami Beach to pick up two more passengers. Old Sea Bee Campbell and Ruth drove up from Bird-in-Hand, Pennsylvania, with Eileen. Madge Finn checked into the local Red Roof Inn, and Camp's two sisters left their husbands and kids behind to tend to the dairy farm so they could see their big brother finally get married.

The early Friday afternoon party started across the street from Karl and Lydia's forty-acre farm and ninety-year-old house. Lydia's Diner closed every day at two p.m., but was now open and teeming with new friends and old family members celebrating unbelievable joy and anticipation.

Karl and Lydia Raines stood front and center, fingers interlocked in holding hands, as their smiles and energy electrified the small diner.

"Hey, look at this," Camp yelled over the sounds of Elvis Presley singing on the diner's jukebox. "General Ferguson just landed in Boston. He's two hours out," Camp said, reading his new text message.

BOX 731

"That'll be interesting," Reuven said, allowing a slight grin to escape his face as Camp gave him an unexpected and random hug.

"Where's your dad-gummed bride?" Sea Bee yelled to the laughter of all around him.

Lydia walked over and unplugged the jukebox as Elvis's voice slowed to turtle speed and then faded. The room focused on Camp, who was wearing a black jacket, black pants, a white shirt with a long narrow black tie, and laced up shoes, just as Reuven had requested.

"Folks, you are in for the treat of your lives and the most incredible afternoon I could have ever imagined. Okay, I just met my future grandfather—and grandmother-in-law, and that was pretty incredible too. The future Mrs. Leslie Raines Campbell is across the street getting into her wedding gown."

"You'd better hurry, Junior, or she's gonna change her mind," Ruth yelled from the front booth.

"We're going to have two ceremonies. My best man, one of the dearest, most incredible friends I have in the world, is going to lead us through an orthodox Jewish wedding ceremony first. Reuven and Dalia will tell you everything you need to know. This is my gift to Leslie. Later this afternoon, we'll have her wedding at sunset, with candles, in the white birch trees. There's snow on the ground, so keep your warm clothes handy."

"Camp, please excuse us. Dalia and I need to go over and help Leslie," Eileen said as she and Dalia walked out of Lydia's Diner, waited for a car, and then crossed the two-lane country highway over to Karl and Lydia's house.

"Reuven . . . it's all yours, my friend," Camp said as he yielded the floor of the diner to Reuven Shavit, director of Mossad's kotsas in the Middle East.

Reuven nodded to the two security officers who were in the diner, and they passed candles out to all who had gathered. Two more security officers were outside guarding and surveying the perimeter as they normally did.

"Friends, I am not an ordained rabbi, but I have studied the Torah since I was a child. This ceremony unites Camp and Leslie not in the eyes of man, but in the eyes of God."

"Did you just say my name again?" Camp quipped as Reuven dismissed him with a hand.

"The orthodox Jewish wedding is a spiritual event. Two souls are merged, bound together physically and spiritually, as one. Camp, come here."

Camp walked up to the center of the floor next to Reuven.

"The *chatan* is the same as what you call the groom. The chatan empties his pockets of every possession," Reuven said as Camp put his change, car keys, iPhone, and wallet on the countertop in front of the green vinyl swivel counter stools. "The chatan undoes his tie and unties the laces in his shoes. They do not marry for physical beauty or for external jewels. She does not marry him for the money in his pockets. They come to each other unbound, with no ties, and no connection to anyone or anything, other than their connection and the love they have for each other."

Ruth started to cry as Sea Bee pulled a napkin out of the two-sided silver dispenser and handed it to her.

"The bride is now preparing herself. She is reading psalms and praying for the ability to crown her husband. Not to be a decoration on his arm or in his house, but to be the tie between his dreams and his consciousness. Just as the crown rises above the head yet connects with it as well, so too does the bride connect the spiritual with the physical. Because she is queen, she allows him to be king."

Camp looked over at Billy Finn, who was also wiping tears from his eyes.

Box 731

"Leslie has removed her earrings, bracelet, and necklace as well. Let us now go over to the house where the *chuppah*, the marriage canopy, waits for the bride and her chatan."

Reuven pulled out a matchbox and lit Camp's candle. He dipped his candle to light Reuven's and the flame was passed until all candles were lit and an illuminated aura of friends and family crossed the two-lane highway and into the living room of Karl and Lydia's home.

Camp walked into the small guest bedroom as Eileen and Dalia slipped quietly past him and out of the room. Leslie's back was turned to him. She was dressed in a beautiful white gown. Camp's eyes filled with tears as he struggled to compose himself. He walked up softly behind her and reached for the opaque veil waiting over her head, bringing it down gently over Leslie's face. He guided her out into the living room where everyone had gathered on all sides of the chuppah.

"They obviously know that they are marrying, which they *can* see, but they are also marrying that which they *cannot* see," Reuven described. "With complete belief and confidence, they know each of them is but only a half of a complete and mutual soul. Mr. Campbell and Mr. Raines . . . would you usher the chatan into the marriage canopy? Mrs. Campbell and Mrs. Raines . . . would you lead Leslie to the outside of the chuppah?"

Camp stood in the middle of the chuppah as Leslie began to circle the canopy three times.

"The bride makes three circuits, one for each of the three virtues of marriage," Reuven said quietly as Leslie looked down beneath her veil at the floor and circled the canopy. "She circles once for righteousness; once for justice; and once for loving-kindness."

Leslie stepped into the canopy and faced Camp. Reuven reached in and handed Camp a glass of wine. He held it for Leslie to take the first drink and then Camp finished it. Reuven handed him the ring as Camp gave him the empty glass.

"Behold," Camp said as he lifted Leslie's veil. "You are consecrated to me with this ring, and I to you, according to the law of Moses and Israel." Camp placed the plain wedding band on the index finger of Leslie's right hand.

"I am a witness," Reuven said quietly as he nodded and signaled Finn to say his big line.

"I am a witness," Finn said quickly.

Reuven handed the wine glass back to Camp, who placed it on the wooden floor by his feet and then covered it with a cloth. Camp stepped down and smashed the glass.

Friends and family yelled "mazel tov" as one of Reuven's security guards started Karl's 1940s era Decca record player.

"Now we dance," Reuven said over the applause and cheers.

The wine flowed as Lydia was crowned with a wreath of flowers and danced around Leslie in the Krenzl dance before Sea Bee begrudgingly shuffled through the Mizinke dance with Ruth, who was beaming from ear to ear. Camp's sisters threw confetti at Camp and Leslie during the "Gladdening of the Bride." The entire wedding party danced the mitzvah tantz as the bride and groom watched and laughed, holding each other's hands in an eternal bond.

Camp and Leslie danced alone for the final song as Lydia, Eileen, Madge, and the other women retreated to the kitchen to start preparing the feast.

The White Birches of Hillsborough County
Weare, New Hampshire

Eileen was the first to notice the arrival of General Jim Ferguson and his two-man entourage of coffee-pouring majors. He was welcomed into Karl and Lydia's kitchen like a conquering king.

BOX 731

"Where's the bride-to-be?" Ferguson asked as Leslie Raines extended her hand. The grizzled general pushed her hand aside and gave her a big bear hug. "Congratulations, Colonel."

"Thank you for coming, sir," Leslie said as Ferguson spotted Billy Finn.

"Billy! You look great," Ferguson said as Camp walked up. "There's the groom! Camp, how the hell are you? Other than the black eye, busted lip, and scratches on your face, you look great. She shot you once and now it looks like she's been beating the crap out of you too. I assume the bride is wasting no time defining who's in charge," Ferguson said with no hint of humor in his voice.

"Yes, sir, I'm officially back in the saddle," Camp said as he quickly moved to change the conversation. "General, you remember Eileen."

"Of course I do. Ma'am it's a pleasure to see you again. Actually, Captain, you're changing saddles," Ferguson said as he handed Camp an envelope.

Camp started to open the envelope until a hint of panic hit his voice. "Sir?"

"I've decided to retire, Camp. Well, actually, the US Army decided it was time for me to hang it up and I agreed."

Camp read through his new orders. "National Security Council?"

"After the election and shortly before the inauguration, President Preston's transition staff asked to see your biography. You were still in the hospital. Logically, I thought you were in trouble . . . again."

Camp looked over at Leslie. "I met Preston in Balad at the trauma center under less than ideal circumstances. He was Senator Preston then and got nicked by some shrapnel when a mortar exploded a bit too close to his Congressional delegation."

"So you know him? Did you actually speak to him?" Leslie asked.

311

"I sewed him up. He winced and moaned like a schoolboy, but I don't remember talking to him really."

"Actually, I was there," Ferguson recalled. "Camp told him to 'shut up and man up' as the rest of the nurses, docs, and patients broke out laughing. It was a classic 'Camp Campbell' moment."

"Geez, is this for real? I'm going to be the deputy assistant to the president and Deputy National Security Advisor for Combating Terrorism? At the White House?"

"Civilian attire, Captain. Better buy some suits this weekend. You'll have an office in the Eisenhower Executive Office Building, and your honeymoon starts with a cabinet meeting first thing Monday morning."

Reuven walked up next to Camp as Ferguson reached out to extend his congratulations.

"General, let me introduce you to my best man. General Ferguson, I'd like you to meet Reuven Shavit."

General Ferguson reached over to greet Reuven. His large smile subsided as he looked deep into Reuven's eyes. "Have we met before?" Ferguson asked rather puzzled. "You look very familiar to me."

"Yes, General . . . you visited my office last year," Reuven answered. "In fact, we were on a video conference call earlier this week as well."

"In Washington, right?" Ferguson asked trying to place the name and the familiar face with a proper location.

"Actually, sir, it was in Tel Aviv, after your short trip over from Palmachim Air Base."

Ferguson looked stunned. For one of the first times in his life, Camp realized the general was speechless. Ferguson looked to Finn for help just as Finn turned and walked away.

"Yes, yes, of course, pleasure to see you again, Director Shavit."

Box 731

Karl and Lydia's Kitchen
Weare, New Hampshire

Leslie Raines, her grandmother Lydia, Eileen, Ruth, and Camp's two sisters worked the oven, the burners, and the serving plates preparing the food for the reception, which would be held across the two-lane highway in Lydia's Diner. Reuven's wife, Dalia, and Madge Finn were already across the street putting up decorations. A young undergraduate student from New Hampshire State University was taking photographs and generally getting in everyone's way as Camp, Billy Finn, Reuven, and old Sea Bee Campbell, Leslie's grandfather Karl, General Ferguson, and his coffee-pouring majors swapped war stories with wine glasses in the empty living room.

Leslie was pulling a sheet of cookies out of the oven as her cell phone started ringing on the kitchen counter.

"Eileen, can you grab that for me?"

Eileen picked up the phone and read the incoming caller ID. "Says Fort Detrick."

"Oh my gosh . . . that's probably Dr. Groenwald. I'll bet he got lost," Leslie said as she wiped her hands on a dish towel and answered the phone. "Dr. Groenwald?"

"Ah, no . . . sorry, ma'am. Colonel Raines, this is Captain Tina Brock in Fort Detrick Medical. I was calling with the results of your medical exam and physical."

"Oh, Captain Brock, you've caught me at a really bad time. Could we have this conversation on Monday? I have a house full of people and I'm really pressed for time."

"No problems, Colonel. I'll put you on my calendar for Monday. Regardless, congratulations!"

"Yes, thank you, Captain. I'm getting married in about an hour," Leslie said with a nervous laugh as she scooped the warm cookies off the tin cookie sheet and onto a serving tray with the phone cradled between her neck and shoulder.

"Oh my . . . well then, double congratulations are in order!"

"Double?" Leslie asked as she handed Lydia the oven mittens from the table.

"Yes, ma'am . . . for the wedding *and* the baby."

Leslie froze. Her legs quickly anchored in the cement of disbelief and shock. She abruptly walked out the kitchen door and into the backyard as she faced forty acres of white birch trees in the brisk cold afternoon air of late February in New Hampshire. The screen door slammed behind her.

"I don't understand," she said quietly as her heart began to pound in her throat.

"I assumed you already knew, Colonel . . . it's very early, but . . . yes, you're pregnant."

"There must be some sort of mistake, Captain Brock. I've been on the pill for almost twenty years."

"You're still on it now?" Brock asked with genuine surprise.

"No . . . no, I actually stopped about three months ago, after my fiancée was wounded."

"And I presume you've been, ah . . . active since that time?"

"Yes, ma'am, both before and after," Leslie said, quietly after a long reflective pause.

"Well, that's how it all works, Colonel. I trust this is good news for you. I'll speak with you again on Monday, Colonel Raines. Good-bye."

Leslie dropped to her knees as the iPhone fell out of her hand and careened face down into the snow. Tears started to pour out of Leslie's eyes that quickly morphed into uncontrollable laughter.

She was overcome with unimaginable joy.

Leslie rolled over onto her back as the snow bunched up around her face. She gazed past the puffy white clouds and blue sky that was fading toward sunset and sent her thanks to the heavens above. She swept out her arms, then her legs, and then her arms and her legs again. Leslie's eyes caught a window full of women as five laughing faces, noses pressed against the cold

Box 731

glass in the kitchen, watched the bride make snow angels an hour before her wedding.

The White Birches of Hillsborough County
Weare, New Hampshire

Dressed in heavy winter coats, hats, gloves, and scarves, the guests gathered in the snow at the edge of the perfectly planted rows of white birch trees. The white birches had been planted one thousand saplings per acre since the 1930s and were spaced exactly seven feet apart in precisely measured formations. Karl would have it no other way.

A fresh blanket of snow covered all the old autumn leaves on the ground. The forest was lit with a heavenly glow as an arc of one hundred candles sprayed patterns of golden light up the white canoe bark and through the shards of the stately trees.

A harpist from the university removed her gloves and began to play the Scottish harp of the Gael, the *clarsach Gàidhealach*, as Karl Raines walked his granddaughter, Leslie, down the snow-packed center aisle. Camp and Reuven stood up front near the local Presbyterian minister who was protected from the elements with ear muffs and an Arctic Cat snowmobile suit. He was wearing thick gloves.

Camp had never seen Leslie look more radiant and beautiful. His love grew as she drew closer to him wearing a tight pair of blue jeans tucked into her lamb's wool boots. Her white cabled turtleneck sweater was offset by a beautiful, multicolored fleece vest and an understated turquoise necklace complemented her stunning appearance. Her hair was down and full.

Karl and Leslie paused and stopped in front of the minister.

"Who gives this woman to be this man's wife?" he asked as his voice echoed through the trees as the magic-hour sunset splashed over the snow with hues of purple, pink, orange, and red.

"Her grandmother and I do," Karl said as he kissed Leslie's cheek and then reached for Lydia's hand in the front row of standing family and guests.

Camp stepped up next to Leslie and took her gloved hand in his.

"I've got something to tell you," Leslie whispered in Camp's ear as a smile streaked across her face.

"Leslie, look around," Camp whispered in wonder as his eyes panned the white birches behind him. "Faces. People's faces. Friends whose names we don't even remember. They're all here, they're all around us. They're watching us. I can feel them."

Leslie took an awkward glance behind her and through the candlelit trees. "I'm not gonna lie. You're sort of creeping me out, Camp," she whispered and squeezed his hand tighter. "Why are they here?"

"I'm not sure."

"The rings," the minister said as the brief ceremony unfolded.

Eileen handed a ring to Leslie as Reuven handed a ring to Camp.

Camp looked deep into Reuven's eyes. He was overcome with pride and admiration for his new Israeli brother. Reuven's eyes fluttered briefly as he reached into his pocket and pulled out the Mossad phone that was vibrating with a new text message.

Camp smiled. No one was ever really off-duty, and certainly not Reuven Shavit.

The minister and the wedding party waited. Camp held up his hand and smiled.

"One second, everybody," Camp said as several people laughed, including Leslie and General Ferguson. "Go ahead, brother," Camp whispered as Reuven quickly read the message. "All good?" Camp asked, smiling.

Reuven looked out at the small crowd gathered in the snow, pushed his spectacles back up on his nose, and smiled

BOX 731

painfully at Camp. "One Agent 15 chemical Scud missile was just launched by Hezbollah into Israel," Reuven whispered without emotion.

Leslie squeezed Camp's hand tighter.

EPILOGUE

FBI's North Miami Beach Field Office
Miami Beach, Florida

The technician from the evidence room burst through the doors yelling for Agent Perez. Perez stood up and ran down the hallway, trailing ten steps behind the sprinting technician.

The cell phone that was bagged and connected to the computer tablet, one the divers had recovered that morning from the body of a murdered Russian woman, was ringing.

"It works?" Perez asked out of breath as he rounded the corner to the evidence room.

"There was so much duct tape wrapped around her and the bag, I guess it was basically sealed," the technician answered. "Do you want to answer it?"

Perez reached for the phone just as the tablet sputtered to life and the screen switched on.

Perez stopped and they both watched. The video jumped around and the picture cut in and out. Fingers appeared as the image spun around and settled on a man's face. He was wearing an earpiece.

"Ekaterina? Ekaterina . . . I know you're there," the man said, almost whispering. "I like New Hampshire . . . I think I will find a nice American wife and retire here."

Perez and the technician watched silently. The man panned the camera around him.

"I'm sitting on the roof of a restaurant. Watch carefully. This is your final. Seven. Three. And one."

The video hopped as the camera swished past a rifle that was sitting on the man's lap, and then stopped and settled before the camera was fixed to the mounting plate on the side of the scope.

"Did you see that?" the technician whispered.

"A Dragunov SVD sniper rifle," Perez answered. "I think we're about to watch a murder."

"Where?"

"Someplace in New Hampshire," Perez said with a slight shoulder roll.

"Seven . . . three . . . one," the man said as he took one final deep breath and blew it halfway out.

FBI Agent Perez and the evidence technician watched the video as the rifle scope panned up from a white cabled turtleneck sweater that was offset by a beautiful, multicolored fleece vest and an understated turquoise necklace, until it settled and focused on a woman's forehead a split-second before the flash.